MASQUE

The Two Monarchies Sequence

W.R. GINGELL

Get the other books in the Two Monarchies Sequence: each standalone but interconnected, and each with a twist of the fairytale retelling to them...

Wolfskin (Prequel)
Spindle
Blackfoot
Staff & Crown
Clockwork Magician
Masque
Castle & Key

Sign up to the WR(ite) Newsletter to keep up with W.R. Gingell and her publications!

This one is for me. It was written entirely for my own selfish amusement.

You can still enjoy it, though. That's okay.

PART I

Chapter One

Ambassadors' Grand Parties are usually huge, glittering, *boring* affairs at best. One daren't do anything untoward (comment upon how fat a grandee of state is getting, for example, even—*especially*—if he is). Despite this tacit prohibition, the hosting ambassador usually spends the evening in a red, sweaty lather, madly running here and there in a desperate bid to be sure that all his distinguished guests are comfortable and sufficiently flattered. Ambassadors' wives, on the other hand, tend to watch the proceedings with an amused eye, and pat their husbands affectionately upon the head every time a harried dash brings them sufficiently close to do so.

There were a great many important guests at this particular Ambassador's Grand Ball; more, in fact, than I knew personally, which was unusual. The daughter of New Civet's ambassador, I had spent most of my life meeting foreign dignitaries, and there was scarcely a noble family in Civet, Glause or the Triumvirate that I was not on nodding terms with.

I was at present talking to the Ambassador of Glause's wife, both of us fanning ourselves with our masks. I could not think that a masquerade was the best idea for an Ambassador's ball, and said so in no uncertain terms.

"The most ridiculous conceit, my dear!" Lady Quorn said, a little pinker than an ambassador's wife is wont to be. "There is nothing more uncomfortable than to dance in a mask! I was dancing with goodness only knows whom, and it felt as though my face were baking! I can only imagine the upsets bound to occur if one of Harroll's precious foreign dignitaries offends another because they don't recognise each other."

"You were dancing with Lord Morsten," I told her, mischief dancing in my eyes. Lady Quorn disliked Lord Morsten.

"I wish I had known! Why, I was positively *polite* to the man! How did you know, Isabella?"

"Only Lord Morsten would think that pink and turquoise are admirable shades for a man to wear together," I said dryly, plying my mask a little more briskly to fan my heated face. "Besides, he wore that particular mask when he tried to kiss me at the Winter's Eve masquerade."

"My dear! Did he really? Why have I never heard of this?"

"Because, Delysia, despite your vast network of spies, we were not seen. I slapped Lord Morsten, who *most* inconveniently chanced to be at the edge of the Markworth's lily pond. It's not a tale he would be willing to tell."

"Lady Markworth told me he had gone home indisposed," Lady Quorn said appreciatively. "I did hear that he was dripping wet, but I thought he'd gotten drunk and fallen in. How wonderful!"

"You wouldn't have thought so if he tried to kiss you," I remarked. "But really, Delysia, why the masks? What was Harroll thinking?"

"Well now, Isabella, that's something that might interest you! Lord Pecus made it a condition of his attending."

"Fascinating! And who is Lord Pecus?" Lord Quorn was nothing if not decided, and the man who could manipulate him was someone I was frankly interested in meeting.

"His family is absolutely *ancient*: they've had a Lord of the manor since before Glause split from Parras," Delysia informed me. "Lord Pecus doesn't usually attend public functions, he's quite a recluse, in fact."

"Curmudgeonly?"

"Oh no! Still the right side of forty, I believe. But no one has ever seen him without his mask." Lady Quorn looked distinctly unsatisfied. "I've never seen his face."

I hid my smile with my mask. "Despite every machination to the contrary?"

"My dear! Every one a failure!" she assured me, vexation and amusement battling for prominence in her face. Amusement won: Lady Quorn had no misapprehensions as to her nosiness, and she was sportswoman enough to appreciate anyone who could outwit her.

"If I've stumbled into him once, I've done it a dozen times! Not to mention popping up behind him unexpectedly, and jarring his elbow when he reaches to adjust the thing. Harroll thinks the man makes me nervous, and now he holds my hand comfortingly whenever Lord Pecus is in the vicinity."

"How trying for you!" This time I didn't hide my smile, and Delysia grinned an enchanting little grin back at me.

"It *is*, my dear! It prevents me from stumbling into him. Never mind, forget about the exasperating Lord Pecus, and tell me who the group in blue is."

I threw her a disapproving look. "Really, Delysia!"

The group comprised of five in all, each with a short blue

cloak that was both fashionable and serviceable, and a blue velvet half-mask trimmed with silver braid that accentuated and protected the cheekbones while exposing the mouth. They wore blue, silver-trimmed tunics that split on either side below the belt: to allow for riding, if I were not mistaken. These five, elegantly battle-ready denizens must be the Glausian Horselords, the riding regiment of Glause's militia.

"Horselords," I said. "The First Regiment, I believe."

Lady Quorn clicked her tongue in vexation. "Of course they are! I forgot that the ladies don't wear skirts; I thought they were all young men."

"They're very graceful about it," I said thoughtfully. I knew a little something about clothes, and the female horselords were dressed to the best advantage; their short cloaks set back in a line that emphasized the feminine set of their shoulders and, more subtly, their breasts. The women did not care to be taken for men. I was a little surprised that Delysia had made the mistake; but then, she hadn't been married to Harroll for so *very* long, and she had never been one to care for learning names.

"Speaking of clothes, how do you like my new dress?" Lady Quorn did a pert turn, showing off a tight, dusky pink bodice, from which sprang an exuberant froth of the finest rosy netting. It set her inky black curls off to advantage and bought out the roses in her cheeks, and the netting wreathed her diminutive figure to admiration.

"It's a creation, as you are well aware," I told her, and two dimples appeared for a moment. "But it does make us clash rather."

"Well, if you will not take advantage of colour spells, you must put up with the disadvantages of red hair," Lady Quorn said firmly. She was a great believer in aids to beauty: her hair had been in quick succession fashionable gold, daring blue, and handsome chestnut before its present raven black. My own hair, long and immensely thick, could never be worn in the high, elegant style that Lady Quorn affected: instead, I wore it in a great, plaited rope down my back. My freckles had all but vanished over the years, but my hair remained a profound, almost fiery, red. Now that I was old enough to be considered an old maid, it was viewed more in the light of whimsy than disadvantage.

"If you are going to insult me, I shall leave," I said loftily. It was time for me to circulate anyway. Delysia bestowed a twinkling smile upon me and allowed me to leave, waving carelessly. I continued onwards to chat with a black-masked individual I knew to be the king-consort of my home country of Civet, and was surprised to find him alone. I had arrived in Glause some months before the royal party, and had been under the impression that the Queen would be part of the second group.

"Has Annabel abandoned you?"

"Hallo, Carrots!" he retorted, grinning. "Still an old maid, I see."

"I *could* say 'I've 'ad me chances!'" I said frankly: "But I haven't! However, if we're being complimentary, *Blackfoot*, you've gained a few more silver hairs since last I saw you!"

Melchior grinned again, more roguishly. "I could have you executed for using that name," he remarked, seizing my hand to pull me into the dance.

"As if Annabel would let you!" I scoffed. I enjoyed dancing with Melchior; and an intimate knowledge of his and Annabel's past made it possible for them to talk to me without reserve. My father had been one of the first statesman to receive a position in the court when Annabel became queen; moreover, she and I had spent some years at school together. "How is she? And why is she not *here*, more to the point?"

Melchior, eyes dancing, leaned forward to murmur in my ear. "Annabel is in an, er, *interesting* situation."

"Again? Aren't you getting too old for that sort of thing?"

"Apparently not," he said cheerfully. "Annabel says it's a girl. Keep whispering, Carrots, Lady Marlow thinks I'm flirting with you."

I peeked over his shoulder at a figure in magnificent red-and-gold. Through the slits in her mask, she was watching us narrowly. "Do you think she knows who we are?" I asked in a theatrical whisper.

Melchior chuckled appreciatively. "I've missed you at court, Carrots. Annabel wants to know when you're coming home."

"If Annabel wants a merger of our militia, she'll have to do without me for a few more weeks. Even I cannot perform miracles."

"How do you find the local wildlife?"

It was my turn to smile appreciatively. "Amusing, on the whole. A little more reclusive than in Civet. I've yet to meet scions of the houses of Gabor, Topher, and, I'm told, Pecus."

"Gabor is the one dripping with gold fringe," Melchior said, curling his lip. He dressed plainly, most often in black, and much to his advantage. The court at Civet had never looked so handsome as it did now that the young men had taken to following his lead. "Pecus is around here somewhere—green velvet waistcoat and matching mask. Shall I introduce you to Lord Topher? He hasn't got a wife, you know!"

"Certainly," I said loftily, disdaining his grin. "Lord Topher is brother-in-law to Sir Coraline, one of the Horselord Fourth, not to mention a distant relative of the king."

Melchior's eyebrows twitched together briefly, then

cleared. "I wish they wouldn't knight females in this place!" he complained. "It makes conversation more than usually difficult."

"I'll be sure to bring the matter up with Lord Topher," I promised, smiling saucily as he bowed to end the dance.

Lord Topher was a rather awkward, gangling boy of not much more than twenty years, and very many freckles. He had to tilt his head to look up at me, but he did so with a touching, boylike admiration, and asked me to dance anyway. Melchior, the wretch, left me with him and sauntered away with his hands in his pockets and a grin below his mask.

"I should be happy to dance with you, Lord Topher," I said kindly. Unmarried indeed! As if I would trap a poor boy almost ten years my junior into matrimony! Melchior would hear a few words from me when next I saw him.

"Do call me Wilfred," he said. His plain face was made rather more beautiful by liquid brown eyes, but they were his one beauty. "Everyone does, you know."

I replied with the obligatory 'That's very kind of you', resolving crossly not to do so even if I were forced to the expedient of 'Hey you!'. I disapprove of familiarity with young men. They tend to fall in love far too easily, and Lord Wilfred Topher was already showing distressing signs of admiration despite my red hair. Fortunately, he was not familiar with the dance he'd chosen for us. If he *had* been so, he would have known that *Raina's Folly* was a four-square dance with two couple to a set, and that most of our dancing would be limited to our opposites rather than each other. My opposite, an immensely tall man with splendidly wide shoulders and thick tawny brown-gold hair tied neatly in a green velvet ribbon, was partnered by a tiny waif of a child, beautiful to look at, but entirely unsuited to dance with such a mastodon. He was too well bred to show his relief at dancing with someone closer to his own height, but the strong, easy grip he held me with was very different from the painstakingly gentle hold he used with his partner. I noticed with some amusement that *she* looked up at Lord Topher with almost worshipful eyes; and with further amusement, that it didn't take long for him to look back down at such a beautiful child instead of at me.

My opposite and I danced in silence: he seemed to prefer it so. At all events, he made no effort to speak to me, and I have never been one to foist my conversation on an unwilling partner. His mask was green, as was his waistcoat, and I did wonder for a brief moment if this were the reclusive Lord Pecus: but there were many men with green waistcoats and matching masks, after all. He looked down at me through his mask with uninterested green eyes, and I, enjoying the sensation of dancing for once with a man who was not shorter than myself, remained content not to ruin the dance with conversation. It was only at the close of the dance, when I complimented him on his mask (the trademark of an obscure Glausian folk hero) that a spark of interest came into his bored green eyes. The arm encircling me stiffened, and he looked down at me properly for the first time, his lips parting to speak, just as the dance ended. I disentangled myself, not without difficulty (the man was carelessly strong) and curtseyed; whereupon he bowed, and closed his lips on whatever it was he had been going to say. I gave a token curtsey to Lord Topher, who looked as if he were pursuing a closer acquaintance with the lovely young blonde, and threaded my way through the crowd to find Father. Perhaps it was my imagination, but it seemed as though I could feel the green-eyed man's gaze still on me. Silly, of course.

I sighted Father in the crowd, earnestly discussing something with the Bromian prime minister, and was making my way leisurely to his side when I was overrun by a pincer movement of blue-and-silver horselords that flanked me on either side and then closed ranks. I had met the First Regiment only a few months ago, during the preliminary talks for the proposed militia merger, and they had taken an immense and wholly bizarre liking to me despite the fact that my seat on a horse was, at the best, laughable.

"Lady Farrah!" They made their bows, and I looked them over with an amused eye.

"What is it you need, horselords?"

"Your company, my lady," said Curran immediately. He was the youngest, at twenty-three or so years, and an unrepentant charmer. The other horselords exchanged guilty grins, and Curran was swatted.

"Actually, lady," Miryum said apologetically, "We were hoping it would not be too early for us to leave. We wouldn't like to offend, but we have manoeuvres in a few hours."

"My goodness, why are you still here!" I said promptly. "You are not indispensable to the party, and besides, everyone is masked. Ambassador Quorn won't feel any insult; in fact, I doubt that he will notice."

"Ah, but will *you* notice?" Curran said soulfully, taking my hand and pressing it to his heart. I flicked his nose sharply with my other hand, and he released me to a chorus of horselords snickering.

"Certainly I will notice: there will be one less buzzing nuisance in the ballroom," I told him, unable to repress a smile. There are advantages to being an old maid; not the least of which is being able to flirt with an amusing man without the matrons of the court coupling your name with his. "Follow me, I'll smuggle you out."

There was an unassuming side door cunningly concealed in an alcove between the musicians and the punch bowl. Delysia had shown it to me just yesterday: it opened into a small, dark library that in turn led to the great hall; and, as she said, there was no telling when one might need a quick exit. It was through this exit that I led my merry band of horselords. Curran danced me through the great hall to the strains of a waltz in the ballroom, much to the butler's disapproval; but the footmen seemed to enjoy the spectacle and since it seemed unfair for them not to have *some* amusement in their night, I allowed myself to be waltzed to the front door. When I left the horselords, laughing and joking in the moonlight, Curran was trying to persuade them to visit the nearest alehouse on the way home.

I strolled back through the great hall, smiling to myself. It was pleasant to be in the company of the horselords; they made me feel young again. Twenty-eight was not precisely *old*, but I had been accompanying Father to ambassadorial functions since the age of seventeen, and hosting them myself for at least as long. I hadn't felt really young for years.

The library was pleasantly quiet when I wandered idly back through it. Someone had lit a fire in the grate, and orangey shadows flickered over the walls, pearlescent and warm. A comfortable-looking settee was set back a little from the fire, big and plush and just right for reading in, and somehow I found myself sitting down. It *was* comfortable, and before I knew what I was doing I had slipped out of my dancing shoes and tucked my feet beneath me as I did at home on a rainy day. I was stretching back luxuriously with a guilty thought that I shouldn't stay too long from the ballroom, when I realised with something of a shock that I was not alone. Green eyes gazed at me from an identical chair opposite mine, and a familiar green waistcoat glowed rich emerald in the firelight: it was the man I had danced with.

"I do beg your pardon," I said, startled. It seemed ridiculous to bleat that I hadn't seen him there, since he filled the chair very obviously, his long legs stretched out in front of him; but I really *hadn't* seen him. "Shall I leave?"

The man stiffened, his head jerking back a little as if he were also startled, but he said quietly: "Not at all." His voice was velvet like his waistcoat, deep with slightly rough edges, but now that I had a chance to really look at him, I found that there was something unnerving in his face.

To give myself time to ruminate on the sense of unease, I said: "I'm sorry if I startled you."

He cocked his head and leaned a little forward. "Most people don't notice me when I don't want to be noticed." He said it more with interest than annoyance.

"I see," I said quietly; and I did see. I saw two things: one, that this man was a magic user, and *that* was why I hadn't seen him at first; and two, that my feeling of unease came from the fact that he was wearing a mask beneath a mask. The lips of it moved, but stiffly, and with imperfect synchronicity. What sort of a man wore a mask beneath a mask? I said: "Lord Pecus, I believe?"

He laughed at that; a low, warm laugh as enthralling as his voice, and removed the green velvet mask. "You have the advantage, my lady."

"Lady Isabella Farrah," I said, inclining my head grandly, just as if I wasn't curled up in a regrettably informal way. I offered him my hand, and he kissed it in the old fashioned way, cold porcelain against flesh. "I believe we have a mutual friend: Lady Quorn." He looked at me piercingly, and I added with mendacious helpfulness: "The one who stumbles." I was enjoying myself immensely. I thought I saw a gleam of answering humour in Lord Pecus's eyes, but it was difficult to tell through the magical mask.

"I think I would like to see your face," he said thoughtfully. "Would it stretch politeness too far to ask you to remove your mask?"

"After you, my lord."

I thought he laughed at me, but again it was hard to tell. "I don't think I understand you, my lady."

I looked at him steadily for a moment, my chin propped up in my palm. "Forgive me if I seem rude, but I think you understand me very well."

He sat forward again, leaning his forearms on his knees. His bulk was so considerable that this manoeuvre put his face only inches from mine, and I found his eyes uncomfortably piercing. "Very well, my lady. Remove your mask, and I will remove mine."

I was burning with curiosity that was tempered by a touch of self-satisfaction that I was about to accomplish something that even Delysia had not been able to accomplish, but I untied my mask with fingers that were steady enough.

"Well, my lord?"

"Charming," he said softly, deliberately misunderstanding. I found myself blushing for the first time in many years. It was annoying to know that he'd intended as much. "How old are you, Lady Farrah?"

"Very nearly thirty, my lord," I told him composedly, ignoring the rudeness of the question. "And a confirmed old maid, so you've no need to waste your compliments on me."

"What brings you to the Ambassadorial Ball?"

"The proposed militia merger, my lord; and I believe you're stalling."

He gave me a slow, considering smile, and I wondered if the face beneath the mask was smiling also. "Is that so? Are you sure you want to see my face?"

Courtesy compelled me to say, albeit with reluctance: "Not if you're unwilling, my lord."

Lord Pecus sat silent for a moment as if in thought, his mask unreadable. "Hm. I don't believe I am," he said at last, as if he had surprised himself. "Try not to scream, my lady."

If he had said it with the slightest theatricality, I would have laughed and gone back to the ballroom, content not to know what his face really looked like. But he said it unemotionally, a plain warning; and I had to take myself firmly to task for the quickly accelerating beat of my heart as he removed the charms that kept his mask in place. I settled my chin a little more firmly in my palm and waited, watching the process with some interest. I had not much talent for magic, and my knowledge was almost as slight: my training had mostly to do with international policy and diplomatic processes.

At last he seemed to be done. He raised both hands to remove the mask—beautiful hands, strong and bare of rings —and it came away cleanly. For a moment I thought he had yet another mask beneath: firelight played on tawny brown hair—no, fur!—in a face that looked like the worst parts of wolf and bear mixed. I blinked once, realising in that instant that it was his face, his *real* face, and no mask. His mask must be magic indeed to have hidden that snout under the pretence of a plain common-or-garden human nose.

"I see," I said into the silent warmth of the room. I dropped my hand back to the arm of the chair and let a small sigh escape. "That explains a good deal."

Lord Pecus gave a short, startled laugh. "Does it?"

"I learned of an obscure, legendary curse in my study of Glausian history some years ago; a curse that passed from father to son."

"Not legendary," Lord Pecus said shortly. I wondered how he spoke with that snout; it didn't look suitable for human speech. More magic, perhaps? He asked briefly: "Do you find me repulsive, Lady Farrah?"

"I've seen uglier," I said coolly. "Lord Morsten, for instance. He has very unpleasant eyes, and of course he has nothing like the splendid facial hair that you do. I don't tend to look for beauty in faces."

His green eyes narrowed at me. They were the only part of his face that looked remotely human, and I found it easier to read his face if I looked into them. At the moment they were speculative, and a little sceptical. "I suppose you'll tell me that beauty is found inwardly, and that you never look at appearances."

"No, my lord. I tend to look more at shoulders. I like nice broad shoulders in a man. Many a man with an ugly face has been rendered attractive by a good set of shoulders. Besides, the courtiers with the most beautiful faces are invariably the ones who are the most inopportune." I saw that he was looking rather startled, and explained kindly: "They get spoiled, you know."

Lord Pecus threw back what I really must call his muzzle, and laughed out loud. "Lady, will you marry me?"

Many young men had said the same thing to me in jest, and I had grown adept at laughing it off with a satirical look. But when I looked into Lord Pecus' green eyes, about to do the same, I found with something of a shock that he was serious. There was no smile in his eyes, just a kind of silent intensity. So I was serious as I said: "No, my lord. I'm honoured, but my father can't do without me."

"I see." Lord Pecus' tone was thoughtful, but I saw no abatement in the determination in his eyes. Used to reading a room of courtiers at a glance, I found that this particular gleam worried me. "Who is your father, who can't do without you?"

"The Ambassador of New Civet," I said, in the no-nonsense tone I use on the younger courtiers. I swept my feet to the floor grandly as if I had *not* just sat half an hour with them curled beneath me, and slipped them back into my thin dancing shoes. I fancied I saw a gleam of amusement—or was it appreciation?—in those emerald eyes of his, but chose to ignore it as the diplomat I was. "Good night, my lord. I should rejoin the dance now; my father will be wondering where I am."

Lord Pecus rose to bow, replacing his mask. It looked distinctly mechanical now that I knew what it was. "Good night, Lady Farrah. I hope we meet again."

I curtseyed with my hand on the doorknob, and said with rather more sincerity than usual: "I look forward to it, my lord."

Chapter Two

By a fortunate coincidence midnight had passed away quietly while I lingered in the library, and everyone was beginning to remove their masks by the time I re-entered the ballroom. I had quite forgotten to retie mine, and after looking vainly about my person for it, I was forced to the conclusion that I must have left it in the library. I hesitated, but couldn't bring myself to turn around and walk back into such a tiny room simply *filled* with Lord Pecus. His less than human face had startled me more than I cared to show and his proposal had thrown me further off balance: leaving me, on the whole, unpleasantly jarred. I gave the mask up as a loss, and merged with the crowd.

I was strongly tempted to find Delysia again, and let drop casually in the conversation that I had talked with Lord Pecus, and *Oh yes, I saw his face, my dear!* But that would necessarily lead to explanations that Lord Pecus had not authorised me to make, and (if I read him aright) would dislike very greatly. In any event, had Delysia known her own country's history better, she would have been aware of the curse. It was no part of my function to educate her as to her country's peers. It might, however, be just as well to let her know that Lord Pecus' mask was magic, and that it was no good trying to jostle it off. No doubt Ambassador Quorn would thank me for that as much as Lord Pecus would.

Father was still talking animatedly with the Bromian prime minister when I caught sight of him. They had not moved away from the refreshment table, but Father was still holding the same half-eaten pastie that he had been working on when I saw him last. If I had a guess, I would say that he hadn't taken a bite of it in the entire time I had been gone. I smiled to myself and made my way through the crowd to the refreshment table for a fresh cup of punch: no doubt Father hadn't sipped his dangerously tilting tumbler of punch either.

Navigating the refreshment table at any kind of a ball is very like bullfighting: you might manage to get through each danger by an elegant turn without spilling a drop, or you might promptly be gored by any number of elbows that jostle your drink all over the front of your dress. It is a sport simply *fraught* with peril. This time I managed the thing with two elegant twirls, narrowly avoiding a fat lady with an enormous corsage of Glausian spineflowers and a young buck who insisted on wearing a ceremonial sword to the imminent danger of passers-by; and arrived whole, if rather breathless, at Father's side. The prime minister favoured me with a precise bow, but did not stop talking. I inclined my head to him with a twinkle in my eye and gently removed both punch and half-eaten pastie from Father's hands, supplying him with the fresh cup I had bought. Father looked pleased to find himself with a free hand and able to gesticulate more freely, but did not otherwise acknowledge my presence. I cheerfully took this to mean that he did not require or desire my presence, and made my way down the room once more, disposing of the pastie and cup into the hands of an obliging footman. I was admiring the dance from a conveniently back-set window seat when Lady Quorn accosted me with a crease between her beautifully arched brows, demanding to know what I had done with Sir Raoul.

I was obliged to bite back a smile at the thought that *anyone* could do something with Sir Raoul. The head Guardsman of Civet was tall and muscled, with a determined jaw and a surprisingly acute mind; and neither force nor argument could sway him to any course of action he had not thought over.

"I danced with Raoul earlier in the evening," I said in amusement. "But if you suppose I have him concealed in my pocket, you're very much mistaken, Delysia."

Lady Quorn sighed in vexation. "Where *can* the man have got to? Missing his dance with me was bad enough, but now his party is ready to leave, and he's nowhere to be found! Be a darling, Isabella, and find him for me! I've got three half-drunk junior guardsmen kicking their heels in the great hall, swearing that they'll walk if he doesn't show up soon."

"The walk might sober them up," I said tartly, rising to my feet again. Knowing Raoul, he might simply have decided that he was tired of standing on ceremony with a pack of courtiers, and wandered off into the night by himself.

"Oh, but Isabella! You know how they are when they're drunk! They're as likely to box the Watch or set off fireworks in the back allies as they are to go home, and if you think that the first really successful day of negotiations is the best day to bail your junior guardsmen out of jail, I suggest you think again!"

I grimaced, acknowledging the truth of the statement. "Send the guardsmen home in the carriage. I'll find Raoul and send him along after them; and serve him right if he has to walk!"

"*Thank* you, Isabella!" Delysia squeezed my hand and bustled off in a relieved rustling of pink netting. I moved leisurely after her, threading my way through the knots of conversing guests that had formed now that masks were off, and went to find another footman. Footmen are very useful people. They stand to attention nearly everywhere in the house, as unmoving as statues, and notice simply everything. If anyone knew where Raoul was, they would.

I collared an obliging young footman who was standing to attention by the great doors. He moved to open the door for me, his eyes averted in polite deference, but I forestalled him with one raised finger. Like the well trained little automaton that he was, the footman went back to attention, arms stiffly by his sides, and regarded the middle distance with avid interest.

"Yes, my lady?"

"Lady Quorn is anxious to know where Sir Raoul is," I said. I was prepared to describe Raoul, but this footman knew his job thoroughly.

"I believe you will find Sir Raoul with the Earl of Horn, my lady," he replied, without pause and without emotion. "They were conversing together a quarter of an hour ago—heading toward the orchestra, I believe."

I thanked him, and though he was too well trained to betray by the smallest smile his pleasure, I saw a gleam of satisfaction in his eyes. I left him to gloat and proceeded up the room once more. I was beginning to feel rather crossly as if I were a weaver's shuttle, going back and forth, back and forth. Of course, Raoul was no longer by the orchestra, with or without the Earl of Horn; and that was just like him, I thought irritably. The night had passed into the wee hours of morning, and I was beginning to feel my tact slipping. Raoul was fully head and shoulders taller than anyone in the room except perhaps Lord Pecus, and he should have been visible by now. I was inclined to think that he was doing it deliberately.

As I scanned the crowd, I saw Lord Topher pushing toward me with an eager smile on his face. I hastily averted my eyes and lengthened my stride: I had not the slightest wish to deal with calf-love at this time of day. I wondered where the beautiful little blonde had gone, and regretted her absence. Unfortunately, Lord Topher's stride was longer than mine, and despite my care not to look in his direction, I very soon found myself unable to ignore him. It is very difficult to pretend not to see someone when they have planted themselves directly in front of you.

I summoned up a welcoming smile from the remaining dregs of my politeness, and said with bright insincerity: "Lord Topher! How nice to see you again."

"I've been looking for you!" he said ingenuously. His eyes were overbright, and I guessed he had been drinking. In Glause, drinking laws prohibited the drinking of alcohol up to the age of twenty years, and it was possibly the first time he had tasted wine. "You disappeared after our dance, and I didn't have time to ask you for another one."

"I would love to dance with you, Lord Topher, but Lady Quorn has sent me in search of my countryman, Sir Raoul."

"He's the tall one with the red sash and rapier, isn't he?" Lord Topher said eagerly. "If I tell you where he is, will you dance with me?"

I laughed, but agreed. By then I would have kissed him if it removed the necessity of walking up and down that room again. "Very well. Where is Sir Raoul?"

"He was talking to the grand old gentleman with big

whiskers, something about battle strategies, I think. Then Sir Raoul went away through the blue saloon and the old gent went back to glaring at the dancers."

That must be the Earl of Horn, I thought satisfied. He had a daughter over whom he kept an eagle eye. No doubt he was engaged in frightening away beaux. It was beginning to look as if I were right about Raoul: the blue saloon was a small antechamber quite often used to set up the card table, with two elegant glass doors leading out to a small terrace. There was no card table tonight, and it would be the easiest thing in the world for Raoul with his long legs, to simply step over the terrace railings. Bother the man! I pursed my lips and glared at the door to the blue saloon as if it were Raoul himself. Why couldn't he call for his carriage like a civilised human being? If he was not in the saloon, I thought, adopting a somewhat militant stance, it would be very much the worse for him the next time I saw him.

Lord Topher, eyeing the martial light in my eyes with some trepidation, said meekly: "You don't have to dance with me if you don't want to, Lady Farrah. It was just a joke."

"Oh, I'm not cross at *you*," I said, quite cheerfully. The thought of wreaking revenge on Raoul had had the effect of turning my mood. Besides, Lord Topher really was rather a sweet boy. "I've no intention of reneging on our dance."

"I feel sorry for Sir Raoul," he said candidly. "What they say about redheads must be true after all."

"*What* do they say about redheads?" I demanded.

He actually grinned. "Nothing, my lady. If you don't mind, I'll walk with you."

I smiled back, liking him a little better. "Very well. But I warn you, he most likely won't be in the saloon, and I shall probably send you to Lady Quorn to say so while I sit and rest my feet."

"It would be my pleasure, Lady Farrah," he said cheerfully. I had a moment's misgiving that I had been too kind to him, but he didn't *look* amorous, and I dismissed the feeling as he opened the door for me, his eyes bright and mischievous as though we were up to no good.

At a glance, the blue room was empty. A careless guest had spilled a glass of rose wine all over the lovely shaggy rug peeping from behind the massive settee, staining the luxurious pile a dark, blood red. I made a sound of annoyance. It was enough to make a person cry, that beautiful rug spoiled, when just a little prompt attention could have lifted the stain right away.

"We'd better clean that up first," I said decidedly. Lord Topher looked surprised, but followed me obediently to the scene of the crime. I stepped carefully over the stain on the carpet, which looked a little too thick and gluggy for a really good wine, and rounded the settee to judge the extent of the damage.

At first I couldn't quite comprehend what I saw. Through a buzzing in my ears I thought I saw more wine: much, *much* more wine, splattered across the back of the cream settee, and the sprawling body of the guest who must have fainted and spilled it all. Then something turned over in my mind with a nasty lurch, and I could see the bloody pulp where Raoul's head had been– Raoul without a doubt, sashed and uniformed as he was. On the wall and the settee back were myriad glistening little patches of something nasty that I could only assume were particles of his brain matter. I didn't kneel to check for life signs: there didn't seem to be much point.

Instead, I turned to Lord Topher, who was peering over my shoulder with a kind of ghoulish enjoyment, and said: "Fetch Lady Quorn, if you please. *Don't* bring her in."

He looked torn between leaving me by myself and doing as I had told him, but evidently decided it was safer doing as he was told. I shut the door behind him and then turned to survey the room, my fingers grasping somewhat convulsively at my skirts. The tall glass doors were swinging open and a fresh, post-rain breeze was beginning to circulate through the room, lifting a pungent odour I didn't recognise into the air. The murderer could not have been gone long: I hoped a little sickly that he was not planning on coming back.

"Hold on, Raoul," I said. "Help is coming." Not that it would do him much good, of course; but it would do me a great deal of good to have someone else in the room with me. Unless that someone was the murderer, of course.

Fortunately, before I had time to frighten myself thoroughly, I heard Delysia's voice outside the door. I was impressed: Lord Topher had been very quick. The door opened a little more swiftly than I expected, and I only just had time to sweep back to it and bundle Delysia out before she saw anything dreadful.

"What did I tell you!" I hissed at Lord Topher, who looked apologetic. "Lady Quorn is not to go into that room!"

"Why should I not go into my own room?" Delysia demanded. "If you're minded to be mysterious, Isabella, I shall tell my footmen to remove you. If there's anything I can't bear, it's a mystery!"

"Delysia, listen!" I commanded, seizing her by the shoulders. "Get Lord Quorn, Melchior, and if you can, someone who knows about magic."

Lady Quorn's eyes went very big. "Isabella, what have you done?" she squeaked.

"I? If you are insinuating that I am a troublemaker, Delysia, may I remind you of a certain affair at Trenthams—"

"Never mind that now!" Delysia said hastily. "Very well, if

you're going to be like that about it, there's no more to be said. I shall fetch Harroll and the others."

I huffed out a breath of relief as she floated haughtily off, and ducked back into the room. A little to my relief, Lord Topher followed me, looking around with great interest.

"It's different now that you know, isn't it?"

He was right. It made the whole room seem different.

"He must have gone out through the garden," I said absently. "The murderer, I mean." I was feeling a little strange. From where I was standing I could see Raoul's feet, and tiny gobbets of brain in the pooled blood. I looked away, and found that Lord Topher had wandered over to the glass doors.

"Maybe he's still out there," he said. He looked too excited, and I felt a stab of unease. "I'll see if I can find him!"

"Lord Topher!" I found that I was speaking to thin air, and threw my hands up in exasperation. A child such as Lord Topher would be no match for a killer who had so violently murdered someone of Raoul's physique and skill. I hoped fervently that the murderer was long gone: I would very much prefer not to have *two* dead bodies on our hands tonight.

Greatly to my relief, Melchior appeared after only a few more moments, entering quietly and unobtrusively with Lord and Lady Quorn close behind him. Following them, much more noticeably, was Lord Pecus. I don't think that man could sidle into a room if he tried.

Melchior said swiftly: "What's wrong, Carrots?"

"Keep Delysia back!" I said, a little fiercely. I was feeling decidedly sick, and Lord Pecus' presence unnerved me. Why was the man here? Delysia was looking slightly pale, and I realised that she could see the blood from where she was standing. Lord Quorn gently sat her down on a small, elegant chair by the door and she averted her eyes to the far wall, as far from the sight of blood as she could.

The gentlemen proceeded around the edge of the settee, Melchior looking back to ask quietly: "Raoul?"

"It's his uniform. And the, ah– corpse is the right size."

There was a rattling at the glass doors that made the men turn as one, and Lord Topher burst into the room, his hair dishevelled. His frock coat had come unbuttoned in his eagerness and large wet spots on his red velvet waistcoat suggested that the rain had begun again without my noticing. Lord Pecus frowned, Melchior looked quizzically at me, and Lord Quorn turned back to the body, uninterested.

"Lord Topher was with me when I discovered the body," I told them.

Lord Pecus' mask still showed a frown, but Melchior only nodded. "Need a bit of air, Carrots?" he asked casually.

"Mm. Perhaps," I said thoughtfully. I was glad for the arm that Melchior put around my waist, since my legs showed a woeful tendency to shake as we stepped onto the terrace. The rain had ceased and was no threat to my coiffure, I noticed, rather absently glad about it. We walked leisurely down the terrace until we reached the rhododendrons, where I proceeded, in the most refined and ladylike way imaginable, to empty the contents of my stomach into the garden bed.

"That's better, Carrots," Melchior said bracingly, the beast. He seemed to have been expecting it, because he was holding my plait back for me, and rubbing my back in a brotherly way.

"Speak for yourself!" I croaked, sitting back on my heels and hoping fervently that the paroxysms had ceased. Melchior laughed unfeelingly as he helped me to stand again, and offered me his handkerchief. "If you ever tell anyone about this," I threatened through the handkerchief; "You will be very, very sorry."

"Behold me, terrified," Melchior said, mockingly. "Which should I be more afraid of, your hatpin or your parasol?"

"Don't underestimate the efficacy of a well-placed parasol," I said darkly, as we approached the glass door again. I re-entered the room with my head held high, and Melchior sauntered after me casually, hands stuffed in his pockets as if he were the scaff-and-raff instead of a royal personage.

"Nothing to see out there," he told Lord Quorn. "No footprints, no disturbance. Any traces, Pecus?"

Of course. He was the magic user I had asked for.

"Lady Farrah and Lord Topher's signatures are around the body, but no others. The curse used to kill Sir Raoul is distinctive magic; dark, but not familiar." Lord Pecus' mask had gone blank, the eyes hooded. "He died only minutes before we got here. I'll be able to tell you more in time."

Melchior nodded. "Any detractors of the military merger, Quorn?"

"An anti-international group and a few individuals." Lord Quorn blinked through his glasses, then removed and polished them, more from habit than need. It was a wonder he hadn't worn the glass away. "The group isn't violent, and none of the individuals have the kind of magic it takes to do this sort of thing."

"Can it be kept quiet?" It surprised me to find that Melchior was looking at Lord Pecus instead of Ambassador Quorn.

Lord Pecus hesitated, then nodded. "I'll put a geas on the entrances, with a diversion clause to misdirect attention. I'll need access to this room for the rest of the morning."

Ambassador Quorn, who was polishing his glasses again, said: "Ring for anything you need, my lord. If Lady Farrah would consent to accompany me back into the ballroom, I'm sure your majesty would– er–"

"Oh, yes, I'll keep an eye on Pecus," agreed Melchior cheerfully, which was *not* what the harried Ambassador had been hinting at. "At the official inquest we can note that the investigation was carried out by delegates of *both* countries."

"Ah, yes– er, of course, your majesty. Lady Farrah, would you be so kind as to–" he stopped short, bewildered, because I was already helping Delysia to her feet without waiting for the request. The poor man really was having an amazingly awful night. Delysia looked distinctly tearful, poor dear; and in good earnest, too. I can always tell when she's putting on the effect to worry Harroll and when she's serious, because her nose tends to go red when she is really crying.

"Powder room, Delysia," I said briskly, steering her toward the door and significantly touching a fingertip to my own nose. She gave a tiny squeak of dismay, hands flying to cover the afflicted area, and forgot about the nasty sight of Raoul's blood long enough for me to steer her through the party-goers without suspicion or further tears. Rather to my relief, it looked as though the party were beginning to break up; I heard the faint, conflicting calls of various footmen for Earl Somebody-or-Other's carriage, and demands of a chair for Lady Such-and-such through the main doors, and to my practised eye the room was getting a little thin of company.

Delysia had brightened by the time we entered the powder room, but she still had a faintly crushed air which suggested she would have unpleasant dreams tonight. I made a mental note to intercept the maid who brought her bedtime chocolate: a nice little sleeping draught ought to do the trick just nicely. I dried her eyelashes as carefully as her painstakingly applied lash tint required and then surveyed my own appearance doubtfully while she powdered her nose. I made myself up in a more subtle fashion than the exotic, colourful way Delysia liked to affect, in creamy colours that blended with my clear skin and made it difficult to tell that I was, in fact, painted. I had every intention of nosing my way back into the blue saloon, and I would need every fortification that being well dressed and well made-up could give me before I dared to go back into Lord Pecus' presence. It was irritating of the man to be so unnerving, I thought crossly, contenting myself with reapplying a touch of lightly tinted lip colour. I was used to men being a little in awe of me. Obviously I would have to work harder at cultivating my inscrutable air if I was to gain the upper hand with Lord Pecus. In the meantime, face colour and a pretty dress would have to suffice.

"There!" I stood back and surveyed myself again. "Will I do, Delysia?"

Delysia, distracted by her own administrations of rosebud pink lip colour, murmured: "Do for what?"

"I'm going to see what Melchior and Lord Pecus are up to," I said determinedly, straightening my green satin bodice with a hearty tug. "I do not approve of the way we poor females were shoved out of the room."

"Isabella, you *cannot* call him Melchior!" Delysia squeaked, showing me a shocked face.

"That's His Royal Highness King Consort of New Civet to you!" I said, with a wicked grin. "Am I presentable?"

"A lower bodice and more colour would suit you better," opined Delysia, forgetting outrage in lieu of more important considerations. "You should try that gorgeous new gold-dust lip rouge, it would suit you *perfectly*."

"Nonsense!" I said, in a businesslike manner. I did not choose to tell her that I had had a tiny tub of the stuff tucked away in a drawer beneath my underthings for quite some time now. It did something for my hair that made it seem less red and more like gold and flame, but I had never quite been able to bring myself to wear it out in public. I found myself wishing I had done so tonight.

"Your guests are beginning to leave," I said to Delysia, peeping around the powder room door. "And about time, too. Wish me luck!"

I left her still expostulating and swept back to the blue saloon. Or at least, I tried to. The geas on the door kept me impersonally at a distance, much to my annoyance: what did Lord Pecus mean by trying to keep me out with the rest! A little meditation was enough to make me certain that it was Melchior who had arranged *that* particular drawback, so I didn't waste time trying to force the issue. Instead, I took myself off into the gardens and began a sally on the back defences with a hairpin and an ever-so-slightly magical thumbtack. My abilities as regards magic have never been particularly elegant, but no one has ever been able to say they are not effective; and in a very few minutes I was letting myself into the blue saloon by way of the garden entrance.

There I stopped, with my hand on the doorknob, because Lord Pecus was the sole occupant of the room. Obviously poor Raoul no longer counted, and Melchior had vanished; there was certainly no sign of Lord Topher. Lord Pecus was kneeling by the body, closely inspecting Raoul's sash with a tiny brush and a pair of tweezers. When I entered he looked up with what I thought was a slight curve to his porcelain lips.

"Lady Farrah," he nodded to me, and added with that lingering smile: "Melchior said you would be back. I thought the geas might stop you, but he said you have a way of insinuating yourself into proceedings."

I thought it best not to reply to such outright provocation, and contented myself merely with pointing out: "I believe your back wards need repairing, my lord."

He laughed, low and soft. "Thank you, Lady Farrah: I'll see to it. Will you assist me?"

I took an instinctive step backward through the door, unwilling to be any nearer to Raoul. "My lord–"

"Do I frighten you, lady?" Lord Pecus asked quietly. His mask had gone blank.

I stepped fully into the room and shut the door behind me with some asperity. "My lord, I have seen many horrible things tonight, and believe me, your face was certainly not the worst of them. How may I assist you?"

"Sir Raoul has something sewn into his sash," Lord Pecus explained, with the grace to look a little ashamed. He paused as if expecting my enlightenment to be immediate. It wasn't. I may have some skill at reading faces, but this does not extend to mind reading.

"And?" I prompted. I fancied that he looked a little sheepish.

"My fingers are too big," he admitted. "Your fingers are conveniently slender, Lady Farrah."

"Of course," I said briskly, though I felt anything *but* brisk. I was not at all anxious to see again the bloody red pulp where Raoul's head had been. As I approached, I heard the quiet whisper of silk, and found that Lord Pecus had covered the remains of Raoul's head with what was undoubtedly a magically treated silk cloth. No blood seeped through the fresh, creamy material, and the sharp, salty scent of blood dissipated somewhat. I looked searchingly at Lord Pecus, but his mask was expressionless.

"It was distracting me," he explained.

I stepped carefully over the pool of swiftly congealing blood without looking too closely at it, and sank gracefully—

or at least, so I *hoped*—to my knees beside Lord Pecus. From there I could inspect the sash narrowly. It was a wide, dashing one in crimson, double-braided with gold in the best Civetan tradition. A length of the braiding had been unpicked by a skilful hand, and close by the shoulder a little bulge could be seen. I felt a cold premonition of trouble: secret pockets are *always* a headache when it comes to international intrigue.

"I tried to get at it with these," Lord Pecus said, ruefully displaying his pair of tweezers. "It went further in, of course, and I don't want to unpick any further for fear of damaging the paper."

"It *is* paper, then?" My heart sank a little. Not Raoul! Lord Pecus nodded unhesitatingly, his silence asking a question, but since I chose to become very busy easing out the piece of paper, I did not have to answer the question. Secret pockets and concealed documents invariably have a single explanation: treason. I didn't want to think it of Raoul, but believing people to be trustworthy has never made them any more obliged to be so, and there is no good hiding one's head in the sand, after all.

A few deft twists, a couple admonitory tugs, and the folded paper was out. My fingers itched to open it, but I said with correct, albeit reluctant, compunction: "Where is Melchior?"

"He thought it best to ah—dispose—of Lord Topher," said Lord Pecus, in a bland way that suggested he could think of a more pleasing method of disposal than the one Melchior had employed.

"Very right and proper," I approved. Lord Topher over-enthusiastically overseeing the proceedings was just what we *didn't* want.

"He kept insisting that he had a claim to a dance with you. It became wearying."

"Well, that really is quite true," I said fairmindedly. "What a good thing Melchior got rid of him! I suppose I shall have to dance with him next time we meet, but at least for now I'm safe."

"I thought that being a diplomat entailed the ability to say no without offending anyone," Lord Pecus remarked, in what I considered to be a quarrelsome tone.

"That," I said firmly, "Is a common misconception. Most often it means having to say yes to things you'd rather not do. Somebody is always offended when you say no, no matter how nicely you say it. In fact, almost the only enjoyable thing about being a diplomat is the rare opportunity to make other people do what *they* don't want to do."

Lord Pecus' mask grinned, showing off a set of startlingly white, even, porcelain teeth. How *did* he manage that! "Lady Farrah, do you always speak so directly? I can't help but feel that it's not entirely ah, diplomatic."

"Oh no!" I said absently, turning the folded paper between my fingers. I wanted to open it so badly that it was a conscious effort to prevent myself from doing so. "Only to the people I like. I'm very polite and correct to everyone else. Oh! Melchior! There you are at last!"

The door shut as quietly as it had opened, and Melchior sauntered toward us, looking sardonic. "Told you she'd get in," he said succinctly, in Lord Pecus' direction.

"I resent the implication of that remark," I said, with dignity. "You should have checked the back wards properly when you went out, Melchior. But never mind that! Look, Lord Pecus has found a paper sewn into Raoul's sash: we were waiting for you to open it."

"I'm surprised at your restraint, Carrots! It must have gone very much against the grain."

I hovered for a brief second between ladylike outrage and

frank amusement. "It wasn't easy," I said, opting for amusement. A mistake, because amusement always makes me grin, and a grin, no matter how small, cannot be said to be ladylike. That was Lord Pecus' fault, of course: if he hadn't grinned that porcelain grin at me it would never have entered my mind. "Do open it, Melchior! You know I'll never be able to sleep tonight if I don't know what it is!"

Melchior's own grin faded a little. "I have an inkling. Intelligence has been steadily leaking from the Capital in the last six months: military manoeuvres, troop training, weapon capabilities, that sort of thing. We know it's passing to someone in the Triumvirate, but I must admit I didn't think it would be through Glause."

"Or Raoul," I said, finding myself suddenly without the faintest particle of amusement.

Lord Pecus was frowning: or rather, his mask was. "How sensitive is the information?"

Melchior did something that buzzed uncomfortably through the room, setting my teeth on edge, and then nodded, satisfied. I do detest anti-espionage magic! "Some of it intermediate, things only of use in a full scale attack," he said. "But then there are the little, unconnected pieces of information that should mean nothing, until you realise that they've begun to form a picture. It's the little pieces that are worrying me."

Lord Pecus' green eyes sharpened suddenly. "National Intelligence Bureau or International Alliance?"

"Neither," Melchior said. "The NIB and the IA have their own ways of dealing with these things: I only get involved when things get too convoluted. This is a crown matter."

"Black Velvet," I said under my breath, and Melchior's brow rose dangerously.

"What do you know about Black Velvet, Carrots?"

"I know enough to not speak of them," I said frankly. "So these unrelated pieces of information have been from Black Velvet operations?"

Melchior nodded. "As far as I can make out. And the things that we thought *weren't*, turned out to be Black Velvet as well. We just hadn't made the connection yet. Someone who knows as much, if not more than we do, is keeping their eye on us."

Lord Pecus said: "It's the same here in Glause. I heard rumours through the IA, so I did a little digging in our own branch of er–"

"Black Velvet," supplied Melchior, with a glint of amusement.

"Black Velvet," Lord Pecus agreed, mild derision in his curved lips. "And I found the same thing that you did: someone has been leaking dribbles of apparently useless information to a Glausian citizen. Where it goes from there is anyone's guess."

"What happened to your leak?" Melchior inquired, with a kind of professional interest.

"I, ah– plugged it," said Lord Pecus, unconsciously flexing his shoulders. "The king authorised an invasive interrogation but whoever was using him was very talented: I barely got out alive."

"So we're both at a standstill."

"Only until I find out who killed your man," said Lord Pecus, carelessly confident. "I've finished my preliminaries, but I'll have to take him to my office. There are avenues I'd like to explore and all my equipment is there."

"And what are these?" I enquired, holding up a tiny glass bottle. As far as I could see, all it held was a hair; but there were more than twenty of the bottles, varying in size and content, on the side-table that had been dragged from its appointed place. Even the stitches Lord Pecus had pulled from Raoul's sash were bottled, stoppered, and marked.

"It's a new branch of inquiry that I'm experimenting with. Magical scans can tell us what a victim last saw—providing, of course, that his eyes are still intact—and find traces of who was last with him."

"Lord Topher and I," I nodded. "Very useful, but incorporeal. These samples are physical."

Lord Pecus matter-of-factly began to slip the little bottles into his pockets. "Yes. Samples that can't be tricked into existence, and that can't be planted without leaving traces that the magic scans will pick up."

Melchior, again with a professional interest, demanded: "What if the killer cleans the body?"

"They don't know to, yet," Lord Pecus said, briefly grinning again. Under my curious eyes, bottle after bottle went into the same two waistcoat pockets and left no bulge. "I've only just begun to experiment with the theory, so the criminal element hasn't caught on yet. They know we've begun autopsies, but this is my own branch of enquiry."

"Speaking of the criminal element—" Melchior added; "No, not you, Carrots, don't look so guilty— speaking of the criminal element, how are we going to get the body out without half a dozen inveterate gossips seeing it?"

"Oh, I've already done that," said Lord Pecus.

Melchior was looking impressed, which interested me: Melchior was not easily impressed. "Smooth shift!" he remarked. "Didn't even feel it. Where are we?"

"Pecus Manor. Lord Quorn will find his blue saloon a little larger than usual for a few days, but it shouldn't inconvenience him too much. I gave them a morning room that I never use."

Lord Pecus held the door open, and I stepped into a wide,

dark hall, gazing around me with all the curiosity that a lady has for the home of a man who has asked her to marry him. There were rich, dark floorboards beneath my thin dancing slippers, and the ceiling was braced decoratively with a series of massive, carved arches of the same wood. It was very large, very simple, and very *male*. At the end of the hall was a man I could only assume was Lord Pecus' butler. He wore the correct air of dignity and deference, but there the correctness of his attire ended. He was in his shirt-sleeves, garters holding his cuffs away from his wrists, and he wore an odd apron that could have been made of oilskin, so shiny was it.

"I am in receipt of your message, sir. Where is the body?"

Lord Pecus gestured briefly at the door we'd recently walked through. "I'll join you once I've shown my guests out."

I was disappointed but not surprised, and lingered behind Melchior long enough to see the butler enter the Quorn's blue saloon with a businesslike air. I expected that we would be shown to the front door, but Lord Pecus took us only a few steps down the hall to another door.

"It opens into the palace gardens," he said, to Melchior's inquiring eyebrow. "It will mean a short walk only."

Of *course* a door in the Lord Pecus' hallway would open into the palace gardens. I have always found magic a little disconcerting, but I couldn't help feeling impressed as well: Lord Pecus was really very clever. The shift between hallway and gardens was barely perceptible, but when I turned involuntarily to catch a last glimpse of Lord Pecus, all I could see was the full moon between the shadowy bars of the palace gate.

Melchior offered me his arm in the best royal manner. "Come, Carrots!" he said grandly, and added in a stage whisper: "Just don't tell my wife I was out after dark with another woman."

By the time we arrived back at the Ambassadorial Quarters, dawn was breaking in a rosy half-light, and the last of the guest were dilatorily straggling out. We slipped in unnoticed, and found Lord and Lady Quorn on the point of retiring to bed, leaving the considerable mess for the servants to quietly and invisibly do away with. Melchior and Lord Quorn melted away in the odious way men do when they are discussing things they think ladies shouldn't hear, and I was left to help Delysia up to her bedroom. Fortunately, this made it perfectly easy for me to slip a sleeping draught into her bedtime chocolate, and before long Delysia was in bed, yawning prodigiously and protesting that she would never be able to sleep. In the midst of her protestations she fell asleep, little pink mouth dropped slightly open, and I left her to the ministrations of her maid.

My own maid was waiting up for me, her eyes round and red from lack of sleep, and guarding my own pot of chocolate. I stripped in a businesslike manner, waving her off to bed, and slipped into one of my more sensible nightgowns, sipping at my chocolate. I wanted to think. My dressing done, I climbed into bed and sat with my arms clasped around my bent knees, staring at the foot of the bed in unseeing contemplation. It was not until I saw the blue rhinoceros peeking coyly around the doorpost that I realised that I, too, had been drugged. *Melchior!* I thought, growing swiftly too sleepy to be as indignant as I would be tomorrow. Unfortunately, the sleeping draught of choice in Glause tends to have hallucinogenic properties for a select few, myself included. In short order, I found myself floating on a downy cloud of softness with the blue rhino and a rather cross-eyed ostrich for company.

"Tomorrow," I said firmly to one of the ostrich's eyes, "Tomorrow, I need to find a new maid."

Chapter Three

"My lady? My lady?"

The voice sounded worried. Good, I thought, in some satisfaction. Marissa, my young maid, was no doubt having horrific visions of an eternally unwaking mistress, and the consequences attached. I toyed with the idea of remaining comatose until she left but it struck me reluctantly as taking things a little too far, so I sighed and sat up with unconcerned grace, as if my head were *not* pounding with a steady and malignant headache. I hate sleeping draughts with a *passion*.

Beside the bed, my tray of breakfast was exuding a delightful, savoury steam that quickly permeated the room with an alluring scent of bacon. Of course, I say 'breakfast' in the loosest sense of the word: it was by now noon at least, judging from the glaringly bright patch of sunlight at present warming my toes through the bedspread. I could just see the searing edge of the middle sun through my window, and I found that my aching head didn't appreciate the fact. The

Triad is no closer in Glause than Civet, but it *feels* closer, with every searing sunbeam.

There was also a city newspaper, but since the headline proclaimed nothing more sensational than the arrival of Lacuna's newest prince, and in smaller print, the newest thing in gloves—*gnau* leather, for the *discerning* lady (and the lacking in taste, no doubt)—I felt that I was at liberty to ignore it.

"My blue and tan walking dress, thank you, Marissa," I said decidedly, wriggling until the breakfast tray fitted just comfortably over my legs.

"Yes, my lady," Marissa said, but she hovered by the door, twisting her apron between her fingers until I was forced to neglect my bacon and eggs to inquire what was the matter.

"Nothing my lady," the girl said, in an irritatingly gormless manner. If it was nothing, why was she still standing there? "That is, are you going out, my lady?"

"I am, Marissa. Perhaps you wanted me to purchase you something while I am out?"

This gentle sarcasm was lost on Marissa. Eyes wide, she said: "Oh no, my lady! But His Majesty asked me to summon you to the royal suite when you woke."

Chewing a mouthful of bacon and eggs thoughtfully, I considered leaving Melchior to stew in his own juice and go out just as I had planned to. But Melchior had an uncomfortable habit of making sure one regretted such decisions; and, after all, he might want to see me about the affair last night.

"The walking dress, but keep the hat aside," I decided. If I was to be wandering through the length and breadth of Delysia's house, I did not want a hat compounding my headache. It was a very smart hat, businesslike in blue with just a bow to add frivolity, but only the great outdoors could make the tightness of the hatband bearable with such a pounding in my temples.

When I was done with breakfast I sat down at the dressing table to allow Marissa to do my hair, absently playing with the haresfoot and powdering my fingers in the process. The remnants of the drug were making my thought processes a little slower than usual, and I didn't notice that Marissa had curled, braided and basket-woven my hair to within an inch of its life until I looked up from my powdery fingers to see my face, pale and big-eyed in the mirror, made distressingly more so by the tightness of my coiffure.

I sighed. "Marissa—"

"It's a royal interview, my lady!" Her eyes were wide and earnest. I have always suspected that I am not respectable enough for Marissa. Her sole mission in life is to see me perpetually coiffed and painted, in which goal I constantly disappoint her. I have earned the right to certain comfortable eccentricities by virtue of being an old maid, eccentricities I have no intention of surrendering, and it was a constant battle between us.

"Very well," I said, rising. Normally I wouldn't think of letting Marissa and her big eyes inveigle me into going out in such a state, but happily, I had thought of a wonderful way both to deal with her and get my revenge on Melchior in one stroke. I took the hat from her hand quite cheerfully, choosing a favourite hair pin to match the blue. "Your fortunes have turned, child."

"My lady?"

"His Majesty is very pleased with your obedience," I told her, ignoring the fact that Melchior couldn't possibly have told me any such thing, since I had not seen him yet this morning. No doubt he *had* been pleased, the beast! Marissa was not likely to call this fact to mind: her face was already glowing with a quiet, saintly pride. *I have received my just reward*, her demeanour said. "You'll be very sad to leave me, I don't doubt," I added mendaciously.

Marissa, the little traitor, was clasping her hands to her narrow chest, her shining eyes raised beatifically to my face. "Oh, my lady! Do you mean–"

"You are now in the employ of the royal family," I nodded. I wondered if she had even objected when Melchior gave her the drugged chocolate to give me. No, she would have thanked him for the honour, with that wide-eyed look of awe. At least I had had the decency not to corrupt Delysia's maid: I had slipped the drug into her chocolate with my own hand. I had no place in my staff for a maid whose loyalties were not all mine. On the other hand, I could not bring myself to let the child go out unemployed, and she would undoubtedly be happier with another master. Besides, it would annoy Melchior immensely. "I congratulate you. You begin tomorrow morning, and you may have the rest of the afternoon to move your things to a room in the royal suites. I will not require your services again."

I left her with a small purse of coins, trembling and still trying to stammer out ecstatic thanks. Really, it was most uncomplimentary. Anyone would think that I had mistreated the child! I found myself grinning as I walked briskly down the wide halls of the ambassadorial palace: Melchior would regret his interference. The footman looked suspiciously at me when I asked admittance to the royal chambers: I wondered satirically if he thought I was the Laughing Assassin, and grinned a little wider. However, by the time I had walked through an excessively sunny morning room that started my headache pounding again, the smile had faded somewhat. When Melchior opened the door to his own sitting room, he frowned at the sight of me.

"You look terrible, Carrots."

"Yes, Marissa did my hair this morning," I said calmly, and swept past him to sit on my favourite seat. I set my hat carefully beside me and began to unpin my hair while Melchior, with a suspiciously mocking smile, sauntered back to his own chair.

"How did you sleep?"

I arched my eyebrows at him, untangling a particularly tiny, tight plait. "That, Melchior, is deliberate provocation. What do you want?"

"Lord Pecus would like a word with us," Melchior said. He was still grinning in a way that warned me I was missing an important detail.

"Very well," I said absently, struggling to reach one integral pin that Marissa seemed to have lodged deep in my skull. "When are we meeting him?"

Melchior's eyes twinkled. "Er, Carrots?"

Oh dear. I dropped my arms and turned, hair half-tumbled down my back, to see Lord Pecus. He was standing just behind me, doing his invisible trick again.

"Good morning, my lord," I said with careful unconcern. Melchior was smiling, horrible man, and I thought I could detect the trace of a smile on Lord Pecus' porcelain mask. Oh, well. No way out but to attack. I said: "There's a pin I can't reach, my lord. Could you remove it for me, please?"

I had the malicious pleasure of seeing his hand hesitate for a brief moment, then gentle fingers felt through the complicated knot Marissa had woven into the back of my head and there was a sense of pressure released. The rest of my hair tumbled down my back, weave disintegrating and tiny braids unravelling. I set to work combing the braids out with my fingers, and said pleasantly: "What was it you wanted to ask me, my Lord?"

Lord Pecus blinked, as if he had been thinking of something else entirely, and said: "The nature of my questions will be ah, rather more *official*, Lady Farrah."

Oho! I thought, with interest. So Lord Pecus was what we in the Capital knew as The Guv'nor, was he? That explained the look the footman had given me: he thought I was a shady type, no doubt. "I never done it, guv'nor!" I said promptly. "I swears it!"

Melchior choked into his coffee. "Carrots, behave yourself!"

"The questions are in regard to Lord Topher, Lady Farrah," said Lord Pecus, a smile curving in his mask. He sat down in a huge leather chair that just contained him, and leaned forward with his forearms on his knees. His eyes were keen, alert and unwavering: if I had been guilty of something I would have been feeling distinctly uneasy. "Your movements have been accounted for all night: Lord Topher's, on the other hand, have not."

Laughter welled up inside me. "You suspect Lord Topher? My lord, let me reassure you; Lord Topher is *not* your murderer!"

"How long were you with him?" The question had a touch of steel to it. Did Lord Pecus not like to be cheeked in official interviews, I wondered, curling a plait around my finger and regarding him limpidly, or was something else in the wind?

I gazed at him long enough to make his lips tighten, and then said helpfully: "You might want to speak to the footman who was manning the doors of the ballroom last night. He saw Raoul with the Duke of Horn just moments before I met with Lord Topher again; after which Lord Topher informed me that Raoul had gone to the blue saloon. I believe you said Raoul was murdered only minutes before we found him."

"Why did Lord Topher feel it necessary to tell you where Sir Raoul was?"

"Possibly because I was looking for Sir Raoul," I observed. "Of course, he *could* have been lying in wait simply in order to tell me, but I rather doubt it. Mostly I think he wanted to dance with me."

There was a twinkle of amusement in Lord Pecus' jade eyes again, which I acknowledged with a small, prim smile. It was nice to know he wasn't a stuffed shirt after all. "And what was your first impression upon entering the blue saloon?"

"That someone had spilt a glass of wine on Delysia's new carpet," I said soberly, all desire to laugh fading like dew on a sunny morning. "I thought that I should clean it before the stain set: and there was Raoul."

My fingers, which had absently been unravelling the last of Marissa's tiny braids, ceased to move; and it was not until Lord Pecus, his gaze averted, said: "Would you like a moment, Lady Farrah?" that I realised tears were gliding warmly down my cheeks. I pulled myself together before Melchior found it necessary to put his arm around me in the sometimes irritatingly older brother way he has. Melchior is a dear, but I felt that I was at a disadvantage facing Lord Pecus as it was, and I positively refused to do so while being cuddled comfortingly in a male embrace.

"I beg your pardon, my lord; my thoughts were wandering. Please continue."

Lord Pecus, who had been thoughtfully gazing at his loosely clasped hands, flicked a quick look at me. "And Lord Topher, my lady?"

"Lord Topher was never in the room without me. I sent him out to fetch Delysia, and once he went dashing out into the garden to see if he could find the killer. In fact, even *I* am possibly a better suspect than Lord Topher."

"*If* you could do more with magic than twiddle locks," Melchior said, with brutal honesty. "Sorry, Carrots; but the kind of skills needed to do what our murderer did are beyond your ken." He thought about it, and added: "For which I am profoundly, *profoundly* grateful."

Lord Pecus made a stifled sound as I glared at Melchior, and said in a rather more strained tone of voice: "Thank you, Lady Farrah. I have no further questions for you."

His voice was a dismissal, which I chose not to recognise. Instead, plaiting the last of my hair and twisting it up into a practical coronet while Lord Pecus watched in what seemed to be a kind of interested speculation, I inquired: "Has your investigation turned up anything interesting, my lord?"

Melchior openly grinned: he would have expected nothing less.

Lord Pecus treated me to a prolonged, thoughtful gaze and said politely: "It's too early in the investigation to say, my lady," which of course meant that even if he did know something, he wasn't saying. I looked up to find his eyes laughing through a suspiciously straight-faced mask, and only just prevented my brows from rising in sudden surprise. So Lord Pecus was not above playing the dense Guv'nor, was he?

Consequently, it was with a buzzing, busy mind that I said: "Of course! How silly of me! Good day, my lord; good day, Melchior."

I thought Lord Pecus looked disappointed, and suspected that he had been anticipating an argument. Melchior said affably: "Oh, there's no need to go, Carrots: Pecus and I were just about to send down for some er, tea and biscuits."

Glausian whiskey, I mentally translated, briefly weighing the chance of either of them accidentally dropping something interesting during the conversation against the significantly better chance of them both guarding their speech until I was gone. Annoying, but unsurprising.

"Thank you, but no," I said decidedly. "Enjoy your *tea*. By the way, Melchior, congratulations on the new addition to your staff! I believe her things have already been moved to the servants' quarters of your royal suite: she was simply *overjoyed*! I'm sure you'll find her just as useful as you hoped."

I beamed a smile into Melchior's thunderstruck face, favoured Lord Pecus with another as I set my hat at a saucy angle over one eye, and took my leave of them. As I descended the stairs beyond the royal suite, the butler was just beginning to toil his way up with a tray, upon which sat a decanter of the best Glausian whiskey; and, insultingly, *two* glasses. Melchior had known very well I would not be staying.

So I said, with parting malice: "Thomas, his highness has changed his mind. They will take sweet tea and biscuits instead of whiskey. Try to find those lovely flowery biscuits that Lady Quorn's cook does so well, I believe his highness is very fond of them."

Thomas, with his usual mournful sigh, descended the one step he had taken, and said in measured tones: "Very good, my lady."

I was still chuckling to myself when one of Delysia's army of footmen presented me with my gloves, which Marissa must have sent down as a last token of affection. I did wish I could see Melchior's face when the tea and biscuits made an appearance.

"Thank you, er—"

"Daubney, my lady," supplied the young footman helpfully. His fresh, clean-shaven face seemed familiar, and it took only a moment longer to recognise him as the footman who had directed me to Raoul last night.

"Daubney! Of course! You were very useful last night."

There was a wicked tingle of mischief in my mood this morning. Giving into it, I said: "I find myself short of a maid this morning, Daubney. If you have no pressing household matters to attend to, I am in need of your services."

As much as a well-trained footman could, Daubney manifested enthusiasm. "Yes, my lady! I am entirely at your service."

"Very well, follow me," I said, and sailed blissfully out the door with the delicious knowledge that when Melchior and Lord Pecus wanted to interview Daubney, they would find him unaccountably missing. Perhaps it would make them think twice about excluding me from an investigation that was eminently my right to assist in, if not by friendship to the victim or merit of sagacity, at least by merit of being first upon the scene.

The triad was bright and warm outside, heating the worn cobbles of the ambassadorial courtyard to such an extent that they fairly radiated warmth and brought a sleepy feel to the air that was untouched by any breath of wind. I found it necessary to bite back a series of successive yawns, and the few people on the streets moved slowly about their various businesses, caught in the stickiness of the day. I had brought along a reticule as if I were about to go shopping, but once out the gate I turned briskly to the left, and followed the main road that would lead me, in time, to the parade grounds of the Glausian Horselords. Daubney looked doubtful, but was too uncertain of himself to inquire if I had mistaken my way, and I continued without enlightening him. The horselords should be finished their morning manoeuvres by now, and ready and willing to talk to me. During peace time there was not much for the militia to do, and despite all the training and manoeuvres that the almost obnoxiously active horselords could squeeze into a day, the only real duties they had were their morning parade and a rotating guard of the royal palace.

As I approached the barracks there was a whoop and a shout, and the small gatehouse door was flung open with a resounding *crack!*

"Isabella! You've come to marry me at last!" said Curran's voice exuberantly. "Or have you come to take my little Paladin for a ride?"

"If that is the name of your new horse, then certainly not!" I said firmly. I still remembered what had happened the last time I tried to ride a horse. No doubt Curran did also, because he was grinning openly.

"He's a sweet little thing, nothing like that scrawny, savage beast of Miryum's. Never trust a white horse! They bite, one and all!"

"I remember!" I said, quite tartly. "I also remember that you all stood laughing at me, and I *distinctly* remember trying to salvage what I could of my new hat from the beast! Without help, I might add!"

"*I* remember the box on the ear you gave me!" promptly said Curran.

"That was bad of me," I allowed. I patted the afflicted member, much to Daubney's well-bred surprise. "But it was my favourite, and it took me a week to make it just right!"

"It was a good, hearty blow," Curran said, pursuing the subject with some glee. "I could almost have mistaken you for one of the horseless regiment. Well, besides the clothes, of course."

"Enough of your tomfoolery!" I said. I had no desire to go into the matter of the horseless regiment— Lacunan soldiers who fought hand-to-hand, weaponless, and, as their name suggested, horseless. They all, male and female alike, wore black bodysuits that were *decidedly* skin tight, and I didn't trust Curran on the subject of skin tight suits.

He said: "Spoilsport!" and grinned.

"Where are the others?" I stepped past him into the barracks, wrinkling my nose at the smell. Daubney, well trained as he was, didn't show by blink or grimace that he noticed.

"Stable. Polishing and saddling up."

"Curran, I am not dressed for riding."

"Manoeuvres," he said, shrugging innocently.

"Don't give me that! I'm perfectly well aware that you can put off the midday manoeuvres for as long as you like. This is important."

"But I do so like watching you try to ride! It's painful, yet entertaining." He maintained the innocent expression for another, sorely tried moment, and then grinned. "Oh, all right. But the ambassadorial poker will have to stay here."

Daubney didn't so much as look at him. My goodness, the man was well trained. "What are your orders, my lady?"

"I think you'll be more useful to me here," I said thoughtfully. He was a young man who noticed a surprisingly good deal, and Raoul had spent most of his time in Glause here with the horselords. Perhaps there was something worth overhearing that I would not learn from the horselords. They liked me, and I liked them, but I was under no illusions as to their *not* cheerfully lying to me if they felt it was in their country's or their regiment's best interests. If and how they lied to me would serve to show me if Glause itself were involved in Raoul's murder.

"You're up late'o'day," Curran said, opening the stableyard gate for me.

"Unavoidable misfortune," I replied, a little absently. The

stableboys do their best, but when horses are allowed to roam free, a certain amount of unpleasantness is inevitable, and it needed all of my attention to safely navigate the cobbles without soiling my shoes. The other horselords couldn't be far away: I could distinctly hear a rendition of *Nelly-O* being performed in a far from tuneful tenor, to the accompaniment of jeers and insults. Brennan never could be convinced that he did not have the voice of an angel, and not even five years with his regiment had cured him of singing while he tended to his horse. I had the feeling that he regarded them as an unappreciative public who would one day warm to his charms, and in the meantime learned to dodge horse-shoes and hammers with great alacrity. I often wondered if this practise had not stood him in good stead in battle, since he certainly seemed less scarred than the others.

"There seems to be an animal in pain," Curran growled, hunching his shoulders as we walked closer. Harness jingled and heavy hooves thumped the ground the nearer we got, and insults of a less than savoury nature began to distinguish themselves through Brennan's warble. "Excuse me while I put it out of its misery."

I allowed him to stride ahead and disappear around the great stone wall of the stable. Brennan's singing abruptly ceased in a wild cacophony of shouts that rose in a crescendo to the accompaniment of the sound of a water butt being overturned. When Curran reappeared, his right arm and the whole right side of his blue tunic were soaked into midnight blue, a circumstance which I thought it better to ignore.

"Come on in, Isabella, I've put him out of his misery."

I entered the corral to find Brennan, as I had expected, still crawling out of the water butt. By all appearances he had been dumped head first into it. Now it lay on its side in a puddle of dirt and horse dung, with Brennan's legs protruding comically from it. The other horselords, ignoring it as a common, everyday occurrence, were variously polishing and saddling at differing points around the stable.

"Don't let Curran convince you to ride Paladin," said Miryum, without looking up from the silvery bit she was polishing. "He's a fiend in horse form."

"I have no intention of riding Paladin," I said, eyeing with disfavour the simply enormous black horse that was watching me with a knowing gleam to its nasty black eyes. "And if that is Paladin, I object to your description of him as *little*, Curran!"

"Not a bit above eighteen hands!" protested Curran, approaching the beast with what I considered to be most inadvisable casualness. In an odious display of duplicity, the animal coquetted and even pranced; trying, no doubt, to lull me into a false sense of security.

"I know your sort!" I said to it severely. "You, sir, are the sort that eats hats! I will not be charmed."

"Now you've hurt his feelings," Curran said reproachfully, but Miryum only grinned.

"To what do we owe the pleasure, my lady?" She put aside the bit and reins, and wiped her hands on a rag of cloth. "Not that we're not always glad to see you, of course. But with the conference this afternoon—"

"I'm afraid this is business rather than pleasure. I need some information. Is there anywhere private we can speak?"

Miryum gazed at me for a deliberate moment, and I could see her weighing up the odds of me asking for privileged information, and how she could courteously refuse if I did. At last she shrugged, and said: "We have wards. The stable should be safe. What information do you need?"

"There are a few things I am *not* going to tell you," I said carefully, deciding that honesty—after a fashion—was the best policy. "I am *not* going to tell you that there was a murder at the ambassadorial palace last night. And I most certainly cannot tell you that it was Raoul who was murdered."

The horselords looked at each other with troubled eyes. Even Brennan, struggling up from the water butt, sat himself down quietly on a hay bale without attempting revenge on Curran. "You think we had something to do with it?" he asked, slicking damp curls back with one hand.

"No," I said, and was pleasantly surprised to find that it wasn't a lie. The horselords had been surprised– and dismayed, if I was any reader of faces. They wanted this merger as much as Annabel wanted it. Together Civet and Glause were strong; apart, we were disastrously isolated. "But you might know something of it."

"Raoul wasn't with us for very long," said Katrina, a tall, dusky brunette. There was a crease between her straight brows, and her hands were clasped between her knees. I had had my suspicions of her and Raoul: Curran said it was because he was the only man she had met who was taller than her, but I had watched them sparring, and I had no doubts that it would have ended in marriage. "He was restless, watching the crowd. I think he was meeting with someone."

I nodded ruefully. It was nothing more than I had expected, but it still hurt to think that Raoul had been a traitor. "Did you see who it was that he met with?"

She shook her head: the other horselords followed suit.

"Saw him with the Earl of Horn later on," Curran volunteered, and Emmett, beside him, nodded a close-shaven head in silent assent. "That was when we were leaving."

"That fits the timeline," I said, sighing. "Keep your ears to the ground for me, will you? Tell me if you hear anything: rebel movement, someone taking credit. Lord Pecus may question you, but I doubt it; Melchior and Lord Quorn want it kept quiet for as long as possible."

Miryum nodded soberly. "I can put out some inquiries, but if Lord Pecus is heading the investigation himself he'll get to hear of it."

That put me at a momentary standstill. "He's that good?"

"He's persistent, and he's clever," she said. "Besides, he knows the right channels, and people are afraid of him."

"I don't want to cause any trouble for you," I said thoughtfully. "Perhaps it would be better if you merely keep your ears open. I'll take care of the inquiries myself."

They looked subtly relieved, and I had a moment's misgiving: I was going to have to walk very warily indeed. *Drat* Lord Pecus! He was becoming a recurring, not to mention inopportune, motif.

"How was he killed?" Katrina asked quietly, as I turned to leave. Her eyes were unemotional and distant, but her hands remained clasped and white-knuckled, and I was not deceived.

"Magic," I said briefly. "If Lord Pecus is to be believed, the darkest and most skilful."

Miryum frowned, and even Curran, light-hearted as he was toward danger, looked uneasy. "Did you touch him?"

"Lord Pecus? I believe not."

Miryum shook her head. "No, Raoul. Did you touch his body?"

"Yes." I began to have the uncomfortably sinking feeling that Lord Pecus had not told me quite everything. "I helped Lord Pecus remove something from Raoul's person. What's amiss?"

"Perhaps nothing," Miryum said uneasily. "But I'm surprised Lord Pecus let you touch a body riddled with dark magic. A lot of the worst killing magic has an inherent tracking clause in the residue that leads the murderer to anyone who might come across the body. Touch the body too soon after the murder, and you're marked. If you catch it in time, it can be worked backwards."

Oho! And he hadn't told me! I wondered briefly if Melchior had known, but dismissed the idea: Melchior might hide any number of things from me, but this was not one of them. Besides, although he had certainly fought a great deal of black magic in his time with Annabel, he had not made a study of it as Lord Pecus must have done.

"That gives me something to go on with, at least," I said pensively. "Thank you, Miryum. Oh, and if any of you so much as *suggests* that I told you about this, I will categorically and absolutely truthfully insist that I did not do any such thing."

I left them smiling with as much of an air of normality as was possible, and rejoined Daubney with great thoughtfulness. He was standing where I had left him, of course, as though made of stone.

"Come, Daubney," I said grandly, sweeping through the gate ahead of him and narrowly avoiding a disgraceful incident with an inconveniently placed pile of horse droppings. "I have an errand in town."

❧

I walked the uncomplaining Daubney through busy intersections and a dizzying array of back allies at a good brisk pace. By the time I had completed an unusually circuitous route to my favourite teashop (that could be conveniently attributed to the fact that I was not a native of Glause) I was satisfied that I was indeed being followed. One of Lord Pecus's watchmen, no doubt. I was not at all surprised: if what Miryum said was true, he certainly wouldn't have allowed me to touch Raoul without the precaution of having me followed. It was a comfort to know that if I found myself in any trouble, help would not be far away. It was less satisfying to know that I would have a great deal of difficulty losing the watchman if I were minded to do so.

I sipped my orange tea pensively at a lacy outdoor table and watched my shadow strike up a conversation with the stallholder opposite in my peripheral vision. I briefly toyed with the idea of escaping here and now, but the teashop was a haven and a sanctuary to me, and I refused to select my tea with the amount of haste requisite to gain a good distance before the watchman realised I was gone. Tea is the only thing I like as well as clothes, and I had no intention of allowing Lord Pecus' importunity to interfere in the selection of a new variety. Instead, I finished my tea and selected a paper bag of Lacunan whole leaf rose-tea to sample, then took to the streets again. I didn't trouble myself to watch for my follower again. Time was running short before the afternoon conference, and I had a great deal that I wished to do. For all the good it would do him, the watchman could follow me all day. It was not where I was going that was important: it was who I was *with*.

"The magic quarter, Daubney," I said briskly, deciding it was high time that he and I had a talk. "Which direction?"

"Due north, my lady. Is there a particular shop you wanted?"

"Something ostentatious and bright, I think," I said. "A shop that deals in improbable love potions and enchanted swords."

Daubney's lips twitched, but he controlled them. "Perhaps my lady is aware she is being followed?"

"Yes, Daubney, I am indeed. Very perspicacious of you. Do you think we could lose him?"

"No, my lady."

"Just what I thought," I agreed. "Is it a long walk to this shop?"

"Yes, my lady."

"Oh, good. I think our fine, upstanding watchman would enjoy a stroll through the magic quarter. Now, Daubney, I want you to tell me exactly what you may or may not have seen last night, *particularly* in relation to Sir Raoul."

Daubney was a concise and accurate narrator, and a more than usually acute observer. The streets were really no place for such a conversation, but he overcame the difficulties with the sublimity that belongs to the best of footmen, and added to my scanty store of knowledge such information that members of rebel factions had been present at the ball. It really was unfortunate that everyone had been masked, else I believe Daubney could have named everyone present without difficulty. The streets passed almost unnoticed but for a nasty moment when I spotted Lord Topher wandering by a street stall and expeditiously stepped down a side street to avoid him. This took us down an interestingly unsavoury walkway that made Daubney unconsciously flex his shoulders in a rather warlike manner, imparting enough wariness into the seedier populace lurking in the shadows, to cause them to let us be.

We had almost reached civilisation again when a small boy was propelled from a shadowed doorway and collided painfully with me. I was just in time to grasp the skinny paw as it removed itself from my reticule, clutching a small silver coin.

The urchin looked at me with wide eyes, then down at his hand, and gulped. "Beg puddin', miss! Force of 'abit, miss!"

An older girl, who had been scrubbing with some determination at a hopelessly stained doorstep, looked up quickly. Sister? No, the boy was too dark: Lacunan blood without a doubt. But there was a relationship, nevertheless; his eyes flickered to her with a little desperation.

"It's no good pinching that, anyway," I said calmly, warning Daubney off with a slight shake of my head. He stood back, and I let go of the urchin. "See?"

The child looked down at the coin, and found himself bemusedly holding a leaf.

"My brother made that for me," I told him pleasantly. "You've no idea how amusing it's been. If you wanted money, you should have gone for my cuff."

I slipped a coin from my left cuff and displayed it.

"Just so, you see? My own invention." I tossed him the coin, and said to Daubney: "Come along, Daubney. I believe you had got to the part where I came and asked you as to Sir Raoul's whereabouts."

"Yes, my lady," Daubney said, managing with an effort not to grin. The urchin dashed to the girl with the scrubbing brush and watched us continue with wide eyes. "I was thinking about it this morning, and it seems to me that there was something strange about it."

"Strange in what way?" I inquired.

Daubney didn't reply. Instead, there was a soft slap behind me: my paper bag of tea hitting the cobbles, I realized, frowning. When I turned, Daubney had a finger in his cravat and was tugging ineffectually at it, his breathing laboured. His eyes were worryingly glassy.

"Daubney?"

I took a step toward him, but a dirty hand caught my arm. "Don't touch him, my lady!"

It was the scrubbing girl, her hands still slick with suds that soaked quickly into my sleeve. Daubney sank to his knees, coughing, and I said crisply: "There's a man just beyond the end of the street; fetch him now."

She nodded, and jerked a thumb over her shoulder for the urchin's benefit. He took off at a run, skinny legs almost blurring, and she knelt beside Daubney, who looked up at me with glazed horror in his brown eyes. "My...lady...help!"

I dropped to my knees beside them both, and the girl said again, sharply: "Don't touch him! Have you got wood, my lady?"

I snapped the beads from my reticule strings without a pang, and the girl made a quick motion with her hand that set them spinning in the air within a complicated web of blue glittery stuff. They revolved once, twice; and then exploded, stinging us with splinters. The girl hissed between her teeth in surprise or fear, I wasn't sure which, and spat: "Get away! Now!"

She was quicker to her feet than me, dashing up and away across the cobbles. I was still forcing myself up when Daubney's eyes flooded red.

"Oh no!" I said, swallowing a horrible lump in my throat; because I knew what was coming. "Oh no, no, no!"

And then Daubney's head exploded.

Chapter Four

I must have closed my eyes. My eyelids stained red as a warm spray stang my cheeks and pattered on my dress. When it ceased I opened my eyes, not daring to look down at myself, and stood very, very still. I was desperately afraid that I would go into a raving fit of hysterics if I had to look at the remains of Daubney that were now decorating my dress. There was a red haze in the corners of my eyes, and a sticky warmth on my cheeks: by which I concluded, with distant logic, that my face was likewise covered with a layer of Daubney.

I closed my eyes again, swallowing, and heard the scrubbing girl say matter-of-factly: "That was a watchman, following you: if you need to scarper, best go now."

A faint smile touched my lips. Perhaps I really did look like a desperate character. "What's your name, child?"

"Vadim, my lady," said the voice, still cheerfully. The girl must have a stomach of cast iron.

"Vadim, there is a handkerchief in my reticule. Please remove it."

There was a gentle tug on my left arm, where my reticule, beadless, still hung.

"Got it, m'lady."

"Do you think you could clean away the worst of it from my face, Vadim? I believe I can do the rest for myself."

Vadim didn't answer, but a gentle dabbing began almost immediately on my face, and after a moment my hat was carefully rather than expertly removed. When I felt deft fingers going through my hair I ventured to open my eyes, and was just in time to see the little Lacunan pickpocket dashing ahead of my sturdy watchman follower.

"Here!" expostulated the watchman, panting slightly and pointing an accusing finger and myself and Vadim. "You're destroying evidence! Stop that, you little baggage!"

I drew myself up to the most dignified height I could, putting myself eye to eye with the man, and froze him with a look. "I *beg* your pardon?"

The unfortunate watchman grew ruddy while Vadim grinned. She didn't stop dabbing.

"Begging pardon, my lady, but I didn't mean you. I meant the young thing snabbling the bits and pieces out of your hair. Lord Pecus will want you processed, and she's destroying evidence!"

"What Lord Pecus wants is a matter of indifference to me," I said. "I will *not* tread the length and breadth of the Imperial City with little pieces of Daubney all over me. I will not, in fact, spend a moment longer than I have to in such a state. I believe you will find quite enough evidence splattered all over the street."

The watchman expostulated at some length, and before long I ceased to listen to him, instead turning my attention to Vadim, who had moved onto my sleeves. A length of clean blue cuff greeted my startled gaze when I looked down, innocent of both blood and miniscule scraps of flesh.

"Vadim," I said quietly, interrupting the watchman; "Are you using magic on me?"

"Yes, m'lady," Vadim said serenely, going on to the other sleeve. "It comes up ever so much nicer when I do."

"So I see." I inspected both arms with approval, carefully avoiding the bodice that Vadim was still working on, and said sweetly to the indignant watchman: "I'm sorry, I interrupted you. What were you saying?"

"I've sent out the signal for Lord Pecus," he said gruffly. "He'll be here in a quarter hour. You may not listen to me, my lady; but I'll wager you listen to him!"

"And so I should if I were going to stay," I said. "But Vadim has finished with my dress, as you see, and I have errands I need to perform."

"You can't leave a crime scene!" protested the watchman. He was beginning to look a little desperate.

"Oh, I'm quite decent again!" I assured him, wilfully misunderstanding. His estimation of a quarter of an hour before Lord Pecus arrived, I held to be generous. I would be surprised if the next few minutes didn't see him here. "I won't cause public consternation like this."

"I'm afraid I'll have to accompany you, my lady."

"How unfortunate!" I kneeled briskly, laying my fingers for a sticky moment on Daubney's stiff shoulder and rising again before I had to look too closely at him. "I do wonder what Lord Pecus will say if you leave a dead body and all this evidence in the street, however. Do you think it entirely wise? Come along, Vadim; you too, child."

I swept away up the street without looking to see whether either the watchman or the children were following, and turned into the main street. After a few brisk paces, I said: "Is he following?"

"No, m'lady," said Vadim, keeping up without effort.

"Very well. Vadim, how would you like to be a lady's maid?"

"Well, m'lady, there's Keenan."

No more than I had expected. There would be no getting the one without the other. "The pickpocket?"

A mutter behind Vadim protested sulkily: "Was n'accident, didn't mean to do it. Force of 'abit."

"That's him," said Vadim, in a grim way I guessed boded no good for the still-protesting Keenan.

"Keenan, would you like to be a page boy?"

"Wiv a lacy collar?" demanded Keenan, in deep suspicion.

"Certainly not," I said firmly. I had a great distaste for the prevailing mode in Glause that dressed little boys in any amount of lace and velvet and called them pageboys: in Civet they were more circumspectly dressed in plain knicker-bockers and a white shirt, and performed duties somewhere between those of a Glausian footman and pageboy. "You will have to fix my pens for me, and fetch things from the market, and I imagine you will have to eat at least three meals a day."

"When do I get to eat, then?" Keenan's tone was one of even darker suspicion than before.

"When we get home, of course." I threw a swift look behind me, saw the look of thoughtful cunning that flashed across the young face, and added calmly: "And not before. Vadim, what do you say?"

"There's a magician trailing us," Vadim said, which piece of information I took to signify her assent. "A good one, coming in fast. I think he's running."

My eyes opened a little wider. The watchman must have

seen me touch Daubney's body and told Lord Pecus. How unfortunate. "Vadim, can you buy us any time?"

The smile passed so swiftly across her face that it was difficult to tell if she really had smiled. "Yes, m'lady. Oh yes."

Keenan watched her with a kind of brotherly pride as her eyes briefly glazed, and said conversationally: "You shouldn't of touched the stiff: you've got a thread of black magic trailin' yer."

"Indeed I have," I said cordially. "And a very fresh one, too. I imagine it will be useful in tracking the murderer."

"You've got two," Vadim corrected absently, her eyes focusing again. "One fresh, one dying. The stiff had one, too, before he died. I've confused the trail for you, m'lady; do you want a tracker?"

"The best you can find in five minutes," I qualified.

Vadim's cheeks took on a slight pink tinge beneath the dirt. "It will take him at *least* an hour to find us," she protested.

"I daresay you're right," I told her; "However, since it's Lord Pecus who's after us, I'd prefer not to take the chance."

I saw the dismay creep into her face. "Lord Pecus?"

"A very possibly *annoyed* Lord Pecus."

Vadim gave a jerky nod, and said tersely: "Against him, it might hold ten minutes. I know someone a few streets down."

"Then we'll walk quickly."

It would not have been ladylike, of course, to trot in the open street. However, the way Vadim took us delved even further into the more insalubrious backstreets of the magic quarter, and there was no one beyond a few stray cats to see me pick up my skirts and run, displaying my ankles in a satisfyingly shocking way. Being the indefatigable walker that I am, my shoes were light and comfortable, and since I do not tend to breathlessly tight corsetry, I was breathing only slightly harder when we turned down a final alley. It was, to my unease, a dead end: I felt that a tracker should have access to at least two directions at any one time. A quick glance at Vadim, however, showed that we had arrived. She pointed at a small, rotting door hanging loosely in a brick archway, and said: "That's her, m'lady. Don't mention the gov'nor, or she won't help you."

My eyebrows went up. Indeed? Lord Pecus seemed to have a very present and powerful effect on the general street populace. I wondered how often he walked the streets on business.

I shook out my coin cuff, and put two silver Glausian *grits* into Vadim's hand. "Get yourself and Keenan some fresh clothes. Mind you wash, and on no account spend any less than what I've given you. I'll have clothes made up later, but you'll need something a little less ragged to get into the ambassadorial palace in the meantime."

Keenan scoffed. "Can get in there anytime, miss! Them bubblers couldn't stop us if they tried!"

"Possibly, but that is not what I asked you to do," I said mildly, scribbling on the back of one of my calling cards. "You must go around by the servant's entrance, and give them my card. Someone will show you to my rooms. Wait for me there."

Vadim looked uneasy, but nodded. "Be wary of Ciara," she said in parting. "She's fair, but hard— very hard."

I waited until they were gone before I knocked, despite the probable shortage of time. My knowledge of magic might be very small, but I knew that what I was about to do was dangerous, and despite the fact that Vadim seemed to be a more than competent magic user, I couldn't bring myself to walk children willy-nilly into danger.

The door sagged beneath my knock, and a voice from

within called faintly: "If that's the supplier, come on in. If it's anyone else, push off!"

Choosing to take the term 'supplier' loosely, I carefully pushed through the spongy door to find myself in a hallway that was excessively dingy, and as narrow as it was long. But if it was dingy, at least what I could see of it was *clean*, and I was able to feel satisfied that Vadim's Ciara was not a shoddy worker.

The hallway opened into a room that was a little larger and a little rounder than I had expected, and I found myself being observed by a pair of steady grey eyes.

"You're not my supplier," remarked the woman. Her look was appraising. She was stretched out on her chair in a manner almost masculine, clothed in breeches and tunic; and the length of charcoal between her fingers was tapping pensively against the top of her desk, leaving little deposits of powdery charcoal.

"Not technically," I agreed, unabashed. I knew ministers like Ciara: they were good at their jobs, and conscientious, but followed the letter of the law down to the very last dash. And as Melchior says, when you follow the letter rather than the spirit of the law, murderers go free, and petty thieves are hanged. Vadim had been right to warn me not to mention Lord Pecus.

"However, I *will* supply you with money in return for your services."

The grey eyes continued to regard me coolly. "Anything illegal?"

That made the third time today! Did everyone imagine I was engaged in some nefarious business?

"Quite the opposite," I said. "I want you to track some black magic for me."

"The thread attached to you?" she asked, one eyebrow rising.

"Is it still strong enough?"

"Yes," she said reluctantly. "But it's dangerous. If the person who cast the original spell feels what's happening and sends a kill spell down the thread, I won't be able to stop it."

"He or she has already murdered two people. Do what you can."

She nodded with a touch of respect. "Very well. Sit down, my lady, and we will begin."

I settled in a solid wooden chair while Ciara, a stick in her charcoal-blackened fingers, drew a circle around me in the dirt floor.

"Once I've begun I can't stop," she warned.

I merely nodded. I wanted to be well begun by the time Lord Pecus arrived. Ciara took my nod as assent, and began swiftly drawing figures about the circle. She had got halfway through the circle when her head snapped around to the door enquiringly; and I realised, with a slight quickening of breath, that she must have sensed Lord Pecus. Oh good! He was too late.

She threw me a look of burning anger, and said evenly: "Why is Lord Pecus pursuing you?"

No 'my lady' there, I thought, biting back a smile that would not have been helpful.

"I imagine he doesn't want me tracking the murderer," I told her. "He seems to be quite proprietary about these things."

"He's the Watch," Ciara said curtly, continuing to draw figures with angry, precise strokes. "It's his *job*."

I gave her a brief half-smile by way of apology. "Raoul was my friend."

She drew around me in angry silence until the door slammed open with a soggy pop, and swift male footsteps declared the entrance of Lord Pecus. He had to duck his head to walk the length of the hallway, and straightened only when he reached us in the main room, the ceiling of which was marginally higher. He wore a hood that confused his face – magically, I assumed, with a certain amount of respect – but as he entered, he pulled it back to display his maskless face. Ciara hissed, and my brows rose: Lord Pecus was trying to intimidate me.

"Lady Farrah, are you trying to make me regret my decision that you are not a viable suspect?" he asked tersely, without acknowledging Ciara by more than a nod. Ah, so they knew each other, did they?

"Not at all, my Lord," I said politely. *More bear than wolf*, I thought to myself, a little more shaken than I would have liked to admit. "I believe, in fact, that I am doing a public service. Careful! You'll smudge the lines."

He abruptly halted, looking down, and took a step back. "Ciara, stop the spell."

"You know I can't," Ciara said through her teeth, and the look she shot me was pure poison. She drew steadily as she talked, completing a final circle, and straightened. "She tricked me, my Lord."

"I have no doubt," Lord Pecus said dryly. I fancied I saw a gleam of amusement in those green eyes.

Emboldened, I said: "It wouldn't have been fair to ask anyone else to do it. Besides, if you had simply done this after Raoul, I wouldn't have had to be sneaky about it."

There was an instant of pause, and then Lord Pecus said: "It was more important to gather the physical evidence at the time, and I didn't have time to run the spell on myself."

"I also touched Raoul– which, my lord, was the point I was trying to make. I had no evidence to gather. The thread only faded this afternoon."

"It's a dangerous procedure, Lady Farrah."

"All the more reason not to expose someone who hasn't already been exposed," I said cheerfully.

Lord Pecus opened his mouth and closed it again with something of a grunt. "My sergeant wants me to have you arraigned for tampering with evidence. He doesn't like having his crime scenes interfered with."

"I imagine he would have liked even less to come upon the scene with a lady in strong hysterics," I said. Lord Pecus was now grasping at straws.

"It's ready to go," Ciara said shortly, tweaking at something in the air. A wall of what looked like heat shimmer sprang up around me. Everything took on a wavering aspect, as though I was underwater, and Daubney's face floated in my mind's eye, pink and choking, his eyes flooding red. I drew in a deep, silent breath, and was surprised when the curtain of shimmer descended again quickly.

"Got it!" Ciara said, wiping the circle away swiftly with one foot. "Clear, no trouble. You can get up now."

I did so, stepping carefully over the freshly swept dirt, and said: "Well?"

"You can't see it?" Ciara's tone was as disdainful as her glance but there was a light of satisfaction in her eye that suggested she was glad to find me deficient.

"I'm creditably informed that Lady Farrah's skills lie in er, twiddling locks," Lord Pecus said, without expression. "Thank you, Ciara."

I was not entirely surprised to see the light flush mantling Ciara's cheeks. Everything made a little more sense now: the hostility, the blind obedience. Lord Pecus, typically male, did not notice. He pulled his hood back up, blurring his face into conveniently forgettable obscurity, and offered me his arm. "I want you where I can see you," he said.

Taking this as a compliment, I smiled sunnily up at him and pointed out helpfully that the passage was too narrow for us to proceed down it together. Lord Pecus looked down at me in silence, and I had the feeling that he was struggling not to laugh though I couldn't see his eyes with any clarity.

"After you, then, Lady Farrah."

Ciara didn't ask to accompany us, and Lord Pecus didn't offer her the chance, for which I was grateful. Three is *always* a crowd when one of those three imagines you to be stepping on her toes.

Once we were outside, Lord Pecus offered me his arm again. This time I took it without comment.

"You move very quickly, Lady Farrah," he remarked as we walked. I was grateful to him for not patronizing me by strolling. I do detest men who stroll.

"As quickly as I could," I answered him frankly, well aware that he was not referring to my walking; "With you chasing me I had to do so."

"You wanted to have begun by the time I got there." Lord Pecus sounded more interested than angry, and I smiled up at him without either confirming or denying the charge. "Who was the young man?"

My smile faded. "Daubney, my lord. He was the footman I was telling you about. I believe I owe you an apology, and Daubney something rather more."

"He was already marked and being watched," said Lord Pecus. "The murderer chose his time deliberately and the mark was in a direct link: had I been there, I couldn't have stopped it."

"Daubney saw something at the ball," I said, by way of

apology. "Unfortunately he didn't have a chance to tell me what it was before he died."

"If I had tried to speak to him the result would have been the same." Lord Pecus guided me around a corner made treacherous with piles of assorted and highly odorous rubbish. The locale was steadily becoming worse as we skimmed the rough edge of the magic quarter and slipped into the river quarter, where summer brought with it a lingering scent of decay and scum from the water's surface. I felt distinctly safer with my hand tucked into Lord Pecus' arm than I had with poor Daubney walking behind me. For one thing, it was a very muscled arm; and for another, the general populace tended to take one look at the splendid physical size of the man, and melt away into the shadows. I wondered how many of them knew him as Commander of the Watch.

The trail ended rather abruptly at a dingy inn-door that was unpleasantly close to the river. The door was swollen but Lord Pecus wrenched it open with casual violence, causing the innkeeper, who was rather gloomily sweeping the floor, to drop his broom. I wondered a little cynically what particular criminal enterprise he was at present engaged in that had made him so nervous, and looked around at the dirty little room with my nose wrinkled. The floor had evidently never seen the business end of a mop.

"It ends here." There was a frown in Lord Pecus' voice.

I smiled sweetly at the innkeeper, who seemed to be actually sweating, and inquired: "Is that unusual?"

"It's certainly unprecedented," said Lord Pecus his gaze roving over the room. "This kind of black mark is almost impossible to hide: to disappear altogether is something I haven't seen before. You there!"

The innkeeper nearly dropped his broom again, recovered

valiantly, and tugged at a non-existent forelock. "Yes m'lud! How can I assist, m'lud?"

"Who came through this door half an hour ago?"

"Didn't see no one coming through the door, m'lud!"

Interesting. One could almost see the whites of his eyes.

"I daresay you turned your back, didn't you?" I said kindly. I was familiar with the concept of lying by telling the exact truth.

"Yes, m'lady," he said, in pre-emptive relief; and then, as Lord Pecus gave a muted snort of laughter: "I mean, no, m'lady! No one came in!"

"No one," repeated Lord Pecus thoughtfully. "A slow day for you, then?"

"Yes, m'lud. No guests at the present."

I slipped my hand from Lord Pecus' arm and advanced a few steps, letting my eyes rest deliberately on the entrance to the taproom, where a ring of freshly-emptied tankards sat around a table that had evidently been the focus of a meeting. The innkeeper saw the direction of my gaze, and swallowed convulsively as I smiled at him again.

"This is the Commander of the Watch," I said confidentially, indicating Lord Pecus. "I daresay you've heard the rumours."

There are always rumours about people like Lord Pecus, of course; notoriety is a great part of how authority works. Be that as it may, I was not prepared for the innkeeper to go *quite* so white, or to sit down suddenly in one of what I suppose he thought of as his parlour chairs.

"Sweet lady, don't let him eat me!"

I very nearly ruined the effect by laughing. With great restraint, I turned in Lord Pecus' direction and inquired in something of a strained voice: "Are you particularly hungry, my lord?"

Lord Pecus let the silence draw out until the innkeeper was shivering, and then said with deliberation: "That depends on the amount and veracity of the information I receive. Speak quickly."

I gave the innkeeper an encouraging smile, and he returned a sickly one, his eyes avoiding the area over my left shoulder that was taken up by Lord Pecus.

"He comes in with six others every week on the same day," he said rapidly. "They hire out the taproom before it opens and have their meetings there."

"Names," said Lord Pecus. The man was nothing if not succinct. The innkeeper seemed to find his brevity ominous, because he swallowed again, more desperately than before.

"I don't know names, m'lud, I swear it! They always give me the same name, Charles Black; that's how I know they're part of the group. Sometimes the meetings are bigger and sometimes they're smaller, but they all give me the same name."

There was a brief silence from Lord Pecus that made me think he knew something of the name, so I filed it away carefully in my memory. Charles Black. I wondered if it was the organization that Raoul had been trying to get into contact with at the ball, but it seemed just a little too...cloak and dagger, really. Seven men meeting at an old, dingy inn under the same pseudonym, quaffing pints of bad ale as they plotted darkly. It was the stuff books were made of.

"The ringleaders," Lord Pecus said slowly: "Were they rich or poor? Noblemen or common?"

The innkeeper, glad to find a question that he could answer without difficulty, said eagerly: "Oh, they were all common, m'lud; old hats with patches of shine in 'em, scuffed boots. All of 'em as skinny as rakes, too; but for the one fat old gent who kept patting his toupee. The kids they bought in sometimes, though, they were all young and posh, if you know what I mean: rubies in the sword handles, gold buckles on their shoes. It wasn't just boys, either," he added darkly, becoming virtuous. "They were poisoning the minds of the young girls as well."

"How fortunate for them that they had such a convenient place in which to do so!" I said.

"S'pose you're going to arrest them all and close me down, then," said the innkeeper sulkily. "Well, you can't arrest me: I didn't do anything!"

Lord Pecus, in a velvet rumble that made the innkeeper's complexion turn two shades whiter, said: "You think I'm going to *arrest* you?"

"Anything you want, m'lud; anything you want!"

"I want you to open and close as usual. I want the meetings to come and go as usual. If you notice a few extra men at the meetings, I would advise you to turn your back and not allow yourself to see. Metaphorically, of course. And," added Lord Pecus, his voice a low growl; "If Charles Black happens to notice anything amiss, I will be...*annoyed*."

"That," I said appreciatively, when we were outside again: "Was *immensely* enjoyable! What beautiful timing you have, my lord!"

"I could say the same of you, Lady Farrah. I would very much like to know where you learned your interrogation technique."

"Interrogation, my lord?" I opened my eyes very wide at him. "Whatever do you mean?"

"That's exactly what I mean," said Lord Pecus. "It's unlike anything I've seen before. May I ask, my lady; do you always involve yourself in the affairs of the Watch, or have you made a special exception in my case?"

"Raoul was one of my oldest friends," I said soberly,

clasping my hands comfortably together on his arm. "And Daubney died before my eyes in a way no man should have to die."

I watched the cobbles pass steadily below my feet with a crease between my brows, and then smiled involuntarily. "Besides, Annabel would never forgive me if I let such an adventure escape me."

"You seem to be on good terms with the king and queen of Civet," remarked Lord Pecus, guiding me through a street that was gradually becoming more crowded. It had not escaped my notice that he was walking us in the direction of the parade grounds: by the time we arrived, there would scarcely be time to catch our breath before the conference began.

"You seem to be on familiar terms with Charles Black," I countered. The name was beginning to rest with some familiarity in my mind; whether because I knew it in some lower part of my mind or because I had heard it so recently, I wasn't quite sure. That Lord Pecus knew something more of it I was certain.

Discouragingly, he said: "I know no one by that name, Lady Farrah. I'll keep you up to date with any important findings in my investigation."

Since I was well aware that this was a promise that was as good as empty, I merely said: "Thank you, my lord," with polite insincerity, and smiled my sweetest up into the blurry region that concealed Lord Pecus' face. After all, I had been steadily planting the seeds of my own investigation anyway, and Lord Pecus' cooperation, though it would have been helpful, was not strictly necessary. I did ask him once what had come of his painstakingly collected physical samples, but was unsurprised when he put me off with a lack of dissimulation which suggested he was happy for me to know that he did indeed have information, but that his lips were sealed. Provoking man!

The horselords were sitting together in a frowning, tight-knit group when I arrived at the conference. I left Lord Pecus at the door and made my way swiftly toward them.

"You look as if you've been caught with your hand in the biscuit-jar," I said, sitting down next to Katrina. "For heaven's sake don't look so worried! I'm beginning to feel that you leave somewhat to be desired as co-collaborators."

"There was a watchman around the grounds all afternoon when you left," Miryum told me in an undertone, leaning forward with her forearms braced on her knees. "He said he was doing a routine half-yearly check of our sewerage and water lines to make sure we were in compliance, but he didn't go anywhere near the pipes or the aqueduct."

"Lord Pecus certainly works quickly." I said, astonished and a little impressed. "If it makes you feel any better, a watchman has been following me ever since I left the house. In fact, I shouldn't be at all surprised if you find surveillance magic about after this afternoon. You'd better not say anything you don't want the Watch to hear while you're on parade grounds."

I left the horselords looking distinctly gloomier than I had found them, and as the meeting came to order, I took my place beside Melchior, who smiled a little wearily at me. No doubt he had been as busy as I had: there would have been communications to send home to Civet and Annabel, and inquiries to make on our side.

"You look tired, Melchior," I said in an undertone, as the Lord President of the Council brought the meeting rather damply to order. His tendency to pronounce 's' as 'th' was well known, though not so well known as his predilection for spraying the assembly at large with a fine mist of spit as he did so. The irony of his name being *Somersby* was the cause of a widespread but overall kindly amusement.

"You too, Carrots." Melchior roused himself enough to grin and whisper: "Perhaps old Somersby will choke on one of those *s's*, and then we'll all be able to go home early."

I laughed softly, but the truth was that the day was beginning to feel particularly long: and to make matters worse, I had an idea that my headache was coming back. I hoped, without much optimism, that the conference would not last too long. Listening a little idly to Lord Somersby's introductory remarks, which tended to be over-long and largely muddled in a morass of desperate alternative words that did *not* contain the letter *s*, I let my gaze run around the table. The King of Glause was there, his heavy-lidded eyes almost closed as if he was asleep and his double chin settled comfortably into the folds of flab at his neck. He didn't seem to be listening, but I knew rather better: there was nothing said around the King of Glause that was not remembered, considered, and sorted into its proper place.

The Glausian Horselords were not the only Glausian troop to be represented; further down the table were the generals of the Foot troops and Mages respectively, looking as different as night and day. General Kropke, commander of the foot soldiers, wore a well-cut black uniform for dress occasions and a rather ragged green and brown uniform on all other occasions that made the foot soldiers all but disappear in anything but the barest terrain, under the maxim that a sighted soldier was most often a dead soldier. Most of the countryside surrounding Glause was hilly and deeply forested, making battles an effort of stealth rather than military might. The Mage General, on the other hand, tended more to spangled gold and massively outsized epaulettes on all occasions, and was of the opinion that anyone stupid enough to shoot at, swing at, or in any way attack a mage was a dead man anyway, so why not be noticed?

The Civetan party, by comparison, was a small one. My father, as Ambassador of Civet, was seated with the Ambassador of Glause, both of them listening with apparently undivided attention to Lord Somersby; but Melchior and I were the only other representatives now that Raoul was dead. The junior guardsmen, I considered, did not count.

Lord Pecus was almost opposite me, arms folded across his massive chest and leaning back with the air of a man at his ease, but I had the impression he was watching me. He had altered the spell in his hood from a blurry facsimile of a face to what amounted to a Keep-Away spell, making it difficult for my eyes to rest on the place where his face should have been. After a little while I gave up trying to look into the hood and looked elsewhere instead, but the feeling of being watched did not abate. It did not make me feel any easier, when, looking up the length of the table to gaze limpidly at Lord Somersby, I discovered that the King of Glause was watching me beneath his eyelashes, his podgy face unreadable and motionless.

It was later than I had hoped for by the time I got back to my suite, tired and hungry. I had all but forgotten Vadim, and I blinked a little at the sight of Keenan asleep on the end of my bed, and Vadim likewise asleep in an uncomfortably straight-backed chair that she had evidently sat in to keep herself awake. They both looked absurdly young, Keenan with his face scrubbed as it had probably never been scrubbed before, his thin body clothed in stiffly new clothes, and Vadim with her hair plaited in a coronet very like my own on a head that looked too slight and delicate to bear the weight. I picked her up without difficulty and put her beside Keenan, covering them both with one of my lighter shawls, and sat down in my favourite armchair to write to Annabel. The chair felt luxuriously comfortable tonight, and I felt my eyelids dropping as I laboriously scratched out the first few sentences. A snore from the bed—Keenan or Vadim?—was the last thing I remember before I fell asleep.

Chapter Five

I was woken by a gentle and really quite expert attempt
to unbutton my bodice and cuffs. Evidently Vadim was
used to undressing slumbering bodies.

Instinctively, my hand slapped over both parchment and
quill from the night before, ripping paper and sending the
quill spinning.

"Careful for the ink!" said Vadim, mildly scolding.

I opened my eyes and gave her an amused smile. "There is
no ink, child. It's a magic quill; the words appear on the other
person's parchment. Much easier than a commlink for two
people with less than the usual amount of magic ability."

I focused sleepily on the torn parchment in my hand. It
said: *Belle, have you fallen asleep? Talk to me! I want to know more
about this dastardly Lord Pecus! And Melchior, of course... Belle!
You've fallen asleep, haven't you? Belle. Belle. Bellebellebellebelle. Oh,
all right. But I want a proper recital when you wake up.*

Annabel.

I stooped for the quill and put it back with the piece of

parchment, while Vadim, with a practised tug and snap, removed the bodice of my walking-dress of yesterday. No doubt Keenan wriggled when she dressed and undressed him, too.

"One of the morning dresses," I said absently, pushing her hands away and unbuttoning the skirt myself. It would be interesting to see which of the morning ensembles she chose for me. I added: "The morning dresses are the loose ones with filmier sleeves."

I would have to write to Annabel again, of course. And then there was the matter of poor Daubney: I would have to find out who he had been friendly with amongst the footmen. Perhaps he had talked to one of them about what he had seen on the night of the ball. All in all, it was morning dress business. I was fond of my morning dresses: foamy and light, they were looser than fashion demanded, but oh so comfortable, with sleeves that were almost scandalously filmy and showed the vague outline of my arms from the shoulder down. One did have to remember not to drape the sleeves in one's breakfast, but the result was ultimately well worth the effort.

Thinking of breakfast...

"Where's Keenan?"

Vadim, who had been going through my morning dresses with reverent hands, turned with a sleeve trailing from her fingers. "I sent him to fetch your breakfast, m'lady. This one?"

I considered it, and nodded, my eyes straying to the wash stand. Vadim had been so prepared as to bring up washing water: I wondered how long ago she had done it.

"I'm afraid it's cold now," she said apologetically, following my eyes.

"Good," I said approvingly. "There's nothing worse than lukewarm water on a summer morning. I have hot water only in the winter, Vadim. Remember that."

Vadim brightened. "Yes, m'lady!"

"Don't think it's all easy, mind you," I told her severely, dousing my face. "I'm a hard taskmaster, and don't you forget it!"

"No, m'lady," she said, grinning.

Vadim was buttoning me up when Keenan charged into the room with an enormous, laden breakfast tray. He kicked the door open with one foot, and scraped the tray edge precariously against the door as he squeezed through, causing Vadim and I to suck in a collective breath.

"Careful!" Vadim said sharply. "That's the lady's breakfast!"

I flicked back the trailing edges of my sleeves, and prodded Keenan toward the small table by my armchair.

"Put it down there and then run off and get breakfast from cook. No, Vadim; I will do my own hair this morning. Go with Keenan."

I had just sat down again to finish my letter to Annabel when a tap at the door brought me to my feet with some exasperation. It was a footman, bearing, of all things, a packet of tea. I received it from him and took it back to my chair thoughtfully, where I discovered a card tucked into the fold at the top, bearing Lord Pecus' name. I remembered my packet of rose-tea that poor Daubney had dropped shortly before he died, and found myself smiling. How thoughtful of Lord Pecus: he had even got the same kind. I turned the card over, but there was nothing on the back of it.

Most men, I thought, with some enjoyment, would send flowers to a lady: Lord Pecus, in his inimitable way, had sent me the very thing I wanted. Well now. I would have to be nicer to him next time we met. Or at least a little less cheeky. One didn't want to overdo things, after all…

By the time Keenan came bursting precipitously through the door again (did the boy not know how to walk?) I had finished with my letter. Vadim followed him with a greater appearance of decorum, but her eyes were sparkling in a way that told me she had *news*.

"I think," I said, with more than one end in mind; "That now would be a good time to measure you for your clothes."

Keenan looked indignant. "I've already got clothes!" His tone suggested that to have more than one set of clothing was at the least indulgence, if not outright profligacy.

"The tailor stuck a pin in him," Vadim explained, grinning.

Keenan scowled and folded his arms. "I ain't having any more clothes."

"Then it's just as well I don't intend to make any more for you today," I said mildly. "However, I must point out that it will have to be done eventually; and be done it *will*, if I have to summon the footmen to hold you down. Do you understand?"

"Yes, m'lady. Sorry, m'lady," said Keenan, his eyes very big.

"Very well. You can go out into the garden while I measure Vadim for a new dress. I want you to find out how many ways there are to get into my chambers from the gardens."

His face brightened almost immediately. "Yes, m'lady! I'll make sure that none of them assassins get in!"

"I have a feeling I shall regret this," I said thoughtfully, as the door slammed after Keenan.

"Thank you, my lady. I didn't want him to hear."

I acknowledged the thanks with the smallest of nods. "What is your favourite colour, Vadim?"

"Er, blue, my lady."

"Good," I said in mild satisfaction. Blue with that chestnut hair and creamy complexion would suit admirably. I set the startled Vadim atop my footstool, fetching out my measuring tape and a bolt of sapphire blue cloth that I had bought a few days ago at a Glausian market stall.

Vadim, standing rather awkwardly on the stool, opened her mouth, closed it, and at last said: "I thought—"

"What did you think, Vadim?"

"I heard something in the kitchen, m'lady."

"Something you didn't want Keenan to hear," I nodded, unfurling my tape. "Arms up, please."

"Then why—"

"I find it best not to lie," I told her pleasantly. "Lying complicates things. Sooner or later you have to lie a little more, and before you know it you're lying to yourself. Turn, child."

Vadim did so thoughtfully. "So I am really to have another new dress? Out of that? But it's so beautiful! What if I dirty it?"

"Then I imagine you will have to have it washed. Beautiful clothes are meant to be worn and enjoyed, not molly-coddled. Now, Vadim; what did you hear in the kitchen?"

The sparkle came back to her eyes. "They were all talking about him that exploded."

"Daubney."

"Yes, him. One of the chambermaids was walking out with him."

"Was she very upset?" I asked, with a swift frown.

Vadim's lip curled. "Not she! She was happy as a cat with cream, telling them all he was a spy for the king, and that's why he was killed."

"An interesting hypothesis," I allowed. I had already cut several pieces from the material, and these I pinned carefully around Vadim. She was far shorter than I was, of course, but it would not be a difficult matter to shorten the skirt. "What then?"

"Helped her clean a few chambers," Vadim said, grinning. "She said he was brooding about something after the Ambassadorial Ball. Said he wouldn't tell her about it, but she heard him muttering to himself."

"I assume you were not left baffled?"

"Well, I don't know about that, m'lady; but she said that *he* said: 'There were two of 'em, I swear! It had to be magic.'"

"Two of *what*?"

"I don't know. Only she did say a lot about the palace being full of spies and traitors, and I didn't want Keenan to hear because if he thinks there's spies about, he'll be trying to catch them."

"Indeed! Does he make a habit of spy-catching?"

"Mostly he catches the milkman, a few charwomen and the street sweeper."

"I see. Your discretion does you great credit: I'm obliged. What else did you learn below stairs?"

"The second footman was Daubney's friend, and the scullery maid was in love with him."

On impulse, I asked: "What do you know about Charles Black, Vadim?"

"What, the brass worker?"

"Perhaps. What do you know of him?"

"He's dead," Vadim said, pleasingly to the point. "He was the best known trumpet maker in Glause when he was alive, though."

"Interesting," I said slowly, filing the thought away for future reference. It might or it might not be the Charles Black that Lord Pecus had recognised, but he had certainly recognised the name. I was very well aware that he intended to keep me out of the investigation as much as possible, and it would be pleasant to find I was able to keep up with him through my own resources.

I was thoughtfully pinning another section of skirt to Vadim's waistband when I caught a sliver of movement from the corner of my eye. Keenan's face, grinning proudly, had just appeared over the edge of my windowsill.

"I can see I'm going to have to grease the windowsill. Well done, Keenan. Is there any other way in?"

He nodded and hauled himself in with a grunt of effort. "Window in the parlour, too. And your chair's in the wrong place. Can see it from the other wing of the palace. Some bloke's up there watchin'."

I gazed at him thoughtfully. "I don't think we need worry about the parlour," I decided at last. The adjoining door had a very good lock, and I meant to see that it remained locked at night from now on: possibly with a small, strategically placed everyday table before it. I fully intended to stir the pot with a vengeance, and if Charles Black did not at some stage try to discover what I knew, I was certain that Lord Pecus would. The idea of watchmen searching my chambers did not appeal to me any more than the thought of revolutionaries doing so. "Where would you suggest moving the chair?"

Keenan put all his skinny might into pushing the chair, and shoved it a foot to the left. "Here. The cobber across the courtyard can't see you from here. Think he's a watchman."

"I've no doubt. I believe I shall have a word with Lord Pecus." Having a watchman trailing me in the streets was bad enough, but for one to be watching my chambers went beyond what was pleasing. "Keenan, you are a treasure."

I had finished unpinning Vadim again when Delysia floated into the room in a billowy cloud of pink satin, waving a stiff, white card of invitation.

"He's giving a ball!" she squeaked, thrusting the card in my face. "Oh, Isabella! It's a masquerade, of all delightful things!"

"Who is giving a ball? The king?"

"*Much* better than that!" Delysia assured me, radiating a bouncing excitement that would not have looked amiss on Keenan. "It's Lord Pecus!"

"And why exactly are we excited?" I inquired. Nevertheless, I was surprised. I could not think that Lord Pecus was the sort of man to enjoy giving balls. What was he up to?

Delysia placed the card reverently into my hands. "There hasn't been a ball at the Pecus estate these twenty years and more! Oh, Isabella! I need a new dress!"

"I'm amazed that Harroll can stand the music," I said frankly. I saw Vadim and Keenan giggling behind the chair, and dismissed them with a shooing motion. "Unless, of course, you are hinting."

"*Dear* Isabella!" Delysia fluttered her eyelashes and looked appealingly up at me. "I have simply *the* most gorgeous material, and no one can make up a creation like you can!"

"Very well," I said, unable to resist. "But I expect to be well regaled with chocolate cake, mind!"

Delysia, ever the thoughtful hostess, had anticipated my demands. Not five minutes later, I found myself alone in one of her many parlours with a mountain of deep crimson material, and a platter bearing the most *enormous* chocolate cake it had ever been my good fortune to meet with. Delysia was easy to sew for– she tended to leave the entire gown to the sewer's discretion, an unconcern I greatly appreciated. It was not unusual for her to see a dress for the first time on the night of the party itself.

I was engaged in cutting pieces of the muslin when Melchior put his head around the door and said: "Oh, there you are, Carrots! I've been looking for you."

He spotted the chocolate cake and a gleam came to his eye. "Pecus is giving a party," he said, helping himself to a generous chunk. Before long, he was dropping crumbs over my bodice pieces.

I swatted his leg. "Buffoon!"

"This your new dress?"

"I do not feel the need to make a new dress for Lord Pecus' ball!" I said, with some asperity. "And if I did, it would certainly not be in this shade! Has everyone run mad?"

Melchior took another bite of cake and regarded me closely. "Thought you liked Pecus."

"So I do," I said firmly. "However, my liking does not entail the necessity of making a new dress."

"Ah. Have one already made, do you?"

I narrowed my eyes at him. "As it happens, I do; but that is completely beside the point. Melchior, if you are going to sit there snickering and eating my chocolate cake, I will trouble you to leave!"

He grinned lazily at me, and cut another piece even larger than the first. "You'll get fat one of these days, Carrots, mark my words. I've never seen a woman put away chocolate cake like you do."

"I do not 'put away' *anything*," I said, with dignity. "I nibble delicately, thank you very much. Kindly remove your foot from the sleeve of Delysia's new gown."

Melchior settled himself casually on the arm of one of the settees, removing himself from the vicinity of my dress pieces, and, more importantly, the chocolate cake.

Casually, I asked him: "What do you know of Charles Black, Melchior?"

His brows flew up. "Carrots, you never cease to surprise me. I know less of Charles Black than I find myself comfortable with, as a matter of fact. The name came up in regards to Black Velvet, but I shouldn't be surprised if the IA knows a little about it, too. Where did you hear it?"

I told him about my afternoon with Lord Pecus as I tacked Delysia's bodice together. I had made a saucy little girdle that would eventually hang on her hips, and I knew Delysia would be very pleased with it. As I pinned it to the rest of the bodice and stood back to observe the effect, Melchior said gloomily: "This is all a bit of a mess, you know."

"Raoul?"

He nodded sombrely, looking unseeingly at the scraps of red muslin; and for a moment I saw the lines in his face, the age in his eyes. "I should have seen it. I've known him for more years than I care to state, Carrots; and I still didn't see it."

"You always think there should have been something that warned you," I said softly, ceasing in my ministrations of the dressmaker's dummy to briefly smile at him. I myself had grown up with Raoul, and I had never seen it. "There isn't. Spies are trained to make friends, they learn to live with their lies."

"I wish it hadn't been him."

I sat down on the seat beside him and leaned my head against his shoulder. "Who would you rather, Melchior? I vote for Lady Farnsworth."

Melchior gave an involuntary spurt of laughter. "I always thought there was something under that wig of hers. It couldn't be such a monstrosity without reason. Who's her contact of choice?"

"Lord Morsten!" I said, with aplomb. "No doubt his mismatching clothes are a code."

"With her mismatching jewellery the counter-sign? Ah, Carrots, you do me good!"

I arched my eyebrows at him. "Missing Annabel again?"

"Wouldn't dream of doing anything so unfashionable," Melchior said. "But between me and you, Carrots, yes."

"Only another few months," I said comfortingly. "Then you'll be home again to the mad babble of four children and Annabel wanting to know how it is that you've forgotten to have your hair cut again."

"It's all noise and no substance," Melchior said, with a faraway and entirely private smile in his eyes. "She likes to cut it herself; says no one else does it the same. Ah, Carrots, I miss her!"

"If it's any comfort, she's missing you too," I offered dryly. "Hold this, will you, Melchior? Perhaps a little less peacefully, but missing you just the same."

"I must say that I find the situation here in Glause less than peaceful, but I hesitate to contradict a lady."

"Melchior, I love your children dearly, despite their inevitable tendency to reduce my favourite gowns to ribbons, but I *cannot* agree that a day with them is more peaceful than the goriest of murders."

Melchior grinned proudly. "They are a lively lot, aren't they?"

"Chips off the old block," I informed him frankly. "Commlink with them all tonight and watch them throw the supper jam-and-bread around the room for a little while. It'll do wonders for your homesickness."

Melchior stood bolt upright. "Speaking of which, I'm late for a linkup with the Lacunan Emperor. I think the Triumvirate may be getting nervous: these blasted Ambassadorial Balls have a tendency to stir up more antagonism than they soothe. For pity's sake, Carrots, you've sewn me into this thing!"

"Hold *still*, you're tangled in the basting threads!" I freed his fingers from the bodice inset he had been absently toying with, and straightened it out. "No, *don't* tread all over Delysia's skirt! Clod!"

Melchior, laughing, took himself off. I was left to my chocolate cake, or at least, what was left of it after Melchior's forays. The silence found me pondering on my own dress for Lord Pecus' party, and whether or not I could bring myself actually to wear that scintillating new gold lip-rouge.

I was not left long to myself: a little after Melchior left, Vadim found me, bringing with her the knowledge that Lord Topher was waiting below to speak with me.

"If I must, I must," I sighed. No doubt, I thought gloomily, he was coming to claim the first two dances at the Earl of Horn's midweek soiree. I found myself hoping fervently that he didn't yet know about Lord Pecus' ball, three nights after, since I would then in all probability have to dance the first set with him there also. At least there would not be a great deal of dancing at the soiree: the earl didn't care to give too many opportunities for young men to dance with his daughter. An idea flashed through my head, swift and bright, and I stopped still in the doorway. The earl! Of course!

Vadim, holding the door open for me, said: "M'lady? Shall I send him away?"

"No, no," I said, and jerked myself into motion again. "Vadim, this Charles Black– did he make horns as well?"

Vadim nodded. "Only two. They were special ones, only for royal use. They're worth a lot now."

"Is this common knowledge, would you say?"

"Oh no, m'lady. Most people wouldn't know; but me and Keenan, we lived in the same boarding house as his grandson when we were little. The old duffer used to show us one of the horns whenever he'd had too much to drink. Someone stole it, in the end."

I went down the stairs in something of a daze. Could it be that easy? The landlord's description of a chubby man fiddling with his toupee suddenly shifted and fit into its proper perspective: the earl was bald, and wigs had not been in fashion for some fifty years. It must have itched *dreadfully*. It struck me that the Earl of Horn had been either very confident, or very stupid. It would be interesting to discover which it was.

Chapter Six

I arrived at the Earl of Horn's soiree in high, sparkling spirits that not even the sight of Lord Topher's eager young face, waiting to assist me down from the carriage, could dampen. The evening was sure to afford some opportunity of slipping away for a little judicious prying, and I had been creditably informed by Delysia that Lord Pecus was gracing the soiree with his presence. In fact, there was little else required to make the evening perfect. Lord Pecus' presence made me a great deal more certain that I was right about the Earl of Horn, and the knowledge gave me a glow which caused even the usually uneffusive Lord Quorn say in measured tones: "You are looking quite delightful tonight, Lady Farrah."

"It's not because a certain someone will be there, is it, Isabella?" enquired Delysia archly.

I disappointed her by laughing without even the suspicion of a blush.

"Yes: Father!" I tucked my hand into his arm and smiled mischievously at him. "We're going to dance every dance together, aren't we?" Father looked vaguely worried, so I kissed his cheek comfortingly. "Don't worry, Father; I shan't make you dance."

"I daresay you'll be too busy dancing with Lord Topher," Delysia said innocently, arranging her chiffon shawl more becomingly across her shoulders.

Melchior gave a spurt of laughter, and said: "Oh, so *that's* who you were talking about. Do you really think so?"

"He's *very* keen on her," Delysia said dignifiedly, resenting any implication that her matchmaking instincts could be at fault.

"And on the beautiful little blonde who was staring adoringly up at him while they danced," I said dryly, depressing pretensions. "Not to mention any female of a marriageable age that he meets with. It's a trying age."

"Isabella, I wish you wouldn't talk as though you were a dowager! Anyone hearing you would fancy you to be–"

"A confirmed old maid!" I interrupted cheerfully. "Which is precisely what I am, I thank you, Delysia!"

Still, it was hard to feel old with that delightful sense of mischief running in my veins. To my disappointment I did not see Lord Pecus immediately: my attention was taken up with Lord Topher and his two dances, and what was not taken up with him was given over to ensuring we left the dancefloor at exactly the right moment and place to collide with the adoring young blonde in a manner sufficiently coincidental. I left them exclaiming the usual *How charming!* and *What a surprise to see you!* and looked around me for the Earl of Horn's daughter. She and I had a slight acquaintance, and while I hesitated to presume upon it with ulterior motives, second thoughts reminded me of Raoul, and hardened my heart. Sadly, I was not given a chance to try out this determination of spirit. Upon catching sight of the young Lady Louisa, I saw with some indignation that the tall gentleman bending over her in what I can only describe as a flirtatious manner, was Lord Pecus.

I stiffened in outrage. Well, really! The little minx was gazing up at him through her eyelashes in the most expert manner it had ever been my privilege to witness, with the immediate effect of banishing any feelings of compunction that I had entertained. It did not look as though Lord Pecus shared any such revulsion of feeling: the lips of his mask had curved in a smile, and as I watched, he led her into the dance. I discounted the dark suspicion that he had monopolized Lady Louisa on purpose to prevent me speaking to her as the improbability that it was, and made a slight alteration to my plans.

The Earl of Horn, watching his dancing daughter with a frown, was shortly startled to find himself the subject of a smiling greeting in my best Ambassadorial manner. He blinked in momentary confusion, and then said pleasantly: "My dear Lady Farrah! How do you do?"

"Tolerably well, my lord. The Countess does not grace us with her presence tonight; I trust she is not unwell?"

I caught a brief flash of something like amusement in the shrewd grey eyes. "My wife is ah, indisposed," he said, with a barely perceptible pause. So the rumours were true, were they? Delysia had told me that the Countess of Horn was fond of her Syrup of Poppies. Actually, what Delysia had said, bluntly, was, "The twinkle in her eyes is the light of fairyland, my dear," and it struck me that it might be expedient to wrangle a conversation with the lady. The only question was how to do it with sufficient craft that I was not dangerously noticeable. The earl was not a stupid man by any means, and while I did not think so much of his guile as to imagine the gimlet eye with which he watched over his daughter to be false, I did suspect him of greater depths.

"Lady Louisa dances very well," I commented, following his gaze. "How firmly Lord Pecus holds her! It must give you pleasure to see her dancing so well."

"Very pretty," agreed the Earl, but gloomily. The dance was a waltz, with no particular order or form but to avoid colliding with the other couples and stepping on the toes of your own partner. A certain amount of confusion was added by the practise of what was currently the height of Glausian fashion— cutting in. It had not yet reached Civet, for which I was profoundly thankful, but in Glause it had become quite the thing to begin a waltz with one man, and finish it with another via a string of different partners. I found it distressingly akin to a hat show, and had learned to dread the moment when a politely smiling face appeared over my partner's shoulder, and a tap on the arm caused the dance to cease momentarily.

Tonight, however, it was a novel custom that I was prepared to put up with and even, to the best of my ability, exploit. "You don't dance tonight, my lord?"

Just as I had hoped it would, the idea ticked over in the earl's mind. With one eye on his daughter, who was simpering up at Lord Pecus, and a tone finely balanced between gallantry and haste, he offered a prompt arm. "If you will dance with me, Lady Farrah, then certainly."

Lady Louisa was not at all happy to see her father determinedly waltzing his way toward her. The rosebud mouth pursed in annoyance and the little jaw set mulishly as we circled closer, whether because she knew what her father was about or because she did not approve of the earl's very robust style of waltz, I couldn't say. I found myself thankful that my legs were so much longer than the earl's, since what he lacked in height he more than made up for in sheer, bustling speed.

Politeness dictated that I had at least a few verses of the waltz before the earl cut in on Lord Pecus (or so I hoped) and, determined to make the best use of them that I could, I asked pleasantly: "What do you think of this military merger, my lord? Have we impressed you with Civet's finest?"

If he really was Charles Black, the earl was at least clever enough not to pretend to an exuberant approval that would have been at odds with his native air of shrewdness. He considered the question for a thoughtful moment, and then said: "I find myself undecided, Lady Farrah. I like to fancy that the enemies of Glause know she can defend herself without help. But this is no subject for a ballroom, or for conversation with a beautiful woman. Let me ask you how you like Glause, instead."

Very nicely done, I thought approvingly.

"Quite well, my lord," I said easily, allowing myself to be swept into closer proximity to Lady Louisa and Lord Pecus. "It rains a little more than I'm used to, but then, the hills are so beautifully green. I must admit that I would have liked to have seen some of the more famous waterworks, but as is usually the case, we have been rained upon each time we set out."

"Then you must ask my daughter to show you our own humble exhibition," said the earl, sounding mildly pleased. "She will be delighted. I fancy our waterfalls are fit to rival anything you'll find in the capital, Lady Isabella: I had them specially commissioned when I married the countess."

"The woman's touch?" The Earl of Horn had married rather late in life, and his house had already been established some years before he did so. The ballroom still had that unmistakeable air of spare, unpretentious manliness to it, despite the profusion of flowers.

The earl chuckled. "A rather unsuccessful attempt, I'm afraid. The countess doesn't care for waterfalls, she complains that they irritate her nerves. Fortunately, Louisa is less nervous."

I threw a glance at Lady Louisa. No, she was not at all nervous. At present she was pouting up at Lord Pecus with what no doubt the male sensibilities considered to be charming playfulness, but that merely gave me a strong desire to spank her. Much to my amusement, the pout became distinctly more pronounced when the earl, with great aplomb, swept us into position to perform the requisite shoulder-tap that signified his desire to cut in. She was forced to concede with a good grace, however, since Lord Pecus, far from showing any aspirations of whisking her away, released her immediately.

A moment later I was being firmly whirled halfway across the dancefloor by Lord Pecus, who was rather more imposing this close to. Despite my previous dance with him, I was not used to having to stretch so much in order to lay one hand on a gentleman's shoulder, nor to tilting my head back at such an angle: most men were conveniently eye to eye with me. I found my eyes on a level instead with Lord Pecus' chest, which was so broad as to obscure my view of the room, albeit in the most aesthetic way imaginable.

We had circled the room once before Lord Pecus said abruptly: "Well?"

I looked up at him with wide-eyed artlessness. "My lord?"

"Lady Isabella, I find myself dancing in an overcrowded and very noisy ballroom when I would much rather be at home with my feet up. I am not in the mood for trifling."

"Anyone who saw you dancing with Lady Louisa wouldn't

have thought so," I pointed out sweetly, and observed as the porcelain lips of Lord Pecus' mask set in a straight line.

"How did you find out about the earl?"

I briefly considered treating him to the wide-eyed look again, but decided against it. Instead, provocatively, I said: "I asked the right person, my lord."

"Then I repeat: well?"

"I believe Lord Topher would like to cut in, my lord."

"I dare say he would," Lord Pecus said indifferently, sweeping me across the room once again. I saw Lord Topher's face briefly: it had flushed red with the righteous anger of youth, and his jaw was militantly set.

"Lady Farrah, are you or are you not going to answer my question?"

I considered this, and said thoughtfully: "I don't remember a specific question, my lord. As I recall, you have barked 'Well?' at me twice, and asked how I found out about the earl– a question I believe I have already answered."

I got the distinct impression that Lord Pecus was grinding his teeth, and said soothingly: "What's amiss, my lord? What has happened to vex you?"

"I spent the day scouring the streets on foot for a man who was already d–," began Lord Pecus unthinkingly, and added with exasperation: "There is nothing vexing me! Lady Farrah, tell me, if you please, what you have discovered in your talk with the earl."

"Not a great deal," I said, relenting. After all, I had told myself I wouldn't tease him so much next time we met. "He changed the subject with great elegance when I asked him what he thought of the military merger, but I gather he is not fond of the idea. He thinks Glause should be able to defend itself, and he's clever enough not to be too enthusiastic either way."

I allowed this information to sink in over a few turns, and then added helpfully: "You know, you should soak your feet in a basin of warm water with a few sprigs of mint and a spine-flower, it takes away the ache *beautifully*."

Lord Pecus gave a snort of laughter. "Obliged to you, my lady. I apologise: my weary feet have frayed my temper."

"Oh, shall we sit down?"

"No, I'd only have to dance with Lady Louisa again," said Lord Pecus gloomily. "I've never met a girl who talks as much with so little to say."

"Then I take it that your interview with Lady Louisa was as successful as mine with the earl?"

"Even less so." Lord Pecus must have seen the amusement in my eyes, because he explained, with a fastidious grimace: "She giggles."

"Most young girls giggle when they flirt," I observed. "A distressing habit, but there it is."

"The flirting or the giggling?"

"The giggling, of course. I quite enjoy flirting, as a matter of fact; it would be very hypocritical in me to condemn it."

"Yes, but *you* don't giggle."

"Ah, but I'm no longer a girl," I said serenely. The fact of that matter was that I knew better. Besides, I have never been able to giggle properly, and the bell-like laugh of the sophisticates is likewise beyond my meagre talents. In polite company I try for a dry chuckle, and am thought to be *terribly* witty and intelligent in consequence.

A great, rich chuckle rumbled through Lord Pecus' chest somewhere about the region of my right ear. "Lady Farrah, despite your protestations of being *nearly thirty* I find it hard to believe that you are more than twenty-seven or eight. You are still a girl."

"I most certainly am not!" I said firmly. I had no intention of losing the – perhaps dubious – distinction of being an old maid. It was a surprisingly comfortable one, and had many uses. "I am an *excessively* cantankerous old maid."

Forbearing to comment as to cantankerousness or not, Lord Pecus said affably: "When you are *my* age, Lady Farrah—"

"There, there, my lord," I said soothingly. "It's only your aching feet speaking."

This time his laugh resounded around the ballroom, turning heads. "I assure you, Lady Farrah, I'm at least eight years your senior. When you are my age you may call yourself an old maid with my right good will."

"That's very good of you, my lord; you can't think how *anxious* I've been all these years without your permission!"

The dance was ending, so all Lord Pecus did was grin, porcelain teeth gleaming in the light of the chandeliers. I found myself wondering how many people knew he was masked. I fancied that I saw the faint fuzziness of a spell about the edges of the mask, but whatever spell it was it was not directed at me, because I could see the perfectly carved coldness of the porcelain quite clearly. I could understand why Lord Pecus did not frequent parties.

I made a mental note to ask some discreet questions of a few pertinent people, and said with wicked glee: "Oh look! Here comes Lady Louisa! What do you suppose she wants?"

Lord Pecus grabbed my hand and dragged me toward the new set that was forming. "You'd better dance with me again."

"I can't tell you how flattered I am," I assured him, slipping my hand free with some difficulty; "However, I have a better idea. Lady Louisa! How good to see you again!"

"La! Isabella!" simpered Lady Louisa. She had an unfortunate habit of addressing everyone by their first names as if they were the general populace and she the lady of the manor.

"How clever of you to monopolize the most eligible bachelor at the dance!"

Lord Pecus' huge form stiffened in shock behind me, and it was with difficulty that I repressed a gurgle of laughter. Lady Louisa was showing her youth.

"It was, wasn't it?" I agreed. "But I'm willing to share, Louisa! The earl told me that you would be delighted to show us the waterfall room."

Louisa, looking anything but delighted, said querulously: "I'm sure Father wouldn't like me to leave the ballroom, Isabella."

"Oh, but Lord Pecus was so looking forward to it!"

Admirably quick to catch on, Lord Pecus bowed. "I hear that your water displays are second to none, Lady Louisa."

Louisa's face was instantly wreathed with smiles. "I would be happy to show you the waterfall room, Lord Pecus!" She insinuated herself gracefully between myself and Lord Pecus, much to my amusement, and slipped her hand into the crook of his arm. Lord Pecus, a distinctly put upon set to his shoulders, silently offered me his other arm, which I took as a mute plea not to be left to the mercies of Lady Louisa and accepted in a spirit of pure mischief. Louisa showed her displeasure at my importunity by tossing her head and addressing her remarks solely to Lord Pecus as we strolled around the dancers, but since this particular tactic left me unmoved I was still tagging along when we left the ballroom.

Unfortunately for my enjoyment of the situation, we met Lord Topher in the hallway. By the time everyone had said their hellos (or in Lord Pecus' case, nodded curtly), he had become one of the party and I was strolling along on his arm instead of Lord Pecus'. I remained optimistic: I could still poke and pry with Lord Topher around. He didn't seem to mind my stopping along the passage at intervals, ostensibly to admire the running mural that decorated the entire length of the hall, but more importantly, to catch a glimpse into any room of which the door stood open. Louisa was assiduously attempting to outpace us with Lord Pecus, her carefully girlish giggles wafting down the hall, and so my investigations went conveniently unnoticed. Unfortunately, they also went largely unrewarded. Very few of the ridiculously many doors along the passage were open, and even less of those were open more than a crack. Through one such crack I caught a glimpse of a gracefully reclining figure that I took to be the Countess, the lacy edges of her train trailing artistically over the plump settee cushions to the floor, and her mouth dropping open to emit a faint snore.

Lord Topher caught the line of my eye and snorted with quiet laughter. "Better than the murals, isn't she?"

"More graceful, certainly," I murmured back. The murals were a distasteful blend of bad painting and painfully bloody battle scenes, and I had not had to feign my horrified curiosity. By and large, though, I was impressed with the earl's taste. Most acts of treason have the simplest of motives behind them: money. If that had been the earl's objective, he had certainly not splashed it about. The rooms were furnished and decorated in a simple, elegant style that was expensive but certainly not beyond his ordinary means: in fact, the only thing I could fault was that ghastly series of murals.

The sound of the waterfalls gradually filtered into hearing as we approached the double doors at end of the hall. At the doors themselves it became a muted roar that made conversation difficult, and as we entered the room, the scent of water wafted refreshingly around us and into the hall. I heard Lord Pecus take in a deep breath through his nose and saw the tension leave his shoulders in the greenish half-light: Glausians do so love their rain and greenery. I had to fight back the urge to helpfully suggest Lord Pecus soak his feet in the frothy pond currently to our right, into which visitors were encouraged to tumble headlong if its position relevant to the door was any indicator.

Lady Louisa did not attempt to speak over the roar, which I thought very wise of her; instead gesturing mutely to the more elaborate of the waterfalls, which leapt from rockeries built high into a central dome and showered us with a fine spray of mist. The dome was glass, through which I could fancy I saw stars if it were not for the glowing orbs of witchlight bobbing against the ceiling, filtering light through fronds of foliage that grew amongst the rocks. I was inclined to stay and gaze about me, enjoying the oddly peaceful roar of the water, but since Lady Louisa showed every sign of disappearing with Lord Pecus if I so much as looked away, I thought it best to keep up. I did not care to be left alone with Lord Topher, who was just young enough to be foolish.

The walkway beneath our feet rose to become a bridge over a gurgling stream, and I found myself smiling. Traitor or not, the earl was an artist. I could almost fancy myself to be in a mountain glen if it were not for the queer way the walls echoed back the sound of falling water. It was a pleasant sound, with the added attraction of making it impossible for Lord Topher to speak with any degree of success, and I was as much annoyed as I was intrigued when the next bend in the walkway brought us into such a sudden hush that for a moment I thought I had lost my hearing. The air was heavy with the scent of water, warm and moist all at once, and I had to force myself not to shake my head like a dog with water in its ears.

"This is the focal point of the room," Louisa said proudly. Her voice had a muffled sound to it that enhanced my feeling of having lost my hearing. "Father had the rocks arranged just so."

Lord Pecus, looking around with critical approval, said: "It took him a full year to get the sound right, did it not?"

Louisa nodded a charmingly water-frosted head of curls. "Father *niggles* at things. If it's not just so, he chips away at it until it is."

I found myself disliking the space intensely. Try as I might, I could not shake off the sense of being deafened with silence, and the rockeries rising around us from troubled pools of water seemed to close in overhead. I took a few steps away from the others, carefully feeling out the cause of my discomfort, but came to the uneasy conclusion that it must be caused by magic. I didn't care for the conclusion. Magic has never been something at which I'm particularly good, and I didn't know enough to accurately guess at the type of magic that had been used. I glanced back at Lord Pecus over my shoulder and his eyes met mine with a definite fizz of warning. I blinked a little, not entirely sure that I approved of him using magic on me, and wandered a few steps further, to where the pools did not so much swirl and gurgle, as gently ripple. The lighting was more discreet here, a gentle ambience of muted witchlight that played on the undulating surface of the water and glanced off the pebbles at the bottom of the pond with a pearly sheen. The stones were a pleasing piebald mixture of dark and light, and it was not until the others began leisurely to turn and walk toward me that I saw the oddity of one of them. Unlike its fellows, it was long and slender, and as I gazed at it thoughtfully, I began to fancy that the blackness of it was metallic rather than stone. In fact, if one looked at it in the right way, one could almost say that it looked like the burnt out shell of a communication device. I flicked a quick glance toward the others to measure the distance, and swiftly weighed the differing merits of the fainting fit and the graceful stumble. Certainly once the little coterie reached me I would have no opportunity of slipping a discreet hand into the pool of water: I was annoyed that I had not seen it sooner, when I might have had a chance of doing so undetected.

The graceful stumble, I decided resolutely; and summoning up a heedless air, I tripped toward the others, carefully and dangerously close to the edge of the unrailed walkway.

"Careful!" said Lord Pecus sharply, and Lord Topher stepped forward hastily, warning: "Mind the edge, Lady Farrah!" but by then the slippered sole of my right foot had grated painfully off the rough edge of the wooden planks.

A jolt rather more painful than I had anticipated twisted my ankle beneath me, dipping the hem of my frock slightly into the icy water, and the hand I put down to catch myself was as instinctive as if it really had been an accident. I gave a sharp gasp of pain, but turned it into a pained cry just in time: making a scene is *always* judicious if one is attempting to get away with a little sleight of hand. The metallic object was there under my hand, shifting dangerously between two rocks, and my fingers closed around it, cupping it between my hand and ankle before Lord Topher, who had rushed to assist me, could see it.

I clasped the other hand about my ankle, bleating a string of distressed inanities, while my mind worked swiftly for the means to conceal my find. I had no reticule, of course, nor even a fan; and the thing was too big to be discreetly tucked down the front of my bodice even if I could have done so without being seen. A quick look beneath my lashes showed Lord Pecus looking exasperated and Lady Louisa, again showing her youth, looking smug.

"Do you think you can stand, Lady Farrah?" Lord Topher urged, a hand beneath my elbow. "The water is too cold, you'll catch your death."

"I believe I've twisted my ankle," I said, with an entirely truthful ruefulness. I was gloomily certain that the bottom of my stocking had torn, and if the tear had not ruined them, the blood certainly would. Bother! That was my last pair of really fine stockings.

I added, with an air of great braveness: "Perhaps I can stand if you give me your arm, Lord Topher."

He did so with alacrity, allowing me the moment I needed to conceal my close-fisted hand in the folds of my skirt, and we regained the walkway with little more than one soaked slipper and a damp length of hemline. Lord Pecus, I thought, looked a little cynical, but Louisa still had the hint of a satisfied smile playing about her lips. "Oh, what a pity, you've spoiled your stockings!" she said, all solicitous sweetness.

"So it appears," I said briefly. I'd done a better job in my stumble than I'd originally thought. My ankle was aching rather dreadfully, and I could feel Lord Pecus' eyes upon me in an uncomfortably searching fashion. I had only taken a few limping steps before he shouldered Lord Topher aside and swept me from my feet with the air of a man doing the only sensible thing. I used the flurry of movement to tuck my treasure into his waistcoat pocket, and he took it without a blink.

Louisa looked annoyed but thoughtful as she trailed behind us. I had possibly just done mankind a great disservice.

Lord Topher, forced to follow behind with Louisa and sounding equally annoyed, said: "Perhaps we should go back to the ballroom, Lady Farrah. You could sit down there."

Lady Louisa brightened. "What a good idea, Lord Topher!

I'm sure Isabella would like to sit down, and take a little wine."

"A cup of tea, thank you very much," I corrected, smiling over Lord Pecus' shoulder at Lord Topher, who took the hint and went ahead to fetch it with a much better grace. The one foot that had been soaked was as cold as ice, and despite the balmy summer evening, I felt the touch of a chill as we entered the hall once again.

Louisa managed to arrange for me to be sequestered away in a little out-of-the-way alcove, which would have been terribly clever of her had it been Lord Pecus' attention I was striving for. Lord Pecus stayed only long enough to set me down in a strong, silent kind of way, before shouldering his way through the ballroom and leaving. Considering my ruined slipper, I thought, he had better keep me appraised as to what I had found, or there would be *trouble*.

I was not kept short of company after Lord Pecus left. Lord Topher stayed by my side through most of the evening, as did the horselords, who did not often dance; and by and by I had gathered a laughing, talking throng about me. Curran insisted on sitting beside me, where he alternately flirted desperately and fanned me with Katrina's fan. I allowed it because it made Katrina smile involuntarily and often as the evening passed. I began to see the audacious Curran in a new light.

By the time Melchior came to fetch me, my ankle was less painful, if a little stiff, and I was not obliged to be carried again; though this didn't prevent Curran from attempting to do so. He was at length dissuaded, and I strolled away with Melchior, who pulled my hand through his arm.

"I know you're up to something, Carrots," he said conversationally.

I drew myself up grandly. "Melchior, you should know by now that I am *always* up to something."

That surprised a laugh out of him. "I can't think why I was expecting a denial! Who did you faint on this time?"

"Faint?" My eyes widened innocently. "Good heavens, no! My dear Melchior, the most unfortunate incident! I fell into one of the earl's pools!"

Melchior thought about this for a moment, and then inquired: "May one ask what was in the pool?"

"Why, water, to be sure! I believe it is usually the case: it comes from the waterfalls, you know."

"One day, Carrots, I will find you strangled, and I won't be astonished. To what purpose did you fling yourself into the earl's pool?"

"Fling? I did nothing of the kind! It was more of a small miss-step."

"Any particular reason the earl is a suspect?"

"Phantoms and ideas," I admitted ruefully. "Nothing that could be called proof."

"Was Pecus part of your little charade, or did he become embroiled by accident?"

"Accident, and a little necessity. Don't worry, Melchior, I'm not corrupting the Watch."

"It wouldn't surprise me," Melchior said, a little gloomily. "Carrots, I wish you'd be a bit more careful."

"That," I said in some amusement; "Is a downright case of the pot calling the kettle black! When I *think* what you did while Annabel and I were at school!"

"All right, all right," he said hastily. "Just don't get yourself hurt."

I grinned at him. "Afraid of causing an international incident?"

"No," Melchior retorted frankly: "Afraid of Annabel!"

I WAS WOKEN SOME HOURS BEFORE DAWN BY A CACOPHONY of muffled yelling, breaking foliage, and a heavy thump.

The door to Vadim's room swung open, and a shadow whispered piercingly: "M'lady? Are you all right?"

I sat up, plumping a pillow behind me into a more comfortable shape. "Ah, Vadim. I take it Keenan remembered to grease the windowsills?"

"Yes, my lady," Vadim said, cheerfully, this time a little louder. She moved into the room and across to the window, her figure a mere silhouette against the opening. There was a mixture of satisfaction and awe in her voice as she said: "There's a man down there in the garden!"

"I rather thought there might be. What is he doing?"

Vadim craned her head further out the window. "Groaning, mostly. Might have broke his arm, m'lady."

"Very good. Don't let me keep you up, Vadim."

She hovered uncertainly by the window. "Should I *do* anything about him?"

"Oh no!" I said easily, snuggling back down into the covers. "I'm sure the Watch will sort all that out. Goodnight, Vadim."

"Goodnight, m'lady."

Chapter Seven

I woke much later to hushed voices and stifled giggles. Vadim and Keenan were leaning perilously out the window, Vadim gesturing with great animation while Keenan grinned. I sat up, yawning elaborately to announce my presence, and they turned eagerly.

"The bloke's gone!" Keenan announced with relish. "Mebbe he made a splint of branches and creepers and hobbled away vowin' his revenge!"

"I expect the Watch took him away," I said, my tone dampening.

Not at all dampened, Keenan grinned. "Maybe he has a– a *comp'ny* of blackguards who are waiting for darkness to storm the keep."

"I certainly hope not," I said, slipping my feet from under the covers to the floor. Vadim, spurred into remembrance of her duties, dashed to offer me my dressing gown. "Since Lord Quorn has never seen fit to fortify the ambassadorial quarters against the onslaught of a battalion, I can only assume they would succeed, and then where would we be?"

"*I'd* protect yer," declared Keenan stoutly. "I got a dagger, you know."

"I feel better already. I may need you later, Keenan; don't wander far. Vadim, I suppose it would be too much to expect my breakfast?"

Vadim grinned guiltily. "Sorry, m'lady. Keenan pinched–"

"Levied!"

"*Pinched* two muffins that cook just took out of the oven, and she kicked us out. She might have calmed down by now."

"Then you had better make sure cook supplies me with a side of muffins," I observed, cocking a brow in Keenan's direction. He grinned. Vadim, shooting him a nasty look, exited to fetch my breakfast.

"Now," I said meditatively, beckoning to Keenan; "I have another job for you."

I took to the streets later that morning, my highly recognisable hair cocooned in a green silk snood and my hat set at a saucy angle that conveniently concealed most of my face. I had a pretty good idea of the way Lord Pecus had taken me when we found Charles Black's headquarters, and I wanted to do a little investigating on my own account. If it was not unusual for young society ladies to play at treason by attending the Charles Black meetings, it might well be possible for me to slip in and observe.

Much to Vadim's injured astonishment, I left her in my chambers. It didn't seem likely that young ladies engaged in this kind of venture would take their maids along. Besides, I had no intention of putting the children in danger: getting Keenan to grease windowsills and cut ropes was one thing, but bringing them to what was likely to be a revolutionary meeting was quite another. The danger involved might be no more than the usual rush out the back door if the Watch showed up to drink an ale in the taproom, but it was the principle of the thing.

As I walked the streets at a brisk march, the only immediate dangers seemed to be that of the threatening storm to my hat, and my one stiff ankle. The ankle could be cared for by a more moderate pace, and as for the hat; well, I had never been terribly fond of it. The streets were quiet and a little muggy, as if the city was waiting in silence for the storm to break around it. I had not yet experienced a Glausian storm: if the horselords were to be believed it was quite an occasion, and I felt a stirring of interest as I picked up my pace.

Much to my satisfaction, I found my way back to the inn without a wrong turning. My satisfaction was destined to be short-lived, however: at the turning of the street I was politely stopped by an excessively good-looking young man, who, if I did not miss my guess, was one of Lord Pecus' watchmen.

"I'm sorry, my lady, but you can't go down there."

I eyed him narrowly for a moment, and then enquired: "Lord Pecus' orders?"

"Yes, my lady."

"May I ask how you recognized me?" The hat should have covered my face sufficiently, and the snood hid the redness of my hair: in fact, I found myself impressed.

The young guard grinned. "Lord Pecus said you would have a veil or a large hat. He also said you would cover your hair."

"Very well: I shall talk to you instead."

"Lord Pecus told me that you would flirt with me and try to persuade me to let you through," the watchman said, with interest. He looked as if he were willing to be flirted with.

I gave him a saucy smile. "How kind of you to put me on

my guard! I do assure you, my dear sir, that were I minded to pass you I could do so without resorting to flirting."

The interest in the watchman's eyes deepened. "I'd be willing to wager you cannot, my lady!"

"No?" A sense of wicked amusement stole through me. "What will you wager?"

"I'd wager my badge on it!" he said frankly. His blue eyes were crinkled at the edges in a mix of camaraderie and enjoyment, and I guessed shrewdly that he had many younger sisters. They were not, I devoutly hoped, as conniving as myself.

"Very well. If I slip past you I shall keep your badge for a day. If I do not, you may name the stake you choose."

The blue eyes crinkled a little more. "I accept, my lady. Do your worst!"

I retreated down the next street, my thoughts moving quickly. He was a clever young watchman: in fact, I was *counting* on him being a clever watchman. Clever enough to weigh options and come to the only decision he could reasonably come to. Hopefully Lord Pecus (who was turning out to be shrewd enough to bring enjoyment to the affair) had not been quite so fore-thoughtful as to provide the young man with instructions for what I was about to do.

I had only to wait a few moments before I espied a possible mark approaching along the walkway. He wore a peaked hood, as if in preparation for the storm, but the manner in which he hurried along the street was most certainly surreptitious. He looked elderly and impressionable, much to my satisfaction. I took a breath, let it out again, and tripped up to him with a friendly and sufficiently vacant smile.

"Oh, thank goodness! You must be here about the meeting, too!"

The old gentleman stopped, momentarily confused. "Madam, can I help you?"

"Oh, you know! Charles Black!" I opened my eyes wide, and then allowed my lashes to drop over them, blushing with all my might. "It's so stupid of me! I've lost my way!"

"Allow me," said the old gentleman gallantly, offering his arm. I accepted it with a becoming simper. "I take it you haven't been to one of the meetings before?"

"Oh no! I have a *particular* friend who told me about them. Only I'm afraid she wasn't very good with directions."

He patted my hand, beaming in the usual way of an old gentleman who is pleased to have a young woman on his arm. "You are safe with me, madam."

We walked right past the watchman, who was lounging casually in a shadowed stairwell, yawning with well-simulated disinterest. I saw his eyes flick toward us, admiration and resignation combined, because there was nothing he could do without frightening off the old gentleman. If I had so chosen, I could have walked into the meeting without being molested by the Watch, and he knew it. But he was a nice young watch-man, and it wouldn't be fair to expose him to the ridicule of his peers for failing to keep a nosey old maid outside his perimeter, so when the old gentleman and I were halfway down the street, I let out a distressful exclamation. "Oh no! I have forgot my veil!"

In vain the old gentleman tried to expostulate that my face was too charming to be hid, and when that failed, that my hat concealed it admirably. Within a few moments I was back in the stairwell that concealed the watchman. He rose to meet me, his face rueful, and I held my hand out, palm up.

"You'll be the ruin of me, my lady!" he said, dropping his brass badge into my hand.

"Nonsense. Another time you will know better, and you will have me to thank for it! You may call for your badge tomorrow, at the Ambassadorial Quarters: teatime precisely." I sailed away serenely: more serenely, in fact, than I felt. It is *so* important to make the right impression on the right people. Besides, he really was terribly good-looking.

Since Lord Pecus had ruined a perfectly good afternoon's fun, I took my revenge in the only sensible way I could. I went to the Royal Library of Magic. The Royal Library of Magic is longer than it is high: a great, bleak monolithic structure built from huge slabs of black marble that are intended to give it a look of stately and learned magnificence. In reality, it gives the impression of glowering fiercely at the two buildings opposite it, as if crouched for attack. One is always surprised to see that the storefronts are still there the next day. It is very well kept on the inside: cold, shining marble floors and dustless bookshelves, each book in its proper order. I had visited the library many times during my sojourn in Glause, and each time I did so, I was surprised all over again at how much I disliked it. Libraries and bookstores ought always to have a decent amount of dust, and to smell pleasantly of mothballs. The Royal Library of Magic felt more like a hospital.

I hoped, by a judicious examination of pertinent books, to discover somewhat more about Lord Pecus' curse than I did at present. It is common knowledge that it is good policy to know as much as possible about one's enemies: what is not as commonly known is that it is even better policy to know as much as possible about one's allies. Lord Pecus had been surprisingly proficient in his knowledge of me, and I would dearly love to repay the favour at an opportune moment. Unfortunately for my plans, the Royal Library of Magic was less than enlightening. After a frustrating hour's search, flipping through countless perfectly crisp pages, I was left wondering just where the Library kept its really *interesting* books. The ones on the shelves were a colourless, unhelpful lot that seemed concerned with magic only as it touched ethereal, high-minded theory.

I left the library shortly before noon with something of an annoyed snap to my step. What a useless piece of infrastructure! Very well! We would see what else the Imperial City had to offer. I returned home briefly to fetch Vadim, who was quietly but fiercely pleased to be walking along with me, and sallied out again with a new determination.

"I need a bookshop, Vadim," I told her. I was beginning to have a very lively appreciation for her talent of knowing exactly where to find everything I asked of her.

"Do you want to buy it, my lady?" Vadim's tone suggested hopeful interest. Heavens! How rich did the child think I was?

"No, Vadim: I wish to purchase a book. Perhaps several books. I shall know more once I have browsed."

"A proper bookshop, or a spiral bookshop?"

"And by spiral, you mean–"

"Magic," Vadim nodded. "We say spiral because they go round and round and never end. No matter how small they are, when you get inside, they aren't."

I allowed myself the pleasure of a put-upon sigh. I knew a little of magic buildings. "Don't people complain?"

"They do if they get out," Vadim said cheerfully. "Missing people don't complain."

"Oddly enough, I don't find that at all comforting, Vadim. Very well, take me to a spiral bookshop. If we become lost and wanting for food, I can always eat you."

Vadim grinned. "Yes, m'lady. Keenan's fatter, though."

"Undoubtedly we should have brought him," I murmured. "However, it's too late to turn back now: I only hope Lord Pecus appreciates the trouble I'm going to."

"Are you trying to annoy Lord Pecus, m'lady?" asked Vadim, unexpectedly perspicacious.

"As much as possible," I assured her. "If I can contrive to annoy the Earl of Horn also, I shall not consider the day to be wasted."

We had walked a street in silence before Vadim, whom I was discovering to be a quiet and penetrating thinker, asked: "I understand wanting to annoy the Earl of Horn, but why are we annoying Lord Pecus?"

"Because he annoyed me earlier today, and I should not like to be backward in repaying the compliment. I wish to know a little more of him."

"He's a good guv'nor," Vadim said, unexpectedly. "Everyone says. My ma used to say that he takes it *personal*, people breaking the law, and around the Sinkhole they say if you do wrong he doesn't leave the trail until he's caught you."

"Like a bloodhound, I expect." I was familiar with the forms of poetic exaggeration, and there was a satirical inflection to my voice, but Vadim answered me in all seriousness.

"No, they call him the Wolf, or the Beast Lord. *I* think he looks more like a bear, though."

I looked down at her thoughtfully. "Why so?"

"He has such big shoulders," Vadim explained, expelling my first, startled thought that she was aware of Lord Pecus' facial characteristics. I did not like the thought that I was one among many privy to the secret. It was grating enough that Ciara had known, and I wondered for a brief, cold moment if he had ever proposed to her. A moment's rational reflection told me the answer: of course not, she would have jumped at the proposal. I found that my lip had curled, and hastily straightened it. Dear me. I seemed to have some rather strong feelings on the subject. I would have to take care.

"You're a positive fount of surprising information, Vadim: cultivate that talent, won't you? What else does the Sinkhole District have to say about Lord Pecus?"

Vadim's eyes sparkled. "That he turns into a wolf every full moon and terrorises criminals."

"Dear me! How enterprising of him!"

"He doesn't *really*," Vadim hastened to assure me, anxious that I should not be put off. "That's just one of the dark ones that gets whispered when there's been too much wine. Mostly they talk about his servants."

I found that we were ascending a set of stone stairs that lead to a dingy shopfront, and waited absently for Vadim to open the door for me. "What about his servants? Are they said to be cursed, too?"

"No, m'lady," said Vadim, cheerfully unaware of her duties with respect to the door. "I met a girl who was engaged to a lad whose sister works nearby, and *she* said that they all have to wear masks like him. What are we waiting for, m'lady?"

My lips twitched. "I haven't the faintest idea, Vadim. Let us proceed."

The door set a little bell tinkling somewhere in the depths of the store, and a breath of book-scented air wafted around us comfortingly. I took in a deep breath and gazed around me with approval. "This is *exactly* what I wanted, Vadim. Well done. I'm sure Lord Pecus will be pleased I took the time to research."

Vadim grinned, but said demurely: "Yes, m'lady! Oh, look! There's the shopkeeper!"

I looked in time to see a colourful vest disappear around the corner. "I should like to be prepared for Lord Pecus' ball,"

I pursued, declining to hurry after the bookseller and instead approaching the dusty counter.

"Shouldn't we follow him?" asked Vadim anxiously. She was bouncing slightly on the balls of her feet with a wholly misplaced zeal to be after the shopkeeper.

"Certainly not!" I said calmly. "It's the first trick. That, my dear Vadim, is the way one becomes lost in any type of magical building. A flash of a vest here, an invitingly crooked finger there, and before you know it, you're lost."

I struck the tiny silver bell that was nestled among the dust, and a single, sweet tone rang out. The sound hung in the air, lightening the shop around us, but before it had time to fade, I heard Vadim gasp. I turned my head to find that the old bookseller was behind the counter as if he had always been there. Of course he had not, and there was no way for him to get there without either Vadim or I seeing him, but that was the third trick, after all.

I smiled at him, my eyes twinkling, and saw the answering smile in his brown eyes. "Fourth trick?" I suggested invitingly, and he chuckled, rubbing his hands together gleefully.

"Fourth trick!" he agreed.

Vadim, her eyes very round, watched in silence as the old man thumped a book down on the counter. Dust flew into the air in giant tickly clouds but I refused to cough: it would only encourage him. As it was, he wriggled hairy eyebrows at me, and leaned forward over the desk. "How'd I do?"

The book's title read: *Book of Interesting Excerpts* in block letters, but when I opened it, the pages were blank.

"I'll be sure to let you know," I said, shooting a look at him through my eyelashes.

For a moment the bookseller tapped his fingers on the wooden counter, undecided; then he grinned. "Oh, all right. Say the name."

I folded my arms on the counter and leaned into it comfortably, ignoring the dust. "Lord Pecus," I said to the snowy pages. There was a moment's hesitation from the book before colour leeched into the pages and three words took form.

Friend or foe?

"I haven't decided yet," I said severely. "Well?"

There was another pause, then a reproachful sentence sprawled into being. ***You're supposed to say 'friend'.***

"And how would you know if I wasn't?"

The book appeared to think about this, and then conceded: ***This is true. Very well, what would you like to know about Lord Pecus?***

I tilted my chin thoughtfully. "Family history first, I think. From ten generations ago, specifically as regards the Pecus curse."

All personal excerpts indicate that the Pecus curse wasn't around ten generations ago. Would you like particulars on the curse, or on family history?

"The curse, I rather think," I said slowly, digesting the new information. My eyes flicked thoughtfully to the bookseller, who was leaning on his counter-top and smirking amiably at me, and then back down at the newly filled page of writing. I skimmed the series of fragments briefly, my lips moving silently, and then looked back up at the man with interest. "I believe the fourth trick is yours. Where did you find such a treasure?"

He looked rueful, and, if I were not mistaken, slightly ashamed of himself. "Truly, lady, I inherited the shop. The books have been here longer than I: they don't belong to me. Four tricks are all I have."

I didn't for a moment believe it. I snapped the book shut and tapped my forefinger on the cover. "How much?"

A smile swept across his face. "Fifth trick, lady. One copper."

I placed a copper on the counter with a snap and said curiously: "What is the catch?"

"You'll find out," the shopkeeper said. There was a glint to his eyes that suggested he had a sixth trick, and that it would pop up at the most inconvenient moment, but I was inclined to risk it. "Good day, lady."

He gave me a last, mischievous, crinkly grin that beetled his eyebrows, and when I looked up again, he was gone.

"That makes six!" I called out through the shelves, and fancied I heard the ghost of a laugh. "Come, Vadim; we have a busy afternoon ahead of us."

We were halfway home before Vadim, tracing the curlicues on the front of the book and trailing behind, said curiously: "What did you mean, tricks?"

I gave her a half smile over my shoulder. "You told me about one yourself."

Vadim frowned. "The way people get lost, you mean?"

"Of course. It's part of the trade. The first trick is the glimpse but never a sight; if you follow the shopkeeper you're sure to get lost. The second is that there's always an easy solution to avoid being lost. In this case, ringing the bell. Once you get past the first two tricks, the rest is easy."

"And the shopkeeper always knows what book you want!" Vadim said, understanding dawning in her eyes. "Then was it just tricks? Not real magic?"

I shrugged one shoulder elegantly. "You tell me. I have no aptitude for magic. What did you think?"

"It was *stuffed* with magic!" Vadim said fervently. "But how did you know about the tricks, then?"

"I have a few tricks of my own, my child. Besides, magic is

like everything else: it has its set rules and regulations. Once one knows the easier rules, one can extrapolate."

"The third trick was his appearing behind the counter!" continued Vadim gleefully, ticking off tricks on her fingers to the imminent danger of my new book. "And the *fourth–*"

"Vadim!" I said firmly, relieving her of the book; "Tell it all to Keenan. We are home, and I have entirely too much to do for one afternoon. I will expect you in my room at four o'clock, and my green-striped walking dress– but no! Will it rain this afternoon?"

"Oh yes!" Vadim said absently. She was still counting off tricks on her fingers. "But not until after dinner, I think."

"Then lay out my blue and ivory calling dress," I decided, with great fortitude. It would be a sacrifice to lose it to the rain, but less than to lose my green-striped muslin; and with any luck, my sacrifice would not be in vain. "Four o'clock, mind!"

Once in my suite, I changed into a comfortable gauze wrapper of many floating layers that was light and cool in the noticeably muggier afternoon, then waved cheerfully at the watchman in the window opposite before curling up in the window seat to peruse my new book. To my malicious amusement, the man ducked his head and pretended that he hadn't seen. I found myself wondering what Lord Pecus would have done in the same situation, and grinned as I settled the book more comfortably in my lap.

"Hello again!"

I'm not programmed for greetings, the book wrote cautiously.

"Well, we all have our failings. What shall I call you?"

Now you're just being difficult.

"I am, aren't I? Never mind. Would you show me the fragments relating to Lord Pecus' curse again, please?"

The information appeared more quickly this time, staining through the pages in blue and gold, and as I read, my fingers worked absently to unpin the snood, tumbling my hair down my back in a frothy mass. I combed it out idly with my fingers, frowning over the text; and then sat back with a sigh as I came to the last piece, which seemed to be an inventory of items required for a facial spell.

"Well now," I said thoughtfully. "This puts a rather different slant on things."

Indeed.

"Just how recent are these excerpts?"

My spell parameters are set to collect excerpts from the latest complete day.

My eyebrows rose. "I can find any written records up until yesterday?"

Yes.

"Any and all excerpts, or merely important ones?"

I have access to any and all written material: my parameters have never been sounded.

"Indeed? How useful! Do you have anything in reference to the latest Ambassadorial Ball?"

Guest lists. A series of communiques to and from the queen of New Civet. A more secret communique between persons styling themselves Angel and Left Hand. Newspaper articles on clothing and famous attendees. Speaking of balls, shouldn't you be finishing your dress for Lord Pecus' ball?

"I shall ignore that. Show me any excerpts from the last two days concerning Lady Farrah."

A paragraph materialised in green and gold, and I read it with my brows raised.

"This is *not* what I asked for," I told the book pointedly.

That is your most probable future, the book said, and

added smugly: ***I am also able to cross-reference and extrapolate.***

"Hm. With dubious accuracy, if you'll pardon me. Besides, my dress is already finished."

The gold one isn't.

"That ensemble is purely experimental," I said. "Besides, I have Delysia's dress to finish, and I absolutely refuse to discuss matters of dress with a book."

Well, there's no need to be insulting. I was only trying to help.

"I think I shall see the Earl of Horn's last month of written history, if you please. Anything *by* him or *to* him."

I am still not entirely sure how a book manages to sulk; but for the rest of the afternoon, the book undoubtedly *did* sulk. It might have had something to do with the sombre colours in which it wrote, or the studied slowness with which it complied with my requests. At all events, by the time Vadim arrived to lay out my afternoon dress, I was feeling the kind of exasperation that is usually only wrung from me by vapour-prone ladies and small, noisy dogs. I put the book down with a grateful sigh, and approached the ivory dressing table to re-braid my hair. "I will wear the cream hat with blue ribbons, Vadim."

I made short work of dressing. The Earl of Horn, if the *Book of Interesting Excerpts* was accurate, had an appointment this afternoon, leaving his wife and daughter at home to receive my call. I wished to make the best possible use of that time. Lady Louisa was pert and talkative, a positive boon to anyone seeking information; and as for the Countess, provided her poppy syrup was at hand, I should be able to turn the conversation whichever way I chose without her noticing any prompting. It's unbecoming in a lady to be smug —or at least to *appear* smug—and one is usually setting oneself up for a fall just when one thinks oneself terribly clever. Nevertheless, when I stepped over the Earl's doorstep that afternoon, my ensemble unsullied by rain, I was feeling that I had managed things very well. Let that be a lesson to all.

It started out quite well, to be fair. The Earl *was* from home– perhaps attending the Charles Black meeting, I thought darkly, feeling again the sting of my grievance with Lord Pecus. The countess was in what the butler chose to call the green room. In the gloom caused by stormy skies it looked more akin to bilious wattle, and Lady Louisa, who was in somewhat bored attendance, did not benefit by the shade. She brightened when she saw me, but her smile lost a little of its brilliance when it became evident that I was unaccompanied.

"Oh! I thought Curran might be with you, or Lord Pecus," she sighed. "We weren't expecting visitors, you know."

I ignored her languorous rudeness since I intended to push the boundaries of politeness myself, and seated myself without waiting for an invitation that would most likely have been given grudgingly.

"Are you very much fatigued after the ball?" I enquired, rescuing the tail of my braid from the countess. She had picked it up with a childlike fascination and was using it to dust imaginary powder onto her face.

"Oh, immensely!" Louisa let herself recline languidly, and gestured with one hand. "The last guests didn't leave until well after midnight. I expected Lord Pecus today, actually: he was *so* attentive last night. What a pity you twisted your ankle in the waterfall room, you looked quite pale and drawn!"

"It's the red hair," I said, smiling at her affably. I sincerely hope I was never so transparently young. "All we redheads look drawn and pale. Your father is out, I believe?"

Louisa's nose wrinkled fastidiously. "Oh yes, father is at his anti-magic meeting."

"No, dear," the countess said in her high, girlish voice, surprising both myself and Lady Louisa, "*Not* anti-magic! Science!" She let her voice trail away dreamily, and then added vaguely: "Dynamos and things."

My mind flashed back to the metallic oblong I had fished out of the earl's pebble pond, and I felt my interest quicken. "Dynamos?"

Louisa waved her hand dismissively. "Power sources, or something. Papa gets quite boring about them, actually."

"Fascinating!"

"Don't let Papa hear you say that!" warned Louisa, her languid demeanour vanishing in sudden alarm. "He'll bore on for hours, absolute *hours*! And all for little boxes that look like pebbles!"

"So useful!" trilled the countess, becoming animated once more with a glaze-eyed fanaticism. "Commlinks without magic and talking boxes!"

"Really?" I turned my gaze on her, but the moment of lucidity was already passing.

"And moving pictures on glass," she said, smiling sweetly up at me. Her eyes blinked gracefully closed, and a moment later, she emitted a faint snore.

"I'm afraid my wife is not herself this morning," said the earl's voice. I turned my head to find him standing in the doorway. "The excitement of last night's ball was rather too much for her."

I was conscious of a flash of irritation mixed with a wholly unexpected embarrassment. In a tone as surprising as it was unwelcome, the earl had managed to infuse a degree of polite puzzlement I had not considered him capable of. I did not blush, however: I am by far too sophisticated to blush unless it is on purpose.

"I wasn't expecting to find you engaged, Louisa," the earl said pleasantly, dropping a fatherly kiss on his daughter's head. His shrew eyes came to rest on me with a suggestion of mockery, but he bowed slightly with punctilious politeness. "Lady Isabella! How can we account for the pleasure of seeing you twice in two days?"

I launched into my excuse without pausing. I had hoped to avoid giving an excuse, and if it had been only Louisa and the countess, I would have done so: it was rather regrettably slim. "Lady Quorn gave me a recipe for the countess," I said, looking up at him innocently. "She's been meaning to send it over ever since the countess asked for it, but what with one thing and another, it never got sent. I thought it best to bring it over myself and make sure it arrived."

I gave the sheet of paper to Louisa, glad that my story, though thin, was true. It was fortunate that I had remembered to bring the recipe with me.

"How thoughtful of you," said the earl, smiling urbanely at me. He sat beside his wife and clasped her hand in one of his. She woke for long enough to smile sweetly up at him and pronounce his name, then dropped back into a gentle doze. Seizing the opportunity, I announced with great solicitude that I was sorry to have tired the countess, and would take my leave. Louisa, hastily jumping to her feet, followed me to the door and said that she would show me out. I was amused, but willing, and unsurprised on the whole when she confided in me some way down the hall: "I didn't really think you needed showing out, Isabella, but Papa *will* talk about his horrid dynamos for hours on end. Mama just nods and smiles, but I have to *listen*."

She didn't walk me all the way to the front door, which

was perhaps fortunate, since I found Lord Pecus on the steps. He looked resigned but unsurprised to see me there.

"I suppose it would be expecting too much to ask you not to interfere in Watch business?"

"Oh, I'm not interfering," I assured him, looking up with my best air of sincerity. "Delysia gave me a recipe that the countess asked for."

Lord Pecus grunted. "I'm sure she did." He managed to make it sound like an accusation, to my fascination.

"Smile at me and offer me your arm," I said, smiling saucily and dropping a curtsey. "The earl is watching us from the window of the green room. He might be persuaded that you came here merely to escort me."

Lord Pecus did so with an air of exasperation, but admitted: "Two visits would look a trifle odd. Lady Farrah, you have ruined my afternoon's investigation."

"But think of the fresh air you're getting!" I smiled up at him sunnily, linking my fingers around his arm, and fancied I caught the glimmer of a smile beginning in the porcelain lips of his mask. "Besides, if you wish to know what that metal pebble is, I believe I can tell you."

"I spent all morning testing that rock," said Lord Pecus, looking down at me narrowly: "And I'm no closer now to discovering its use than when I began. I was beginning to think that your instincts were at fault, my lady."

"But?"

This time the smile was more than a glimmer. "Nothing is this impenetrable. It's dense, metallic, and gives off a force that isn't magic."

"In the earl's waterfall room," I began, pursuing an interesting thought; "Was it magic you sensed? Certainly and absolutely?"

He hesitated. "I couldn't swear to it. I would have said so

at a pinch, but the resonance was slightly off. Does it have some connection to the pebble?"

"I believe so. Louisa mentioned an anti-magic meeting that the earl attends, and the countess mentioned dynamos; commlinks without magic and talking boxes, that sort of thing. I thought at first that the pebble was a burnt out commshell, but I'm beginning to think it might be a dynamo. Louisa did say they look like rocks."

"It's certainly not a commshell," Lord Pecus agreed. He was frowning. "If it's a dynamo, I'd like to know exactly what it was powering."

I felt a flash of dismayed understanding. "You think the earl will notice it's missing."

"Let's just say I have a sinking suspicion that he might." Lord Pecus absently covered my linked fingers with one huge hand. "You've already taken some precautions, I believe?"

I allowed myself a smile at the tacit confession of surveillance as we mounted the steps to the ambassadorial residence, and released Lord Pecus' arm.

"I have, my lord."

"Double them," he said.

❧

THIS TIME WHEN THE CRASH CAME, BOTH KEENAN AND Vadim dashed into the room to witness the disturbance. I had only just come to bed from the sewing room, where Delysia's almost-finished dress was draped on a dummy, so I had not had time to fall asleep. I watched their glee with an indulgent eye.

"Well done, Keenan," I said.

"I fink the awning's cut him in half!" Keenan said, with indecently ghoulish enjoyment. "Right down the middle! His legs are twitchin', though, lady: he *might* still be alive. I loosed all them screws right out!"

"You did, Keenan; and very well, too! I don't know what I ever did without you."

"Slept in peace, I reckon!" said Vadim, grinning. "Who did you annoy this time?"

"The Earl of Horn, I rather think," I said thoughtfully. "Make sure your doors are locked tonight, my children."

Chapter Eight

I had time to complete Delysia's gown before my young watchman of yesterday was ushered into the room with his rounded hat tucked bashfully under one arm. He scrubbed up very nicely, but in spite of his excellence in uniform he was looking rather sheepish.

"Do sit down!" I said invitingly. "I've ordered tea for us."

He looked at me beseechingly. "Lady–!"

I couldn't help laughing. "Oh, very well! *There* is your badge: take it and be comfortable. I have ordered tea, however, and I wish to have someone with whom to share it."

"I would be honoured, lady."

"Besides," I added agreeably, "I have some–"

"–questions to ask me!" finished the watchman, nodding. He was grinning. "I thought you might."

"Of course, I realise that as an officer of the Watch it is your duty to take all such questions in stoic silence and not give away a thing, but I was hoping that Delysia's *very* fine chocolate cake would be enough to test your stoical reserve."

The tea tray arrived as I spoke, and it was clear from the

gleam in his eye that the chocolate cake was already having an effect.

"I trust it doesn't count as a bribe if I am terribly obvious about it."

"Lady, you know the way to a man's heart!" said the watchman ruefully, gazing at the cake with longing.

I poured him a strong cup of tea and briskly passed him an enormous serving of the cake, reserving one just as generous for myself. This time the look the watchman cast me was as respectful as it was admiring. "You have a hearty appetite, lady."

"Yes, Melchior says it's a wonder I'm not as fat as a carthorse!" I said cheerfully, causing him to choke on his tea. "Now, it's all very well for you to know who *I* am, but I've not the least idea who you are. Since we've no one to introduce us, I'm afraid I shall have to be terribly indelicate and ask you for your name outright."

"With pleasure, lady. Lieutenant Trophimus Holt at your service!"

I tilted my head, considering this, and came to the conclusion that I knew the name. "Is it the fashion in Glause for Earls to join the Watch, Lieutenant?"

The Lieutenant grinned. "Those of us without any money to speak of, yes. Besides, any man would be proud to serve under Lord Pecus, lady. The king tried to set him up as a Commander in the Glausian army, you know."

"Lord Pecus didn't care for the idea?" I stored this fact away for later consideration, and offered the Lieutenant another slice of cake.

He shrugged, but accepted the cake. "He says the worst enemies we have to face come from within."

"How very philosophical of him! Poetic, too. Do you agree?"

"A country can crumble from within just as disastrously as it can be over-run from without," he said bluntly. "Charles Black is only one group among dozens that threaten to do so."

"Was your surveillance of the meeting productive, Lieutenant?"

His blue eyes regarded me thoughtfully. "You like to skim the boundaries, don't you, lady? I don't think Lord Pecus would like me to say. He was very particular about you not being allowed to pass."

"Very well," I said equitably; "We won't quarrel. Tell me about Lord Pecus instead!"

He looked relieved, but wary. "What would you like to know, my lady?"

"Oh, nothing very sensitive or top secret," I assured him, doing my best to appear appropriately innocuous. "Have you known Lord Pecus for very long?"

"All my life. I was one of the first to sign up under him when the Watch was granted Royal sanction by the King."

I nodded without surprise, because I had heard that the Watch House in Glause was not long officially established. It had previously been a privately run corporation formed of a medley of spies and investigators who looked into certain affairs for a fee, and the general task of policing of the realm had previously been assigned to the military.

"Is his manor as gothic as they say?" I enquired, allowing a slight, ghoulish interest to creep into my voice. I did not think it constructive to tell the Lieutenant that I had visited Lord Pecus' domain once before: people are always so much more willing to expound when they believe they are doing so to ignorance. Besides, the visit had been less than lengthy, and could be said, without stretching the truth, not to count. To add to all other arguments, I had not had a moment then to indulge my inquisitive nature, and no one could reasonably expect me to count it as an actual *visit* without doing so. "I've been told that all the servants wear masks. So intriguing!"

The Lieutenant looked amused, but willing to pander to my macabre interest. "The servants have worn masks at Pecus Manor for centuries, ever since the first Lord Pecus was cursed and began wearing one to hide his face. He chose to make an affectation of it by masking the entire house, and it's become part of the tradition of Pecus Manor. I think the servants would be disappointed if it *weren't* done: it gives them a certain distinction that not even the king's servants can pretend to."

Another triumph for Vadim! I thought amusedly. The girl was a treasure. I made a mental note to buy her a pretty frippery when I went out to choose stockings for Lord Pecus' ball.

"It must give the Manor somewhat of an eerie air," I pondered, with interest. If the masks were anything like Lord Pecus', it would give one the surreal feeling of being surrounded by people who were not quite alive. "Not to mention the danger of thievery! No one would know if one didn't belong. Why, one could be surrounded by vagabonds and murderers and never have the slightest suspicion!"

His eyes danced appreciatively. "Lord Pecus thought of that eventuality, my lady: I'm surprised, however, that *you* did. I'm inclined to think that Lord Pecus was right when he told me your character borders very narrowly on the criminal!"

"I should think you would, by now," I said admonishingly. "Let it be a lesson to you never to trust in appearances. I may *look* like a meek old maid, but I am devious and very possibly nefarious into the bargain!"

"My lady, you do not look at all like a meek old maid!" he said, laughing out loud. His laugh didn't have the rich, magnificent resonance of Lord Pecus' laugh, but it was a nice one in its own right. "You're more akin to a siren, beautiful and chancy."

"You see how well I've deceived you!" I said, nodding portentously. "And how adroitly I fish for compliments!"

The Lieutenant grinned. "I hold to my remarks, lady! What else would you like to know about Lord Pecus?"

"Has he always worn that porcelain mask?" I asked thoughtfully, running a finger along the edge of my teacup. Despite being curiously lacking in a few key areas, the *Book of Interesting Extracts* had surprised me a great deal in what it had had to proffer about the Pecus Curse, and I had reached a few conclusions of my own with regards to the withheld information. Acting on one such conclusion, I said: "It's almost unnoticeable– a family heirloom, I suppose?"

"Lord Pecus designed it five years after the Watch was royally sanctioned," said Lieutenant Holt, raising another host of interesting possibilities in my mind. "He says it was the most difficult thing he's ever done. His father, the twelfth Lord Pecus, was a genius with magic: he designed the first mask Alexander ever wore. Until he was twenty-four I didn't even know it *was* a mask."

"What happened when Lord Pecus was twenty-four?" I inquired, tucking away the interesting fact that Lieutenant Holt was on intimate enough terms with Lord Pecus to slip into a first name basis.

"He and I were out hunting on his birthday. Lord Pecus was ahead of me and fell through the floor of some old ruins: when I found him the mask had split." He was silent for a moment, and then added reflectively: "I almost killed him, Lady Farrah. I thought he was a demon."

That would explain Lord Pecus' attitude when I drew back at the Ambassadorial Ball, I thought compassionately.

"It took him seven years to design and make the new mask, and until then he kept to Pecus Manor, directing the Watch House from behind closed doors. It's only in the last year that he's begun circulating in society a little again."

"I assume, then, that Lord Pecus has wards of a magical nature in place about Pecus Manor?"

"He does," said Lieutenant Holt cautiously. I thought, with some amusement, that he actually seemed to think I might attempt a break-in. "The wards are quite advanced and difficult to slip past."

"Oh, I've no talent for magic," I assured him cheerfully. "If it can't be undone with a hairpin and a thumbtack, I'm powerless against it."

He laughed again. "You are a surprising woman, lady. How often can you meddle with magic using a hairpin and a thumbtack?"

"Oh, it's only useful when it comes to magical locks and Keep-Away spells. I've always suspected that my skill has something to do with my inquisitive personality."

"Lord Pecus did say something of the sort," said the Lieutenant, with a twinkle to his eye.

"Are you sure the term he used wasn't 'meddlesome old maid'?"

"I believe he said 'taking, but as nosy as a terrier'."

"*Well!*" I said indignantly. "Taking! He could at least have stipulated *beautiful!*"

I comforted myself with another slice of cake and gazed balefully at Lieutenant Holt over my teacup. "Why are you laughing, sirrah?"

"I find it amusing that you don't object to being called nosy," explained the Lieutenant, grinning. He put down his teacup and regarded me thoughtfully. "You're not asking the questions I expected you to ask, Lady Farrah."

"Which questions did you expect me to ask?"

He shrugged. "Oh, about the Earl of Horn, about the meeting, anything about Charles Black."

I threw him an amused glance. "Would you have answered them?"

"Of course not. I was warned about your feminine wiles."

"Then what would be the use in my asking them? I asked you a testing question about the meeting, and you drew back. Very well. There was no use in pressing the issue."

I couldn't help feeling a little pleased with myself. It would have been useful to know about the Charles Black meeting, of course, but my chief interest was in finding out what I could of Lord Pecus. A reputation for inquisitiveness was sometimes a useful thing: if a person thinks they are being pumped with regards to one thing, it is the easiest thing in the world to prompt them to talk about anything else. So I gave Lieutenant Holt my sweetest smile, and said: "You're just too clever for me, Lieutenant."

"And yet, lady," said the Lieutenant frankly: "I worry!"

I WAS JUST SHOWING THE LIEUTENANT OUT WHEN LORD Pecus arrived. He looked exasperated but unsurprised, and the Lieutenant looked distinctly sheepish again as he bowed over my hand.

"I hope I shall see you again!" I told him mischievously, but not entirely mendaciously. He was a lovely boy.

He blushed, bowed again, and said: "I certainly hope so, lady!"

I waved him off airily and turned to Lord Pecus, who had given his hat to the footman and was regarding me narrowly.

"Lady Farrah, I suppose it would be too much to ask of you not to corrupt the Watch?"

"Nonsense!" I said loftily. "Lieutenant Holt is a charming boy, and I object to the idea that I am in any way a corrupting influence on him. Have you come to see Melchior?"

Lord Pecus opened his mouth, evidently thought better of what he was going to say, and nodded. "Yes." He hesitated, then said roughly: "Lady Farrah, the Watch is capable of conducting an investigation competently."

"I have no doubt you are, my lord!" I said soothingly. Not entirely to my surprise, Lord Pecus did not look soothed.

"We are not playing games, my lady! My protection only—"

"Pecus!" Melchior was leaning over the balcony, his eyes alight with mischief. I wondered suspiciously what he had been up to— or what he was *about* to get up to. "I thought I heard your voice!"

I gave Lord Pecus a roguish smile and took myself off while I could. "Goodbye, Lord Pecus; so nice to have seen you!"

I was quite pleased with myself as I entered the sewing room. I now had a good working knowledge of Lord Pecus to be going on with: Lieutenant Holt had been *extremely* helpful. He had confirmed a suspicion that the *Book of Interesting Excerpts* had planted in my head, and I found myself entirely satisfied with the progress of my different investigations. It occurred to me that a letter to Annabel was long overdue, but I was in the mood for sewing, and before I knew what I was about, I found myself meditatively shaking out my half-completed gold dress. There was no time to finish it of course: Lord Pecus' party was tomorrow night. But I couldn't help setting the second sleeve, or unpinning a flare that was not quite right, and repinning it. By the time lunch was announced with the resounding boom of Delysia's ancient

Lacunan gong, I had finished the last of the pinning. I sat deep in thought, considering the dress, then rang the bell in sudden decision. When the footman had been dispatched to fetch Vadim, I resigned myself to going without lunch, and swept the dress off the dummy. It swirled beautifully with flares of gold and red, and I couldn't help smiling: it was exactly as I had imagined it.

Vadim entered the room to find me holding the dress up to myself in the long mirrors, and for a moment I saw pure longing in her eyes as she looked at it.

I shook my head. "No, Vadim. Blue, and possibly pink, but never gold for you."

"Oh, it's too fine for me," she said. Vadim evidently had no pretensions to the higher classes. "But it is *beautiful,* lady!"

"It should be!" I told her frankly: "I spent a week just designing it. Can you sew competently, child? I'm a little short of time."

"Mm'no," she said slowly, her eyes not leaving the gown. "I can do better than that, though."

"You perplex me, Vadim. What is better than sewing?"

Vadim grinned, and suddenly looked very like Keenan. "I'll show you."

She flicked the skirt inside out with a professional flour-ish, and pinched one of the seams together half an inch from the selvage, avoiding the pins. I watched as she ran her fingers the length of the pinned pieces, and saw the fabric weave itself together after her, leaving no seam.

"Vadim, I don't know what I ever did without you!"

Vadim was removing the pins in a businesslike manner, but I fancied that her cheeks went a little pink with pleasure.

"I trust I won't come unstuck at any time during the party?"

"Oh no!" she said, through a mouthful of pins. She put

them one by one into my porcupine pincushion with dainty precision, and said more clearly: "I wove it together, you see: it's all one piece of fabric now. There's nothing *to* come unstuck."

I considered the seamless pieces for a moment, and arrived at a potential setback. "What of my flares? The seams make them sit right."

"I'll iron them in," Vadim said, looking the dress up and down with a professional eye now rather than a longing one. "Then they'll sit flat when you're still and flare out when you dance. Leave it to me, lady."

On the whole, I found I approved of Vadim's method of sewing. My creation was finished a few hours after we started, with only a few minor missteps and one nasty moment when we discovered that an error in Vadim's joinings, once cut apart again, left significantly less fabric than before. Most opportunely, the only two pieces ruined were shoulder-ribbons of gauze, which were easily cut and attached again while Vadim apologised, explaining with amusing naivety that she had never discovered the flaw before because she had never done enough sewing.

We were finished with the dress by mid-afternoon; just, in fact, as a footman came to inform me that Lord Topher had enquired if I were at home. I counted myself fortunate to have finished so coincidentally, because as long as Lord Topher didn't know what I was wearing to Lord Pecus' ball, I had a good chance of escaping a dance with him until the unmasking. I briskly cleaned away a few scraps of gold cloth and informed the footman that he could send Lord Topher up, while Vadim bustled the dress back to my own chambers. However, this time Lord Topher knew his stuff. He had brought a rose for me, and he presented it, brown eyes shy, with the ingenuously expressed hope that I would wear it tomorrow night.

I eyed him with some severity. "Lord Topher, I believe you are attempting to cheat!"

He laughed and blushed, but disclaimed all accusations of cheating. "Don't forget, Lady Farrah, you owe me a dance! How can I claim it if I don't know who you are?"

"If that's the case, I'm surprised you didn't enquire after my costume," I said.

"Oh no!" protested Lord Topher disarmingly; "That *would* be cheating."

I couldn't help laughing– which, as the event proved, was a mistake, for Lord Topher, who had been hovering a little uncertainly near the door, took heart and sat down. I tempered my annoyance with the comfort that I hadn't promised to wear the rose, after all, and sat down opposite him.

"Have they found the murderer yet?" he asked, changing the subject summarily. His manner had become positively buoyant, and I reflected with a silent sigh that my first impressions of Lord Topher had been all too correct: he was well into the throes of calf-love. If I had thought it would do the least good, I would have sent him right about his business, but I have found from experience that pointed disinterest and outright impoliteness have never dampened the ardour of the young. I steeled myself for a long and perhaps tiresome visit, and picked up the subject that Lord Topher had begun. "Not to my knowledge, my lord; but I've spoken only in passing with Lord Pecus today."

"Did you hear that they've taken the Earl of Horn in for questioning?" he asked, his eyes sparking with mischief. "Coraline told me that Lord Pecus took him in this morning because the Watch found a witness who saw him go into the room after Raoul."

A simmering anger flushed my cheeks. The cheek of Melchior! He had been meeting Lord Pecus earlier for this very reason, no doubt; and had not seen fit to include me in the briefing! And Lord Pecus had not given any indication when he met me on the steps, either.

"Well now, that's very interesting!" I told Lord Topher lightly, swallowing my anger for a better time. Lord Pecus would be very, *very* sorry, if I had any say in the matter. "Did Coraline say who the witness was?"

"A footman, or a butler: one of the liveried servants, anyway," said Lord Topher, his eyes bright and enthusiastic. "Do you think he did it? The earl, I mean?"

I smiled a little and indulged him. "He's a good suspect. Lord Pecus thinks the murder was politically motivated, and I'm inclined to agree with him."

"But he's so old and round! He couldn't have done it, Lady Farrah, it would be too disappointing!"

"I shall look about for a better candidate in my inquiries," I promised, amused again. At this point, it would have pleased me very much to find a suspect that Lord Pecus hadn't; but despite the fact that the Earl of Horn was rotund and unromantic to the youthful eye, he was still a very likely suspect, and I didn't hold out much hope.

Lord Topher's eyes sparkled again, bringing life to his otherwise quite ordinary face. "Are you trying to find the murderer too, my lady?"

"If you won't give me away to Lord Pecus, yes!" I said, laughingly. I had enough ire left to add: "He doesn't approve of me investigating, if you please!"

"You like excitement, don't you, Lady Farrah?"

"Certainly I do!" I told him briskly. "It strengthens the

constitution and makes one much less likely to fall into fainting fits. I highly recommend it for today's less resilient youth." I stood while he was trying to decide whether or not I was joking, and said in a friendly tone: "Do greet Sir Coraline for me; I believe I met her at a soiree last week."

Lord Topher stood politely, if not enthusiastically, taking his cue like a gentleman, and assured me that he would say everything proper to his sister-in-law. It was only at the door that his grown-up air deserted him long enough to say: "Don't forget our dance, Lady Farrah!"

I shooed him out with laughing promises that the dance should not be forgotten, and returned to my chambers. Vadim was there before me, peeping from behind the partitioning door between our rooms to say excitedly: "Lady, my things have arrived!"

I observed dispassionately that they had, and crooked a finger at her. "Show me."

Vadim entered the room fully, and did a turn. "It's so light, lady!"

I looked her up and down in critical approval. The girls below stairs had sewn the pieces together very competently, and the sapphire cloth suited her as perfectly as I had known it would.

"Very satisfactory, Vadim: I believe blue may be your colour. May one ask where Keenan is, or would it be unwise to enquire?"

"He's under the bed," Vadim said, with a scowl over her shoulder. "He says he's making something for you. Keenan! The lady wants to see you! Come out, or I'll drag you out!"

I laughingly declined any need to see Keenan, ignoring his mutinous muttering, and said: "I believe I shall go out, Vadim. You will accompany me— no, you may continue to wear what you have on; now is as good a time to start with your new things as any other."

Vadim left Keenan to secrecy and dust without a backward glance, and dashed to help me dress. "Where are we going, lady?"

"To see the horselords, I rather think," I said thoughtfully. If Lord Pecus was not sharing information I certainly wouldn't give him the satisfaction of going over old ground in an attempt to keep up. The Earl of Horn and Charles Black were old ground, and now beyond my power to explore. No, I must branch into new line of investigation, one that Lord Pecus had either not considered, or not seen as important. As an afterthought to Vadim, who was attempting to perch the wrong hat on my head, I added: "But to Raoul's chambers first. Vadim, are you determined to make me a laughingstock?"

My lips twitched at the consternation on her face. "Widebrimmed hats are only for mornings, child. As the day wanes, so do hat brims; and as it is now approaching late afternoon, any brim in sight must be a small curled one."

Vadim held up another hat tentatively, this time a small, curved confection that dipped toward one eye and displayed a charming curl of sapphire blue feather. I nodded my approval and allowed her to place it while I changed my overdress to something more nearly matching. By now, Raoul's room ought to be unguarded: the Watch had finished their inspection yesterday, and I should be able to walk in without attracting notice.

Vadim, for once conscious of her duties, opened all doors for me. I would have been more favourably impressed if I had not had a strong suspicion that she was merely eager to break and enter, but it made a nice change. I found myself suddenly thankful that Keenan was not with us, and wondered briefly if

I was setting a bad example for impressionable children. However, a moment's reflection was sufficient to remind me that Keenan's criminal tendencies were already fully formed by the time our paths crossed, and that Vadim was very nearly as bad. Much to my amusement, she showed herself proficient in the art of the search, lifting and replacing each item just as it had been before she touched it; and displaying a talent for hidden niches and drawers. Nevertheless, adept though she was, not even Vadim could produce useful information out of thin air— or perhaps she could, for all I knew, with those ever-useful magical abilities of hers. At any rate, there was nothing to be gained from poking about a room that had already been divested of any relevant clues, so I signalled to Vadim, and we left as carefully as we had arrived.

"Why are we going to see the horselords?" she asked, when we were safely out of the house and strolling along the streets.

Curbing the tongues of one's servants may be dignified and lofty, but it is rarely useful, so I merely said: "I want to know if Lord Pecus has found out about Katrina yet," and allowed her to chatter.

I left her at one of the tables in the mess hall, where she was fussed over by four huge guardsmen who should have known better. They teased her and provided her with far more sweets than she could possibly eat, and treated her, in short, like a younger sister; leaving me free to wander in search of Katrina, whom I found in one of the recreational booths. She was hunched over a chessboard and fiddling with the pieces while Curran, a lazy smile on his face, sprawled back into the padded seat with his arms spread on the seat top each side. This, I knew as well as Curran himself did, would see him with his arm around Katrina when she sat back from her turn. How interesting! So Curran was courting in earnest, was he? For all his talk, Curran was not in the habit of putting an arm around his ladyfriends unless he was dancing with them.

It was Katrina who looked up and saw me first, her dark face lightening with a rare smile. Curran, drawing his eyes away from her, winked at me and said: "Isabella, my darling! I hear you've been obstructing the Watch."

I flicked a pointed look at the arm around Katrina's shoulders, but forbore to remark, since his eyes held as much warning as his smile did audacity. So Katrina didn't yet know she was being courted. Also interesting.

"No: corrupting it, apparently," I told them. "Or so Lord Pecus informs me."

"I think Lord Pecus is fond of you, Isabella," said Katrina unexpectedly, gazing up at me with quietly curious eyes. "He told us not to encourage you."

"I dare say he did!" I remarked, with feeling. I was conscious of disappointment. "Lord Pecus already spoke to you, then?"

Curran looked at me with a faintly mocking smile. "He spoke to all of us, yesterday. But if you mean to Katrina in particular, no. None of us felt that her business was pertinent."

I chuckled with a touch of malice. "Lord Pecus will most likely beg to differ when he finds out. And he *will* find out, Katrina."

"I know," she said, smiling faintly. "I didn't want it gone over just yet, that's all. Have you come to question me?"

"Yes. I'm sorry."

She shrugged, and unconsciously leaned back into the circle of Curran's arm. "Don't be. I want the swine who did this caught and executed as much as any Civetan could, but I don't know how much use I can be."

"Neither do I," I said ruefully. "Perhaps I'm clutching at straws. I wondered if Raoul ever said anything to you about Charles Black, or perhaps Black Velvet; or if there was a single place you used to meet in more than any other place."

"When we didn't meet here in the mess hall, we'd go to a small eatery in Rooker's Square— the *Pig's Squeal*," Katrina said, turning a queen over and over between long fingers. She didn't look up. "It's the only place we went to. The king-consort thinks Raoul was a traitor, doesn't he?"

"Yes," I said regretfully. "Raoul *was* carrying sensitive papers."

This time Katrina did look at me. "Lady, he was no traitor. It carries no weight from me, I know, but I knew him. He was troubled—something to do with papers, like you said—but Civet was always first in his thoughts. Look for any other motive but treason."

"It gives me no pleasure to think of Raoul as a traitor," I said sombrely, sighing a little. "I won't close my mind to the possibility, but it has never sat well with me."

"He said you grew up together," said Katrina, inclining her head in a nod. "There's another motive somewhere: find it, Isabella."

"And so I shall!" I said, infusing a cheerfulness that I didn't quite feel into my voice. "The *Pig's Squeal*, you say?"

I left as Curran was showing Katrina sleight of hand with the chess piece—no doubt because this entailed playing with her fingers—and couldn't help but smile. Katrina, so strong and independent, had stood shoulder to shoulder with Raoul: it was intriguing to see her leaning on anyone, let alone on so precarious a support as Curran. I stifled a chuckle as I crooked a finger for Vadim. Garrulous Curran and silent Katrina! They would make an odd pair.

When Vadim rejoined me, we took to the open street

again. Dusk was drawing near, but fortunately Vadim knew Rooker's Square well, and it was barely a ten minute walk to find the *Pig's Squeal* eatery; where, if its signs were to be believed, one could enjoy the best bacon in the city. I raised a sceptical brow at this, but since the same sign informed customers that strongboxes could be obtained for their varied (and possibly illegal) possessions, I subdued my misgivings, and entered. Declining to seat myself at any of the tables, I approached the counter and showed the tender my Civetan chit.

"I believe a countryman of mine had a lockbox here," I said pleasantly, as he examined it. "His name was Raoul."

The tender passed the chit back and nodded. "He was here last week, lady."

"He's dead," I told him bluntly, because I was moderately sure that he knew already. "I need to open the locker."

The tender eyed me for a brief, ruminative moment, no doubt debating between the dual possibilities of successfully shaking me down for a bribe and starting an international incident, and went with the safer option. "I'm not supposed to let anyone but the renter in, lady." He rubbed unnecessarily at the already clean counter, and shot another look at me. "He hasn't paid the last lot of rent, you know."

I slid a coin from my cuff and flashed it at him. "Open the locker: I'll settle the rent."

He left me with the key, and I left him with the coin. Vadim, bouncing with barely contained excitement, hung onto the wooden, magic-grained door, and peered in.

"Huh!" she said in disgust. "It's only a card, lady! I thought it would be secret papers."

I reached in and plucked out the oblong of stiff cardboard, but it was blank. "Vadim?"

She took it, and her eyes brightened. "Oh! Clever! Watch,

lady." She passed her hand over the face of it, then tapped it sharply on the side of the lockbox. "It's a carnival trick. Look!"

Ink trickled into being like sand through a timer, forming the words: *Today at dusk. Order tea for two.*

"Very well!" I said sharply, flicking the card back into the strongbox. "Now we achieve something! We have arrived just in time, I think. Vadim, wait for me at another table."

Vadim, her eyes very big, took the coin I passed her. "Lady, perhaps you'll be kidnapped!"

"Nonsense!" I said cheerfully, though her fear had not fallen too far from my own rueful presentiments of danger. "You will sit at another table, and watch carefully. If we leave the table you will stay, but I'll take a sip of tea before we leave and you will know all is well. If I drop my teacup instead of sipping, run for the nearest watchman. Do you understand?"

She repeated it back to me, and I left her to take a table while I harassed the counter tender once more. "When was the message left?"

This time I prefaced my question with the sight of another coin, and the tender didn't hesitate. "This morning. A message boy poked it through the slots. Can I take your order, lady?"

"Tea for two," I said, and sat down.

Chapter Nine

I sipped my tea with a tranquillity that was only slightly more than skin deep, and reflected with an inward sigh that the day was becoming another long one. Well, it was all in a good cause, after all. One couldn't let someone like Lord Pecus get the better of one, and Raoul's murderer certainly must be brought to justice.

There was a flash of red to my right mid thought, and someone sat down opposite me in a slither of satin. Female, my periphery told me, with a jolt of surprise.

"You're not what I expected," said the woman, crossing her legs. Her scarlet Lacunan cheongsam pulled tight across her shapely legs in a way that would not have been permissible in a Glausian or Civetan woman, displaying one ankle and a good deal of calf shamelessly.

"From the message I expected a man."

I shrugged a little and sipped my tea. "Assumptions are dangerous things. Will you take tea?"

"I prefer to deal with business first. Did you bring it with you?"

I thought of Raoul, with a folded paper sewn into his sash. I had no papers with me, treasonous or otherwise. "It's somewhere safe. I'll tell you where it is after we've settled accounts."

One eyebrow rose, rousing my admiration with its exquisite arrogance. I would have liked to have raised my own in reply, but it has never been one of my talents, and I had to be content merely to give her look for look.

"Do we have an accord, lady?"

She hesitated only a moment. "Not here. Upstairs."

She rose as languorously as she had seated herself, and moved gracefully past me to the back of the café. I took a sip of my tea, my eyes dwelling thoughtfully on a potted plant just to the left of Vadim, who had stiffened, and rose to follow her.

The shadowed staircase was narrow and dusty, no difficulty for the Lacunan lady in her close-cut cheongsam, but distinctly troublesome to me. I found myself in a losing battle for clean skirts and began to feel that I had been somewhat hasty. It was all for Raoul, of course – not to mention discomfiting Lord Pecus – but I did not feel that I should have to sacrifice my skirts to the cause. There is no reason people cannot have clean stairwells, if only they will take the trouble to *sweep*. The room above stairs was not much tidier, but at least it was of sufficient size to allow me to stand in the centre and thus avoid the rampant dust bunnies that freely populated the corners. I heard the door click shut behind me with ominous loudness as the Lacunan lady sat down elegantly on one dusty table corner and lit a cigarillo.

"Who are you working for, lady?"

"Myself," I said pleasantly, watching the curl of greenish smoke. I wondered where I had slipped: for slip I certainly had. Unless I was very much mistaken, the herby smoke quickly drifting through the room was *hash*, commonly thought of as a potent truth drug, and I was now in no small amount of danger.

"You are not my contact," remarked the woman, issuing a thin stream of smoke from scarlet lips. Her eyes ran over me calculatingly, but I remained calm by reflecting that at least she was not a magic user: no one would use *hash* if they had the choice between it and a truth spell. "Who are you? Who are you working for?"

Firmly, I said: "I work for myself."

I was familiar with the green form of *hash*: it was not so much a truth drug as it was an intoxicant. The green smoke produced a bubbly confusion that gave issue to an unconsidered and unceasing chatter of anything uppermost in the victim's mind. While the drug was usually effective, however, it was also unfortunately undiscriminating. An unwary questioner could find himself thoughtlessly answering more questions than he asked, if faced with a clever opponent; and there were ways of cheating it outright if one had enough determination of mind. I was nothing if not determined. Nevertheless, she was smoking the drug, and it would, paradoxically, take longer to affect her: I would have to be more than determined. I wished I had had foresight enough to sweep my teacup off the table instead of taking a sip like a silly little sheep.

"I have all day, you know," said the Lacunan woman. I took a small, light step backwards toward the door, and she slid off the table. "It's locked. A friend of mine followed us up."

It was no less than I had expected. "What gave me away?"

"Payment was made some days ago," the woman said, circling me. Another thin stream of smoke drifted toward me, and I couldn't tell if she had answered willingly or under the influence of the *hash*. "We get requests for more money often, but not for an original payment already made. Who are you?"

"'*Poet, philosopher, queen*'," I told her, with a sparkling smile. The quote was meant to be spoken straight-faced, but the smoke was beginning to make me dizzy and a little happy, and I couldn't quite manage it. The trick with *hash* is to fill one's mind with so many pent-in, separate thoughts, that when an interrogator begins questioning one, the only reply they gain is nonsense.

I allowed my thoughts to sharpen for a moment while the Lacunan woman frowned. "I'm not your first Civetan contact, am I? Who else do you have?"

"We began with the Harper family," she said, without thinking. "Then six months ago another operative took over."

"Raoul?"

"Yes. But his information wasn't as useful as we had hoped."

"Did you kill him?" My voice was too sharp, and the woman blinked.

"You're familiar with *hash*, I see," she said, more watch-fully. She blew a meditative stream of smoke into the ceiling. "What a pity I have no magic: I was hoping it wouldn't have to come to this. I'm afraid I will have to hurt you, lady. Claude!"

Claude was a small, wiry man with well-trimmed mutton-chops and a face that was almost waxen in its quiet stillness. I allowed him to tie me to a dirty chair without demur because I had met his kind before: he would take pleasure in hurting me if I resisted. While he tied me, the Lacunan woman put out her cigarillo and opened a window to let in air of a dubious freshness. I heard the rattle as the window rose in its frame behind me, and though the breeze was warm and muggy, I felt a cold chill. I was very much regretting that I had not given Vadim the signal to call the Watch.

"This is Claude," the Lacunan woman said, stalking into my line of sight once more. The introduction was unnecessary, but my respect for her went up: she knew how to build tension. She slid one of the decorative sticks from the inky black upsweep of her hair, disclosing a sharp poniard at its further end, and tapped it lightly against the back of my hand. It was sharp enough to draw a painless drop of blood.

"You can call me Chi. You won't get the chance to talk about us to anyone, so we may as well be informal."

Ah. A little clumsier. Death threats give no incentive to talk.

"Isabella," I said coolly, nodding. "You've begun wrongways, lady. Talking becomes less attractive when I've only death to look forward to."

"Would you believe me if I told you I would let you go?"

I laughed. "No, lady; I would not."

"Then lying would be pointless," she said, shrugging. "And I can make you wish you were dead. If you talk, I'll make sure death is quick and painless; if not, I'll leave you to Claude's tender care."

"I think you underestimate the desire of the living to keep on living," I said. Was that a footstep in the other room? "Are you familiar with Lord Pecus, lady?"

Chi's eyes had gone to the door, but at this they snapped back to me. "All of Glause is familiar with Lord Pecus."

"He asked me to marry him last week," I told her, quite truthfully. I didn't feel it necessary to inform her that I had replied in the negative. "I am not unprotected."

Chi gazed at me long and thoughtfully. "I can't tell if you're lying or not, but I do know you're stalling. I would have liked to have someone like you on our side, lady."

Claude was looking at the inner door, somewhere over my shoulder and out of sight. "She heard a footstep. So did I."

"Go have a look," Chi told him, without taking her eyes off me. "I'll stay with the lady."

We waited in silence, Chi leaning gracefully against the wall despite the dirt. I spent a little time regarding the toe of my shoe. It was regrettably soiled, and very possibly ruined. That would teach me not to meddle in treasonable affairs: they seemed to be dirty in more ways than one. I wondered briefly if Vadim was getting restless, but the thought was not helpful and I dismissed it: there was no use dwelling on things that could not be changed.

Into the silence fell quiet, shuffling noises from the next room; then, abruptly, sounds of a violent scuffle. Chi's fingers closed around a wooden chair top. The scuffle was followed just as suddenly by an ominous silence, then there was a gentle pattering on the door as if someone had drummed their fingers lightly against it.

Chi said sharply: "Claude! Did you take care of it?"

Silence.

"Claude, come out at once! I am in no mood for your sick fancies!"

One scarlet fingernail tapped the top of the chair; ceased. Chi took an impatient, uncertain step toward the door.

"Don't go in there," I warned her, bracing my hands almost unconsciously against my bonds. I thought I might know what had happened in the room, and my feeling of danger had intensified tenfold. "It's not safe."

"It's only Claude and his twisted little tricks," she said impatiently, but I saw the shade of fear in her dark eyes. She was not altogether convinced. She flounced past me with an exaggerated stride, trying to regain her confidence, and I heard the door fling open behind me. Perhaps she gasped; I wasn't quite sure. But the door slammed shut again almost immediately, and there was that ominous stillness again before the pattering began, as if early spring rain were falling on the door.

The door opened with gentle snick of door lock against jamb, and I resolutely fixed my gaze straight ahead, fingers curling around the chair arms.

A voice spoke behind me, startlingly close. "Lady Farrah."

His voice was an unfamiliar tenor tone, with a light, lilting touch to it that sounded as if it could rise to the pitch of madness without much provocation. I heard him draw in a deep breath, very close behind me now, and came to the disturbing conclusion that he was smelling my hair.

"I believe you have the advantage of me," I said quietly. Movement teased my periphery, but I looked steadfastly ahead, refusing to turn my head.

"Don't you want to know who I am?"

Petulance. I said, hardly daring to breathe: "That would ruin the suspense."

He laughed. "I knew I liked you! Why did they tie you up?"

"They didn't want me to run away."

Even a child of ten years would have protested that I hadn't given a proper answer, but he didn't. The cold feeling in my stomach spread in an icy rush to my outer extremities: I was at the mercy of a man whose homicidal mania was governed by a childlike whimsy.

The movement in my peripheral vision died away as he moved behind me again. "Did you know them?"

"Barely." I had the distinct impression that this man would know if I lied to him, and so I told the exact truth. "A countryman of mine was killed a short while ago, and we had reason to believe that it was in connection with a leak in our covert affairs. Those two were encouraging me not to follow up the investigation."

"Oh." It sounded as though he was thinking. At length, he said: "I didn't kill him for *that*. You're playing with me, aren't you? You know it was me."

"As soon as I heard Claude die," I said, nodding. "But I don't know why you did it."

He chuckled mischievously. "I'm not going to tell you. You have to figure it out for yourself."

"How delightful!" I managed to say. My throat was becoming steadily drier, but I didn't dare so much as lick my lips to moisten them. I knew instinctively that he would take it for a sign of weakness.

"Who's that at the door?" There was a sudden scuffle of dust as he spun sharply to face the door. "Someone's coming. A little girl."

I closed my eyes. Vadim. "It's my maid," I said. "I would prefer if you did not kill her."

He huffed out a breath of discontent. "It would be so easy. One little *pinch*; then splat! You couldn't stop me, you know."

"I know." The balmy breeze had brought a prickle of sweat to my hairline, and the air seemed suddenly too thick to breathe. "We are at your mercy, Vadim and I. You can let her live."

He sounded thoughtful. "I could, if I wanted to. I wonder if I want to?"

I drew in another breath of warm air and repeated: "I would prefer if you did not kill her."

He didn't reply but I was aware that he was suddenly very close, and in an instinct of pure self-preservation I closed my eyes, gripping tight to the arms of my chair. A light kiss was pressed on my lips, then there was a gust of air behind me, setting dust bunnies tumbling, and speaking of sudden aloneness.

It lasted only for a moment, then Vadim was tumbling into the room, breathless and distressed. "Lady! Oh lady, he didn't kill you!" She threw her arms around my neck, all but choking me, and the chair creaked dangerously.

"Vadim, I am flattered, but I will not have my hair rumpled!" I told her tartly. I did not care to have her see the sweat dotting my brow, or the paleness to my cheeks.

Vadim pulled back apologetically, but her hands twisted themselves into the fabric of her new dress as she stood before me, and I smiled faintly. "Well, Vadim? What is it?"

"Lord Pecus, m'lady." The fingers tightened until I was half afraid that the material would rip. "He must have felt the first one die, same as me. He's not far off now."

A jolt of energy shot up my spine.

"Untie me! Quickly now!" Her fingers pulled a little jerkily at the ropes, and I sat still to allow her to work, frowning in thought. "Are you able to hide any traces of our being here?"

"You won't leave a magic trace," Vadim said, tugging determinedly at a knot. She was rather pale, and I felt a stab of guilt at having pulled her into this dangerous shambles. "I can hide mine."

"Lord Pecus has other methods of investigations," I said curtly, glad that I had been present to see it in person. "Any hairs, any dress fibres: they have to be gone, Vadim."

"Yes, lady. No one will know you've been here."

I freed my wrists with a jerk, singeing a light burn across one of them, just as shouts began to ring out below stairs. Apparently not all of the *Pig's Squeal's* patrons were entirely easy in their consciences as pertaining to the Watch. I locked and barred the door, and told Vadim: "I'm afraid it will have to be the window."

There were heavy footsteps on the stairs, running steps, and I ran to the window in quick, cold haste. "Vadim, is it done?"

"It's done, it's done!" Vadim panted, hurrying across the room. I lifted her out and she found her feet on the ledge outside, clinging to the window frame for a moment. "We can reach the ground, lady. It's a small drop."

"I should like to mention," I said, climbing out with less than my usual dignity and a heady amusement that was no doubt a lingering effect of the *hash*; "That I find this situation unrefined in the extreme! I'm ashamed of you, Vadim; you've led me into dangerous company."

Vadim gave a panting giggle. "Yes, lady. Sorry, lady. You're showing your stockings, lady."

I emitted a strangled giggle of my own. "We will not mention the matter again, Vadim. Now, jump!"

I believe I heard the door splinter open as we jumped. It was a longer distance that I had imagined it to be, and the jolt of landing sent shocks of pain up my shins, but I didn't dare hesitate to check for injuries. We limped around the corner in haste, and I heard Lord Pecus' voice snarl: "To the window!"

"Nearest teashop, Vadim!" I gasped, propelling her around another corner. I did not put it past Lord Pecus to send someone after us while he attended the crime scene. I had an uneasy feeling that he had seen the flurry of our gowns as we leapt. "Am I untidy?"

"There's dirt on the border of your skirt," Vadim said briefly, darting a cautious look around a corner. "This way, lady: only two blocks. I've fixed the dirt."

"Very well," I said, following at a brisk walk. "No, walk now, Vadim. We must not appear flustered. If we are caught up, we are simply strolling to tea."

We retired to the powder room of the nearest teashop to

tidy ourselves. Vadim, ever thoughtful, had traced a new colour into my gown to confuse any would-be questioners; and I was pleased to discover that although there was a dash of colour to my cheeks, it was merely a becoming one, and not a flustered one. I sent Vadim out to secure us a table while I delicately swabbed away the tiny beads of sweat from my brow and powdered lightly. I found myself smiling, and reflected that it was no use deceiving oneself: I had always enjoyed a good game of cat and mouse. Killer or no killer, it was certain that I would not do differently if another occasion arose. Besides, I had gained valuable insights: Lord Pecus might hold the Earl of Horn in highest suspicion, but although he *could* have been the man behind me, I very much doubted it. The earl was nothing if not sane. Dangerous, yes; but perfectly sane in his methods. Besides, if this madman was to be believed, Raoul had not been killed because of treasonous documents. I was quite sure that besides his wife and daughter, the earl would not care enough about anything to kill for it.

I replaced my powder box with a thoughtful frown, dusting the powder from my fingers, and turned from the mirror only to discover that the powder room window was swiftly being populated with horselords.

Emmett climbed through, filling the window, and gazed about him in interest as the others followed, jostling him as they came. "It's all a bit pink, isn't it?" he said.

"Move!" snapped Miryum, stabbing his ribs with an ungentle finger. Emmett jumped, looking more sheepish than a man of his size ought to look, and stood aside. Curran and Brennan followed close behind, Curran turning back to help Katrina, who didn't need the help but accepted it quietly.

Brennan looked around disparagingly, but said laconically: "I've seen worse."

"When?" demanded Curran. "Spend a lot of time in powder rooms, do you?"

"A bit," Brennan said equably, unshaken. "Laura meets me in the powder room."

"*Which* powder room?"

Brennan shrugged. "Any powder room. Her father doesn't like me."

"I'm not surprised, if you're in the habit of frequenting ladies' powder rooms!" I said tartly. "Is there a reason I'm being invaded by a regiment of horselords?"

"The Commander is on his way," said Emmett briefly, nodding toward the door. "He could be here already."

"He arrived but a moment or two after you left: someone must have told him about Katrina," Miryum said. Her voice had a delicate undercurrent of anger to it. "We had to account for her whereabouts and I don't appreciate the fact that one of my people had to be vouched for."

Emmett shrugged, and I gathered that it was a point of contention between them. "He was doing his job."

Unusual. Emmett and Miryum usually had one thought and one agreement between them. Curran, quick as ever to sense contention, said mockingly: "Mum, dad, don't fight!"

This had the effect of turning Miryum's steely gaze away from Emmett to Curran, and I was at leisure to ask Emmett: "What happened?"

"He must have planted a monitor on you. He was questioning Katrina when something fizzled. The Commander knocked over a table and took off running."

I remembered suddenly Lord Pecus patting my hand—absently, I had thought at the time. Not so absently, then. The beast!

"That's *terribly* interesting," I remarked thoughtfully; "However, I should like to know exactly how Lord Pecus knew where I was. I'm no expert in the affairs of magic, but I was under the impression that a monitoring spell was only capable of monitoring."

"Katrina had to tell him about the café," Curran told me. His voice was light, but if I were not mistaken, he was just as annoyed as Miryum. "Interestingly enough, he seemed to know that that was where he would find you. Sweet Isabella, this man knows you too well. We saw you dashing down the street and followed: he won't be far behind."

"Well, he didn't find me," I said primly. "And I would like it to be clearly understood that I was never there. I have been enjoying a quiet day of shopping and have just stopped for tea."

"You haven't got any bags," said Brennan, with what I considered to be an entirely unnecessary interest.

There was a brief silence before Miryum said: "Well, if even *he* noticed it, Lord Pecus certainly will."

I ignored Brennan's protests of *what do you mean if **even I** noticed it?* and gazed narrowly around the room. "Turn out the cushions," I told them, resolutely, heading for the powder room seats. "There is always an assortment of packaging in a powder room."

Curran nudged Brennan and said: "Should have known *that*, shouldn't you?" but they both turned out cushions with the greatest good humour, and in a very few moments I was provided with an assortment of varied papers and string bags.

"*Cussons* and *Percy's*," I said, pointing out the pale blue and bright red papers. Curran gathered the others, as if to throw them in the waste chute, but I stopped him with a wave. "Padding, my dear Curran; padding." I held up one of the papers to demonstrate, and wrapped it around one of the balls of paper that had been too crumpled to be believable. I tied it with a tag end of string, and presented it to the group. "Well?"

Curran looked at me in admiration. "You're frighteningly criminal, Isabella."

"So I've been told." I tied two more bundles; one long, the other fat and square, and stuffed them into one of the string bags. I dangled the string bag from my reticule arm, and held it out for inspection. "Will I pass muster, Brennan?"

He grinned and assented.

"Is there anything else I should know?"

The horselords looked at each other.

"He'll be angry," said Katrina. "Be careful, lady."

"I'll bear that in mind," I said, smiling. I found that I was a little nervous, and put up my chin. "I'm obliged to you all."

Curran shrugged cheerfully. "Oh, anything to annoy the Watch!"

Miryum grinned in agreement, but only said: "Good luck, Isabella."

I left the horselords to disperse through the window once more, and re-entered the teashop. Vadim was standing stiffly by a table for two, while Lord Pecus, dwarfing the spindly table and chair alike, glowered at the tea counter. My poor Vadim! I made a mental note to buy her an especially nice present when this meeting was over, and sauntered over to the table, swinging my string bag jauntily. Lord Pecus saw me from halfway across the room, and regarded me with a scowl as I walked the last few yards toward them. He stood curtly but sat down again almost immediately, whether as a deliberate insult or because his mind was on other things, I was not sure.

I smiled cordially at him and gave my string bag to Vadim to hold. Bless the child, she took it without a blink.

"Lord Pecus! What a pleasant surprise!"

"I'd like to say I find it surprising," said Lord Pecus disagreeably, declining to comment as to the pleasantness or otherwise, of the situation. "But I don't. In fact, I'm beginning to expect to see you whenever I find trouble."

"You are surely not suggesting that I cause trouble!" I said, with dignity. "Vadim, is our tea ready? Perhaps you should order for two; I'm sure Lord Pecus is thirsty."

Lord Pecus' porcelain lips opened, no doubt to repudiate the charge, but he changed his mind, and instead growled: "Tea and biscuits for me. Wait for your mistress outside."

Vadim put her chin in the air and didn't move. Lord Pecus gazed at her in exasperation; and, at length, grinned. "I would like to speak with you privately, Lady Farrah. If you please."

I smiled approvingly at him. "Since you ask so nicely, my lord! Vadim, would you wait for us outside, please?"

Vadim lowered her chin and said: "Yes, m'lady," just to show how well she took orders from those she considered worthy, and left us alone.

The tea arrived almost immediately after, so there was no awkward silence. I poured out for Lord Pecus and then sat back in horrified amazement as he dipped his biscuits into the teacup and gulped them down whole. There is a way to drink fine tea, and dipping biscuits in it is *not* that way. I sipped my own tea in an admonitory fashion but Lord Pecus did not seem to notice, because after he had gulped down a final biscuit, he said: "I was at a crime scene this evening."

"How distressing for you!" I said sympathetically. "Was it terribly gruesome?"

"The odd thing about it," continued Lord Pecus meditatively, licking his fingers without acknowledging my question; "Is that I could swear I saw a girl in a blue dress climbing out the window."

"How very odd!"

"It was, wasn't it?" Lord Pecus smiled at me affably. "I would hate to think that you were interfering in a Watch matter again, Lady Farrah."

I didn't treat him to my wide-eyed look because I didn't think he would believe it, and I felt that I would rather not share what I knew at this stage. Instead, I let my brow furrow ever so slightly, and said: "I find myself somewhat at a loss, my lord. You did say that this girl had on a *blue* gown, did you not?"

Lord Pecus brushed crumbs from his shirt for a long thoughtful moment, gazing at my now pink skirts, and then said: "I did. You may or may not be aware of this, Lady Farrah, but I put a monitoring spell on you some days ago."

I allowed my very real anger to show through. "Lord Pecus, you come very close to what is unacceptable!"

"I'll do whatever it takes to keep you safe," he said shortly. "Half an hour ago there was a spike in your heart rate that corresponded with two murders at the *Pig's Squeal*. Can you explain the spike?"

Again, my anger prompted me to action. I had sunk my chin on the palm of my hand, the better to look narrowly at Lord Pecus, and now I traced a finger lightly across my lips, gazing into middle distance with a lilting smile. "I met an acquaintance," I said, a little dreamily. I didn't dare overplay it with his eyes on me, so I had to trust Lord Pecus' very finely tuned intuition to catch the inference. I would much rather he thought I was stealing a kiss with a sweetheart than that I was at the centre of his crime scene.

The handle of Lord Pecus' teacup snapped with a tiny tinkle, and I felt a jolt of pleasure. How wonderful! He *had* caught it. I held out my hand across the table and said evenly: "Take the spell off."

Lord Pecus looked at me without expression, but took my

hand and ran one huge, rough finger across the back of it. Something fizzed gently and then died away. "It's gone."

I tried to pull my hand back, but Lord Pecus tightened his grip. "Lady Farrah, I won't allow you to run constantly into danger."

"If I *were* running into danger it would be entirely my own business, thank you very much!" I said, with something of a snap. It would have been undignified and less than useful to try and tug my hand away, so I contented myself with glaring at him. "However, as I have already informed you that I was otherwise engaged, my lord, I fail to see any point to your remarks!"

"Let me make it clearer. If you continue to involve yourself in my investigation, I will do something about it."

With an effort, I subdued my anger and smiled brilliantly at him. "Now, now, Lord Pecus, I'm sure you're not threatening me! Diplomatic relations are good for something, after all."

Lord Pecus smiled briefly. "No threats, lady; but I will keep you safe by whatever means necessary. Despite what you seem to think, I find it very much my business."

He really was rather sweet. I rested my chin on my free hand and regarded him thoughtfully. "You and I are friends, Lord Pecus: don't let's quarrel. I've tried to stay out of your way, and I shall endeavour to do so still."

"That's what I'm afraid of, lady," he said ruefully, loosening his grip on my fingers at last. "I'm beginning to think that you're safer when you're in my sight."

I could have pulled away then, but an impulse made me press the huge hand instead. It was a comfortingly warm, rough hand; and besides, he looked a little forlorn. "You shouldn't worry about me, my lord. I've come through worse peril unscathed."

I took my hand away gently, and Lord Pecus sat back with folded arms, regarding me with a curious smile.

"Do you always recover your temper so quickly, Lady Farrah?"

"Anger benefits no one, least of all oneself," I said dismissively. "You must do as you must do; just as I must do what *I* must do. I might as well be angry with the tide for shifting itself from dawn to dusk."

"I wish I knew why you feel you have to involve yourself in my investigation." The words were contentious, but he was still smiling and it wouldn't have been useful to take offence.

"I want to be involved in catching Raoul's murderer," I told him candidly. "But I would be lying if I said that was my only reason. I enjoy the thrill of the chase."

Lord Pecus gave a soft snort of laughter. "Of course you do. What am I to do with you, Lady Farrah?"

"Well, you can walk me home, if you wish," I said agreeably, rising and delicately shaking a few crumbs from my skirts. "That is, if your crime scene can do without you for so long."

"I think the Lieutenant can manage for a little while longer," Lord Pecus said.

I dismissed Vadim from accompanying me with a small gold coin and an adjuration to buy herself something nice. She scowled up at Lord Pecus with touching dislike, and said in a deliberately loud aside: "Will you be comfortable without me, lady?"

Lord Pecus grinned widely, but I merely said: "I would not have told you to go otherwise, Vadim. Don't hurry to return: Keenan will fetch my dinner."

She departed with a last scowl at Lord Pecus, and he and I walked on together in the darkening evening. It was a comfortable walk, for I took it upon myself to question him delicately about the crime scene, and I do believe that by the time we reached the ambassadorial quarters he was more or less convinced that I had not been present. My task was made easier by the circumstance that I had not, in fact, *seen* the crime scene: both Claude and Chi had died out of sight in the next room. I do not love to lie; and since it may be said that telling the exact truth in order to deceive is, at the heart of it, lying, I took care to confine myself to questions and didn't offer any unnecessary information. Lord Pecus took his leave of me at the front stairs with a cold, porcelain kiss to my hand, and a quiet remark that he would see me tomorrow night. I agreed sunnily, pleased to find the day ending so well, and made my way upstairs in a more buoyant frame of mind than I had left it early that afternoon. Lord Pecus' ball, I thought, sucking in a deep, thoughtful breath, was sure to be interesting.

Chapter Ten

Father was already in the breakfast room when I went down the next morning. I dropped a kiss on the bald patch that was just beginning to show, and said: "'Morning, Papa."

He looked up from his paper and smiled absently. "Good morning, kitten. Where have you been?"

"Busy, Papa," I told him, sitting down and reaching for the fruit bowl. Glause, unlike Civet, does not present fruit whole and unpeeled; it presents a glorious medley of tropical fruits chopped into bite-sized pieces, tossed as a kind of salad. "Have you missed me?"

"Very much," he said; and added with an uncharacteristic interest: "What mischief have you been making?"

"I've been about Raoul's affairs." It was not necessary to mind my tongue with father; he had a touching faith in my ability to manage, and rarely remonstrated with me. "I think he may not have been killed for a few papers. Oh! I meant to ask you: what *was* that paper?"

Father put his newspaper down and said mildly: "I don't think Melchior wants it discussed with you."

"I daresay he doesn't, Papa," I agreed, looking at him beneath my lashes. "But we needn't let that worry us, need we?"

"Well, you know better than to do anything that would cause an international incident." Father polished his glasses and leaned his elbows on the newspaper. "The document was different from the others we found missing."

"Different in which way?"

"It's an early draft for a speculative air assault in war scenarios."

I pondered this. "Useless?"

"Absolutely useless. The plans are about four years old, and they've changed times out of mind: Melchior told me that the only reason they were kept was for our records."

"Then it's not out of the question that Raoul might *not* have been a traitor?"

"Not out of the question," Father said, cautious as usual. "He may not have known which papers were significant, however."

"Papa, you're a wonder!" I said warmly. "You might look like a tubby, absentminded little gentleman, and you're forever wearing mismatching stockings, but it's only because your mind is occupied with greater things."

He didn't smile this time. "Kitten, I know I don't always notice, but tell your old Papa what you've been up to."

I gave him a brief summation, beginning from my morning with poor Daubney to the whirl of excitement yesterday. He frowned when I lightly touched on my encounter with the murderer, but didn't speak, bless him; and when I finished, he sat in silence for a few minutes.

Then he asked: "Would you stop all this if I told you to?"

"Of course, Papa." I leaned over to kiss his cheek. "You know you don't have to ask. I do hope you won't, however, because I should hate to give it up; especially now that things are getting so interesting."

Father laughed suddenly, creasing his face with the laugh lines that were always a surprise though I knew them so well. "You were always the same. You and Annabel, dashing into danger with poor Melchior running frantically behind to keep you safe."

"And didn't I always come back to you?"

"Well, yes," he admitted. "Bruised knees and torn petticoats, if I remember rightly. Do what you must, Kitten, but be careful."

"Very well, Papa." I finished my fruit and twinkled at him. "No torn petticoats, and no bruised knees. I promise."

❦

Keenan had emerged from under his bed by the time I began to prepare for the ball. If the dust caked on the front of his shirt and trousers was any indicator, he had spent the night there as well as the balance of the previous day. He sat down on my bed, scattering dust and cobwebs on my linen, and followed Vadim's ministrations with a concentrated scowl as she buttoned me into my gown.

I watched him in the mirror with an amused eye. "Keenan, are you unwell, or do you disapprove?"

There was a moment's frowning silence before he offered: "Hair's wrong."

Vadim looked offended. "There's nothing wrong with her hair, you snotty little boy! I did it myself!"

I stood up from the vanity chair, fluttering gauzy red and

gold ribbons. "Well, then, Keenan? How shall I wear my hair tonight?"

"Oh, no, lady, you're never going to listen to him!" said Vadim in despair.

"Certainly I am!" I said calmly. "It is *always* sensible to consider the male opinion. Go ahead, Keenan."

Keenan chose to take the invitation literally, and darted up on the vanity chair. Ignoring Vadim's protests, he pulled out every last pin with gleeful abandon, tumbling my hair down my back.

I inspected myself in the mirror. "A novel approach. Vadim, do you think you can pin some of the ribbons in?"

She swatted Keenan off the chair, and in a moment the ribbons were fixed among the huge curls that remained in my hair from its recent coiffing.

"I think that might do," I observed thoughtfully. "Well done, my children."

I was applying the gold-dust lip rouge when there was a knock at the door: heralding, if I were not much mistaken, Delysia's arrival. I spared her a glance, and noted with amusement the elegant twirl she turned through the doorway.

"Isabella, you're an inveterate flirt!" she said, presenting an armful of flowers. "This one is from a Lieutenant Trophimus Holt, *very* nice; and this one is from Curran; and *this* one–"

"Enough, enough!" I protested, laughing. "Vadim, put them with the others. Well, Delysia, and how do you like your gown?"

"Absolutely *delicious*! It's missing just one thing, *dear* Isabella!"

"You may have whichever of the flowers you choose, Delysia. Just be sure to leave the single red rose."

Delysia's blue eyes opened very wide. "Oooh, whose are you wearing?"

"Lord Topher's," I sighed. "I half promised. Besides, it's the only one that will go with my dress."

"Well, if you will wear gold, Bella!" Delysia sorted through the flowers critically, and turned with a dancing smile. "There are two red ones, you know. Which do you want? I shall take the other."

I gave them a brief glance, but there was nothing to choose between them, so I said: "Ask Keenan. He's our male authority."

Delysia giggled and held them out to the boy. "Choose one for me, there's a dear. May one enquire why your pageboy is a cloud of dust, Isabella?"

"Certainly one may. Keenan, why are you dusty?"

Keenan, who was scowling as darkly at the roses as he had scowled at my hair, said: "Been under the bed. You 'ave *that* one, lady."

Delysia giggled again, and curtseyed to him. "Thank you kind sir!"

"Which brings us to the question of why you were under the bed," I prompted Keenan, accepting the other rose. The deep crimson would never work in close conjunction with my hair, but it would be charming pinned to my dress. The gold dress and lip rouge had done something to my hair: tonight it seemed red-gold instead of plain red, and the flame-like flares in the skirt were swirling just as I had envisioned them. All in all, I was excessively pleased with it.

"Been makin' stuff," Keenan said gruffly. "*You'll* see."

"I am breathless with anticipation," I told him. "Vadim, where did I put my mask?"

She brought it over with care: it was spangled gold, and the spangles had a distressing habit of floating away and adhering to anything and everything. No doubt I would be covered with them before the night was out.

I allowed myself one last peek in the mirror once my mask was on, and found myself pleased. "Well, Delysia, how are the men progressing?"

"When I looked down on them, Harroll was just beginning to pace," Delysia said, with wifely affection. "Poor dear! I shall wait until he starts fiddling with his watch before I put my mask on."

Poor Harroll indeed!

"There's no need to wait on my account, Delysia: I'm perfectly ready."

"Oh yes, but if we wait a little longer he'll start clutching at his hair, and he's so adorable when he does that!"

"I warned him not to marry you, you know," I said severely. "See how right I was! Plagued by a wife who finds it necessary to arrive fashionably late, he'll no doubt fall into an early decline."

Delysia pouted. "Oh, very well! But you can't ride in our carriage, Isabella; I shall have to rumple his hair myself, and Harroll won't let me if we're not alone."

I laughed. "I did wonder how Harroll's hair always managed to be so elegantly ruffled."

"If I left Harroll to his own devices, he would be neatly boring!" Delysia said tartly. "Isabella, men are nothing but trouble!"

"So I've heard," I murmured, pushing her gently but firmly to the door. "Let us go down before he pulls his hair out. Vadim, you need not stay up for me."

There was a determined gleam to Vadim's eyes, suggesting that she intended to stay up and make herself a martyr to duty, but she only nodded.

Keenan, sidling closer to me in a furtive manner, peered around the door to make sure Delysia had gone, and said loudly: "*I* ain't tired!"

Since he chose that moment to try and sneak his hand into my hidden pocket, I was not deceived.

"Keenan, I allow you to be dusty and very possibly flea ridden because it doesn't concern me. If, however, you insist upon inflicting your dirt upon my best clothing, I shall have you bathed in the horse trough."

I withdrew the item he had tried to deposit in my pocket and observed it in distaste. It was difficult to tell exactly what it was: I could pick out a tangle of string, three twigs and a thimble, but the rest of the bulk was made up of what appeared to be an amalgamation of cobwebs, dust, and possibly even hair.

Keenan's sharp eyes gleamed: he looked, if it were creditable, *proud* of himself. "Made it meself!" he said complacently. "'S'protection."

"Protection against what, pray?"

Keenan thought about it. "Stuff."

"How very useful. It must needs have been made out of dust and cobwebs, I suppose?"

"'S'the only way I know," he said sulkily.

I sighed, but found myself unable to disappoint him. After all, it was quite small, and wouldn't make a bulge in the smooth lines of my skirt. "I'm sure it will be very useful. Good night, my children: don't forget to take precautions with the doors and windows."

I made my way downstairs, hoping that I wouldn't come home to find the doors boarded up. One never knew with a child like Keenan. I turned the spiral of the grand stairway, sweeping into view of the gentlemen, and noticed with some amusement that Delysia was too late: Harroll's hair was already rumpled.

Melchior whistled. "Carrots! You scrub up quite well!"

"Good heavens, Melchior! What are you?"

"Winter," he said solemnly. He was dressed all in white, almost blindingly so. "Or perhaps a ghost. I haven't decided. What are you, Flame in the Wind?"

"I was going to call myself Fire, but Flame in the Wind is *much* better!" I said approvingly. "Thank you, Melchior! See if you can guess what Delysia is."

Harroll, looking distinctly ruffled, asked: "Is she coming down, Lady Farrah?"

"When I saw her last she was about to fetch her mask," I said soothingly. "Look! Here she is!"

Melchior whistled again, and Delysia fluttered her eyelashes at us all. "What do you think, Harroll?"

Lord Quorn, for once not at all diplomatic, said: "I think we're late. The carriages are waiting."

The masquerade was in full swing when I strolled in on Father's arm. He had declined to dress a part but had ceded to the occasion by wearing a plain mask, and was looking very decently understated.

"Now, Papa," I said severely, with dancing eyes: "You're not to flirt with all the beautiful women just because you're masked. It will never do: people will talk."

Father chuckled. "Off you go, Kitten. If you find Georges, send him my way."

"Certainly, Papa." I kissed his cheek and danced away through the crowd. I found my eyes flitting from side to side in hopes of a sight of Lord Pecus and decided that it would not do: I must find something productive to do.

In the event, I was not forced to productivity. The horselords found me and I danced with each of them in turn, beginning with Emmett, who was not a good dancer but swept all before him, and ending with Curran, who *was*, and knew it. We made a laughing group at the refreshment table, where I found Delysia, who told me with great complacency that she had been constantly complimented on her dress.

"Even Harroll likes it, my dear," she said, with sparkling eyes. "And you know how he never notices one from the other."

"Yes, I thought your lip-rouge was a little smudged when you got out of the carriage," I said wickedly.

Delysia went pink, and giggled. "That was my fault: I was nibbling his ear and he got carried away. It's a good thing I carry a handkerchief with me, or Harroll would have been as rouged as I. Oh, look, Isabella! It is Lord Topher!"

I gave her a quelling look but turned to greet Lord Topher with a friendly smile. It is never of the least use to be snide to boys suffering from calf-love: they seem to take it as a challenge. The only thing to do is be polite and elder-sisterly, and hope that they recover quickly.

"How do you do, Lord Topher? Are you enjoying the masquerade?"

"Now that I've found you, I am!" he said ingenuously. "Will you dance with me?"

I agreed pleasantly, leaving Delysia, much to her chagrin, alone at the refreshment table. Delysia has never been anything less than resourceful, however, and by the time the sets formed for the new dance, she was being led into it by a black-masked individual. She whirled past me a little later with a knowing smile at Lord Topher, and I frowned her down, but she only winked at me. Lord Topher, noticing this, enquired as to the cause.

"Oh, Delysia thinks we make a very pretty pair," I said cheerfully, but with only half my attention. If I were not very much mistaken, Lord Pecus had just joined the dance. Those massive shoulders could not belong to anyone else: and his partner was undoubtedly Lady Louisa.

Lord Topher smiled shyly. "*I* think we do, too," he said. "I would like to call on you tomorrow, Lady Farrah."

Oh, dear.

"Now, Lord Topher, don't make me dislike you," I besought him laughingly. "I am an old maid, and a happy one. Don't let's talk about it."

"I didn't really think I was exciting enough for you," confessed Lord Topher, engagingly. "But I wanted to try."

"I'm sure you're very exciting, Lord Topher."

I caught Lord Pecus' eye over the heads of the dancers and smiled involuntarily. He smiled back, annoying Lady Louisa with his inattention, before the dance sent us in opposite directions.

"I notice *one* young lady in particular seems to find you very exciting," I remarked, allowing myself some amusement. "She rarely takes her eyes off you."

He followed my eyes to where the young blonde—Miss Emily Dewhurst, I was creditably informed—was dancing, and I fancied I saw a blush rise in his cheek.

"She's very beautiful," I observed impartially, inching slightly to the right so that the beauteous Miss Dewhurst was in clear sight over my left shoulder. "She's also quite well off, I'm told."

I let him digest this for some minutes, and by the end of the dance he was looking thoughtful.

"You think I should marry Miss Dewhurst, then?" he asked, bowing over my hand.

"I think you should do just as you choose," I corrected, curtseying. "But certainly Miss Dewhurst is a very good catch."

He opened his mouth to reply, but before he could do so Lord Pecus had approached, and said without preamble: "Lady Farrah. A word, if you will."

"Of course." I curtseyed again to Lord Topher, and took Lord Pecus' arm. "What is it, my lord?"

"Have you been shaking any cages today?"

I found myself startled. "I beg your pardon?"

"There are men in one of my card rooms," he said, in a low voice. "My security spells picked them up as they entered the garden room. Once again, Lady Farrah, have you been stirring any pots that I should be made aware of? They are waiting for someone."

"Goodness me!" I said meditatively. I was quite often accused of causing trouble, but it was not often that I was *falsely* accused of causing trouble, and I was a little at a loss. I was unsure if I should appear flustered or indignant. "What an unusual circumstance! I appear not to be guilty. If there is trouble, it has nothing to do with me."

"That *is* unusual. You can understand how my thoughts immediately went to you."

I inclined my head. "Certainly, I can. In nine out of ten cases, you would be correct, but— oh, good heavens!" I stopped in dismay. I seemed to remember Delysia sweeping out of the dance, pink with anger over a torn hem that her clumsy partner had trod on. She had gone to one of the empty side rooms to pin the material. "Delysia! It must be Delysia!"

Lord Pecus must have been using one of his Look-Away spells, because nobody looked askance when I picked up my skirts and ran for the door at which I last saw Delysia. I don't know quite how it happened, but he reached the door before I did, and thrust it open with a single movement, restraining me with his free arm. It took a moment to make sense of the scene, but when I had done so, I could see Delysia sitting on one of the sofas, looking pale and considerably rumpled in the midst of a chaos of broken furniture and glass. I pushed Lord Pecus' arm aside impatiently and ran to embrace her in relief, because I had really thought the worst for a moment.

She gave a sob of relief and clung to me. "Oh, Isabella! A horrible man trod on my skirt, and when I tried to fix it in here those nasty men just *grabbed* me and tried to make off with me, and oh, Isabella, they've *ruined* my beautiful dress!"

I gave a watery chuckle at Lord Pecus' bemused face, and patted Delysia's cheek. "The dress is not ruined, Delysia; I can pin it in a trice. Now be calm and tell Lord Pecus exactly what happened."

Her lip trembled, but she gave a defiant sniff and said: "I came in to pin my dress, because of that stupid man! When I opened the door someone said: 'That's her, grab her!' and they pulled me into the room. They took my mask, then one of them held up a candle to my face and swore, and said I wasn't the right one after all, so they threw me down and ran out."

"My poor Delysia!" I said soothingly. The furniture was in a deplorable state, suggesting a struggle of some magnitude. "You must have given them a little trouble, my dear."

Delysia looked vindictive, and declared darkly: "One of them will have a black eye, or I'm no judge! How *dare* they ruin my dress!"

Lord Pecus almost disgraced himself with a smothered laugh that he turned hastily into a cough. "The intruders are gone now, Lady Quorn. You are quite safe. Can I fetch Lord Quorn for you?"

She nodded and Lord Pecus left us alone. I began to tidy Delysia's hair, beginning with the rose that was now nestling at a drunken angle in her curls, and then her crimson hair ribbon. By the time I finished pinning the torn hemline she was calm again, and tied the strings of her mask with fingers that shook only a little.

At last I sat back beside her, and clasped cold fingers in my lap. "Delysia, how long has Lord Pecus been gone?"

She looked startled. "Perhaps a half hour. He *has* been gone rather a long time, hasn't he?"

"Perhaps Harroll was difficult to find?" I suggested, half-heartedly. There was a wrongness in the air, and Lord Pecus' ball was beginning to feel very perilous to me.

"Harroll is *never* difficult to find." Delysia pursed her lips, and stood with resolution. "I shall go and find him. If masked intruders have tried to make off with Harroll as well, they will be very, *very* sorry."

I accompanied her back to the ballroom in a little relief. I didn't like leaving her alone so soon after such a shock, but there was a nasty feeling in the pit of my stomach and I didn't think I would be comfortable until I saw that Lord Pecus was safe. Raoul's murder had begun to spiral into a messy, confusing vortex with neither sense nor direction, and there was no telling what could happen next.

I couldn't see Lord Pecus among the dancers or in any of the cardrooms that were lit and in use, so I expanded my search further and ventured into Pecus Manor's great hall. There was no one in sight along the hall, but candlelight was flickering from one of the doors further down, and an urgent babble of voices told me that there was something afoot, so I hurried toward the light with my heart pulsing breathlessly in my ears. The first person I saw was Harroll, standing by the door with his hand white around the knob, but that was surely Melchior kneeling on the ground beside a huge, prone form that could only be Lord Pecus. I pushed past Harroll, who was too glaze-eyed to stop me, and sank to my knees beside Melchior. Lord Pecus' mask had been wiped of all expression, and through the slits of his mask I could see that his eyes had flooded red.

Father said sharply: "Isabella, no!" but I already had Keenan's protection spell in my hand, and I pressed the thing into Lord Pecus' palm, closing his fingers around it and cupping his huge hand in both of mine.

He shuddered and gasped, and Melchior said in a low voice: "Carrots, I'd murder you myself if that hadn't worked! Don't you ever do that to me again!"

"I knew it would work," I tossed at him, my eyes on Lord Pecus. I hadn't known anything of the sort, of course. I had simply hoped that Keenan's spell would be strong enough, and trusted to my instincts that the murderer would not kill Lord Pecus if I were physically linked to him. He had shown a strange reluctance for killing me. "Who did this? Did anyone see?"

"Pecus must have," Melchior pointed out. Like Father, he was very pale, and I knew I hadn't heard the last of touching a cursed person. "He seems to be coming back quite quickly. What was that you gave him?"

"A protection spell," I said shortly. Lord Pecus' eyes were beginning to flow back into their native green, and I slid one hand under his head, levering it up. "Wake up, my lord! I refuse to kneel on dusty floorboards a moment longer than necessary. Like Delysia, I object to my best things being ruined."

A spasm of amusement rumbled through Lord Pecus' chest. "Lady Farrah. I wonder why I'm surprised." His eyes, showing a heartening movement, flicked toward Melchior. His voice was rough and exhausted. "It's over."

Melchior and Harroll helped him to his feet, and then to a huge leather armchair where he stretched out with a sigh of relief; and I moved over to comfort Father, who wrapped his arms around me with suspiciously shiny eyes and kissed my brow.

"No scraped knees, Papa," I said softly.

"I'm getting too old for your tricks, Kitten."

"Did you see who it was, Pecus?" Melchior had drawn up a chair to face Lord Pecus, and was eyeing him narrowly.

Lord Pecus was silent for a moment, and then said carefully: "I saw him. I didn't trust my eyes, so I marked him: he won't get rid of it in a hurry."

"Someone you knew, then?"

"I saw Ambassador Farrah's face." I looked at him incredulously, but he was frowning down at his clasped hands. "It seemed ridiculous; and as I said, I marked him."

"You'd better run a scan, then," my father said quietly. "The sooner this muddle is cleaned up, the better."

Melchior made an impatient hissing sound. "Oh, no one really suspects you, Dominic; but someone seems to have made a significant effort to cause trouble. You'd better do the scan, I think, Alexander."

Lord Pecus nodded, and a gentle humming pervaded the air. I tucked my hand into Father's and squeezed it, cold inside. The evidence I had gathered didn't support the idea that Raoul had been killed in the pursuit of treason, but the implication of my father in the attempted murder of Lord Pecus would drive a wedge between Civet and Glause nevertheless. It was ridiculous to think that my dear little Papa could be guilty of such a murder: therefore, someone was still playing games with us. The question was, had the murderer been lying to me when he claimed he had not murdered Raoul for the papers? I didn't think so. Yet treason was beginning to look more and more likely.

The humming stopped short, interrupting my musing, and I felt Father's fingers twitch convulsively in mine. There was a blotchy red rash rapidly populating his left cheek when I looked at him, forming a paw print or perhaps a rough rose shape, and I gazed at it stupidly, blinking, because it didn't make sense. Father had gone quiet and a little pale.

"What does this mean for me?"

There was silence. Then Lord Pecus, without looking up, said gruffly: "I have to take you into custody."

"This is nonsense!" I snapped. I was feeling very close to tears, and that would never do, so I glared around at them all. "Melchior, Harroll– you both know my father! You *know* he would never do this!"

Melchior rubbed the bridge of his nose tiredly. "Can the mark be passed on, Alexander? Duplicated in any way?"

Lord Pecus shook his head. "If the attacker wore a glamour, the mark would have settled on his real face. As I said, I mistrusted my eyes. *That* is the skin I put the mark on. It can't be erased, and it can't be duplicated– if the attacker somehow managed to duplicate it and mark the Ambassador, he would still be marked himself. The scan would have picked him up."

"What of the merger?" Harroll asked. His fingers were digging agonisedly through his hair, creating a disorder that would have pleased Delysia immensely, could she have seen it. "If the Watch takes Ambassador Farrah into custody, the merger is as good as lost. Public outrage, protests– it doesn't bear thinking of! I demand that the king be informed!"

"Might it be kept quiet?"

I opened my mouth to expostulate, but Father patted my hand chidingly. "No, Kitten; let me finish. Keep me in custody until this is cleared up: let Isabella handle the merger. She's capable."

Melchior shook his head. "Harroll is right, the merger would never go through. No offence, Carrots, but once it leaked out – and it *would* leak out, one way or another – the merger would be off. Can he be released on his own recognisances?"

Lord Quorn raked his fingers through his hair once more, biting his lips. "No. Glausian law doesn't allow for the release of murder suspects on bail."

"Then the matter seems to be simple," I said briskly. There was an angry ache in my throat that meant I was only minutes away from tears, and I was not sure who I wanted most to beat for stupidity; Harroll, Melchior, or Lord Pecus. "Glausian law doesn't allow for recognisance with relation to a monetary value: it does, however, allow for a hostage to be taken against the risk of flight."

"Absolutely not!" Father said, with a very good assumption of authority. "I will not have my daughter held in gaol!"

"She would be given a suite of rooms here and every polite attention would be paid her," said Lord Pecus, speaking for the first time in many minutes. "I'll carefully let leak the information that an attempt has been made on her life, and the merger can continue. In the meantime, I'll continue my investigation. When you are cleared of all charges, Lady Farrah will be released."

"You see, Papa?" I said softly to him. "I'm to be an honoured guest of Lord Pecus."

For the first time in many years, I saw his gentle eyes angry. "You're to be a guest of the Watch, Isabella. I can't allow it!"

"You can and you must, Papa." I smiled a little ruefully at him. "Our first service is to Civet: I've heard you say it a thousand times, and you wouldn't want to disturb my views on the uprightness of your character, would you? Lord Pecus will investigate thoroughly, I'm certain; and Annabel won't let the matter be, you can be sure."

Father said absently: "She was always a good girl. I don't like it, Isabella."

"No more do I, but there's nothing else to be done. You'll send Vadim and Keenan over to me, won't you?"

"Anything you need, Kitten. May I visit her, Lord Pecus?"

Lord Pecus nodded. "One visitor, once a day; and none after dinnertime. Will that suit?"

"It will have to, won't it?" I said briefly, my eyes resting steadily on him. His mask was bland, but his green gaze flickered away, and I felt obscurely pleased. "Perhaps you had better have someone show me to my rooms."

"There's no need for you to leave the masquerade early," Lord Pecus said, startled. "My housekeeper will make up the rooms for your convenience."

"If my attempted murder is supposed to have occurred now, my presence will be remarked," I told him crisply. "Kindly have someone show me to my rooms. Papa, come along and see me settled in."

In the end, they all came along. Melchior linked his fingers through mine and swung my hand as if we were on a jaunt, and Father shuffled along silently on my other side with Lord Pecus striding ahead. The housekeeper had been dispatched to find fresh sheets by that time, so I sent them away again once I had explored the suite. Father was the last to leave, and after he did I sat myself down in the window seat and gazed through the glass at the lighted garden below. The housekeeper came and went with sheets, and I let her do so without speaking: no tears had fallen yet, and I fully intended to keep it that way.

Vadim and Keenan arrived some time later with a small trunk packed with my night things and a few changes of clothes. All my other clothes, or so Vadim informed me, would be sent over tomorrow afternoon. They both looked wide-eyed and anxious, so I shared my cocoa with them when we were nightgowned, and tucked them into bed with me.

"Are you alright, lady?" Vadim asked timidly, at last.

I looked down at her big eyes, and felt a laugh welling up. "Cheer up, child! It's not the end of the world." I gave Keenan an absentminded kiss, which made him scowl to hide his pleased smile, and said: "Your spell saved my life tonight, Keenan. Well done."

Vadim nestled into my arm and sighed sleepily. "What will you do now, lady? About your investigation, I mean."

I regarded the ceiling thoughtfully. "I shall think of something, have no doubt. Goodnight, my children."

PART II

Chapter Eleven

I woke up in a strange bed as the night began to lighten into morning and the first sun of the triad peeked over the horizon. I gazed up at the four massive posts of the bed thoughtfully, sifting through last night's memories, and wriggled my shoulders uncomfortably. Keenan had burrowed under the mound of pillows, pushing them up under my right side and making further sleep impossible, so I climbed out of bed and curled up in the window seat instead. Vadim, charming child, had packed my inkless scroll-and-pen with my night things, and since dawn arrived in Civet a little before Glause, it was not inconceivable that Annabel would be up.

Accordingly, I put pen to scroll, and wrote. *Annabel, are you up?*

After a few minutes, one word inked into being. *Unfortunately.*

I laughed softly. *Morning sickness?*

No: Melchior. Belle, what have you been up to?

The Glausian Watch thinks my little Papa murdered three people,

I wrote. *I'm collateral. Annabel, I refuse to be held prisoner by a man who dips biscuits in his tea! Get me out of here!*

You know I can't. Besides, Melchior thinks it might be for the best.

I sighed, but I wasn't really surprised. *I know you can't. As for what Melchior thinks is best, all I can say is that Delysia is possibly the only one who doesn't understand his 'veiled' references. You're sniggering, aren't you?*

Yes, Belle. Yes I am. Don't let it get you down; I'm sure it won't be long before Lord Pecus clears your father. Then you'll be free as a bird.

Unless Lord Pecus decides to suppress a little evidence in order to keep me out of the way, I scribbled glumly. *I wouldn't put it past him. Annabel, this is war!*

Well, that's what we're trying to avoid, isn't it? wrote Annabel practically. *Be a big girl and manage. I know you can.*

Oh, I'll manage very well, I wrote vengefully. *Lord Pecus will just **see**. I'll not let my little Papa be suspected any longer than I must.*

Just don't get arrested for treason yourself, Belle. I'll go into premature labour, and it will be all your fault.

***Very** premature*, I told her dryly, chuckling. *You've another seven months, by my count.*

And I fully expect you to be home again by that time. I have to go, Belle; Jenny is beating up James. When you're back you'll have to teach her how to negotiate.

Keenan stirred and muttered as I laughed aloud. *Very well. My love to the children.*

I rolled the scroll up with a sigh, tucking the quill into the roll. Golden light was beginning to spill into the garden below me, glinting on dew-soaked lawn and lush greenery, and it was not long before I heard the clatter of a coal scuttle. The maid who entered was masked, and I found myself surprised, though it was hard to say why. After all, my information had suggested as much, and every servant at the ball last night had been masked. It was perhaps, I thought amusedly, that one didn't expect a *chambermaid* to be masked. She didn't see me huddled in the window seat, and set about her business with a brisk efficiency, whisking dust and stone chips away from the hearth and setting wood in order. It was evident that this fireplace had not been used in months, perhaps years: unsurprising in the warm, muggy Glausian climate. Nevertheless, this early in the day there was a distinct coolness rising from the massive flagstones that formed the floor, and my clothes no doubt would be grateful for the prospect of airing out. Certainly the damp would do them no good at all, and good clothes should always be pampered.

I was eyeing the huge wooden wardrobe somewhat thoughtfully, debating internally upon its possible dampness, when the chambermaid turned to pick up a few fallen scraps of wood, and saw me. She gave a muted exclamation, scrambled to her feet, and curtseyed in a flustered manner.

Her mask was a very pretty one, the perfect brows of which were at the moment arched in dismay. "My lady! Oh dear, the master's going to be cross that I woke you!"

"Well, you didn't wake me, so you've no need to worry," I told her soothingly. Her voice pronounced her to be younger than I had thought, perhaps only just in her twenties, and I tucked away for later consideration the thought that the masks in the Pecus household could prove to be deceiving if I wasn't careful. "Keenan woke me, as a matter of fact. I'll acquaint him with Lord Pecus' displeasure when he crawls out from beneath the pillows."

The maid eyed my bed in fascination. "Are they– are they your *servants*, my lady?"

"At times I find myself wondering, but by and large, I believe so. Who are you?"

"Damson, my lady."

"And you're a chambermaid?"

"Yes and no, lady. There aren't enough occupied chambers to tend to at Pecus Manor, so I help out in the scullery after I'm done with the fires."

"And then on to making the beds, I suppose?"

She nodded.

"Your life must be one round of festivities after another, Damson."

A small, ladylike grin appeared for a moment. "Yes, my lady. There's poached peaches and porridge for breakfast this morning, you know. Imported all the way from Civet!"

"Dear me!" I murmured. I wondered if Lord Pecus was trying to make me feel at home, or if he usually ate on a sumptuous scale. Either way, for the first time in very many years, I found myself without the slightest desire to eat. "It sounds luxurious to the extreme, but I find myself without an appetite. You need not send up a tray."

Damson curtseyed with a lowered head, but I thought I saw a brief flash of sympathy in her brown eyes. "I'll tell cook," she said, smiling shyly. "Can I bring you anything, my lady?"

"No, Damson; thank you."

She curtseyed again, then took herself and her scuttle away, pausing only to say around the door: "The gardens are beautiful of a morning, my lady." She gave me another shy smile, and disappeared.

I cast a thoughtful look out the window at the gardens, where the first sun was flowing warmly through the manicured trees, and rose to dress myself. Vadim could sleep a little longer today.

My sateen slippers were soaked in the heavy dew before I had taken more than three steps through the lush grass, but the early sunshine had warmed the air sufficiently to make catching a chill a negligible danger, and I quite cheerfully gave the slippers up as a loss. Damson had been entirely right; the gardens *were* beautiful, though I found myself rather unnerved by the blank masks of the gardeners that turned to watch me as I walked. Evidently I was not the only one up early this morning. It was interesting to note that none of the gardeners had felt it necessary to display a mask with more humanity than a basic nose and chin structure: if it were not for the different body shapes, I would have assumed them to be one man in many places. The baffling anonymity of the men only added to my feeling of unsettled balance, and I quickened my step until I had passed through the gardeners and into another section of the garden that was wilder and charmingly tangled. There were fruit trees here, with broad, low-hanging branches that were easy and comfortable to sit on, and provided a bewildering array of tropical fruits. I settled myself on one of them, enjoying the cool of the shade that seemed to vanish all too soon in Glause, and absentmind-edly picked some of the dark red prickly fruits that hung nearby. The skin was tough but only paper-thin, and my fingernail was enough to puncture it, revealing to my fasci-nated gaze plump, translucently white flesh. I took a cautious bite and let it rest for a moment on my tongue, since in Glause fruit is not always safe to eat; but the flesh was sweet and juicy, and I let it slip down without further hesitation.

I had eaten a great many more, dropping the smooth almond-shaped seeds beside me on the ground, before I heard the sound of a hullabaloo approaching through the garden at speed. I wiped my sticky hands in the dewy grass and waited for events to unfold; for if I were not very much mistaken, it was Keenan's voice that I could hear whooping along the lanes.

Keenan was in full cry when he tore around the corner, just inches ahead of three large, angry gardeners. When he saw me he changed course with a gleeful laugh, leaped the branch I was seated on, and from this position of safety made faces at the stymied gardeners, who had come to an abrupt halt before me.

"Well, Keenan?"

He gurgled wickedly. "Got yer some flowers, lady."

A handful of decidedly windblown roses was thrust under my nose, causing me to blink a little, and I saw one of the gardeners clench a fist in my peripheral.

"An' they tried to make me wear one o'them masks, but I was too quick!"

"I daresay you were," I said mildly. "But that is no excuse to go about butchering Lord Pecus' gardens. I don't suppose it was any one of these gentlemen who were trying to make you wear a mask?"

"No, my lady," said one of the gardeners. "That would be the footmen. They're very particular."

"They've got Vadim trapped in the courtyard," reported Keenan, with the beginnings of a scowl. "I got away, said I'd bring you back."

"Then I suppose you had better do so," I told him, rising leisurely to my feet. I smiled in what I hoped was a melting manner at the gardeners, and said: "I apologise for Keenan, he lacks artistic temperament. Would you mind very much if I kept the roses for my room?"

The gardener who had already spoken bowed. "You're very welcome to them, my lady. I can send some up fresh every morning if you'd like."

I gave them a very real smile in passing. "Thank you, yes! Now, Keenan, where are these footmen who are holding Vadim hostage?"

The gardeners watched us go with blank masks, but I thought I heard one of them chuckle. I ignored it in my best ladylike fashion and followed Keenan back along the garden lanes until the grass met with neatly paved flagstones and the hedge gave way to a stone wall. There was a babble rising in the early morning air, suggesting that Vadim was not being co-operative; and as Keenan and I entered the courtyard, I had the felicity of seeing her seize one of the footmen by the ear, and twist scientifically. The footman yelped and staggered to his knees as Keenan winced in vicarious pain beside me, so I thought it best to come to the rescue without more ado. It was not quite clear whom I was rescuing by that time: the footmen were more in number than Vadim and Keenan, but Vadim seemed to hold the balance of power presently.

"What is the meaning of this fuss?" I asked briskly, motioning Vadim to release the footman. She did so with a venomous look, and he clapped a hand over his glowing ear as he rose, backing away hastily. The other footmen as hastily bowed and murmured the necessary respectful 'my lady', but they did not look pleased by any stretch of the imagination.

Vadim said, panting a little: "I was just teaching this silly little footman a lesson." She was still glaring at the footman, who, now that his ear was no longer in imminent danger of being twisted off, was looking back at her in distinct admiration.

"So I see," I said pleasantly. I gazed for a thoughtful moment at their astonishingly pretty masks, allowing them to fidget uncomfortably while I pondered whether or not they were so beautiful beneath the masks, and then asked, as pleasantly as before: "I wonder why I find it necessary to come to the rescue of my maid while staying as a guest at Lord Pecus' Manor? Can anyone enlighten me?"

The footman whose ear Vadim had twisted, said beneath his breath: "*She* didn't need any rescuing."

I let my eyes rest on him, but the glint in his eye was one

of humour, not of disrespect, so I remarked fairmindedly: "That is quite true, I suppose. However, I believe that I would still like to know what the fuss is about."

"She wouldn't put on one of the masks," said another of the footmen, with an undercurrent of belligerence to his voice. "It's Lord Pecus' order that any servant in the house shall wear a mask."

"I doubt, however, that he intended for you to hunt down the servants of his guests and tie masks on them by force," I told them, with a tinge of cold anger. "My servants will not wear masks. No doubt his lordship will mention the matter to me if it is as important as you seem to believe."

There was really nothing left for them to say, so they did the only thing they could: each man bowed respectfully, murmured another 'm'lady', and took themselves back into the Manor. Vadim's footman lingered a little behind the others, but she was still stiff with anger and before long he gave up and followed the others. I waited until we were quite alone, then wiped the charming rustic bench dry with my handkerchief, and sat down.

"Now," I said gently, swinging one foot and looking in turn from Vadim to Keenan; "I would like to know why it is that two of my household are involved in a brawl the very first day I spend away from home."

Vadim flushed, and even Keenan looked momentarily subdued. "Sorry, lady."

Interesting. I gazed at them with a sense of quiet fondness, absentmindedly rearranging the somewhat battered roses in my lap. No excuses, and no protests: just a 'sorry, lady'. They were both still young enough, however, to have that look of swelling injustice.

I found my lips twitching. "Tell me what happened, children."

"I came down to fetch water for you to wash with, lady."

"You wasted your time, then, Vadim: Lord Pecus has indoor plumbing, and our suite is very well equipped."

"That's what I found out when I got downstairs. The footmen were sitting around the table eating breakfast, but they stopped when we got there. They all stared at us and one of them said to cover up because we were ugly."

"*I* told 'em to get stuffed!" proclaimed Keenan, with the air of one proud of his efforts.

Vadim glared at him, but he didn't look abashed, and she continued, ignoring him: "I told them that we didn't want masks and they said that we *had* to, or else."

"Then she told 'em *'or else what?'*" Keenan said gleefully. "And the skinny one said 'Or else we'll make you', and got up."

"Cook said not to have a smash-up in the kitchen and threw us out," Vadim said. Her brow darkened stormily, turning her eyes an even darker blue. "The skinny one tried to grab me in the courtyard, so I kicked him and sent Keenan away; but he tried again, just when you came in."

"The ear," I nodded. "Very well. I would naturally prefer to begin my sojourn at Lord Pecus' residence in a more peaceful manner, but the issue does seem to have been forced somewhat. Who taught you how to twist an ear, Vadim?"

She tried, unsuccessfully, not to grin. "Mum, lady. No one could twist an ear like she could."

"Judging from your young footman's reaction, I believe he would beg to differ," I said dryly. I could imagine the energy that must have gone into the reprimand: Vadim was not beautiful, but she was quite pretty, and it would have rankled to be jeered at as ugly. "Have you eaten yet, children?"

They shook their heads gloomily, and I heard the rumble of Keenan's stomach as he patted it disconsolately.

"In that case, back to the kitchen with you!" I said,

shoving them onward. "Return to our suite when you're finished."

"Will you be all right by yourself?"

Vadim's tone of doubtful anxiety brought a smile to my lips. "Certainly I shall, child; do you think I'm made of glass? Off with you both!"

I left them to the mercies of Cook, and leisurely made my way back to the suite, abandoning my dew-soaked slippers on the little terrace that had led me into the garden. The triad had begun to work on me, and I was feeling warm and a little sleepy, but the flagstones were invigoratingly cool when I stepped on them with my stockinged feet, waking me enough to wonder where Lord Pecus was. No doubt pursuing his investigation while I was becalmed, horrible man. I wondered if he had released the Earl of Horn yet, now that my poor Papa was prime suspect, and found myself doubting it. With a furrowed brow, I retired once more to the window seat, this time with the *Book of Interesting Excerpts* under my arm. I was perusing it with some interest when Damson returned to the room, bearing an enormous tray laden with breakfast.

"What's all this?" I asked, in some amusement. "I'm not hungry, Damson; do take it away!"

She set her tray on the chubby little table that squatted beside the wardrobe, and twisted her apron between nervous hands. "Please, lady; Lord Pecus says you're to have a tray anyway."

"Does he so? What a very particular man he is!"

"He's not so bad, once you get to know him," Damson said, with an encouraging smile. "He's a good master, lady."

"I daresay he is," I agreed mildly. I wondered how much the servants knew. Certainly Damson was not under the impression that I had been attacked: she undoubtedly knew that I was a prisoner of the political type. Servants have a way of knowing everything that goes on in the household. I wondered if the Earl of Horn was here also, but there seemed to be no way of finding that out from Damson without Lord Pecus finding out that I had asked. It would perhaps be judicious to explore the manor a little before asking too many questions.

The first visitor to break the monotony of my incarceration was Father. He brought with him my trunks—all five of them—and sat rather absentmindedly on the edge of my bed to watch as Vadim and I unpacked them.

"Now, Papa!" I began, shaking out a silken scarf that billowed in the early afternoon breeze: "What has been happening in the outside world today?"

"Not a great deal. Discussions are still going on about the military exchange that Annabel wanted."

"Oh, have they agreed to it?" I asked, willing to be distracted from the investigation of Raoul's murder for a few moments.

"Yes, with reservations. They feel that a turnaround of seven years is too long, even if the soldiers are spending the greater part of the time in their own army."

"Annabel will be a little disappointed, perhaps, but some time is better than nothing. Our soldiers will need to know how to fight to Glausian conditions if we're to aid them, and I fancy that the Glausian foot soldiers won't be as hardy as they think they are when faced with a Civetan winter. What timescale are they willing to stipulate?"

"Three years," Father said ruefully, rubbing his chin.

"Oh dear! I don't think it will be enough, Papa."

"Neither do the horselords; they're suggesting a turnaround of five years."

"I didn't think the horselords were one of the regiments

put forward for the scheme," I said, frowning. "Not but what they're right."

"They put themselves forward: Miryum said that it would be a challenge for them."

I hid a smile behind one of my dresses. "Good heavens, imagine Emmett on one of our long-haired ponies! His feet will trail on the ground!"

Father was surprised into an uncharacteristic snort of laughter. "I thought I'd find you downhearted, Kitten! I see that I should have known better."

"Indeed you should, Papa! When have you ever known me downhearted?"

"Not for many, many years, my dear."

"So the horselords are in favour," I mused aloud, carefully smoothing gloves on my bedspread. "Or at least the first Regiment are, and where the First lead, the rest will follow. What did the King say?"

Father shrugged. "Oh, you know what he's like: he sat and smiled, and listened and watched. I wouldn't bet either way on his decision, but I'm certain he's made one already. We'll have to wait and see."

"I think he likes watching us all run around like ants," I said thoughtfully. The King of Glause was something of a favourite of mine, but even I had to admit that he could be infuriating. He was one of the few people I found it difficult to read, and I had the uncomfortable suspicion that he could read me only too well. It said something for him that I liked him in spite of it.

"Who are the chief naysayers?"

"Sir Pentus and the Earl of Horn," Father said, leaning back against the pillows. He was watching me a little pensively. "The Mage General is also causing some difficulties. Isabella, am I being pumped?"

"Oh, not yet, Papa!" I assured him, twinkling a smile in his direction. "I thought I'd make some casual conversation first and just *edge* into it."

"I'm glad to know you still give adequate warning when you're about to dig for information."

"Well, it disarms people so! Now, Papa: was the Earl of Horn at the meeting today?"

"No, but he's been released. I believe he spent the morning with his wife and Louisa."

"Did it cause a stir, Lord Pecus arresting an Earl?" I enquired. Glause was class-conscious to a greater degree than Civet—perhaps because New Civet was still predominantly a nation of revolutionaries, despite being a monarchy once again—and I was curious to know if the nobility were suitably enraged.

"Less than I expected," Father said, frowning a little. "Most of the upset was caused by bewilderment and sheer disbelief that the Earl could be guilty. The question of his nobility didn't arise."

"How very egalitarian of everyone!" I said admiringly. "And you, Papa? What do you think?"

"I'm afraid I'm not an unbiased judge, Kitten. I've a larger stake in the affair than most people, and I find myself wishing him guilty if only to prove my own innocence."

I dropped a kiss on his head in passing, and said bracingly: "It's very horrid for you!"

"Oh, nonsense! When I think that you're locked away here—"

"Now, now, Papa!" I scolded. "I won't have you upsetting yourself. Tell me about the party last night instead."

Father moved restlessly. "You were there, Kitten; you saw as much as I did."

"As much," I allowed; "But differently. You're the one who taught me the importance of differing perspectives, after all."

"I didn't see anything out of the ordinary."

I looked at him severely. "You're not trying, Papa! Feeling, then: did you *feel* anything out of the ordinary?"

"You're a dreadful bully," Father complained, but he couldn't help smiling. "I'm still not entirely sure that I want you mixed up in this business, Isabella; too many people have died already."

"I'm already mixed up in it, and as for dying– certainly not! Pecus Manor is the safest place I could possibly be."

A thoughtful light came to Father's eyes. "Hmm. I might have done Lord Pecus a slight injustice."

"I doubt it," I said dryly. I thought I heard Vadim giggle, but when I glanced over at her she was solemn-faced. "I daresay Lord Pecus is quite able to bear the brunt of your displeasure. Now, out with it!"

"Bully," Father reiterated, but he sat a little more at his ease. "It was a few minutes before Melchior and I came across Lord Pecus. I was in the great hall looking for Melchior, but it felt as though I was somewhere else as well. I put it down to the whisky, but the more I think about it, the more I remember the wallpaper."

"Wallpaper?" An involuntary frown creased my brow. "The great hall is stone, Papa."

He nodded. "That's what I mean. I felt for a moment as though I was surrounded by wallpaper in vines and flowers."

"Like the wallpaper in the room where you found Lord Pecus," I said, in a low voice. A prickle of cold crawled down my neck. "You met Melchior only a few seconds later?"

"Yes. He was running; he said that something was happening and that we needed to stop it."

"Then you're placed at the scene without a witness. How convenient for someone!"

"It's worse than that, Kitten."

"You're beginning to think you might have done it, aren't you?"

He nodded again. "I felt the pain in my cheek before Melchior got there. I didn't know what it was at the time, but I can only assume that it must have been Lord Pecus' mark."

"I won't have Lord Pecus bullying you into thinking you've committed murder!" I said indignantly, my eyes flashing. "Just you *wait* until I see him next!"

"It was just a thought, Isabella. I know I didn't do it, but all the facts together buzz in my head until I'm not sure anymore."

"How are you managing by yourself?" I sneaked a look at him over the top of a morning dress I was shaking out, and caught the worried crease between his brows.

"Oh, very well, Kitten," he told me, with a very good assumption of ease. I narrowed my gaze at him but didn't call the bluff. I would have to get my brother Kit on a commlink and have him over here as quickly as possible. Father needed someone to manage things for him.

"When is the next conference? I seem to remember that there were three scheduled for this week."

"We reconvene this afternoon," Father said. "We've only broken for recess. I think this one might last all day."

"Papa! What are you still doing here?"

He looked mutinous. "Melchior can manage without me."

"You know very well that he can't! Melchior is good for diplomacy only so far, and then he loses his temper. Oh, Papa, it was sweet of you to come, it really was! But do go back now, and finish your meeting."

Since Father did not look convinced, it was perhaps fortunate for the wellbeing of the conference that Damson tapped at the door that moment, with the information that visiting hours were over. She looked unhappy and flustered despite the beautiful mask, and I gathered that she was expecting to be railed at. I bestowed a warm smile upon her, and said: "Thank you, Damson. You will show my Father out, won't you?"

Father opened his mouth to protest, but I pulled him to his feet with an admonitory look and kissed him above the left eyebrow. "Off you go to your conference, Papa. Make us proud!"

I spent the rest of the afternoon and much of the evening unpacking my wardrobe. It's an extensive one that takes an army of maids several hours to unpack, so I was somewhat surprised when it all fitted into the closet provided for my use. Surprise turned to unmitigated approval when Vadim showed me the scrolling trick that presented all of my ensembles in a sliding display at the wave of a hand, and I spent far longer than I should have grandly sweeping a hand sideways to send the skirts and bodices whizzing past in a flurry of material. I found myself wishing that I had had something of the sort when I was at Trenthams: though perhaps it was just as well that I hadn't, since I could very well imagine Annabel convincing me that we ought to ride the clothes rail to see where it led.

Damson appeared again some time later, while Vadim and I were still gleefully observing the closet. Keenan had disappeared underneath his bed once again, but he scrabbled out with great dispatch upon Damson's announcement that dinner was ready. I had sent away my lunch tray untouched earlier, too preoccupied to eat, and it now occurred to me that I was really quite hungry.

"Send a tray up," I told her, closing the closet door with

some slight discomfiture. It was a little off-putting to be discovered playing with a magic bauble as though I were eight instead of twenty-eight. "Vadim, leave the wardrobe alone, you're too old to play with such things."

Vadim gave a short, surprised giggle, but said a suitably submissive "Yes, lady" with a bowed head.

I glanced away from her to find that Damson was still just inside the door. Her flawless mask was unemotional, but her clasping fingers and taut shoulders told me she was steeling herself to make an unwelcome announcement.

"What is it, Damson? It won't get any more palatable with waiting."

"Lord Pecus' orders, my lady–" she hesitated.

"He seems to give quite a few of those," I said, refraining from pursing my lips by great effort of willpower. After all, it was not Damson's fault. "Which particular orders are these?"

"The master says you're to accompany him at dinner," Damson said, in a gasp.

"Is. That. So?" I said, slowly and lightly. Damson took a fresh grip on her apron, but this time I was too angry to show her the consideration she deserved. "You may tell Lord Pecus that I'm not inclined to accept his invitation."

"My lady, please!"

"I'm sorry, Damson. Return to your master and tell him just what I said. I've lost my appetite."

She left in a distraught whirl of apron, and I threw a quick, narrowed look around the room. Two pot-pourri bowls– wonderful! I would have to make sure I was near enough to the dressing table to reach one without difficulty.

"Vadim, get my night things, quickly! Keenan, begone!"

I scrambled into my nightdress with more haste than elegance, counting myself fortunate that Lord Pecus ordered his dinner for such a late hour. My nightdress would not be out of place.

"What are we doing, lady?" Vadim asked, panting a little as she bundled up my discarded outfit for washing.

"Getting ready for bed," I told her unhelpfully. She looked disappointed, but I only smiled saucily at her and said: "Off to bed with you, Vadim! If you should hear a little noise in a moment, feel free to disregard it."

I was sitting at the dressing table, brushing out my hair, when a loud, abrupt tattoo was pounded on my door. I smiled at myself in the mirror, and rose from the low stool. My bowl of pot-pourri was to hand: I was ready.

"Who is it?" I called out.

"Dinner is ready," said Lord Pecus' voice. It sounded as though he were speaking through clenched teeth. "You have five minutes."

"I'm not coming down," I retorted. "Go away!"

"Lady Farrah, if you're not out of your room in the next few minutes, I'll fetch you out."

I winced, but it had to be said. "You wouldn't dare!"

The puerility of it was embarrassing. Fortunately, Lord Pecus was too annoyed to notice. "Two minutes, Lady Farrah!"

"I absolutely refuse to come out!"

Of course he burst through the door. It cracked against the massive slabs that formed the stone walls, sending splinters flying, and I didn't have to try very hard for the startled jump as Lord Pecus strode into the room. I gave a maidenly shriek, and in a moment of truly inspired acting, snatched my dressing gown from the bed to my chest and assumed pose #35, *Maidenly Horror.* Hands clasped below the breasts and clutching my dressing gown as if to protect girlish modesty, eyes wide– maybe finishing school had been useful for something after all. I thought I might have gone too far, but Lord Pecus, who at my shriek had stopped two strides into the room with a look of horror on his mask, hastily turned his face to the wall. He tried to utter a disjointed apology but I threw one of the pot-pourri bowls at him, and it smashed satisfyingly on the wall, cutting off the attempt. His shoulders hunched, but he didn't dodge. I was enjoying myself immensely: after a debacle of this magnitude, I was *bound* to have my evenings to myself. Lord Pecus made another essay at an apology, his massive shoulders still hunched like a schoolboy, but gave up and slid hastily out the doorway with his head ducked when I threw the second pot-pourri bowl disconcertingly close to his left ear.

I tried to shut the door behind him, but it hung limply like a broken wing on a bird, so I left it where it was and took my silly giggles to the pillows where they wouldn't be heard. I was crying tears of laughter when Vadim's big eyes appeared over the footboard of the bed.

"Are you all right, lady?"

"Oh, Vadim, Vadim! I have never been better! Go to bed now, there's a good child: tomorrow is a bright, bright new day!"

Chapter Twelve

Damson was somewhat subdued the next morning. I took it for granted that Lord Pecus had been sharp with her and was surprised, since I had never thought of him in the light of an unreasonable master. However, as the morning wore on it began to be impressed upon me that Damson was showing me the cold shoulder.

I was amused, but willing to placate, so I said with a faint smile: "Am I forgiven yet?"

She dusted the hearth with some energy. "Forgiven for what, lady?"

"That's what I'm trying to discover, Damson. I have the lowering feeling that I've hurt your feelings."

"Oh, no, lady!" she said at once, melting with pleasing promptness. "Only the master was upset, and he's so lonely; we all thought you'd be company for him, you know. And if that weren't enough–"

She stopped short, and I prompted: "And?"

"Nothing, lady."

I was further amused to note that she was blushing. "I

take it you're experiencing problems with a gentleman friend?"

"Oh, it's nothing that would interest you, lady," Damson said hastily.

"You greatly underestimate my interest in the affairs of others," I said frankly, drawing a surprised giggle from her. Since she really didn't seem to want to discuss the matter, I asked instead: "How are Vadim and Keenan doing below stairs?"

Damson was cautious. "Too soon to say, lady; but I hope you won't judge us all by the footmen."

"If I were in the habit of judging all by a few, I wouldn't be a very good diplomat," I told her comfortingly. "Mind you, there *are* people who have voiced their doubts as to my skills before, so you never know. Oh, are you finished? Very well; send Vadim up to me, if you please."

I entertained Melchior as my sole visitor that day. He consoled with me, but absentmindedly; and patently disbelieved my innocent gaze when I informed him that my stay had been so far uneventful.

"But it really has, Melchior!" I assured him. "I only threw a pair of pot-pourri bowls at Lord Pecus, and as they were *very* ugly I do think I've done him a good turn! If he tells you anything else, it's a shocking untruth!"

Melchior grinned. "You want to be careful I don't give Pecus some pointers on how to handle you, Carrots."

"You've never been able to handle me," I pointed out, and added: "Or Annabel, for that matter. Lord Pecus is doing quite well on his own."

"You mean you have him wrapped around your little finger," retorted Melchior, still grinning. "How's the investigation going?"

"Slowly." It was one of the particular sore points that I

nursed against Lord Pecus: situated as I was, it was almost impossible to continue my investigation, and it really had been stimulating. I looked up to find Melchior smiling impishly, and demanded: "What is it, Melchior?"

"I may be able to help you with that," he said. "Alexander said I could fix you up with a semi-detached commlink, since you can't produce 'em yourself. What you use it for has nothing to do with me."

"Melchior, you wonderful man!" I said warmly. "I need to contact Kit for Papa, and see if Su can manage on her own, and oh! very many other things besides!"

"Your firstborn is the usual payment, Carrots. Hmm, on second thoughts, maybe not: that might be more trouble than I'm prepared to take on. What do you want the link fixed to?"

I ignored the first part of this exchange as beneath notice, and looked around swiftly for an object with a sufficiently mirror-like surface. At length I selected my hand mirror: it was pretty, and I was a little sorry to lose it, but I had the bureau mirror after all, so I tossed it lightly to Melchior and sat down at the bureau chair to observe him.

There was a moment of heavy silence before he looked up distractedly from the mirror. "I wish you wouldn't stare at me."

"I know," I said simply, propping my chin on the palm of my hand. "That's why I do it. It's taken me a long time to perfect a silence this loud. One doesn't achieve excellence without practice, you know."

"Yes, but must you practice on me?"

There was a note of real pleading in his voice, so I left him to it and wandered out onto my stone balcony. I found it pleasant to lean lazily against the cool stone balustrade: the warm Glausian air had become somewhat stuffy inside, and though the triad glowed around me there was a light breeze sweeping through the tops of the trees that was very refreshing.

Melchior's voice said behind me: "The gardens are nice, you know."

"You must have been talking to Damson," I called back, in some amusement. "One *might* think you were trying to get rid of one, Melchior. One *might* be offended."

"One would be right," he retorted, without glancing up. "Be off with you, Carrots, and cause your own particular blend of madness and mayhem elsewhere."

I would have pointed out, with great dignity, that it happened to be *my* suite of rooms that he was currently occupying, but Melchior was doing me a good turn after all, so I let the bait go unmolested and wandered out into the garden once again. The gardeners were still as interested as ever, looking stealthily over hedges and bushes to watch me walk, but once I passed beyond a last manicured hedge into the wild tangle beyond, there was a pleasing lack of gardeners. I should perhaps have wondered why: but the most sensible explanation for the absence of serfs unhappily did not occur to me until I was strolling down a crumbling walkway that converged on the large form of Lord Pecus. He was standing with his back to me, forearms propped on ancient masonry that must once have been the balustrade of a charming outlook, but when I turned silently to retrace my footsteps, he said with uncanny perception: "Lady Farrah. Good afternoon."

No way back but forward. I moved forward again and said pleasantly: "It *is* a good afternoon."

Lord Pecus turned, leaning his hips casually into the parapet, and observed my approach with folded arms. I gave him a politely enquiring look, and he said: "I have to congratulate you, Lady Farrah."

I raised my brows. "Indeed, my lord? I can't imagine why."

"Can't you? It was a beautiful job of acting: I was out the door before I realized."

I was betrayed into a giggle. "How unfortunate! I *was* afraid it might not work on you."

"Should I be flattered?"

"Certainly!" I tucked my hand companionably into the crook of his arm and linked my fingers together. "It works with most people."

"Do you throw pot-pourri at all your suitors?"

I threw him a sharp look, and found that his eyes were glinting down at me in something very like challenge. "Oh no!" I assured him lightly, smiling guilelessly up at him. "I treat my suitors very well! My friends, on the other hand, frequently inform me that they find my, ah—pot-pourri—decidedly off-putting."

"Oh, are we friends, Lady Farrah?"

"Certainly we are!" I gave Lord Pecus a real smile this time, friendly and open; and his porcelain brows rose.

"I thought you'd be angrier," he said thoughtfully.

"Oh, I've *been* angry. Now I am merely determined."

"Why is it that I find myself more apprehensive than before?"

"I can't imagine, my lord!" I looked at him through my lashes and said confidingly: "I'm inclined to believe that it points to a sadly suspicious side in your nature. I'm sure you struggle to overcome such defects in your character, so I feel no scruple in pointing them out."

I distinctly saw a tremor of laughter shake him, but he said: "Then I feel no scruple in adding that if you refuse my dinner invitation again, you'll be carried down, nightdress or no."

I gave a tiny sigh. "May I ask why?"

"It's...necessary," he said, after a brief pause. "I'm sorry to insist, but I do insist."

"Very well," I said consideringly. "I have a stipulation, however."

"Which is?"

"You dine with me unmasked."

There was a short silence, then Lord Pecus took in a slow breath. "Do you know what you're asking?"

I levelled a steady gaze at him. "I believe so. I may add that I think it only fair in the light of what *you* are asking, my lord."

He gave the low, rumbling chuckle that I liked. "I think we will get along very well, Lady Isabella."

"I'm sure we will," I agreed cheerfully, allowing myself to be pulled away from the wall. Melchior should be finishing the detached commlink by now, and if Lord Pecus was inclined to walk me back to the suite, I was quite content.

Instead, I found myself being drawn irresistibly down the left-hand fork of the path, *away* from the manor.

"It's a little stuffy inside," explained Lord Pecus blandly, when I turned my head to look at him. "Cook tells me that your meal trays have been returning to the kitchen full, Lady Farrah."

I blinked a little, then chuckled suddenly. "Oh, I see! I assure you, my lord, I am not attempting a hunger strike!"

"Is there a dish you prefer, then?"

I shook my head briskly. "I never manage to eat on the first day in a new place: I can't settle myself to it while the clothes are unhung and the trunks are out."

"Ah." Lord Pecus nodded solemnly. "Then it must have been rats."

He saw the look of amused comprehension that swept across my face, and explained with limpid kindness: "My *lechias* trees suffered a raid yesterday morning. Clever little rascals: they skinned the fruit and tossed the seeds."

I couldn't help laughing. "You know perfectly well that it was me! I didn't intend to eat your fruit, it was simply *there*."

Lord Pecus' porcelain teeth showed in a grin. "*Lechias* is not often palatable to Civetans, Lady Isabella. I was keeping an open mind."

"What a fib!" I said, too amused to be indignant. "You thought that I was refusing my meals to spite you and gorging myself in the garden instead, where my depredations would go unnoticed!"

"Perhaps I did. In my defence, you're not like other ladies."

"Well now, I'm glad you made that point!" I said immediately. "It leaves me free to ask without fear of surprising or shocking you, just how your investigations are proceeding."

"I wondered how long it would be before the conversation was wrangled in that direction," remarked Lord Pecus amiably, assiduously helping me over a tree trunk that had fallen into the path.

I allowed myself to be swept back down onto the path in his capable hands, and smiled sunnily at him. "Well, one does wonder how it is that you're home *quite* so early? I was given to understand that the Commander of the Watch was never off duty. I would also like to point out that I object to your use of the word 'wrangled'."

"I apologize: 'inveigled' was the word I should have used. As to being off duty, it may surprise you to know that there have been six tentative forays on my wards since you joined me in the garden."

"Interesting," I said thoughtfully. "Who was it, do you think?"

"I don't have the foggiest idea," he said ruefully. "But I

would be prepared to swear that they were six different people. This situation goes from one mad extreme to another."

I traced the pattern on Lord Pecus' cuff with one forefinger. "It appears that our murderer would like to lend truth to your lie by attacking me. Are we setting a trap?"

He frowned. "No."

"Oh, but it would be such a good idea!" I cried, in disappointment. "We could close the investigation!"

I thought he smiled. "No, Lady Farrah."

"I think you are *very* chicken-hearted!" I said accusingly. "*I* am willing!"

"I don't think I've seen you anything but willing to put yourself in harm's way," Lord Pecus remarked, leading me back toward the manor. "You wouldn't be trying to swindle me into agreeing with your plan, would you?"

I looked up at him with a suitably shocked expression. "Oh, no! I would never try to swindle you into anything, Lord Pecus!"

"Do you really think so?" asked Lord Pecus meditatively. "My experience seems to suggest otherwise."

"Oh, you're far too clever for me," I assured him soulfully. The lowering truth was that he just might prove to be so, but it is always productive to plant a little doubt in the mind of— well, not the enemy; but perhaps the competition.

"And yet I find myself uneasy! Strange, isn't it?"

We rejoined Melchior in my suite just in time to hear him swear and drop my hand mirror.

"Clod!" I said cheerfully, and picked it up for him. Fortunately it had fallen on the rug beneath my bureau and wasn't broken. Melchior was too busy wringing one hand in the other and muttering to take it back at once, but when he did, it glowed briefly to finish the spell.

"Was that you, Pecus?"

Lord Pecus manoeuvred his bulk through the long, thin windows and trod lightly across the flagstones. "The manor wards sometimes interfere with spell-casting indoors. What happened?"

"Don't know. I was just finishing up when a shock came through the powerlines." Melchior massaged his hand again in remembered pain, and passed the mirror back to me. "It's done now, Carrots. What have you two been up to?"

"Strolling through the gardens: Lord Pecus thinks I'm up to something."

"Sensible man."

"Even though I assured him that he's too clever for me, and that I wouldn't *dream* of trying to swindle him," I continued, in gentle melancholy.

Melchior's brows professed surprise. "Even then? Strange man!" He grinned at Lord Pecus and remarked: "I'm surprised she didn't tell you she's only a poor female. That's where the conversation usually goes from there. I'm sorry to say I know it from experience."

"I was just getting to that bit," I told them, looking up demurely through my eyelashes. "Of course, I feel bound to point out that my bashful nature wouldn't allow me to do anything so bold as swindle you. You being so big and frightening, *you* know."

Lord Pecus looked startled. "Pardon?"

Melchior grinned a little wider. "She can keep it up for days until you're convinced that she's misguided but sweet and that you've been a beast to her, and then she pinches your best invisibility spell and makes off with your fiancée."

"She wasn't your fiancée then," I pointed out primly. "Besides, if anyone was 'made off' with, Annabel made off with *me*. I was merely an innocent bystander who got caught up in the general confusion."

"I suppose my invisibility spell got caught up in the confusion as well?"

"How did you guess?" I marvelled. "Your grasp of the matter is really commendable, Melchior!"

Lord Pecus' shoulders shook as Melchior glowered, remembering past wrongs. "I think I begin to understand," he said.

"You *think* you do," said Melchior with heartfelt conviction; "But you understand nothing until you're standing in the middle of a draughty old mansion with a battered top hat instead of a first class invisibility spell. That's when you begin to understand. You begin to understand even more when a cohort of Old Parrasian councilmen take you prisoner because you're not as invisible as you thought you were."

I put my nose in the air. "That will teach you to tell us not to do something when you intend to do it yourself. Besides, we rescued you! I do think you're ungrateful!"

"I would have been more grateful to have my invisibility spell," retorted Melchior, but he was grinning again. "You haven't got any invisibility spells, have you, Alexander?"

Lord Pecus touched a finger briefly to his temple. "Only up here."

How interesting! I knew that Glausian spell-casting was different from the orderly, item based spell-casting of Civet, but I hadn't expected Lord Pecus to remember *all* his spells on demand. I would have less in my environment to rely upon. I bit back a sigh. Really, it ought to be good for me. At Trenthams any and all items of a magical nature had been kept strictly out of reach of students, and at one time I had been quite ingenious. We would see if I could be so again.

"That's her conniving look," Melchior observed, nudging Lord Pecus. "That's the one that means trouble."

I blinked myself out of my thoughts and paid attention. "I'm sure I don't know *what* you're talking about!"

"Of course you don't; you're the innocent, injured party," mocked Melchior. "You've been duly warned, Alexander."

"I think I can manage." Lord Pecus was smiling at me, and I thought for a moment that I saw his eyes—his *real* eyes—crinkle at the corners through a suddenly thin veneer of porcelain mask.

"And *that*," continued Melchior, his eyes sharp: "Is her look of startled realization! What did you just understand, Carrots?"

"I feel faint!" I said firmly, sitting down at my bureau chair. "Go away, both of you!"

"You don't look faint."

"I'm about to drop any minute!" I reiterated, with even greater firmness. "Vadim! Vadim! Bring the smelling-salts!"

Vadim brought the bottle in with an impressive amount of bustle that caused Melchior's eyebrows to rise as he and Lord Pecus took their leave. "A girl after your own heart, Carrots!" he said around the door, and vanished before I could do anything but scowl at him.

Vadim ceased her flurry of activity and sat lightly on the edge of the bureau. "Did you want me for anything, lady?"

"No, I think that was just enough. Well done, Vadim. How are you making out below stairs?"

A bright spot of colour appeared high on each cheekbone. "Very well, thank you, lady," she said stiffly.

"Oh, that badly?"

She huffed a small, angry breath. "It's that footman, lady."

"He's making a nuisance of himself, is he? I thought he might."

"But *why?*" wailed Vadim. "I haven't done anything to him!"

I wondered whether I should remind her of the ear-twisting incident. Had that really been only yesterday? Time seemed to have lengthened and stopped: or perhaps it was simply that too much had happened in too little time. "I would advise against ignoring him," I said mildly, running my finger lightly around the surface of my newly magicked mirror. It was cool and smooth, and tingled just a little. "I would also advise against any more slapping or ear-twisting: it encourages them to do the same, and scuffling with boys is rarely dignified in the end. If you simply *must* engage in violence, kick him; it will put a little distance between you."

Vadim opened and closed her mouth, then puckered her brow. "I don't understand."

"That's the joy of growing up, Vadim; you are at liberty to discover things for yourself."

She looked gloomy. "I don't *want* to discover anything about him. He's skinny and sharp, and too clever by half."

"They always are, my child. He may improve upon closer acquaintance, you know."

"I don't care if he improves or not," Vadim said, with an annoyed swish of her skirt; "I only want him to stop making snide little comments, and flicking things at me!"

"Alas, all good things eventually come to an end, Vadim," I said, with a small, private smile. "I won't need you again until I dress for dinner: perhaps you and Keenan could explore your new surroundings? I would like you to feel...*at home*...in the manor."

Vadim's eyes brightened and narrowed. "You want to know where the exits are, lady?"

I smiled dreamily at her. "I'm sure I don't know why you should imagine so, Vadim! I shouldn't like you to think that

I'm at *all* interested in any other prisoners, or the kind of spells that Lord Pecus wards his manor with. It would be excessively impolite of me as a guest to put my nose into the running of the Commander's household."

She took in an exultant, satisfied breath. "*Yes*, lady!"

I wasn't sure if her antipathy for Lord Pecus and a particular footman was at the root of her satisfaction, or if it were merely her natural joy in looking for trouble, but I congratulated myself on giving her thoughts a happier direction. Of course, one had to wonder if it really were a *happier* direction as such: one would hate to think that one was leading one's underlings into pernicious ways, after all.

"Oh, Vadim?"

She paused at the door, and looked back enquiringly. "Lady?"

"Be a little careful, yes?"

I spent most of the afternoon leafing through the pages of my *Book of Interesting Excerpts*. Really, I should have been connecting a commlink with Kit, but I could only contemplate my newly made commlinker with a distinct lack of enthusiasm. Kit had never cared for politics, and he would no doubt be unwilling to be called into Glause (whose climate he referred to as *wet enough to swim in*) to assist Papa in anything so boring as discussions for a military merger. Besides, my talk with Lord Pecus had reminded me that there were avenues of investigation still open to a person who owned a magical artefact such as the *Book of Interesting Excerpts*. Interesting Excerpts such as a Watch Commander's confidential report on crime scene details...

I called it up, waiting impatiently for the ink to fully leach into the pages, and pored over it at length with a furrowed brow. Most of it was, unfortunately, unintelligible. There were small, ovular black spots made up of thin, swirled lines that were marked in Lord Pecus's decisive handwriting as *finger-prints*, and which fascinated me completely. One set were written down as unknown, the other, as *Lady Farrah*. There was even a set marked as Raoul's. Goodness, how could he tell? They looked so exactly alike! The rest of the report was a miscellany that was as comprehensive as it was useless. Of what use was it to know that Raoul had been carrying some twenty-odd Glausian grits and a curlicued ruby ring in his pockets? I read through the pages once more, unaccountably annoyed at Lord Pecus for refusing to tell me anything of his discoveries when he knew perfectly well that he hadn't *made* any.

Ah well, the commlink must be made, I thought at last, sighing as I closed the *Book of Interesting Excerpts*. Papa needed the help, and since disagreeable things never became the more palatable for letting them sit, I at last took up the mirror. However, when the blank intermediary screen of my mirror focused, it was Susan's enquiring face that I saw. She was looking untidy and a little cross, and when she saw me her eyes grew speculative.

"Hallo, Belle. What have you done this time?"

"I wonder why it is," I began plaintively; "That everyone I talk to seems to assume that I'm about to do something, *am* doing something, or *have* done something! My own sister, too! You're supposed to look up at me with wide-eyed admiration, Su, and wait eagerly for the pearls of wisdom that drop from my lips. It's a sad reflection upon your upbringing, I'm inclined to think."

"You should have taught me better, then," said Susan cheerfully. "Besides, I can't do wide-eyed looks, and since you've been away, all I've had are Mrs. Higgins' words of wisdom."

"Which particular words of wisdom has Mrs. Higgins

been sharing?" I enquired. Mrs. Higgins had been our cook for most of my life and all of Susan's, and she had become something of a fixture.

"Wait, I want to get it just right; the wording has to be fully appreciated." She concentrated, curling a section of escaped chestnut hair around one finger. "Oh yes! I believe her exact words were 'Sling it in yer ear!' With regards to the drayman who splashed her second-best boots with mud."

"I've always admired her ability to vocalize so effectively. Was the drayman abashed?"

"Don't know," said Susan, watching me thoughtfully and continuing to twirl the one curl around her finger. "He was hunched over his horse and driving away so quickly it was hard to see his face. I think the peach she hurled at him might have had something to do with that."

"Susan, am I to understand that you merely stood and watched as our servant peppered a drayman with fruit?"

"Of course not," said Susan. "I passed her a dew-melon."

"I'm glad to think that at least *some* of my training remains. How are you and Kit coping?"

Was I mistaken, or did a watchful gleam come to those grey eyes?

"I've been out riding most of the day," she said, accounting for her windswept appearance. A little worm of suspicion began gnawing away somewhere in the woodwork of my mind. Susan didn't go in for wide-eyed innocence or deflectors: her particular type of deception was much harder to spot— particularly since she didn't *try* to deceive. She simply mentioned what she thought was relevant, and left anything else out. Therefore what she said was not so much important as what she *didn't* say. What hadn't she said?

"What happened, Belle? Is it Papa?"

"Yes and no," I said, letting the little worm chew away

until it churned up something useful. "Have you heard about the murders?"

"Everyone has," she said, matter-of-factly. "Haven't they caught him yet?"

"That depends upon whom you ask," I remarked. "Lord Pecus certainly thinks so. He arrested Papa."

Susan's eyebrows went up, highlighting a smudge of dirt above her right eyebrow. "He must be an idiot. Or is he angling for something?"

I drummed my fingers thoughtfully on my knee. "I haven't decided yet."

"But Papa isn't in prison, is he?" said Susan slowly. "No, I would have heard about it; Annabel would have told me. Glause doesn't allow bail, so...Belle, you're in prison, aren't you?"

"Something of the sort," I remarked, my lips twitching.

"I always knew you'd end up in prison."

"I'm an honoured guest of the Watch House Comman-der," I corrected her loftily. "*Thank* you very much! Officially, I was attacked by the murderer, and am being housed here for my own safety. Which brings me to my reason for calling you–" I stopped, because I had realized what it was that Susan had not said earlier. There was a sinking feeling in my stomach as I asked: "Su, where is Kit? Papa needs him."

"I was hoping you wouldn't ask that," she said candidly. "Kit's gone off on one of his explorations. He left yesterday."

"*Well!*" I said wrathfully. "If that isn't just like him! What are we to do now, I should like to know?"

"I'm coming over, of course." Susan tucked the few strands of loose hair away behind one ear in a businesslike manner, her eyes distant. "I can be there in three days– less if I ride, and let the coach follow."

"Absolutely not!" I told her firmly. "Kit must be fetched;

and you, young madam, shouldn't be travelling alone, not to mention being home alone!"

"He can't be fetched, he's gone offlink," said Susan, shrugging. "You know how he is. He probably sensed you'd call: he did leave in a bit of a hurry. Will I need party things, or just meeting things?"

"If you think you're going to do the job, you're very much mistaken!"

"I don't see how you're going to stop me," she pointed out. "Unless you get time off for good behaviour, of course. You know I can do this, Belle."

"I know you can *do* it," I said. "Su, I was pushed into this life without a choice in the matter, and I won't let it happen to you. You're only seventeen."

Susan gave me a level look. "*You* were hosting parties when you were fourteen, and ambassadorial hooplas by seventeen. I want to do this, Belle. Kit never liked politics. I do. It's my chance now."

I did a quick mental rearrangement, resigned to circumstances beyond my control. Susan would do a much better job than Kit ever could have, but I did wish she could have been older before she made such a decision.

"Stick with the horselords and you won't go wrong. You've not met the king, have you?"

She shook her head, undismayed, and I felt a smile playing about my lips. Nothing ever did dismay Susan. "Papa's next meeting is at the end of the week: can you be here by then?"

"Kit's been working on a travel spell to shoe a horse with," said Susan thoughtfully. "He won't mind my borrowing it."

I thought that this was dubious, but Susan did tend to know Kit better than I did. Besides, he had no business going off and leaving Susan in the first place, so if he didn't like it he only had himself to blame. "Don't commlink with Papa before you come," I warned her.

"Good grief, no!" she agreed at once. "He'd tell me not to come. Do you know, Belle, sometimes I think Papa is entirely too selfless to be an ambassador."

"Then it's a good thing he has two conniving females on his side, isn't it?"

There were light footsteps along the hall, if I were not much mistaken; and I flicked my eyes sideways just as the door to my suite opened, admitting Vadim. I found myself startled. Was it dinner time already? I didn't feel quite ready.

"Belle? What's wrong?" Susan's voice was sharp.

"Nothing, my darling; merely the call to dinner. Come and see me when you get here, won't you? And for heaven's sake bring me some drinkable tea!"

She grinned at me, and closed the connection. I looked down at the mirror for a little while in pensive silence, then sighed and turned my gaze on Vadim.

"Is it time, Vadim?"

"An hour until dinner is served, lady. I thought you'd want the time."

"Very perspicacious of you, Vadim. We're presenting dulcet harmlessness tonight: do you think you can manage?"

Vadim nodded with an eagerness that suggested she knew the game was afoot, and stood ready as I pulled the combs from my hair and confined the resulting curls loosely at the nape of my neck with a moss green ribbon. The red mass puffed softly around my ears and left a few curls drifting free; adding, I thought in some satisfaction, a touch of youth to my face.

"Which brings us to the most important business of the evening: what shall I wear?"

Chapter Thirteen

I was late to supper after all. It wasn't that I had nothing to wear: my problem consisted in an *over*-abundance of somethings to wear, and in deciding which one made me look sufficiently innocent and trustworthy. I am a devout admirer of the *long* con.

I thought Lord Pecus was regarding his watch with a porcelain frown when I arrived, but if so, he whisked it away so quickly that I didn't even catch a flash of gold. I was pleased to find that he had provided his dining hall with light orbs: I have never appreciated having to hunt around my plate in the dark for the last mouthful. A footman was holding a chair away from the table, and I sat automatically.

The servants seemed to hold their breath as they served. I wondered if they were nervous of me or of Lord Pecus, and was irrationally put on edge by the loaded silence until the small, mischievous part of my mind reminded me that I had done the same to Melchior just this afternoon, and made me chuckle. Still, it was a relief when they left, taking the air of expectancy with them. I looked down the length of the table at Lord Pecus, who, as promised, was removing his mask, and belatedly realized the enormous amount of tabletop between us. I frowned in disapproval: if there was one thing I hated as much as searching for my food in the dark, it was shouting across the tabletop at my dining partner. I wondered if Lord Pecus had done it to be imposing, or if he had been putting distance between us because he must remove his mask. Well, that sort of thing had better stop right *now*, I thought determinedly; and, picking up my plate and utensils, I trod to the head of the table. I sat down at Lord Pecus' right hand just as he pulled the mask away, startling him; and was strangely unsurprised to see the involuntary snarl that curled his lips and showed long, pointed teeth.

"Lady Farrah—"

"I can't talk to you from all the way down there," I said firmly, interrupting without compunction. "Besides, who will pass the salt?"

He looked pained, as far as I could tell beneath all the fur. "I didn't think it would be an insuperable difficulty!"

"Lack of salt is *always* an insuperable difficulty unless there is more salt," I said, delicately laying out my napkin. "I have to say that I didn't take you for a bashful man."

I watched with interest the tremor of movement that passed over his face, and decided that he was trying not to laugh.

"I didn't want to frighten you." His green eyes glowed with a touch of— what was it? Reproach?

I assumed so, and said pleadingly: "You wouldn't be so unkind as to send me all the way back down there, would you? I've just become comfortable!"

One of Lord Pecus' big hands curled around the stem of his wine glass, swallowing it. He said dryly: "I would hate to think I'd made you uncomfortable, Lady Farrah."

I chuckled, startling him again; but this time he controlled the snarl. "No, you wouldn't. You're finding me more trying than you expected, aren't you?"

"Not trying," he said, and again I thought I could see a very human crinkling in the corner of his eyes that suggested he was smiling. "Unsettling, perhaps. I have the feeling you're trying to discomfit me."

I flicked a look of genuine surprise toward him. "Not at this stage, my lord."

"We're still friends, then?"

I hadn't thought I was being *un*friendly. I thought about it critically, and came to the conclusion that Lord Pecus was more self-conscious about his condition than I had given him credit for. Evidently I had erred in judgement. "I didn't intend to make you uncomfortable," I said, regretfully. Throwing him off balance in a spirit of mischief was one thing: making him genuinely uncomfortable was quite another. "Please, dine in the manner you find most agreeable. Forgive my malapertness, it wasn't maliciously meant."

This time it was Lord Pecus who looked taken aback. He regarded me for a moment in pensive silence, and then pinched the bridge of his nose between his long fingers. "We seem to have started out at cross-purposes, Lady Farrah," he said. He sounded tired. "You're very welcome to join me at the head of the table."

"You've had a bad day," I said, in sudden realisation. Father tended to drop things and huff into his evening coffee if he had had a bad day, and I had become so used to it that I had neglected to consider that it could manifest in any other way. Lord Pecus must have gone back to the Watch House after he and Melchior left me to my fainting fit.

Lord Pecus grinned, showing a great deal of long, pointed teeth. It would have been frightening if I hadn't seen his snarl and recognised the difference. "Perhaps a little," he admitted. "There was a disturbance down in the Sinkhole. Most of my men were down there trying to keep peace—at least, as far as peace *can* be kept in the Sinkhole—so of course there was another incident in the city centre."

I regarded him interestedly over the top of my wine glass. "What happened?"

"A half-drunk drifter backed into the wrong store window," he said. "Or the right one, depending on which way you look at it. Burglar spells went off with a roar all through the Watch House, so Trophy and I went to see what the fuss was about."

I frowned. "Trophy?"

"Trophimus Holt," Lord Pecus explained. "My Lieutenant."

"Oh, the lovely boy whose badge– that is, the lovely boy I had to tea with me!" I corrected myself, with aplomb. "Go on, my lord. I've got the feeling you're just getting to the interesting bit."

Lord Pecus took a meditative sip of his wine (really, I don't see *how* he did it; it must have been something to do with the magic, or those jaws could never manage to sip) and eyed me quizzically. His beast face was amazingly mobile, with disturbingly familiar fluctuations of emotion that reminded one without hesitation of a human face.

"Well, when we got there the drifter was rolling about in glass and pearls from the shop window," he continued, keeping his reflections to himself. "He was muttering away to himself, so I thought I'd lock him up for the night as drunk and disorderly; give him a square meal or two. When he saw us he bolted for it, so of course we chased him down."

"Of course!" I echoed, fascinated. "Is it usual for the Commander of the Watch to chase down disorderlies?"

Lord Pecus gave me another of those fearsome smiles. "Drunks don't run. They mumble at you and ask what's on the menu tonight, and if they should dress for dinner. People with guilty consciences run."

"You mean they set off alarms on purpose to have a meal and a roof over their heads?"

He nodded. The stiffness in his face was now completely gone, and as I watched the play of movement over his mobile features, studying each different expression, I flattered myself that he had entirely forgotten that he was no longer wearing his mask.

"I've never had one run away before. Something felt *off* about it, so we chased him." A muscle in Lord Pecus' hairy jaw twitched through the fur, as if he had clenched his teeth at a galling memory. "I was chasing him down an alley so that Trophy could head him off when someone emptied their washing water over me."

I choked off an involuntary laugh a little too late to turn it into a cough.

"I'm sorry, did you say something?" asked Lord Pecus coldly.

"Nothing in the world, my lord!" I said, in somewhat of a strained voice. "Did he get away?"

He gave a brief shake of the head. "Trophy had him in his sights by then."

"Will you let him go tomorrow?" Lord Pecus was silent, and I found my curiosity roused. "No? What do you suspect him of, my lord?"

He grinned. "I don't suspect him of anything as such, Lady Farrah; I merely suspect him."

"I've warned you about the lack of trust in your nature," I noted mildly, covertly sequestering a few stray peas beneath crisp, cheesy slices of potato. I've never much cared for peas, but since I'm far too old not to eat all the greens on my plate, my diplomatic skills extend to the point of concealment. "Did he tell you anything sufficient to allay your suspicions?"

"No." The corners of his mouth pulled back slightly in a way that I was beginning to equate with quiet amusement. "He's spent the last few hours bawling drifter's drinking songs into the garden. Very usual, very unsuspicious, but–"

"But perhaps a little too drunk to be true?" He nodded, eyes glinting amusement, and a little cog in my mind whirred, then clicked. "The garden? He's imprisoned in the cells *here*?"

Lord Pecus shrugged. "The Watch House cells have been turned into a second Sinkhole district: I'm told they've already split into two factions. It wouldn't have been safe. I didn't take you for the nervous type, Lady Farrah."

"Not nervous," I told him; "Merely grateful that *I* have a suite of rooms rather than a draughty cell."

I wondered how difficult it was to get to the cells. I would have to confer with Vadim. I was inclined to trust Lord Pecus' instincts that there was more to the drifter drunk than met the eye, and I have never been a great believer in coincidence. Our murderer had a long reach, and I wondered very much if he had been behind either or both of the disturbances today.

I left the dinner table in a thoughtful mood. I flattered myself that Lord Pecus hadn't noticed my preoccupation, but his own thoughts had to have been running along similar lines, and I wondered what plan he had concocted in order to induce the man to talk. I smiled mischievously to myself as I climbed the stone stairs back to my suite, because I already knew what my plan was...

"Now, Vadim: report, if you please."

"One of the doors in our hall is locked," said Keenan glee-fully, interrupting Vadim without compunction. "Bet it goes somewhere excitin'!"

I suffered the interruption long enough to ask: "A grand old door, I presume? Big and foreboding, with great, dusty carvings inlaid?"

He nodded with glinting eyes, and I had a moment's relief that though his upbringing may have been a little lax, he evidently hadn't descended to criminal enterprise– or at least not the housebreaking sort. A thief would know better. I found it a refreshing innocence in Keenan.

"What do you think of this locked door, Vadim?"

"I think I could pick the lock," she said, pleasingly to the point; though evidently as misguided as Keenan. "It'ud take a while, though, lady."

"Is it a magical lock, Vadim? Or mechanical?"

"Both," she told me, with a grimace. "I can do the magic bit, *just*, but I'm not much for mechanical ones."

"I have a feeling that I would *just* be able to pick the mechanical bit," I said thoughtfully. It was almost insulting of Lord Pecus. At any rate, I could be reasonably certain that anything that I might wish to explore was not to be found behind the mysteriously locked door. Lord Pecus, like Melchior, was not the sort to hide his secrets behind an impressively and obviously magical door: no, if there were secrets to be found in Pecus Manor, they would be found behind ordinary, everyday doors. It was more than likely that one would never know that there *were* any. However, if Lord Pecus was trying to keep me busy with a false trail, then it stood to reason that there *was* something to be found around and about the Manor. I found myself cheered.

"Tell me about the cells," I requested, observing Vadim over my plump feather-pillow. I was reclining shamelessly at my ease on the bed, shoes and all, fresh from my dinner with Lord Pecus. I was in the mood to think and plan.

"There are two prisoners," she said. She was sitting back-to-front on my bureau chair with her legs crossed, leaning over the back of it in her eagerness, and she looked like a street urchin instead of a lady's maid. "One is a hairy drifter who can't decide if he's drunk or not, and the other one I couldn't see. It looked pretty smashing, but I think the cells must have been servants' rooms that someone altered."

"Do they sit on an outer wall?"

She nodded. "Not reinforced, or anything, lady: just plain stonework. There's something there, though."

"A magical something?"

"Yes. But I can't tell what it is."

Protection, most likely, I decided, and lost interest. "Was it easy to find the cells?"

"Not *easy*."

"It was a ruddy nightmare," opined Keenan, with a dispassionate air well beyond his years.

"It was all slippy little Keep-Aways and things like that," Vadim elaborated. She had gone slightly pink, and I had an idea that she was pleased with herself for having made it to the cells. "Don't think he wants anyone down there."

"Shouldn't have put cells there, then," Keenan grumbled, unconsciously echoing Lord Pecus; "People like a good night's sleep."

"Wasn't anything compared with how hard it was to get back out," Vadim said shortly. I gazed at her narrowly and discovered that Vadim had been really scared for a moment in those cells. The knowledge cost me a pang of conscience, and determined me to attempt this enterprise, at least, with Lord Pecus' approval.

"Well done, my children," I said, sitting up. It was enough

to be going on with. "Keep your eyes open, but don't go anywhere you can't get out comfortably. And do not disturb Lord Pecus' private quarters."

I tossed them a coin each, with instructions to please themselves in the disposal of it, and they went to bed with bright eyes full of plans for tomorrow. I was no less full of plans, but mine would have to wait until dinner with Lord Pecus tomorrow night. It went against the grain to bring him into my plans, but I was hardly equipped for an assault on the cells, and involve the children again. I could only hope that Lord Pecus would consider the idea favourably.

I found myself alone the next morning. I had given Vadim and Keenan permission to go into the city and spend their coin, and they had left me with an alacrity that could have been construed as insult. I was not long left alone, however; and before I had had time to do more than flip a few pages of the *Book of Interesting Excerpts* (snooping on Lord Pecus, of course), Miryum was ushered into the suite. She was looking grim about the mouth, but her eyes were tinged with an unaccustomed amusement, and I allowed surprise to show through my pleasure.

"Miryum! What brings you to see me?"

"Perhaps we could take a stroll through the gardens, lady?" she said bluntly, throwing a cursory look around the room. I found it amusing that she suspected Lord Pecus of listening in on our conversation, but showed her through the long glass doors into the garden without demur.

"Something has come up," she explained, when we had passed a little way through the garden. Her stride lengthened, and it occurred to me that I was being led nearer to the outer walls.

"You're not attempting to break me out, are you?"

She grinned. "I'll admit we thought of it. Well, Curran did, anyway, and Brennan was all for liberating you for the afternoon. We were heading over from Cottesloe way to try what we could do when someone tried to slice through the Glause-Civet boundary without stopping for the Waypoint."

I experienced a sinking feeling that was only partially alleviated by the almost certain knowledge that Susan couldn't possibly have made it to Glause since our commlink yesterday. I found myself wondering just how good Kit's travelling spells had become since I had last seen him. "I take it that the matter concerns me?" I remarked, looking sideways at her. This time I thought the amusement was more prominent than the grimness.

"We had a great deal of—" she paused momentarily, increasing the impression of humour by a slight curve to her lips; "Er, *difficulty*, cornering the fugitive. I don't know what magic she was using, but it was fast. And then when we did corner her, we almost lost her again. We have to report all border-jumpers or I swear I would have let her go, lady, just for the pleasure of seeing her give Emmett a bloody nose."

Oh dear. Kit's travel spells must have significantly improved: it certainly *sounded* like Susan.

"We bought her to you," Miryum continued, approaching the front gate. It was large and impressively scrolled in black barwork, and through those bars I could see the blue-clothed backs of three more horselords. "Said she knew you, so we thought we'd call her bluff."

Susan's voice said conversationally, through the wall of bodies: "Let me go, or else."

I curled my fingers around the bars, leaning languidly into the gate. "All I can see is fine, upstanding horselord, Miryum."

They turned at the sound of my voice and parted, but warily; and I was treated to the view of Emmett, his nose bloody, sitting on a remnant of what must have been the previous boundary wall. Susan was perched on one of his knees, her arms pinioned to her sides by Emmett's huge hands, and he was grinning at her. "Or else, what?" he said.

"I'll take that as a refusal, then," Susan said. Her voice was quite pleasant, but she had her head on one side in a way that I knew boded ill for Emmett. She gave me a sliver of her attention. "Hello, Belle. Surprised?"

"Not particularly," I said, my lips twitching. "I must say that I find it a little hypocritical of you to animadvert on *my* criminal tendencies, however. Emmett, do let her up."

"And let her draw Curran's cork as well? Tempting, but no."

"Last warning, lummox."

He gave her a rough shake. "Less of the insults, pipsqueak. I'll let you go when I'm sure you're not going to hit anyone else."

"Belle, do you mind?"

"Go ahead," I told her, watching with interest. "It's been a few years since I've seen you work. I trust your technique will reflect the years."

Emmett gave her a cool look and tightened his grip on her forearms. It must have hurt; but Susan, who had a far higher threshold for pain than I, only smiled. Then she leaned forward and planted a robust, smacking kiss on his lips. Emmett gave a muffled yell and leapt to his feet, shoving her away, and Susan leapt away with perfect timing, landing like a cat. A moment later she had surrounded herself with a wall of translucent blue fire. The horselords shouted with laughter at Emmett's discomfiture; but they, like myself, had evidently experienced the pain of that blue fire for themselves, because they kept a respectful distance from Susan. Young as she was, she was a force to be reckoned with.

"Emmett, my sister Susan," I said, flourishing one hand in

her direction. I reversed the flourish. "Susan, my friend Emmett."

"Very entertaining," said Miryum, still grinning. "I would like to know what we're to tell the border guard, though, lady."

"Susan? Was there a reason for your hostile invasion?"

She shrugged, and drifted over to me in a shimmer of flames. "We made good time over the mountains, but something went wrong as we got lower. I would have stopped if I could."

"Would you?" Miryum's voice was dry. "I wonder? You didn't spare any punches, child."

Susan cocked her head in Miryum's direction, but evidently decided to let the epithet pass unmolested. "The lummox wouldn't let me go. I was in a hurry. I told you who I was."

Curran looked at me, grinning. "It didn't seem likely, Isabella: a relative of yours, astride a horse? So we brought her in."

"Tried to," put in Brennan, with greater accuracy. "Where'd she learn to hit like that, Bella? Not from you, I'd swear."

"Certainly not!" I said coldly.

"No, Belle is more ladylike than that," Susan observed. "She doesn't *have* to use her hands."

She let the blue-fire spell drop as Emmett approached cautiously, and smiled up at him with a perfect good humour that held no trace of either animosity or smugness. It was one of the traits in her of which I most approved.

"Truce, pipsqueak?"

He was holding out his hand to be shaken: she clasped it and did so. "Truce, lummox."

Susan sauntered toward the gate, kissing me through the

bars, and I found that I could only just see over the top of her head. The commlink had not done justice to her height and health, nor the sheer abundance of her chestnut hair, which had grown several inches since last I saw her.

"Good heavens, Su!"

"I think it's all the horse manure," she said cheerfully, grinning. "I've been growing ever since Kit went away, anyway. You're looking as slim as ever."

"I think it must be all the tea," I retorted, unable to hold back an answering grin.

Behind us, Curran muttered in an audible aside: "Heaven help us, there's two of 'em now!"

LORD PECUS WAS SURPRISINGLY AMENABLE TO MY tentative suggestions regarding his prisoner. He had the faintly amused look of one humouring a small child, for which I only forgave him because I was getting my own way. After all, it is never productive to cavil at receiving what one asks for on the grounds of the manner in which it is given. Moreover, he made no objections to my questioning the drifter without his presence, and though it was obvious that he didn't expect me to be successful I was pleased to have a little privacy in which to work. His only stipulation was that I should not enter the same room as the prisoner, and since I had no intention of doing so, it was no hard promise to make. I borrowed one of Damson's sootiest aprons for the occasion, and wore it over a plain dress of brown wincey that I had used in not a few of my less grand adventures. It was a little tight across the shoulders, but I had done my growing early, and overall it was a good fit. With my hair carefully tousled and a light dusting of soot on my face I looked suitably urchin for my part, and nodding at my reflection in a satisfied manner, I proceeded downstairs to give commands to a very surprised footman.

It didn't take Lieutenant Holt very long to arrive, puzzled but willing to help. When he understood what it was I wished him to do, he grinned, and enquired: "Does Alexander know?"

"I'm not to enter the prisoner's cell, but otherwise I may do as I choose," I said, with perfect truth. "Will you help me?"

"Happily!" he assured me, replacing his hard-topped Lieutenant's helmet with every sign of enthusiasm. "How rough would you like me to be?"

"Oh, throw me in!" I told him blithely. Drunk or no, drifters were a shrewd clan with a nose for deception, as versed in it as they were themselves; and I didn't want to ruin things at the outset by being handed into the cell like a ladyship.

"He'll need to hear the key turn, so you'll have to lock the door. Don't activate the magic lock."

Trophimus nodded obediently. "Throw you in, lock cell door, don't activate the magic."

"Very good. Vadim! The blood, if you please!"

Lieutenant Holt watched in interest as Vadim drew one finger along my right cheek. A few beads of bright red appeared in my peripheral, large and heavy.

"It won't dry," she warned me, standing back to observe the effect. "So you can't stay too long. They're noticing people, them drifters. If you have to stay longer than it should take to dry, wipe it away and it'll show a cut for a while."

"Did you make that spell yourself?" asked Lieutenant Holt, fascinated, but I forestalled him with one raised finger.

"Later, if you please! I have a cell waiting for me, and

blood that won't dry on my face. Vadim will tell you all about it when I've finished."

"Nervous?" he enquired with a grin, marching me down the stone stairs.

"Oh no!" I said, as we approached the basement door. "This is not the first cell in which I have been imprisoned, after all."

"Now that is a story I want to hear!" remarked Lieutenant Holt, pausing before a door in massive oak. "Are you ready?"

I took a moment to gather a few, precious tears in my eyes, and settled my shoulders in a suitable slump. "You may proceed."

I was thrown into the cell with perhaps more violence than originally intended, and scraped my knee painfully on the flagged floor. Fortunately Trophimus was a better actor than I gave him credit for: he didn't look back, though he must have heard my exclamation of pain. I spat at his retreating back as I clutched my knee, not allowing myself to enjoy the scene too much for fear that my amusement might show through. Already the drifter had wandered over to the bars that adjoined our cells, and was regarding me with a kind of interested sympathy.

"Hungry, was yer?"

I gave a defiant sniff, and tossed a few straggly locks back. "No. I ain't a drifter, I'm a good girl. I never *done* it!"

"Much they believe yer, in here," the drifter offered, with doubtful comfort.

"*Much* they do!" I agreed, a single tear quivering on my eyelashes. I was very proud of that tear: it is not as easy to cry on demand as the regrettable multitude of tantrum-throwing children would suggest. "One rule for the likes of them, and one for the likes of us!"

He watched the tear fall, and advised: "Dry up yer bubblin' chicky; it never helped a soul."

"I ain't bubblin'!" I said indignantly. "An' as for helpin', well, I reckon I can help meself!"

I tilted my chin at him and removed my hairpin and thumbtack from their hiding place in my corsets. For the first time, the drifter showed real, sharp interest.

"What you doin', chicky?"

"Them as has sharp peepers gets 'em put out," I told him pertly, fiddling with the door lock. It was a rather delicate four-tumbler job, but not beyond my skills; and before long I heard the unmistakeable click that meant the lock tongue had slotted back into its hole. I grinned my triumph back at the drifter, and he licked his lips.

"Go on, chicky. Let a cellmate out, eh?"

I gave him a look of carefully melded suspicion and hesitation. The door is unlocked, my demeanour pointed out, and I should be off: however, I was a good girl, and my mam had taught me never to leave someone in distress. "'Ow do I know what you done, then? You might be a murderer, you might, and then where would I be?"

"Ah chicky, does I *look* like a murderer?"

"You *looks* like you're avoidin' the question," I said sharply. Mam's girl was no fool. "You want out, you tell me what you're in for."

"Wanted somewhere warm for the night," he said easily, gazing earnestly at me.

"It's no good lying to me, cobber," I told him, with perfect truth. I tapped my head, signifying the possession of superior, if not magical powers of lie detection. He went quite white, and swallowed.

"My aunt were one of your kind," he said quietly. "You see the future as well, chicky?"

"Enough," I said, again with perfect truth. Enough to know that potato soup would be the opening course at dinner tonight, at least. Not to mention the *Book of Interesting Excerpt*'s powers of extrapolation, which, though its power was not strictly mine, at least *belonged* to me.

"No more lies, cobber."

"I was driftin' through the Sinkhole, just markin' time: cobber came up to me and asked if I'd like to make a bit of coin. *Nat'rally* I said yes."

"Nat'rally," I murmured, fascinated. Perhaps I really could see the future. The conversation was going exactly as I would have predicted. For the sake of the part, I added darkly: "Told you to kill summun, did he?"

He gave me a reproachful look. "Now, chicky, don't be saying things like that. All I had to do was break a window, and run. Told me where to run, and all, he did."

"That's daft," I opined, but I was almost certain he was telling the truth. "Orright, then: what else?"

"That's it, chicky. He told me not to get caught, though; and he's not the kind you want to cross. Least he paid right up, eh?"

"Makes yer wonder," I said quietly. Was that Trophimus' step outside the door? Surely I had not been that long? I stepped closer to the bars and said to the drifter: "Want to know your future, cobber?"

His eyes pleaded with me. "Let me out, chicky; we can take him down!"

"You'll get out," I told him crisply, hardening myself against the plea. "Soon. But don't you wait around, cobber; you run as far and as hard as you can, savvy?"

Trophimus was stepping through the door, and the drifter's eyes bored into mine for a loaded moment before he said: "Savvy," and walked away, distancing himself from the prisoner who was clearly about to be removed. I had seen it a dozen times at Trenthams; the way a group of girls would suddenly dissipate in the face of authority, distancing themselves from the unfortunate who had called down said authority on her head. It was amusing to find that schoolroom logic held true in the prison system.

Lieutenant Holt removed me from the cell with a none-too-gentle shove and a rough adjuration to move myself up the stairs. Accordingly, I moved myself, and emerged at the top of the stairs to the eager countenances of Vadim and Keenan. They gazed avidly at me, but it was left to Lieutenant Holt to ask: "Well? What now?"

"A bath, I rather think," I said disparagingly, lifting a strand of my grubby hair and eyeing it with fascinated horror. "Vadim, I think you might have done just a little too well."

"Don't be unkind, Lady Farrah!" Trophimus pleaded laughingly. "You know what I meant."

"Isabella, if you please!" I said firmly. "Once one has been imprisoned by someone it seems a little silly to stick to formalities, after all."

He grinned shyly. "You can call me Trophy, my lady. Isabella, I mean."

"To answer your question, Trophy: let him go."

"Let him go?"

"Let him go, Trophy, let him go!" I repeated, waving an airy hand.

"I don't know if Lord Pecus would like that," he said dubiously.

"Oh, live a little! And it might be as well to send someone to question the woman who poured a load of dishwater over Lord Pecus. Discreetly, of course; don't burst in on her wearing your Watch uniform."

"Perhaps I should put *her* into a cell," remarked Trophy

humorously. "Since you seem to be doing so well. What did you get out of him?"

"He was paid to set the alarm off. He was also paid to run in the direction that he ran."

Trophy blinked several times, rapidly. "It was a *jape*? Someone thought it was a good idea to run a practical joke on the *Commander* of the Watch?"

"I don't think it was a joke, exactly," I said slowly. The murderer had struck me as definitely unbalanced, and with a distinct interest in me: was it a stretch of the imagination to think that he could consider Lord Pecus in the light of a rival? "I believe I need to speak with Lord Pecus."

I frowningly considered this for a moment, and added: "But first I must have a bath."

Chapter Fourteen

It was a week later that I awoke to the sounds of vigorous dusting and numerous determined sniffs: Damson was evidently still experiencing problems with her gentleman friend. I forbore to question her, since she had been disinclined to discuss the matter earlier, but I did wonder briefly, gazing up at my ceiling in quiet meditation, if the hearth had been in a sufficiently dirty state to justify the vigorous scraping I had heard. I rather fancied not. It would seem that my morning rest was at the mercy of Damson's gentleman friend. Since it didn't seem likely that I would get any more sleep, I roused myself sufficiently to decline the presence of a fire in the newly swept hearth. It was the second month of summer, and hot as the days already were, they would daily increase in mugginess until not even the dawn or dusk would offer relief from the heat of the triad. As it was, the morning coolness had not even managed to pierce my light coverlet, and the thought of a fire, no matter how small, was decidedly disagreeable.

After Damson had flounced her way back below stairs, I

climbed languidly out of bed and into a warm, soupy morning that seemed to wrap itself around me like syrup.

"Insupportable!" I said firmly: but since it was also insupportable to remain any longer in my somewhat sticky nightdress, I ruffled through my wardrobe for a light summer frock and was dressed before Vadim and Keenan had even stirred. It had occurred to me last night, in the time before I fell asleep, that I had not been making the best use of my resources, and with that thought in mind, I curled myself up in the window seat with the *Book of Interesting Excerpts*, to await breakfast.

The Book was in a contrary mood, however; sulky and slow with its information, and when the children awoke fractious and quarrelsome, it began to be borne in on me just what the day was liable to be like. Evidently I was not the only one who found the first real day of summer a trial. Eventually I sent them outside to bicker, and changed focus in my perusal of the *Book of Interesting Excerpts*. I had been trying to get a little more history on the Earl of Horn, who, though not in my estimation a truly viable suspect, was certainly a Person of Interest. It was he, I strongly suspected, whom Lord Pecus and I had followed to the Charles Black meeting. But the Book was vague and confusing, inking out diverse and contradictory written reports from Watch occurrence books (and, disturbingly, personal diaries) that could not possibly have been true in conjunction with each other. When I pointed out as much to the Book, its ink sank into a sullen black, and it sputtered out a short, messy sentence.

Can't help it, that's what happened.

"It can't be what happened!" I said, with some asperity. "Look, you've got the Earl at home *here*, according to the time of this little note he wrote, and over in the Sinkhole District *here*, on the same date and at the same time!"

I don't write it, I just research it, said the book, its writing growing smaller and more crabbed. It looked as though it were about to throw a temper tantrum, if such a thing were possible.

I sighed. "Very well, if *that* is too difficult, show me all communications the day the Pecus Curse took effect."

The Book paused, its writing fading in and out uncertainly. At length, a sentence formed.

I don't think that's allowed.

"What do you mean, it's not allowed!"

You're concerned in breaking the curse, the Book scrawled. ***It would be considered cheating. This is outside my parameters.***

"I am most certainly *not* concerned in breaking the curse!" I told the book firmly. "It has nothing in the world to do with me. Lord Pecus can look after himself."

Lord Pecus seems to have chosen you to break it, smugly said the Book. ***That means you're not allowed any help. You wouldn't want to cheat, would you?***

"Of course I would!" I said. "What a ridiculous question! I quite often cheat, thank you very much; sometimes it's the only way to get things done. For example: how may I break a curse if I'm not given any information?"

It's meant to be hard, inked the Book, sulky again. ***That's the way it is. All the True Love curses are like that.***

"I utterly refuse to be involved in anything so trite as a True Love Curse! And if you dare to tell me that 'Lord Pecus seems to have involved me', I shall begin ripping your pages out!"

There was a brief, pregnant pause; then a few, cautious words swirled onto the page. ***I can show you excerpts that record when it started, but that's all.***

I felt a glimmer of light. "Lord Pecus' twenty-fourth birth-day, I believe?"

If you knew, you shouldn't have asked, the Book scribbled irritably, whisking away the fragments that had been collecting on one page.

"Oh, never mind," I told it, my mind no more than half concentrated on soothing it. "You've been very useful. Thank you."

I closed the Book with a snap, ignoring the half formed words that had begun to spell out another complaint. It was evident that the Pecus Curse was not a hereditary thing. One, and only one of his ancestors, had suffered under it, and had originally brought masks to Pecus Manor. No doubt it had become the expected thing for Pecus Manor's servants to be masked. Was it, as the Book had suggested, a True Love curse? I found it reasonable in light of the circumstances. I wondered if Lord Pecus knew it to be so, and thought, with something of a snap to my eyes, that it was very likely he did. Well! If he thought I was going to break it for him, he was very much mistaken. True Love curses had a tendency to be inconveniently binding, and I had no mind to be inveigled into marriage when there was so much work to be done. Besides, the climate of Glause did not suit me. I would have to speak with Trophy again: I was sure it was he who had told me something of Lord Pecus' twenty-fourth birthday, when the mask had been broken. I had one or two suspicions about that 'mask'; a mask so good that it had not been recognised as anything other than Lord Pecus' face for the first twenty-four years of his life. Lord Pecus, I had been creditably informed, was one of the fore-most magic users in Glause. It struck me as unlikely that he had not been able to produce anything so lifelike as his orig-inal 'mask'.

Some time later I was roused from a pensive, daydreamish state by Susan's arrival.

"Twice in two weeks!" I said admiringly, rising to kiss her. "My, aren't we the family fond!"

"Well, you're technically in durance vile, so I thought I'd better."

Susan seated herself on the windowsill nearest her, swinging a leg. She was wearing a pair of borrowed horselord breeches and had managed to acquire a very nice pair of boots and a smart new tunic since last I had seen her. She looked young and boyish.

"I left the lummox outside."

"Oh, you brought Emmett? Wonderful! I have a job for him."

Susan grinned. "I thought Curran was joking when he said they were in your employ. Do the horselords usually take orders from a foreign power?"

"When they know what is *good* for them, they do. And if it comes to that, Su, I should like to know why you've got one at your beck and call."

"Oh, that's because I'm a Delicate Flower of the Highlands," Susan said. "The King is afraid that I'll be 'attacked' as well. Well, publicly he is. Privately, I'm certain he knows that you're in no more danger than the average Glausian who roams the streets. If you ask me, he's sitting back to enjoy the show."

"Well, I'm glad someone seems to be enjoying it," I remarked, with great insincerity. "When did you become so satirical, Susan? I'm sure you were nicer when you were younger."

"No, I wasn't," she said. "I was just out of the way more. Anyway, it's all your influence; I thought you'd be proud."

I laughed, and sat beside her in the window seat with my

feet up and my arms clasped around my knees. "I'm simply bursting with pride. I have missed you, Su!"

The corner of her mouth turned up in the lopsided smile I knew so well. "I suppose I've missed you, too. It's never as fun when you aren't at home. How's the Beast Lord treating you?"

"So they really do call him that on the street!" I said, with interest. "You've acquainted yourself with the gossip very quickly."

"I have a thousand eyes and ears," she told me airily. "Actually, I spent the morning lounging about the Sinkhole district pretending to be a *hash* runner until the lummox found me. They're a wary bunch down there; your Beast Lord has 'em all in the fear of being eaten or worse."

"He's managed quite well, I think," I allowed. "He does have certain natural advantages to work with."

"Does he mean to marry you, Belle?"

I considered deflecting the question, but it has always been difficult to deflect anything in the face of Susan's grey gaze. "I believe so. Of course, I shan't do anything of the sort; the man dips biscuits in his tea. Besides, Papa needs me."

"He doesn't, you know."

"Of course he does," I said. "I've seen him do it myself."

"I've got my chance now and I mean to keep it," Susan continued serenely. "And so I warn you, Belle."

"Very right and proper of you. This may perhaps alter things. How is the merger proceeding?"

Susan tilted her head. "Are you changing the subject?"

"Certainly I am. I want to know how we're doing."

"It's still going slowly; Papa moves to raise the year limit, someone vetoes, and so on. Do you know, General Kropke is *quite* the dancer. I think it must be all the legwork he does over the Glausian hillsides. The Mage General is trying to ramrod us, and Papa has begun taking sugar in his coffee again."

I laughed. Father and sugar were a notoriously bad combination. "Do you have enough money for clothes?"

Susan gazed at me in silent consideration for a long moment. "I always forget how much I love you until we're together again. You never interfere. You know a thousand ways to get around the Mage General, but you won't tell me unless I ask. You'll let me go on and make my own mistakes. I appreciate that."

"I can't *imagine* what you're talking about. You're more than capable of taking care of things: why should I try to interfere?"

She slipped off the windowsill and bounced down on the seat beside me, crushing my skirt. "How do I get past the Mage General, Belle?"

"He ramrods." I shrugged, and gave her a roguish grin. "Simply make sure that when he shoves, he shoves in the direction you want him to go. He doesn't have a terribly athletic mind: it will be enough for him if he thinks he's opposing you. Create something for him to fight against, put a few conditions for surrender in place—things you really want—and he'll push all before him."

There was a gleam in Susan's eyes. "I think I may have an idea. What do you want Emmett for?"

"Are you leaving me already?" I tried for an indignant tone but couldn't quite manage. Susan grinned.

"Work to do, Belle. You of all people should know how busy things get."

"There's a person I need the horselords to see for me. Nothing formal, and strictly no uniforms."

Susan looked knowledgeable. "A flighty witness?"

"Something of that sort."

"Is it something to do with Raoul's murder?"

"Perhaps. I think someone is trying to get my attention."

"You've made some unusual friends since I last saw you. Does the Beast Lord know you're investigating?"

"I certainly hope not!" I said frankly. "He doesn't care for interference. Tell Emmett that the thing needs to be done quietly."

"Of course."

"Oh, and Su?"

Her tone was resigned. "Yes, Belle?"

"*Don't* do it yourself."

I DIDN'T SEE LORD PECUS UNTIL DINNER THAT NIGHT. HE arrived dishevelled and tired, and it seemed to be no far stretch of the imagination to assume that there had been trouble on the streets again. He applied himself to his food in silence, leaving me at leisure to study his face. I did so at length, my chin propped in the palm of my hand while I nibbled at sweetmeats, and fancied that I began to discern the suspicion of lines about the corners of his eyes. It was nonsense, of course, since nothing could possibly have shown beneath all that fur; but I couldn't rid my mind of the notion. Once, I thought I saw the movement of a clean-shaven jaw as he ate, and my thoughts began to tick over interestingly as the second course was brought in. It was an odd curse—True Love or otherwise—that worked as fitfully as this one seemed to do. Unless, of course, I was already involved. Oh dear.

I was engaged in discerning the faint line of Lord Pecus' human nose through the fur, with the quickly growing certainty that I had in fact become involved, when he turned his head and caught me at it.

"Am I interrupting you, Lady Farrah?"

I may have blushed a trifle. "Not at all. I was merely wondering when you would join me for dinner."

A smile curved his lips, perfectly synchronized with the overshadowing tooth-baring grin of his beast face. "Did you miss me, my lady?"

I only had time to think faintly: *Oh my, he has a dimple!* before his outer face solidified and made him the Beast Lord again. I may have grown a little pinker than before. It was in the consciousness of this that I said firmly: "Absolutely not! I've been far too busy to do anything of the kind."

Lord Pecus grinned a somewhat ferocious grin. "Up to no good, my lady?"

I looked at him primly. "Certainly not. I've been improving my mind upon the subject of modern history – not to mention Damson's difficulties with her young man."

Lord Pecus said cautiously: "Should I know who Damson is?"

"She's your chambermaid," I told him helpfully. "I have yet to ascertain all the details, but the matter has already deprived me of some little amount of sleep. As you can see, I've had far too much on my mind to think of causing mischief. I only cause mischief when I am bored."

A gleam appeared momentarily in Lord Pecus' jade eyes, and I knew that he was thinking of that one, locked door in my passageway. I wondered if he fancied I had been attempting its challenges. I gave him my most demure smile in the hopes of encouraging the thought, and sipped the last of my fruit nectar. To be *really* elegant, of course, one ought to drink wine: but I've never cared for the taste, and so I drink fruit nectar with great spirit instead, which answers very nearly as well when it comes to polite society.

"Did you let the drifter go?"

He nodded. "I could have tracked him but it didn't seem worth the trouble. He'll have to shift for himself."

"I should imagine that he's well out of the city by now," I said. The drifter had not wanted for sense, and I was tolerably certain that he had taken my warning to heart.

"Then I only hope he has sense enough to stay out," remarked Lord Pecus. "People dealing with this madman have a tendency to turn up dead— if it *was* our man he had dealings with."

"I think it very likely. No doubt if you questioned some of the rioters you would hear the same story."

This time his smile was a trifle bitter. On his beast-face it looked intimidating. "If it's all the same to you, Lady Farrah, I'd rather not find out that all this chaos was caused by a single man. I dislike the notion that one man can influence the Imperial City at will. And to what purpose?"

I remembered the bright, wild lilt to the murderer's voice as he had talked with me, and shivered. He had murdered not just at will, but on whim. "At will, by whim, according to plan— there's no sense to it. He changes from one moment to the next, but he always has a wide reach. Why Raoul? If it was because of treason, why you? Daubney was murdered because of what he knew, but your attack makes no sense. If we consider them apart, there is *some* reason, but none at all if taken together."

"There's one connection you've forgotten," Lord Pecus pointed out. His teeth were showing in a faint grin, as if he had expected me to see something I had not, and was quietly amused at my lack of comprehension. "All of them are connected very clearly by one thing."

"Indeed? And what is that, my lord?"

The grin grew a little. "By you, Lady Farrah."

A tea tray was brought in after dinner, much to my

surprise. I could have been mistaken, but I rather thought that Lord Pecus was as surprised as I— which was, of course, nonsense, for what servant would send in a tea tray that had not been requested? I found myself wondering if perhaps a *very* devoted servant might not do so, and wondered again just how much the servants in Pecus Manor knew. It was no part of my bargain to stay for tea; and yet, I did stay. It couldn't have been Susan's blunt assurance of Father's no longer needing me that influenced my decision: it must have been the wonderful aroma of Civetan Winter's Dream blend rising from the tea canister that swayed me to stay. And then, just as I was making up my mind, Lord Pecus had suddenly looked so *hopeful*, in a puppy like manner that no man approaching forty has any right to look…

Lord Pecus drank his coffee with his boots off and his feet up, without making any attempt at decorum. I felt myself likewise free to do so, and curled my feet under me on the plush velvet to enjoy my tea luxuriously. The servants had happily possessed intelligence enough not to steep the tea before it was brought in, and so I was able to enjoy it properly brewed by my own hands. I offered Lord Pecus a cup, but he only shook his head.

"Smells like fruitcake," he explained.

I don't quite know how it happened, but before the evening was very much further advanced, I found myself reading the *Sondeim Sonnet* aloud for Lord Pecus' entertainment. It was an old number of the *Sonnet*, and its humour therefore dated, but Lord Pecus was not so young that it was unintelligible to him, and every so often he would give a short bark of laughter. Some time later I was amused, but unsurprised, to hear him emit a gentle snore. His chin had dropped to his chest in repose, his arms folded comfortably; and I could once again observe the two warring aspects of his face.

I let my voice sink until it was a mere murmur, and ceased. Poor boy, he'd been working himself too hard.

I allowed myself a few moments of pensive study before I retired to my suite, where Vadim and Keenan were still bickering. I closed the door quietly behind myself, and said to the room at large: "It would appear that I have given neither of you sufficient to do, if you are now reduced to quarrelling with one another."

They looked around guiltily with heat-flushed faces and miserable eyes.

"Sorry, lady."

"Sorry, lady."

I gazed at them thoughtfully, and then trod lightly across the room to the garden window. "Come with me, both of you."

Vadim edged after me, shamefaced, and Keenan trailed dumbly behind her, rubbing a hand through his sticky hair so that it stood up in spikes.

I took them to the courtyard. The fountain there was a deep one with a low wall around it, and despite the profusion of brightly coloured fish, there were no inconvenient lily pads to tangle a small child who might happen to find himself or herself floundering in it.

"Up you get," I told them crisply, and they climbed onto the parapet, surprised but uncomplaining.

"Wot's happenin'?" Keenan demanded. They were still looking at me in confusion when I pushed them in. Vadim gasped, Keenan yelled, and there was a splash sufficiently large to dampen my dinner dress pleasantly before they surfaced, spluttering.

"Wot didjer do that for?"

"Do you feel better now?" I asked, ignoring the question.

Vadim gave a gurgle of laughter. "Yes, lady. Thank you, lady. Are you coming in, lady?"

"Certainly not! I'm surprised at you, Vadim! The idea!"

"There's no one watching at the windows," she said persuasively.

"Oh, in *that* case!" I sat myself down on the parapet and took off my shoes and stockings. "Just a paddle, mind; and if there is any splashing, I shall be excessively unhappy."

Dusk remained in half-light for some time, and I eventually left the children paddling and frightening the colourful little fish with their splashes, while I retired to my suite with rapidly drying legs. It was sultry and dark indoors, and not even the bobbing lights overhead managed to convey anything but a sense of dullness. The first real day of summer. I bit back a sigh and thought dismally that I seemed to have a headache coming on. Fortunately for my melancholy frame of mind, I was not given time to dwell on it: my commlink buzzed almost immediately as I entered the dressing room, and displayed Susan's flushed face.

"Kit's right," she said, with something of a gasp. "The place is humid enough to swim in. Belle, what have you gotten yourself into?"

"I suppose she's dead?" I felt my heart sink, and I was not sure whether to be glad I had told the drifter to make himself scarce, or afraid that in doing so, I had led to the death of the washer-woman.

Susan nodded. "Remember how you said not to go there myself?"

I closed my eyes.

"All right, all right, I went there myself. The lummox went with me, if it makes you feel better."

"Perhaps slightly," I allowed. "But only *very* slightly."

"It was all rather nasty," Susan said ruminatively, gazing

into the distance with a small line between her brows. She sighed and pulled herself together with a small shake of her head. "The lummox thought I was going to faint, or at least that's what he *said*. I think it was just an excuse to drag me out by the scruff of the neck before the Watch caught up with us. Oh, and Miryum said to tell you that some friend or other of yours is like to get married. She seemed to think you'd be relieved. Been flirting again, have you, Belle?"

"Certainly not!" I said, with dignity. "And let me tell you that if you imagine I'll let you change the subject so easily, you're very much mistaken!"

"You would have done the same thing," she reminded me, grinning.

"That's quite true," I admitted, fairmindedly. "I should like to have you know, however, that *I* did not at any point come close to fainting."

"It came pretty close." Susan was looking reflective. "It gave me a bit of a buzz through my head, anyway. You're a better man than I took you for, Belle."

"I should hope I'm nothing of the kind! No, I did not come even close to fainting. I did, however, lose my dinner in the hydrangeas."

Susan gave a spurt of laughter. "Did anyone see you?"

"Only Melchior, and I threatened him with dire consequences if he ever revealed it to a soul."

"I respond better to bribery," Susan remarked. "Especially if you're offering me some of those wonderful Glausian Chocolate Oranges. I've never seen so many luscious chocolates, Belle: it could be worth even the humidity. I had the lummox carrying bags and bags of them back home for me."

I gazed at her in some amusement. The thought of Emmett carrying *anybody's* bags, not to mention chocolate bags, was not one I had previously encountered. "I'm certain that when Emmett was assigned guard duty, he was not of the opinion that his duties would include carrying your shopping bags. Does he complain?"

Susan grinned wickedly. "No. He just stands there like a mountain: a sort of strong, silent mountain. I even took him shopping for my court things, and he carried my stocking bag without a blink."

"The poor boy! Have the others teased him dreadfully?"

"No," Susan said thoughtfully; "But I think that might have something to do with the attacks."

I blinked twice, rapidly. "Which attacks?"

"In the Sinkhole," she said easily. "And once when I was out shopping for tea for you. I thought you should have some of the comforts of home, and someone else thought that they should have your comforts of home instead."

"Glausian streets have become strangely perilous since I was taken off them," I said, with a great deal of dryness. "Who would have thought it? Or did you just *happen* to walk into the most dangerous of Glause's citizens yesterday?"

"Well, Emmett was bored, and the others were starting to tease him, poor lummox. So we had a few adventures, and now everyone thinks I'm a difficult handful to guard."

"Where did you manage to find characters desperate enough to attack you with Emmett standing by?"

Susan looked demure with a little difficulty. "I must have stepped away *just* as the lummox turned to look at a display of street fighting that I may or may not have pointed out to him. A pickpocket and an enforcer were on the make, and somehow or other I ended up in a little side alley." Susan paused, and added meditatively: "It really was impressive, Belle. I don't think I've seen a full-grown man scale a ten foot wall quite so quickly before. Of course, by then the lummox had all but thumped him through the alley wall, broken his nose and hung his partner by the ankles, so I don't know that I blame him."

I raised my brows. "Emmett did all that?"

"He was a bit upset," Susan explained. "I don't think he likes it when I wander off."

"I'm not surprised, if that's the sort of thing that happens when you wander off! I expect Emmett will have grown a few grey hairs by the next time I see him."

"I expect he will. He could have already for all I know, with his head shaved so close. He says he doesn't like having to wash hair. Belle, is the Earl of Horn mixed up in this business?"

"If you're trying to take me by surprise, you'll have to try a little harder," I said. "Besides, I would have told you anyway."

"No ambushes," protested Susan, spreading her hands in manifest innocence. "It just sprang to my mind. Emmett's bald head reminded me."

I choked on a laugh. "I would advise against calling Emmett bald to his face."

Susan grinned. "Or at least without a nice thick wall between us. The earl, Belle."

"The earl is very much mixed up in this business, unless I am greatly mistaken. Why do you ask?"

"Bits and pieces here and there." Susan frowned, marshalling her thoughts, and perched her chin on the palm of her hand. "You're not often mistaken, and unless *I'm* entirely in the wrong, the earl is a staunch albeit quiet dissenter of the military merger. He doesn't say much, but he moves about behind the scenes, and suddenly things fall apart, or come together: and when they do, there he is in the background."

"I suspected as much," I said. "What has changed?"

"Well, he's understated, but he's never missed a summit.

Not a meeting, not a session: and then all of a sudden, he misses three in a row."

"What of Louisa?"

Susan made a face, and I bit back a smile. So Susan had not got along well with Louisa either. Unsurprising. "Miss Twinkles-and-Bells has been sent away to the country for her health," she told me, with a toss of the head that was purely Louisa. "By all accounts she's not too happy about it."

"I imagine not. And the Countess? Has she been sent off too?"

She shook her head. "Just Louisa. I *had* heard that the earl tried to send her away as well, but if so, the Countess has for once stood obdurate. People are funny, aren't they?"

"Positively side-splitting. What else has happened this week?"

"Suspiciously little," said Susan, shrugging. "It's been a bit boring, really."

"Aside from your encounter with the desperate scaff-and-raff of Glause," I reminded her. "What do you think the earl is up to?"

Susan considered the question for a brief moment. "I think he's about to run. Lord Pecus has taken him in for questioning four times this week. He's no fool."

"Lord Pecus or the earl?"

"Both. I think it might be a good time to meet with the earl."

I huffed a small sigh, thinking rapidly. The earl would be either ready to run or ready to talk, and in either case, it would be as well to strike while the iron was hot.

"Could you arrange it, Su?"

"Maybe. Could you entertain him without being heard?"

That took a little more meditation. "With difficulty. I might have to er, break out."

"How *daring* of you!" said Susan, with a wicked gleam to her eyes. "Is the Beast Lord that easily outwitted?"

"Not easily," I said ruefully. "It is possible, however. If you can contact the earl, I think I might be able to arrange to slip away."

Susan raised a brow. "Time? Place?"

"A picnic, I rather think. As to time, it might be expedient to let the earl decide: you can visit me when you know for sure."

She nodded. "I'll let you know. In the meantime, your bubbly little friend wants you to commlink with her. Try and persuade her that I really don't want full court dress, will you?"

I narrowly avoided an unladylike snort. "Delysia is ever the optimist."

"I can't think why she believes it will suit me," Susan added, indicating the length of her body with a wave of the hand. "Court dress is not for tall women."

This time I allowed myself to grin. "Well, as you so elegantly put it earlier: people are funny, aren't they?"

Chapter Fifteen

Breakfast is undoubtedly the most important meal of the day. A good, hearty breakfast, eaten in the privacy of one's own chambers, allows one to nibble delicately at one's lunch as a lady should, and leaves the male populace in general under the impression that females are a delicate and tender species. It was therefore puzzling to find, some two months after the disastrous masque at Pecus Manor, that I had begun to look forward to dinner as *the* event of the day. I was observing myself in the mirror to test the effect of a newly designed dress when the thought occurred to me, and it left me gazing blindly at my own reflection for some minutes before I roused myself.

"Did you need something, lady?"

"Pardon, Vadim?"

Vadim paused in her folding. "I thought you said something."

What I had said, in quiet astonishment, was: "Bother!" Now I said, with sudden energy: "I've decided I won't wear this one, Vadim. Bring me the cream and pink sheath."

She gazed at me in open surprise. "But you said it makes you look like a strawberry strawbiscuit!"

"Well, there's more to life than one's clothes, after all!" I protested. It was high time I ceased to dress myself to the best advantage for Lord Pecus' benefit. It wasn't at all healthy for me: I was becoming maudlin.

"Are you ill, lady?"

"Very possibly. You're right, that pink sheath is an abomination. Throw it in the incinerator and bring me the ivory beaded ensemble instead, the one with the gauze wrapper. It's useless to expect a chill in the air, I suppose, but it might serve as protection against rain draughts."

"The rain draughts are warm," Vadim assured me, with an entirely misplaced solicitude. "It's only the first month of autumn."

"I am regretfully aware of that, Vadim!" I said. "In Civet, excepting a few evergreens, the trees will already have begun to lose their leaves."

Vadim looked as if she were not quite sure whether to believe me or not. "What do they want to do that for?"

"So that the snow doesn't gather on the leaves and drop a snowball down your collar," I told her, not entirely mendaciously. "Where is Keenan? It seems that whenever I can't see him trouble is quietly gathering a snowball to drop down *my* collar."

"He's still with Lady Susan."

"Still gone? My, my, Susan has certainly been busy this morning. We can only hope that the time has been well spent. Persuading Keenan to stand still for some new clothes, for instance."

"She'd be lucky," opined Vadim pessimistically.

"Oh, Susan is *very* lucky," I told her. "Keenan may well have met his match. In the meantime, I suppose I had better go down to dinner. If Keenan arrives home after I've gone down to dinner, you must keep him up for me."

Vadim nodded, laying the scarf of ivory gauze across my shoulders. "Will he have news?"

"Now, Vadim, if I knew *that*, I wouldn't go down to dinner." I regarded the mirror thoughtfully. "I wonder if it's too late to have the headache?"

Nevertheless, I was very shortly making my way downstairs to the dining hall. I was conscious of looking really quite nice, and it was pleasant to feel Lord Pecus' eyes resting on me appreciatively. It was no part of my plan to play the love-struck maid, however, and I pulled myself together by saying firmly to him: "I am not well, and I shall be very unsociable."

Amusement sprang to his eyes, lightening the green, and the now-familiar laugh lines creased beside them. It was becoming easier and easier to see his real face, and I had not failed to notice the covert glances of the server who brought in the different courses as each dinner saw Lord Pecus' face a little clearer. It was a nice face, with a strong nose that must have once been broken, and a firm jawline that was dark and stubbled. I liked the lines by his eyes, and the creases that curved beneath his cheeks when he grinned, meeting the corners of his mouth. In fact, if I could have imagined a face for him, it would have been this face. Really, the only thing I had not been expecting was the single, deep crease that served as a dimple.

It was in play now as he said affably: "What a pity. I thought we could talk about some new information I have regarding Raoul's murder."

I put my nose in the air. "No you didn't. You thought you could tease me with it."

"You're a suspicious woman, Lady Farrah."

"So I've been told. Very well, what is this news?"

"You already know the washing-water woman is dead: but what you don't know is what I found in her rooms."

I leaned forward, eyes sparkling. "Intriguing! *Do* tell!"

"Well, I could, but my feelings are hurt," explained Lord Pecus.

I blinked twice, rapidly, and then gave vent to a peal of laughter. "What a very fine poker face you have, my lord! I had a nasty moment there."

"You're very good practise for me, Lady Farrah."

"Oh no!" I rested my chin in the palm of my hand and smiled companionably at him; "As I said to Trophy, once you've out-bluffed me, it's time to drop the formalities. Although in his case, it was pitching me into a cell; but the principle is the same. There is to be no more Lady Farrah, thank you very much: I would much rather be called Isabella."

A smile swept across Lord Pecus' face, creating the indent in his cheek. "I'm honoured. My name is Alexander."

"Oh, I know!" I told him airily. "Trophy told me. I was pumping him for information about you: poor boy, he thought I was trying to learn about the case."

"The more I learn of you, the more I find myself thankful that Glause and Civet have never been at war," remarked Lord Pecus. "I can only imagine that you would have taken to the field as a spy, and I'm certain that Glause isn't equipped for the onslaught."

"I will ignore the insult of being referred to as if I were a disease," I said coldly; "Because I want to know what you found in the washing-water woman's room, Alexander."

I ignored the brief smile that lit his face, acknowledging the use of his name, and narrowed my eyes at him. "If you don't mean to tell me after all, I shall be most indignant!"

He grinned. "I think you'll appreciate this; I certainly did. We found a tiepin belonging to the Earl of Horn."

I tilted my head to one side. "Then *surely*–"

Lord Pecus continued smoothly without giving me a chance to finish: "Beside the tiepin, lined up neatly so that we wouldn't miss them, were a fob belonging to Raoul, a flea-bitten scarf I can only imagine belonged to the drifter, and a watch chain with your father's signet on it. Very convenient, I thought."

"He's playing with us," I said, nodding. "Mocking us: telling us that we haven't got the right one yet, and that he's still pulling the strings."

"Or he's throwing suspicion off himself by implicating himself along with everyone else."

"Now you're just being difficult, Alexander. Did you find anything else?"

"Well, I thought that would be enough," he said, smiling. "But to answer your question, no: there was no other sign that anyone had been there besides the woman herself."

"How vexing!" I said sympathetically, if a little automatically. Something was niggling at the back of my mind, distracting me. Lord Pecus raised an amused brow, aware of my preoccupation and inviting information, but I didn't enlighten him. There was still a certain, cautious part of me that objected to revealing all; besides which, I was by no means certain what it was that had made me uneasy. I continued to muse on the matter as I climbed the stairs to my suite, but Keenan was bouncing on the bed in a state of high excitement when I returned, and all my attention was needed to elicit a coherent tale from him.

The Earl of Horn, it seemed, had indeed made a run for it as Susan had predicted. He had evidently left before the Countess expected it, for she remained at home and unavailable to visitors. It occurred to me, with a faint surprise, that he had done the right thing by her. One didn't expect a suspected revolutionary to love his family quite so much: it made them seem uncomfortably like oneself. The earl had not been observed visiting his wife or his daughter; and Susan, from what Keenan told me, expected Louisa to be called home to support the countess in the not-so-distant future.

I wondered if Lord Pecus had known about the earl and simply neglected to tell me, but concluded from Keenan's somewhat garbled account that Susan's intelligence was the very latest. No doubt Lord Pecus would know by morning. I would have to practise my expressions of surprise.

"Was Su able to arrange a meeting?"

Keenan paused in his bouncing for long enough to say breathlessly: "She says not yet, but it won't take long. Says you should set a picnic for the end of the week, and she'll comm-link a time."

"Very well. Off to bed with you both, now."

Keenan bounced one last time, launching himself in the air, and landed on the rug with a flourish.

"Lady Susan belted me," he said.

I looked at him, amused but unsurprised. "Did you deserve it?"

"Yus. Picked her guard's pockets."

"Well, then, you have no reason to complain," I told him, reflecting that Emmett's life must have become one of considerable aggravation in the last month or so.

"I wasn't *complainin'*," said Keenan, releasing himself from the one suspender that was still attached and stripping off his shirt without regard to present company. He was as filthy as ever, but he was not quite skin and bones any longer. "I was just *sayin'*. Lady Susan's orright."

My eyes met Vadim's above his head: she was grinning.

"Says she's got as good an arm as our mum had," she explained, when he had left the room.

"It's good to know what Keenan respects in a mistress," I said dryly. "I must try to make an effort to beat him once or twice a week. How are things progressing below stairs?"

Vadim's eyes flicked momentarily beyond me, and back to meet my eyes. "Very well, lady."

How amusing! She was keeping something back. I looked at her for a long, smiling moment, and decided to let her have her secrets: after all, she must learn how to look after herself at one stage or another. Of course, Vadim had always known how to take care of herself—and Keenan, too!—but I didn't think she had had to take care of a young man as well. Her footman must be continuing to make an impression. Determined young upstart! I wondered if I should intervene a little, but regretfully decided against it: I may be nosy and somewhat prone to insinuate myself into the affairs of others, but I am not *entirely* a busybody.

So instead of giving into the temptation of winkling answers out of Vadim I sent her to bed, and enjoyed a cosy evening commlink with Delysia, who was able to bring me up to date with the latest news– the newest of which concerned Lord Topher's marriage to his beautiful young blonde.

"It's a great pity," said Delysia, inclined to be resentful. "I was *sure* he favoured you, Belle! There's no understanding it!"

"Delysia! Of all the unkind tricks to play on a boy of only twenty or so years! To marry him to an old maid at least seven years his senior, when such a beautiful young creature was around!"

"Well, I dare say he married her for her money," she said, with dark foreboding. "No doubt she'll sink into a decline when he runs through it all, and die a young mother."

"What a delightful picture of wedded bliss! I must

remember to send them a homecoming gift: when are they due to come back?"

"Oh, some time this week," replied Delysia airily. "He's had his townhouse all new-furnished, you know, just for her."

"I'm glad to hear it!" I said frankly, remembering vaguely a description of Lord Topher's quarters as sailor like and sparsely furnished. That would never do for such a beautiful young thing as Miss Dewhurst; even if she *was* merely a Miss. I hoped he had had enough sense to furnish in blue and acorn shades of wood to complement her. "What are you sending for a homecoming gift, Delysia?"

Delysia shrugged elegantly. "A vase, perhaps. Something ugly for their children to break. Oh, Isabella! It's horribly boring here without you! Harroll is gloomy and tiresome, and I'm in need of stimulating conversation. What is Annabel doing about this business? And is Lord Pecus horrid?"

"Lord Pecus is *quite* horrid!" I confirmed, my lips curving. I never tired of Delysia: perhaps because she had the attention span of a squirrel. *Isn't my fur nice and glossy this morning, and the grass is so green— ooh, a nut!* "He teases me, and takes great delight in putting me at a loss. However, since he sees fit to purchase the most luxurious and delicious blends of tea, and has the *dearest* little teapot besides, I find it easy to forgive him. Why is Harroll tiresome, my dear?"

She tossed her head. "Oh well, I'm sure I'm a bad wife, but Isabella! I do so *detest* children!"

"Harroll wants children?"

"It's not as if *he* will have to change the vile little things!" continued Delysia with a martial gleam in her eye, completely disregarding the fact that it was unlikely in the extreme that she would ever be called upon to do so. No, if I knew Delysia, any child in her home would be recurrently attended by a nurse.

"No, he will sit with them after dinner and bounce them upon his knee, and say 'What a good boy you are, eh?' and send them off to bed!"

"Perhaps you will have a little girl?" I suggested, for once all at sea. Delysia's reference to more than one child was confusing: she could not be certain that she would have twins.

"No, it is two nasty little boys," she said obstinately. "Ugly little things, too, Belle!"

"I'm sure they will not be ugly, Delysia!"

She opened her eyes wide at me. "But they already are! Two of the nastiest little urchins I ever laid eyes on! I'm not surprised their parents died, no doubt they wanted a bit of peace and quiet!"

I repressed a strong desire to giggle. How like Delysia. "Which of Harroll's relatives have quit this mortal coil?"

"The only coil I can see at present is my own!" she retorted. "They're well out of it. And they are *not* Harroll's relatives, Belle, they are *mine*! One should be allowed to disown one's own relatives, after all!"

"Certainly one should." I said soothingly. "But Delysia, only think how charming they will look when the picnic season is upon us. Dressed in white, you know, with their collars freshly starched."

"I know exactly how long fresh-starched collars will last with William and Colin," said Delysia tartly, but a thoughtful gleam had entered her eye. She curled one midnight black curl around a finger. "They will have to wear blue, and that is convenient, I suppose; since it means I won't have to dye my hair. I'm quite fond of being a brunette."

"Now," I said meditatively, as much in my own interests as to take her mind off the iniquitous William and Colin; "*Speaking* of the picnic season–"

"We weren't, and I won't!" said Delysia at once. "What–

ever you're trying to do to Lord Pecus, I won't be pulled into it!"

"Delysia, you shock me! In fact, you injure me!" I gazed at her for a long, melting moment. "To imagine that I would attempt to do anything to my protector, my dinner partner; in fact, my provider of tea-and-biscuits! They are not merely biscuits, Delysia, they are works of art!"

She pursed her lips and returned my melting gaze with a shrewd one. "Well, I've never known you to risk a good biscuit. What do you want?"

"The tiniest favour, my dear! Merely that you allow Susan to come to me for a picnic near the end of the week, without forcing a footman upon her. I assure you that I don't mean the least harm to Lord Pecus."

"I'm sure I don't know how to *force* Susan to do anything!" returned Delysia, stiffening. "Isabella, she will *not* mind me!"

"She doesn't mind you?" I raised my brows, mildly surprised. That didn't sound like Susan. "Well, she has been a long time at home alone, thanks to my erratic and highly unreliable brother. She doesn't like to be dictated to if she thinks she knows better."

"We-eell," Delysia admitted, in a milder tone; "She doesn't *refuse* to do as I say, exactly. She merely ducks out of the house before I have a chance to tell her things! And *then*, Isabella; and *then* when I go to tell her what she's doing wrong, somehow I never remember what I was going to say! Mind you," she added fairmindedly, "I do have to thank her for the tip she gave me on removing that awful wine spot from my favourite white crepe. And the sale at Purcell's was where I got that simply gorgeous hat, *you* know."

I did know. It sounded very like Susan: *Misdirect and Conquer* was her watchword. I, of course, had had absolutely *nothing* to do with teaching her any such thing.

"I've even tried sending her notes!" said Delysia, beginning to smile in spite of herself. "She says she hasn't received them."

I bit my lip: that particular trick I *had* taught Susan. Footmen by and large are obedient and unwilling to put themselves forward. It is, consequently, the easiest thing in the world to officially *not receive* a note. One need only direct a footman to place it on the sill of an open window (where it might, unhappily, chance to be blown away) or give instructions for the note to be placed with others on a desk (where it most likely became lost in the other papers). So long as the note has not been passed into one's hands, one is able to say legally (and really quite truthfully), that one has not 'received' the note. Evidently Susan had become a past master at not receiving communications. Fortunately for my blushes, Delysia did not probe further. Instead, she fell into a fit of reminiscence regarding the hat she had worn with her riding habit before the advent of that simply wonderful hat from Purcell's; and before long I was able to bid her goodnight, severing the commlink.

It buzzed again almost immediately, much to my annoyance. To my further annoyance, the face that clouded and formed in Delysia's wake was that of Lord Topher; who, even if he were no longer in love with me and making a nuisance of himself, was still a nuisance in and of himself. I wanted to go to bed meditating smugly upon my own cleverness. Instead, I met his sparkling brown eyes, wary at their high good humour, and said a polite good evening.

"I did as you said, Lady Farrah! You were right, she is beautiful!"

I wondered if he had been drinking again, or if it was merely the fact that I had become embittered and elderly that made him seem so uncommonly alive. I supposed a bridegroom should be happy the month of his wedding, but found in myself a wish that he could have done so in the company of his wife, and left me to my bed.

"I'm entirely happy to hear it," I told him truthfully.

He gave me a glittering smile, leaning into the commlink, and said confidentially: "I knew you would be. I think we shall be very happy, you know: this makes everything perfect."

I couldn't help smiling a little at his exuberance, and since I was quite soon able to extricate myself from the commlink without hurting his feelings, I was left to think that the evening hadn't gone so very badly after all.

I undressed and slipped my nightgown over my head with a thoughtful languor, forbearing to wake Vadim for such a trifle, and settled myself luxuriously into bed just a few moments later. It had been a day of interest, leaving me feeling decidedly cat-with-cream-ish because it seemed as though I finally knew my way forward again. I had been slowed but not stopped by my residence in Pecus Manor: I was once more rising triumphant. Of course, it would be a different matter entirely if the Earl of Horn had nothing helpful to add; but at that moment I felt that I had truly begun again to find Raoul's killer.

I woke with the same warm feeling of satisfaction, and breakfasted with great energy upon a Glausian specialty I was beginning to love: thick slices of fried bread topped with bacon and a wonderful kind of sugar-sauce I had never before encountered in Civet. I had been dubious at first, since the idea of sweet with savoury was an unfamiliar one, but I had been won over with the first warm, sweet mouthful, delighting in the subtle hints of cinnamon and nutmeg, and savouring the glazed orange and fresh strawberries that decorated the dish. It was only, in fact, by an extreme exercise of self-control that I contained my appetite for the dish. It would be unfortunate if I were to become fat and comfortable under Lord Pecus' roof. Perhaps that was his intention, who knows? Certainly if I were comfortably plump I would have neither the energy nor the inclination to make a nuisance of myself.

It was with an air of expectancy that I dressed myself before the children began to stir. I was sure I would hear from Susan today. Nor was I disappointed: shortly after my breakfast tray was taken away, and Vadim had made an appearance to brush and pin my hair, my commlink sprang into life, displaying Susan's grinning face.

"You owe me about two gross of trayed chocolates," she said. "Set your picnic for the day after tomorrow, Belle, and lay out places for three."

She was preoccupied and didn't talk for long, cutting off the link after a few brief instructions on the best place to meet the earl, and how to smuggle him through Lord Pecus' wards (how she had gained the information was a mystery to me); and I wondered amusedly just what she was up to. I refrained from questioning her since I would hardly have relished enquiries if I were in her place, and took myself out into the garden. It was peaceful under the shade, and I wandered through the labyrinthine hedges until I came across a side of Pecus Manor I had not before encountered. There the laundry, flapping to a light breeze in all its unabashed glory, fluttered laces and underwear to the surrounding courtyard while Damson grimly pegged with all the good humour of an elephant with a head cold. Her lips were set in an annoyed line, and there was a snap to her eyes, suggesting that her problems with her gentleman friend had not abated.

"So this is where you exist after fire-lighting," I said, gazing around the little courtyard with interest. It was ridiculous, of course, to assume that Damson's only duties were those regarding the fires and scullery; but I *had* assumed it.

Damson's head snapped around, and she pegged her finger instead of the stocking she was holding. "My lady! I didn't see you there!"

My eyes danced. "No, you were too busy pinning down the washing."

She planted one fist on her hip, regarding me in silence, and then gave an angry laugh. "It's more than enough, so it is, my lady, when your beau begins to tell you what to do."

"Beaux have a tendency to do so," I told her sympathetically. "It's part of being in love."

"Well, I don't call it love to tell a person her face isn't good enough!" Damson said angrily. "I know it's not my own face, but what does he want with my real face?"

I readjusted my ideas and found myself intrigued. "Your beau wants to see your real face? Well now, that's not quite what I was expecting. Can you not remove your mask?"

She shook her head. "It's part of the Manor. Only the master can un-spell the masks, and that won't happen until–"

"Until?"

"Until forever!" Damson rejoined darkly, sniffing. "It's comfortable, lady. I *like* wearing a mask."

"I take it your gentleman friend is less favourably inclined toward the masks."

The lip of her mask trembled. "He showed me his real face. He said that he's going to keep his mask that way now."

So I had been right: the servants *could* change the appearance of their masks as they pleased. "I begin to quite like your young man, Damson. Didn't you like his face?"

This time a tear trickled down her porcelain cheek, and I watched it in fascination. "I didn't, lady! What does he want to go and do that for? I won't show him my face, I won't!"

"What is it you're afraid of, Damson?"

Damson sat down beside her wash basket and hugged her knees. "I don't know." She traced the paisley of her skirt with one finger, and gave another sniff, this one more watery. "What if he thinks me as ugly as I think him?"

I sank down beside her on the mossy tiles, resolutely not thinking of the damage to my gown, and rested my back against the Manor wall. "What if he does?"

She gave a surprised hiccough. "I don't want him to think me ugly!"

"Oh, it's too late for that now," I told her quietly. "Now that he's started thinking, he'll never be satisfied with a pretty canvas again. Do you love him?"

"Yes!" she said, too surprised to equivocate. "Oh yes, lady!"

"Well then," I said briskly, rising and sorting through the washing. "It seems you have only two choices."

I pegged a second stocking beside the lone one Damson had left, and she trailed after me. "What do you mean, lady?"

"I mean that you must either lose him, or show him your face and begin to learn his."

"I don't understand, lady."

Promising! She hadn't given the idea of losing her beau a moment's consideration: she really did love him. "There's a disadvantage to your masks," I told her, pinning to the line a pair of drawers of a truly impressive size. "You've lived so long with them that you've forgotten the way a real face moves; all the little lines that make up an expression, and all the shades of colour. You see perfect white and perfect smiles, and perfect teeth. I see walking marionettes."

"I used to have nightmares like that," Damson said, looking rather thoughtful. "When I first came here I used to dream that every night. Then I forgot."

"Now you must begin to remember. Show him your face.

Don't be afraid: he will think you beautiful. And you— begin to learn what his face looks like when he's delighted, or when he's angry, or happy. Study him."

Damson wrapped her arms defensively around herself and rocked on the balls of her feet, thinking in silence. She flicked a look up at me. "Can I show you first, lady?"

No doubt Damson's beau would have been jealous of the first sight, but no doubt also he would prefer her to show him her face at all.

"Certainly," I said, appropriating the last stocking. Now there remained only sheets to be done: a two person job that would be very useful in just a moment. Damson spread her hands over her mask, heaving a sigh, and then pulled them away.

"Well, lady?"

"Sheets," I prompted her gently, sorting corner from corner. Damson had apple pink cheeks and blue eyes in a face that was slightly round but pleasant; a face which at present looked startled as she darted to help me. It was a very different proposition from the mask, with its flawless porcelain features and high, delicate cheekbones.

"Yes, lady. Sorry, lady."

I snapped my side of the sheet briskly, observing her, and then said: "I like it."

She smiled as though she couldn't help it, making her cheeks plumper, and colour glowed. "Would you say that I'm beautiful, lady?"

I considered her for another moment. "No. But then, I don't know that I like beautiful people particularly well. You have a pleasant face— it smiles even when you're not smiling. Any boy worth his salt would be a fool not to appreciate it."

Damson gave a surprised laugh. "I knew you'd tell the

truth. That's why I wanted to show you. Do you think Jason will like me?"

"Dear girl, he showed you his face!" I said tartly. "He opened himself up to you, which means that he will love you no matter what you look like. As to whether he likes your *face* or not, you'll simply have to find out."

She grinned, and for once I saw the true Damson, with lights in her eyes and dimples in her cheeks. "Yes, lady. Thank you, lady."

❧

THE DAY OF THE PICNIC ARRIVED, BOTH WARM AND cloudless, with a light summer breeze that teased through my hair when I stepped briefly out onto my terrace. The weather didn't matter in the slightest, of course, since my objective for picnicking was purely investigative, but I found myself cheered despite that fact. I hadn't been woken unseasonably early, by which I inferred that Damson and her beau were getting along well once again. I found myself very well pleased with the change, though I did wonder if she had begun to wear her own face yet.

In fact, it was promising fair to be a wonderful day out, when I received a rude shock in the shape of Lord Pecus' large form. I was walking briskly through the great hall, pinning my hat as I went, and found myself startlingly face to face with him as he entered the great hall from the opposite end.

"Alexander! What a pleasant surprise!"

I gave him my hand to kiss, and he did so with a quirk of the lips.

"Is it? I'm glad to hear it." He gave me a proper smile, and added: "I have a few hours free this afternoon, and cook mentioned your desire for a picnic. As you can see, I'm fully prepared."

I blinked a little at the perfectly huge picnic basket that three footmen were presently struggling to fit through the door. "I shouldn't like to disturb your day," I told him firmly and insincerely. Drat the man! Was it a particular foible of his to always show up when he was least wanted?

He grinned, and said with an even greater firmness and insincerity than mine: "There's nothing I would like better. I insist on accompanying you."

Now where had he learned that I was to meet the earl? For learn it he certainly had: there was no other way of accounting for his sudden and curious presence in the middle of the day. I felt a single pulse of pure anger sear through me, right to my fingertips, but it vanished as suddenly as it had struck. It occurred to me that I knew now how Lord Pecus felt. I gave a chuckle, and resigned myself. Lord Pecus laughed too, but his eyes held a warmness that told me he had noticed the coming and going of the anger, and that he approved of my response.

I was ridiculously pleased at his approval, and so I said pertly: "Very well, but be it upon your own head, Alexander. I shall pick daisies and wildflowers and thread them into positive *ropes*– ropes which you will be forced to hold, mind."

"I will do my humble best," Lord Pecus promised solemnly, and offered his arm.

Much to my surprise, the afternoon was a pleasant one. Susan slumbered peacefully under a conveniently shady tree with her disreputable hat over her face, showing no sign that she had expected quite a different addition to the picnic party, while Vadim and Keenan romped through the daisies, beheading them with joyful kicks and hopping energetically with the cheerful corpses between their toes. I flirted enjoyably with Lord Pecus and let him thread wildflowers through my loose hair. I kept a sharp eye out for the earl, of course, but was not at all surprised when he didn't make an appearance. I let my eyes slit to filter out the triad's rays, leaning on my elbows while Lord Pecus plaited blue and yellow buds into my hair, and thoughtfully considered just how he had come by his knowledge. Had one of the servants overheard Susan and I talking? Worse still, had Vadim, like Marissa, been reporting to a higher power? I didn't like to think so, but since the idea of Lord Pecus listening in on a private commlink was not only laughable but impossible, it must be either one of the two. I made a note to mention the leak to Susan, hoping that the lapse was from her side and not mine, and that the meeting was able to be reset. No doubt the afternoon would afford an opportunity to speak with her, though Lord Pecus watch us never so closely. Meanwhile, there was no reason that I shouldn't enjoy myself.

Susan woke a little after I had sneakily finished the last of the chocolates, and discovering herself bereft, began flicking flower-heads at me. I laughed and fended them off, realising in some amusement as I did so, that the flowers came in volleys of three, then two, then three again. Susan was using an old code of ours to tell me that she needed to speak to me. I rolled my eyes at her as if to say *Of course you do, ninny!* glad that Lord Pecus was behind me where he was unable to see my face. I flicked four flower heads back at her, then scattered the entire contents of my lap in her general direction. It meant: *Pay attention. Final instructions to follow.* If I recalled the code aright, and Susan recalled it as correctly, my next remark should consist of a new meeting place and time.

"This reminds me of the time we sneaked out of the house to attend the third annual village fair," I said lazily, and not entirely mendaciously. There had certainly been a lot of flowers thrown, but it had been dark, and there had been lights threaded through the lanes of the fair.

"It wasn't so hard once we got past the two ticket-collectors, was it?"

Susan laughed, and I knew she had understood. Day and time were established. "We were beastly little kids, weren't we? Where did Papa catch up with us?"

I shrugged carelessly. "Oh, somewhere near that fountain in the square. Don't you remember? I pushed you in."

There was the rumble of Lord Pecus' laughter behind me. "You have my sympathies," he said to Susan. "Your sister constantly does the same thing to me."

"I've yet to push you into a fountain," I reminded him mildly, tilting my head back to smile at him.

"No," he agreed; "But the general sensation is much the same. Cold shock, followed by a moment of wild splashing before I find my feet."

I gave him another companionable smile, presenting as innocuous an appearance as I could, and turned my head to wink naughtily at Susan. Three days away, two o'clock in the morning, at the fountain in the city square. The meeting was set. Now I had only to discover exactly how Lord Pecus had gained his intelligence, and prevent such a thing from happening again.

Chapter Sixteen

Susan left us not long after the chocolates ran out. When I berated her upon the fair weather nature of her companionship, she admitted it cheerfully and refused to be contrite as she untied her horse. She had obtained a tiny, broad-backed little pony from heaven only knows where, since Glausian horses tend more to the large and grand. It had a hard, speculative gleam to its black eyes that suggested that it didn't like you, and that you'd better watch out if you knew what was good for you. Much to my own surprise, I found that I quite liked the beast, and though it bared its teeth and shook its head when Lord Pecus approached too near, I held this to be indicative of an intelligent nature rather than a defect.

Lord Pecus, of course, did not move out of earshot from us: I had expected nothing less. I made it easier for him by tucking my hand through the crook of his arm and including him amiably in the conversation, which made Lord Pecus grin a porcelain grin, and Susan smirk. We walked her as far as the front gate, where Emmett had come to meet her, his figure and his horse both dwarfing hers; but Susan's pony was a quick, determined trotter, and before they had shrunk from view the pony was jogging in the lead. Emmett, evidently resigned to the indignity, did not attempt to push his horse.

"It must run in the family," said Lord Pecus, as we turned to stroll back to the house.

I gave him a sparkling look. "What is that?"

"The desire to nose-lead the rest of the world," he explained, removing his mask. "It's your most similar feature."

I chose to leave this sally unmolested, and merely grinned up at him. I was not sure quite how it had happened, but somehow my hand had become clasped in his instead of tucked in the crook of his arm, and the absentminded stroke of his thumb against mine tickled. "Just think how bored you'd be without me," I said instead, swinging his hand gently. "Well, what shall we do with the rest of the afternoon?"

Lord Pecus looked rueful. "I have reports to read," he said.

"Oh, and I thought you were so lacking for something to do this afternoon! What a shame we wasted so many hours picnicking!"

He gave me a startlingly roguish grin. "I can't say that I've ever considered time in your company to be wasted, Isabella. Added to the benefit of learning something new every time I speak with you is the thought that while my eyes are on you, you can't be getting up to mischief."

I could have begged to differ, but since the act of doing so would have left myself open to some rather difficult questions, I forbore to remark that I had managed my mischief under his eyes quite well, and instead offered sweetly to read the reports with him. "Just think how quickly we'd get through them with two sets of eyes!" I told him. I didn't expect him to agree, of course, nor was I really averse to being left alone: there were affairs that needed to be attended to and snares that needed to be laid.

"While I have no doubt I would enjoy that more than poring over the reports myself–"

"You must decline my assistance," I finished for him, nodding. "Very right and proper of you. The Watch must be delighted to have such an unerring and upright Commander."

I could see his face suddenly very clearly: the brows had pinched together momentarily in a stricken look, prompting me to add severely: "I am *hoaxing* you, Alexander, not being snide. If you're going to be serious and boring, I shall have to treat you like a dignitary, and that would be a pity."

"I'm not so delicate," he said calmly, as if he had not just gone perfectly white. The line between his brows vanished, and it occurred to me with some amusement that he didn't know I could see his real face. Well now, *there* was an advantage. "I can't say that I've noticed a great deal of difference in how you treat dignitaries, however. Melchior seems to agree."

"Melchior exaggerates: I am perfectly diplomatic when it comes to dignitaries. I'm also usually quite bored, and I can't say that I've ever been bored in your company, Alexander. You make me work far too hard to be bored."

"I'm glad to know that you have to strive for the level of importunity you've achieved," remarked Lord Pecus. "If you were only amusing yourself, I would hate to think what you would achieve when you really set your mind to it."

"Chaos!" I said simply, gazing at him with limpid eyes. I took the first step toward my suite, but couldn't climb any higher than this because Lord Pecus seemed still to be holding my hand. He chuckled and kissed the hand that was still clasped in his, holding it against very human lips a little longer than was strictly necessary.

It was with a slight flush, therefore, that I skipped away up the stairs, waving carelessly and trying to suppress the tingling his kiss had elicited. I arrived at my suite without having done so with any success, but fortunately I was given no further chance to meditate on the matter. When I entered my suite, Keenan was sprawled on my bed, leaving dirty smudges on my sheets and levitating a suspiciously familiar rock above his head while Vadim watched with narrow-eyed interest. Good heavens! They had been exploring Lord Pecus' private chambers! I opened my mouth to tell them in no uncertain terms that they were a pair of desperate characters who would no doubt end up in the Watch House, but before I could do so, Keenan saw me, and with bright eyes declared: "Look, lady! No hands!"

"Very clever of you," I said, suddenly thankful that Lord Pecus had not chosen to walk me up the stairs. "What are you doing with the Earl of Horn's dynamo?"

"S'not me, see?" grinned Keenan. He pawed with both hands at the space between himself and the dynamo. It revolved, slowly at first, and then more swiftly. "It's sort of *pushin'* against me magic."

"As interesting as I find your discovery, I must ask again: what are you doing with the Earl of Horn's dynamo? Where did you get it?"

Keenan gulped, but to do him justice, did not attempt to prevaricate. "Got it from the Beast Lord's rooms."

"Do you know, I'm almost certain I warned against entering any of Lord Pecus's private rooms."

Vadim by this time was pink and ashamed, but Keenan said with the air of one making a discovery: "I fort you just meant not to get *caught*."

"Did you so? Then let me undeceive you at once! Lord Pecus' rooms and any subsidiary thereof, are strictly out of bounds. Is that clear enough for you?"

The little imp actually thought about it for a moment. Then he said with judicious slowness: "Yeah, I reckon. Want me to put it back?"

I strove momentarily and successfully for a straight face. "Certainly I do."

"Only I don't think I can," Keenan confided, with the air of one about to relate an anecdote that should be of interest to his hearers. "'E's there."

"I beg your pardon?"

"'E's *there*, whenever I go back. Just sittin' and readin'. I think 'e knows."

"I've no doubt that he knows," I said crisply, repressing the desire to pull Keenan upright by his ears. "No doubt he knew as soon as he entered the room. Which of Lord Pecus' rooms did you remove the dynamo from?"

"The office one," Vadim said, clearing her throat. "Only, lady, he didn't have any traps set. There was nothing on the dynamo, and no wards on his doors."

"Lord Pecus undoubtedly has other methods of securing his privacy," I told her dryly, remembering a little ruefully the early days after Trenthams. Papa and I had travelled quite extensively in the name of New Civet and Annabel; and many of the further countries we had visited had not yet discovered magic and its many uses. Consequently I had become versed in many of the alternate methods of security: some of which I still implemented after my own fashion. "In fact, I'm quite certain that any door in Pecus Manor that is heavily enough warded to attract attention will not prove to be worth the bother of unwarding."

Keenan blinked a few times and then stared ferociously at a bedpost, his chin tucked in one palm, lost in thought. At length a grin crept subtly over his narrow little face, and he rubbed his hands together. "Ooh, that's good, that is!" he said, in admiration. "Wot's 'e use, then?"

"You can ask him when you take the dynamo back," I said firmly, motioning him off the bed and toward the door.

Keenan stopped short at the door, looking doubtful. "Wot if 'e eats me?"

"Then he'll still be hungry for dinner," muttered Vadim caustically. "You're no more than a mouthful. Do what you're told, you nasty little boy."

"I'm more'n a mouthful!" objected Keenan, deeply offended. "I'm *tough*!"

I ignored Vadim's aside of: *'Stringy, more like'* to inquire somewhat sardonically if Keenan was so anxious to be eaten. Upon his wide-eyed, gulping shake of the head, I said calmly: "Then it is a moot point. I will accompany you, if only to make sure that your sticky fingers don't attach themselves to anything else."

Keenan was subdued as we strolled through the labyrinth of corridors. I could have reassured him, I suppose, but I didn't think it was a bad idea for him to live in fear for a few moments. He was becoming a little too cheeky for his own good. I was rueful but resigned to the idea of Lord Pecus finding out the profligate habits of my servants: that he found out from my own lips was essential. I didn't want him to think for a moment that I had encouraged my servants to pry about his private quarters. Of course, I *had* encouraged them to pry around the house in general, but that was another matter, and quite acceptable etiquette for a house prisoner. Still, I wasn't entirely calm as we approached Lord Pecus' office. I wasn't sure if my unease related to the fact that Keenan had been looking around his personal office, or if it was because of that kiss. It was a lowering thought, but I was beginning to think it was the kiss. Ridiculous! He had kissed my hand, and if that kiss had lasted a little longer than it should, what of it? There was nothing in it to make me lose my reason. I gave myself a mental shake, and pinned a glare on Keenan, who squirmed and offered a glum: "Sorry, lady."

"Not as sorry as I, believe me, Keenan. You are a hopeless case."

He seemed to take this as encouragement, for he beamed, and said in a satisfied manner: "*Yes, lady!*" as I raised my hand to knock at the office door. It was sturdy Glausian oak, perhaps several inches thick, and my bold knock was swallowed up and regurgitated into an unimpressive tapping.

Despite the softness of the sound, Lord Pecus' voice called immediately: "Enter!"

He was leaning back in a massive leather chair by a garden-facing window, maskless and with a small sheaf of papers held casually in one hand, but when we entered he put them on the arm of his chair and observed our approach, one eyebrow raised. He couldn't have missed the dynamo in Keenan's grubby hand, but it didn't seem as if his eyes left my face.

"I shouldn't be surprised," he said. "I know I shouldn't. But I am."

Keenan's mouth opened in an 'o' of surprise at the first sight of Lord Pecus' dual faces. He managed to say: "Oi! Your face is all—" before I curled a swift hand around his mouth and jerked him back admonishingly. Lord Pecus' amused eyes travelled from me to Keenan and back again, and he tilted his head, inviting explanation.

"Keenan seems to have wrangled one of my prohibitions into an invitation," I informed him, responding automatically to the smile in his eyes with one of my own. Keenan mutely held out the dynamo, his eyes very wide over the gag of my hand. "I do apologise, Alexander. It won't happen again."

"I did wonder exactly what you wanted with it," he admitted, still with that lurking smile. "And why you thought I wouldn't notice."

"I wonder why you thought I would do such a thing," I retorted. "No, don't answer that question; I don't want to know. No, Keenan, I have not forgotten you."

Keenan made another muffled noise, and then, disgustingly, licked my hand. I wiped the defiled member pointedly in his hair. "Yes, Keenan? Do you have a question?"

"Couldn't breeve!" he protested sulkily. "Wotcher do that for?"

"Keenan, have I ever given you any indication that my actions are open for questioning? No? Then I will trouble you to keep silent."

He subsided, shoulders hunched, and looked so crushed that I found it necessary to lay my hand on his head again briefly.

"Keenan apologises most humbly," I said to Lord Pecus.

"Yes, I can see that. I think you said something about my face?"

Keenan threw a cautious look up at me, and said judiciously: "Well, it's a bit ugly, innit?"

I choked, and Lord Pecus' grin widened.

"So I'm told. Your mistress thinks otherwise, don't you, Isabella?"

Keenan shrugged, indicating the unreliability of females in the matter of judging looks. "Well, she's a girl, though."

"I believe I said that I had seen uglier," I told Lord Pecus reprovingly.

"Mm." Lord Pecus leaned back in his chair and folded his arms. "Comparing me with Lord Morston, if I remember rightly. Thank you for that, by the way."

"Favourably," I reminded him, with a touch of amusement.

"Come, Keenan. Now that you've apologised,"—here I had to ignore Lord Pecus' one pointedly raised eyebrow—"We can be going. I shall turn you over to Lord Pecus' mercy if it happens again."

Lord Pecus was still grinning, suggesting that his mercies were nothing to be feared, but Keenan didn't notice and was suitably subdued as we left the study: a state of mind that was not, alas, likely to last long. By the time we regained my suite he had already begun bouncing impatiently along the hall, and when I sent both he and Vadim off to bed, it was with a distinct feeling of relief. I had forgotten the unpleasant habit children have of sweeping the rug out from under one, and Vadim was looking a little pinched and quiet, reminding me that I had been rather quiet with her myself since the picnic. I simply couldn't help feeling a little cautious, and poor Vadim was going to have to suffer for it.

Fortunately she didn't raise the issue, retiring to bed quietly while I settled myself in my most comfortable chair for the purpose of a quick conversation with Annabel via my inkless scroll. It would only have been for the dubious pleasure of laughing at my own discomfiture, however, and I instead found myself meditating quietly on the events of the day. I had the niggling idea that I'd missed something important. The idea grew on me, and I unaccountably called to mind the remembrance of Keenan, spinning the Earl of Horn's dynamo above him. I followed the thought, and found myself wondering just what this particular dynamo powered. The countess had warbled about boxes with moving pictures and commlinks without magic, and I wondered if it had been powering something like a commlink. Someone in the earl's business (which I firmly suspected to be treason) would find it excessively useful to have a communications device that was unable to be eavesdropped upon magically. With all that falling water in the room, it would be next to impossible to maintain any kind of espionage magic. No doubt that explained the one quiet point in the room: the waterfall room was the earl's council-of-war chamber. I thought about this for some minutes, regretting the unlikelihood of finding any Interesting Excerpts on treasonous conversations that would likely not be referenced in any other way than verbally, until it occurred to me that it was very remiss of the king not to be up to every discovery of the day, magical or otherwise. No, the king was not remiss. Could it be possible, I wondered, in kindling excitement, that some of the king's agents had managed to use the earl's own inventions against him? An open commlink that wouldn't show up on a magical scan was rather a double-edged sword, in fact: the earl would most likely never have known it was there.

I bounced out of my chair and dashed to fetch the *Book of Interesting Excerpts.* And, do you know, there *were* surveillance reports from the earl's waterfall room. I gave a naughty chuckle as I made myself comfortable for a long evening in my chair, wondering if Lord Pecus had known about these reports and shrewdly suspecting not. The king did tend to keep his own council.

I skimmed the reports with both interest and a steely determination not to be distracted by the juicier paragraphs. Good heavens, had the earl really been in contact with persons unknown in both Civet and Broma? I blinked a little and continued to scan. I was more interested in who had been in contact with the earl than the content of the conversations, but unhappily for me they tended to use code names even in conversation—exasperating man, the earl!—and I was only able to make the wildest guesses. The content of the reports, however treasonous, didn't seem particularly pertinent to my case, however, and by the time I had read to the last report I found myself less inclined than ever to believe that the earl had had any part in Raoul's murder. Sighing, I closed the *Book of Interesting Excerpts*, and went to bed with only the vaguest feeling of impending unpleasantness on the morrow.

GOODNESS KNOWS IT HURT TO DO SO, BUT AFTER MARISSA I couldn't take the chance: the next morning I sent Vadim to Susan with a message to be prepared tomorrow night with the earl. Susan would know it to be false, and if Lord Pecus knew my plans a second time, I would have my leak. I found myself fervently hoping that he did not: I had become quite fond of Vadim and Keenan.

When they were both gone, I opened a commlink to Susan, who was not at home but had evidently expected my link, for she answered at once.

"Wotcher, Belle!" Her face was flushed with exercise for all that she was sitting demurely at a café table, and I wondered for a wistful moment what she had been up to. I had been too long out of the action.

"How's the merger proceeding?" I asked her. Whether or not my call was simply for the purpose of running tests, there was no reason for it not to be informative. Besides, I wanted to know how Susan had managed with the Mage General.

She grinned. "Oh, pretty well, pretty well. The General's going on in great strides, swinging his little swagger stick for all he's worth and barging along. You were right: he doesn't seem to care in which direction he goes striding, so long as he's striding."

"What madness did you have him chasing?"

"He seems to be under the impression that the Civetan

Council is trying for small Embassy-like plots through the length and breadth of Glause; *you* know, Civetan soil and so forth. He got quite testy, actually. I think they might have been a bit embarrassed, Belle; in the end poor little Harroll got very red in the face and told the General to shut up before he embarrassed Glause thoroughly, and while the General was being bemused at that, he accidentally gave his vote for all our measures. We've gotten to the second stage at last."

"Oh well done!" I told her approvingly. Poor Papa! Whatever had he done to deserve two such conniving females? I could not have done any better had I been there myself. "How is Emmett holding up?"

Susan tilted her commlink to include Emmett's large, stoical form, and put an arm chummily through his. "What do you think, lummox? Are you managing?"

Emmett took it with an unmoved demeanour, but unbent enough to grin at me. "Hallo, Belle."

"You shouldn't let her get away with it," I warned him. "She'll only get worse, you know."

"I shudder to think," he said, closing his eyes for a brief moment. "If your mother was anything like the two of you, I'm surprised it was she and not your father who went to an early grave."

"So was everyone," I nodded, causing Susan to grin. "If you become too overwhelmed, just say furlough. Furlough is good for a half-holiday every week, but they don't accrue, so make sure you take them."

Susan laughed. "Oh, I remember that. Whenever we got too much for Mama, she'd claim she had a furlough due, and we all got locked out."

Emmett threw her a look that was at once tired and a little bit fond. "Sensible lady."

"There you go, lummox; whenever I become too much to handle, just call a furlough."

He sat back, folding his arms in an unspoken, definite negative.

Susan beamed at him. "Lummox! I knew you loved me! Isn't he sweet, Belle, he doesn't want me to get hurt."

"I'm more worried about the citizenry of Glause," muttered Emmett.

"Don't try denying it, lummox, you'll only make it worse for yourself. Speaking of lummoxes, how's the Beast Lord?"

Emmett choked on a mouthful of ham sandwich, and I chuckled. "As sharp as ever, I'm afraid. I've been obliged to send Vadim to you, Su: but I find that I've told her the wrong day. So thoughtless of me!"

She cocked one eyebrow at me. "Careless of you, Belle! What day should I expect her to say?"

"Tomorrow night."

"I see. Do we make it for tonight?"

"It's as good a time as any other," I said prosaically, and Susan's grey eyes rested on me for a thoughtful moment. I felt a slight breath of relief: she had understood me. "I don't suppose there were any leaks on your end?"

She shook her head, and I shrugged. "It was worth the question. I'm a trifle annoyed, Su."

"The Beast Lord keeping you on your toes, is he?"

"Regrettably so. Scintillating though an even match of wits is to me, I find myself wishing he were just a *little* less perspicacious."

"You don't mean that, Belle, I know you don't," Susan said, grinning. "You'd be bored out of your mind in no time. What will you do when it's all over?"

I frowned a little, feeling oddly off balance. "What do you mean?"

"After you catch your murderer. What will you do then?"

"Go home, I suppose," I told her, trying to shake off the sudden gloom that had fallen on me. "Now that you've got the merger well in hand I can go visit Kit in whichever far-flung corner of the world he's fetched up. That should provide ample opportunity for excitement, I imagine."

"Oh. I thought you were going to marry Lord Pecus." She elbowed Emmett, and jerked a thumb at me. "Didn't you think Belle was going to marry Lord Pecus?"

"Yes," said Emmett, without quibbling.

"I don't know why you should imagine so, since he hasn't asked me!" I said tartly, but was forced in good conscience to add: "Lately, anyway. I must say that I've been tempted to spread rumours."

Susan nodded at Emmett. "Told you she'd be thinking about it. I hate to say it, Belle, but I think you're right at the centre of all this."

"Yes, Lord Pecus said the same thing some time ago: hence, my idea of rumours. I wonder if I should be flattered or worried that a bloody and quite probably insane murderer has a fixation on me?"

"Curran says you're two of a kind," said Susan, causing Emmett to smirk.

"No doubt that accounts for it," I replied calmly. "Now, if you're *quite* finished insulting me, I have a delicate job for you."

"Rumours," nodded Susan, unsurprised. "I don't want to be the one to put a kink in your plans, Belle, but it's not going to be safe."

"I believe that's the point," I said. "We *want* the murderer to come and find me."

To my surprise, Susan still looked mulish. "Investigating a

murder is one thing: luring a deranged killer to come and get you is another. What does Lord Pecus think of it?”

“Lord Pecus doesn’t know,” I said, narrowing my eyes at her: “Of which you are very well aware. I've no intention of drawing the killer after Alexander, if that’s what you’re thinking.”

“The Beast Lord can look after himself.” Susan sounded impatient. “He’s a big boy. What will you do?”

“Try not to die,” I said, and closed the link. I would have been annoyed if the unexpected sweetness of Susan’s concern hadn’t tickled my sense of the absurd. I only hoped that she would spread the rumours for me despite her objections: it was time to become proactive in my approach. It is all very well to sit back and wait for your perpetrator to make a wrong move, but so far as I could see, all *that* approach had achieved was more bodies.

Shortly after Vadim returned to me from Susan, just a little more silent than last night, Delysia arrived with much pomp and splendour in a simply enormous hat which was plumed so high that it brushed against the ceiling.

“How very dramatic!” I said admiringly.

Delysia paused to clasp her hands and cast her eyes heavenward. “Isabella! You’ll never guess! There’s been another murder!”

“I would have guessed,” I told her dryly, and she abandoned her pose to put a hand on either hip.

“That’s not the part you’ll never guess, silly! Who do you think it was?”

“Delysia.”

Delysia was petulant. “Oh well, if you *will* look at me like I’m a naughty little girl!”

“I refuse to guess the identity of a murder victim, Delysia. What has happened?”

"You're no fun since you've been locked up, Isabella," pouted Delysia, ignoring my question. "It's bad for your constitution: you should get out more."

I favoured her with a long, drawn-out smile. "Yes, Delysia?"

"*Yes!* Oh." She bit her lip. "I'm sorry, Isabella, I didn't mean it like that."

"I shall carry on, wounded but brave. Who has been murdered?"

"Poor Lady Topher! The servants found her this morning, all over the bedroom floor. The maids haven't stopped having hysterics yet."

I sat down with rather a jolt. Ideas were spinning in my head, round and round, making no sense. Right at the back of my mind was the horrible thought that somehow, this was my fault. "The poor child! Married barely a month! How is Lord Topher taking it?"

"He doesn't know yet," Delysia said, sombre now. "The Watch has been trying to get in contact with him all morning."

"Where is he?"

"I don't know," said Delysia, a dissatisfied line between her brows. "Harroll won't tell me."

"Typical! Lord Pecus is just the same. I can guarantee he won't mention the matter to me tonight unless I mention it first. Something ought to be done about it!"

"You're *always* doing something about it," opined Delysia unexpectedly. "Ever since I've known you you've been doing something about it, no matter what *it* happens to be at the time."

"Do you know, I think you're right. How very proactive and forward-thinking of me! Will future generations erect a statue to me, do you suppose?"

"More than likely," she said frankly; "But not for the reasons you suppose, Belle! I'm only surprised that it's taken this long for someone to lock you up."

"For crimes not my own," I pointed out, firmly. "Don't forget that, Delysia!"

"It's probably all they could get you for."

"I wonder if Susan knows?"

Delysia bristled. "She hasn't come home since yesterday, Isabella! If that is *your* idea of proper behaviour there is nothing more to be said, of course; but it is not mine!"

"Susan was out all night, was she? You had better look out, Delysia, there's undoubtedly something in the wind."

"Yes, I thought so," she said darkly. "The trouble is, I'm not sure whether the horselords are a bad influence on her, or if she's a bad influence on them!"

"A little of both, I should imagine. Is she with Emmett?"

"Always! I even have to feed him, Isabella! Do you *know* how much a fully grown horselord eats?"

"Rather significantly less than an overgrown one, and Emmett is nothing if not overgrown. I am surprised, however, to hear that you're suffering from a lack of food, Delysia. Alas, you will have to begin to economise on the plumage of your hats."

Her bosom swelled. "My plumage is not an inordinate expense, thank you very much!"

"Oh, so Harroll has mentioned it, has he?" I remarked, with something very close to a smirk. "Never mind, Delysia, I won't tease you. I am glad, however, that Susan and Emmett seem to be managing together."

Delysia sniffed and seemed unconvinced, but let the matter drop. "Harroll is unaccountable, Isabella!" she said instead, reverting to her former grievance.

"Oh?" I raised my brows invitingly, and patted the seat beside me. "Do tell!"

She popped down next to me on the window seat, the enormous plumage in her hat bobbing perilously close to a gently drifting cobweb that had evidently been too high for the maid. I watched it breathlessly, stifling the urge to giggle like a schoolgirl as Delysia continued crossly: "He's already sent for those wretched children, Isabella! I've told him and I've told him I won't have it, but it makes no difference."

She gave herself an annoyed shake, twitching her skirts, and the feather swayed nearer to the cobweb, stirring it with a light breeze. I had to bite my lip before I could say with any attempt at an even tone: "How very barbaric of him, my dear."

"Well, it is!" declared Delysia, tossing her head. This sent the feather scurrying briskly across the wall and finally carried away the cobweb, much to my delight, leaving the clinging strands to trail behind in the breeze.

"I can't imagine what it must be like to have Harroll do something you don't want him to do," I said, eyeing the feather in fascination. It nodded, and the cobweb floated.

"Now you're just being difficult!" she complained.

"Yes, so I've been told. I enjoy being difficult, it gives one something to strive for."

Delysia gave me a soulful look that almost rivalled that of Keenan begging for food. "You *could* talk to him, Isabella."

"I could," I agreed, laughing; "But I won't. You and Harroll must fight it out between you, I'm afraid."

It could never be said that Delysia is anything but determined. Therefore, it was no surprise to me that she was still trying to inveigle me into speaking with Harroll by the time Vadim arrived to help me dress for dinner. In fact, she was determined enough to follow me when I insisted that I must go down to dinner, and only left when conversation with Lord Pecus' blank, polite mask faltered without any idea of his inviting her to remain for dinner. I gave her a saucy smile as she left, which she returned with a narrowed gaze and pursed lips, and turned to rejoin Lord Pecus. If I were not mistaken, his green eyes were laughing behind the holes in his mask.

"I thought I heard the sounds of trouble," he said. He sounded quite as usual, and the realization that I had been quite right, and that he was *not* intending on telling me about the murder of Lady Topher, cost me a little pang. I debated briefly within myself upon the merits of mentioning the matter myself, and decided, taking my seat with a decided swish of my skirts, that I would not do so. After all, the idea that Lord Pecus was hiding certain information from me was not a surprising one, and I found that I still felt guilty about poor Vadim. There was no good in being unable to take what one, in the vernacular, dished out. Lord Pecus might very well begin to tell me more by-and-by. As for Vadim and the message I had left with her, all that was left to do was wait—and hope that Lord Pecus did not find out.

It is impolite to show too great an interest in what one is served for dinner. It is, of course, equally rude not to notice at all; but a few, light compliments upon the aesthetic quality of the course is generally the extent of such politeness. Lord Pecus, however, had chosen to serve a first course of creamy potato soup, topped with curls of leek and tiny bacon pieces, followed by beautifully crisp vegetables served over potato rosti and tender beef, attended by a perfectly done *jus*; and if he expected to be attended to while I was savouring such delights, he was very soon made aware of his mistake. Perhaps he didn't intend to be taken notice of: he didn't make any great attempt to start a conversation, and once or twice I caught him watching me with a decided smile to his eyes. At last, tipping the last few drops of *jus* onto my tongue, I sighed contentedly and said: "Am I amusing you, Alexander?"

"I've been trying an experiment," he explained, his eyes narrowed in amusement. "It's been a great success, I have to say. It's come to my attention that when your dinner is particularly good, you seem to talk less."

"Oh yes!" I told him airily: "My proclivity for poking my nose into other people's affairs can be traced back to the lack of food in my youth. It was a terrible time, you know; school dinners and a dreadful lack of sweetmeats. When there is nothing for me to eat, I invariably become bored and look about me for something to do. You may safely keep your secrets when I have an excellent dinner."

"I haven't noticed that a good dinner produces miracles, Isabella. It merely makes things easier."

"A *jus* this wonderful is worth contemplating in silence. Besides, the investigation is going quite well—" I acknowledged his raised brow with a small, prim smile, and continued: "And I would have no qualms about continuing at Pecus Manor for as long as your cook continues to produce a *jus* in which I can taste both the butter *and* the wine."

"Is that so?" demanded Lord Pecus with interest, leaning forward on his forearms and observing me with a smile that, much to my annoyance, made my heart skip a beat. "That being the case, I have no scruple in once again inviting you to remain as my wife."

"Alexander, are you *seriously* proposing to me with the enticement of an excellent *jus* each night with dinner?"

"Well, I thought it might make a difference."

I resisted the urge to tell him that if he added the wonderful battered toast-and-bacon for breakfast every morning, he would have a deal, and likewise bit back a number of rash things that I felt very tempted to say; contenting myself merely with observing: "You're hard to discourage, Alexander."

He remained thoughtful for a moment, and then asked: "Is it this?" gesturing briefly at his face with its superimposed beast-face.

"Indirectly," I said. "But you're asking the wrong question."

"So I'm beginning to think. What would be the correct question?"

I opened my mouth to reply, closed it again, and sighed. Drat the *Book of Interesting Excerpts*! It was quite right.

"I don't think I'm allowed to tell you."

Lord Pecus looked speculative. "Would you marry me as I am?"

"Oh yes!" I said encouragingly. "Do go on."

"*Will* you marry me, Isabella?"

I shook my head.

"No, my lord." He looked quizzical, though not discouraged, so I explained. "You're asking the wrong question again."

He took a meditative sip of port. "Do you know how to break the curse?"

"I believe so. There, you see how much *easier* things are when you ask the right questions!"

"I suppose it would be too much to ask of you to tell me how to do so?"

"That's another of the things I don't think I'm allowed to tell you," I said regretfully. "I'm terribly sorry, Alexander; but I'm afraid you're going to have to work it out on your own."

Lord Pecus grinned, and suggested: "But just think, Isabella: you could add truth to your rumours!"

My immediate feeling was one of clear, sweet relief that Vadim had not been the leak. My second thought was one of cold rage: Lord Pecus *had* been listening in on my commlinks! "How. *Dare*. You!" I said, through my teeth.

Lord Pecus set his port glass down carefully, and ran one hand ruefully through his hair. "Yes, I was afraid you'd catch that. I expected you to catch me out sooner, as a matter of fact."

"How dare you listen to my private conversations!" I said, in a voice so tight with rage that the words had to be forced out. I was terribly afraid that I would begin crying in sheer anger, and that would never do. Heavens above, how often had Susan and I discussed Lord Pecus? Or Delysia and I? "They were never meant for you!"

I had blindly risen to my feet somewhere along the way, and now I felt my thighs losing the strength to hold me up. I was never one to faint, and it puzzled me in a distant way, so I curled my fingers around the ledge of the table and leaned my weight on it. "I didn't expect this of you!" I told him, panting with the effort of standing.

Lord Pecus was silent for a long moment; then he said, without looking at me: "You forget that you're a prisoner here, Isabella. Well treated, as I like to think, but still a prisoner. I took what precautions I felt to be necessary."

The anger drained away, leaving me empty and weary. "I see," I said, in a voice that seemed to come from a long way away. It sounded cold, though I had not meant it to. "I did forget. I won't do so again."

I pushed myself away from the table and tried to walk to the door. I say 'tried', because after the first few steps my legs gave way, and I found myself being held closer to Lord Pecus' massive form than I was entirely comfortable with. I pulled myself away with the last of my strength and sat down rather less than gracefully in the nearest chair, supporting myself more by an exercise of will than anything else. I looked up to find that Lord Pecus was watching me, his face carefully emotionless, and I said in that strange, distant voice: "Alexander, what have you put in my wine?"

"A sleeping draught only," he returned, quietly. I thought he pulled at the bell, but it was beginning to be difficult to tell exactly what was happening. "I couldn't trust that I'd be able to stop you slipping out. The servants will carry you to your suite."

"I see." I let the words hang there, more because it was becoming hard to speak than for the effect, and made a last defiant effort before the potion took me. "Then it is perhaps...incumbent upon me...to bid you goodnight."

I thought I heard him give the ghost of a laugh, and then all was darkness.

Chapter Seventeen

I may perhaps have mentioned that I do not take kindly to sleeping potions. This aversion is based on more than a mere dislike of being rendered insensible by persons known or unknown, however; and since my reaction to most of them is to commence being violently ill as soon as I regain consciousness, I will draw a discreet curtain over the first few hours of the next day.

Vadim, charming child, attended me the entire morning, methodically dampening strips of cloth which she laid alternately across my heated forehead; and although she was still quiet she showed no signs of sulking, which I greatly appreciated. Keenan sat at the end of my bed and watched with great interest, but I was too exhausted to send him away; besides, he had no qualms about emptying my sick bowl when it was required. When at last the paroxysms had ceased and I felt brave enough to sit up cautiously against my pillows, I beckoned to Vadim, who was tidying away the various strips of cotton.

She looked doubtfully at the cotton, and I said: "Never

mind that now; Keenan can take them down with the sick bowl." As Keenan obligingly did so, I patted the bed beside me. "Sit down, Vadim. I think that we should have a talk, you and I."

Vadim sat down readily enough, but there was a slight line between her brows.

I gave her an enquiring look. "Well, child? What is it?"

"Did you send me away to Susan because you thought I'd been telling Lord Pecus things I shouldn't?"

"I was afraid you might have done so. Lord Pecus knew too many things he should not have known otherwise."

"I never did, lady!"

"So I have found. In my last commlink with Susan I mentioned in jest that I would be meeting with the earl last night. Lord Pecus subsequently drugged me to prevent my leaving the manor. I apologise, Vadim: I've never been more glad to be wrong."

Vadim frowningly considered this for a moment, and then said: "That wasn't right of him, was it?"

"I'm hardly likely to be the most unbiased opinion upon the subject, child: suffice it to say that there are different opinions upon the matter. Lord Pecus seems to find himself perfectly justified. I am not so certain."

My tone must have been less than cordial, because Vadim threw me the kind of cautious look that one gives to a dog one is not certain won't bite. "You're angry," she said. "I don't remember you being angry before. Not really."

"Well, I'm hurt," I told her. "And perhaps just a *little* piqued. I think Lord Pecus is sorry, however. He will certainly be more so by the time the week is out."

This earned a grin from Vadim, bloodthirsty child that she was; but it was Keenan, arriving with zest into the late sick-room, who demanded to know Who was going to be sorry and Could he help?

"Certainly you are going to help," I said. "You are my secret weapon, Keenan."

Keenan grinned a wide, fierce grin, quickly divining his target. "You want I should magic his boot soles?"

"As amusing as that might prove, I believe I've thought of something more elegant," I told him.

He looked dubious but willing to compromise, and curled his arms around his knees with a conspiratorial look.

"Wot we goin' to do to him, lady?"

"Vadim?"

She shook her head, instantly comprehending. "No one can hear. I checked."

"Very well."

I cast my thoughts back to the one time I had been in Lord Pecus' private office. There were two brown leather chairs set by the vast, arching windows; and one behind the solid desk that seemed duller but not so battered. I frowned, considering the remnants of my memory, and turned to Vadim once again. "Which chair does Lord Pecus most often sit in?"

"The right hand one by the window," she said, without blinking. "He puts his feet up in the seat of the other one."

"Of course he does!" I murmured. I had rather thought that one of the window seats, with their shiny, well-worn seats was most likely, but with so much riding on the correctness of my memory, I would much prefer to be sure. "Keenan, do you know your right from your left?"

Keenan wrinkled his brow, as if suspecting the presence of a trick question, and then ventured: "Wossat?"

I closed my eyes for a brief moment. "You use both hands, don't you?"

"'Course!" said Keenan, in a scoffing tone. "*Everyone* does."

I ruefully considered my options and said; "Perhaps we could still attempt it if we were to tie a piece of string about your right arm."

"Um, Lady?"

"Yes, Vadim?" I enquired, with the humorous certainty that my ignorance was about to be shown up. I was not mistaken.

"He'll know which one. It's the one with Lord Pecus all over it."

"And by 'all over it' you mean—"

"He's got a very distinctive signature," she nodded.

Interesting. The disadvantages of a lack of natural magic were manifold, I thought regretfully, not for the first time. I wondered briefly whether Lord Pecus' signature was so very strong because he was the Commander of the Watch, or if he had become the Commander as a result of the strength. I could see both the advantages and the disadvantages of magically inclined felons knowing one's signature, if one were the Commander of the Watch.

"I begin to feel myself very fortunate to have the services of two such competent magic users," I remarked, not entirely tongue-in-cheek.

Keenan looked smug. "*Yes*, lady."

I spent the rest of the afternoon avoiding Lord Pecus. It was not as easy a task as I would formerly have supposed: he was not at the Watch House (the reason for which I declined to guess) and seemed to be always just around the corner no matter where in the Manor I betook myself. I was even forced to the expedient of refusing to answer his knock at the door when I retired in annoyance to my suite once again. I felt a little guilty at this last ruse and more so at the stab of ill-natured pleasure it gave me to do so. I would have to be careful tonight at dinner: it would not do to lose my temper. I had not done so properly in many years, and the last time I had done so, a man had died. It was, in fact, the sort of thing that made one think twice before allowing one's red hair to catapult oneself into a towering rage. I certainly wished Lord Pecus to think I was decidedly out of charity with him: it was quite another thing, however, actually to be so.

I will admit to some measure of trepidation as I went down to dinner. It was nothing that I hadn't expected, however; and in anticipation of this very feeling I had dressed myself very carefully in the grandest, most forbidding of my dinner gowns. It was dull gold, with a high, filigreed collar and gracefully long sleeves slit right to the shoulder, from which inner sleeves of more gold filigree clung to my arms right down to the wrist. It was girdled around my hips with a golden cord, and cut open at the front to display an under-skirt of dark yellow; all in all presenting a great deal of gold, and conveying a pleasing sense of dignity. Vadim looked at me with wide eyes as I turned to observe myself in the mirror, but busied herself with my hair without commenting.

It was Keenan who said: "You look diff'rent, lady."

"Very good," I said, looking at him from the corner of my eyes. Vadim had achieved a precarious arrangement of my hair that sat grandly atop my head, and I didn't dare move before it was properly affixed. "That is just what I want. Where have you been?"

"Makin' stuff."

"By 'stuff', am I to take it that you are referring to another spell?"

"Yeah."

"Hm." I applied a few dabs of golden lip-rouge with one finger and thoughtfully eyed the effect. "I've been meaning to ask you about those. Are these spells of yours an impulse of the moment, or a carefully implemented plan?"

Keenan shrugged. "Make 'em when I need 'em."

A slight smile touched my lips. "Are you feeling particularly fearful of your health, Keenan?"

He gave me a pugnacious look that told me he was perfectly well aware that I was teasing him, and said distantly: "'S'for you, lady."

"I see. I seem to remember that the last time you gave me one of these, I found myself in no inconsiderable danger shortly thereafter."

"That's the way they work," Vadim put in, tucking in a few pins with a light touch. "That's Keenan's sight."

"Is that so? In that case, my appreciation knows no bounds."

Keenan looked as if he were not quite sure whether or not I were joking. While he decided, I took a final look in the mirror and swept downstairs to dinner.

The dinner was a particularly fine one, once again suggesting that Lord Pecus knew me rather too well. After my exertions this morning I found my stomach dreadfully empty, and the immediate delicacy of it faded away very quickly under the influence of an excellent course of roast beef. Lord Pecus didn't attempt to engage me in conversation, for which I found myself vastly thankful. If he had tried to do so I would have had to be quite short with him, and it was difficult to be short with Lord Pecus. He would be expecting something of me, of course; and since the best way to succeed in my plan was to make sure that he thought I was up to something else entirely, I made up my mind to ignore him. Unfortunately, it was not as easy to ignore the fact that Lord Pecus' green eyes were observing me steadily each time my eyes chanced to fall in his direction. After encountering his gaze for the third time in a row, I elected not to turn my gaze toward him again. It seemed safer.

He spoke to me once at the end of the meal, to ask if I would take a little tea, but didn't look surprised at my quiet negative; and before long I found myself wearily climbing the stairs to my suite once again. Vadim was there to help me undress once again, for which I was surprisingly grateful. I allowed her to unbutton and unpin to her heart's content, merely stepping in and out as the occasion required, and betook myself to bed with Keenan's spell under my pillow. Keenan seemed inclined to stay and watch anxiously but was shooed away by Vadim, and I was left in peace to look rather listlessly over the *Book of Interesting Excerpts* to see what I could discover about poor little Lady Topher. There was nothing out of the ordinary: nothing, that is, apart from the now-familiar confusion that seemed to exist between different accounts which put one servant in multiple places. I had thought long and hard about that dual presence that had ailed the Book, trying to piece it together with poor Papa's predicament, but the Book had been adamant that the excerpts were correct and complete; and my thoughts had led me to the reluctant conclusion that something in its internal magics had somehow decayed or gone wrong. It left me unsure if Lady Topher's servant had really been in the room with her, or in her own bed—or perhaps neither!—at the time of the murder; and I at last put the Book aside in frustration, ignoring its sulky protests that ***It isn't my fault!***

I sat blindly in thought for some time longer until it became apparent that someone was waiting respectfully by the door, waiting to be acknowledged. I looked up. "Yes, Vadim?"

"I've put Keenan to bed," she said. "Is there anything I can do?"

I gave her a faint smile, and remarked: "Bored, are you?"

"No, lady. I thought you might need something, that's all."

"Not tonight, I think. Tomorrow will be a different story, however. How good is your memory, Vadim?"

"Middling, lady. Is it a message?"

"Something of the sort. You've studied Lord Pecus' wards, have you not?"

Vadim gave me a sharp glance. "In or out, lady?"

"Both, I rather think," I said thoughtfully. "For instance, how would I go about getting out without setting off alarms? I assume there must be a way, since the servants are not kept prisoner. How does Keenan manage?"

"Oh, *that*," Vadim said dismissively. "That's just Lord Pecus letting him out. The servants have their masks: they're all recognized by the house wards."

"Indeed!" My heart sank, and then rallied. "There are unfitted masks, aren't there?"

Vadim's eyes grew sharp, and she nodded. "The footmen were going to fit us with masks, so I think so, lady. Would you like me to find out where they are?"

"No, I think not," I said, considering it. "I have another task for you."

I sent Vadim off with a message quite early the next day. She looked at me doubtfully. "Enough Dozy Brown to lime a perch? That's all?"

"Believe me, it's more than enough," I told her. "Susan will know what you mean. And if she asks you if it's a big perch, tell her it's *very* big."

Vadim grinned. "Oh, I understand that bit," she said. And after all, it turned out to be not terribly difficult to appropriate one of the spare masks. By appropriate I mean, of course, *steal*; but if Lord Pecus thought that keeping them in the butler's closet was good security, it was just as well for him to be shown his error. No one looked amiss at my presence below stairs. I had learned long ago that if one walks as though one belongs, one will invariably not be questioned. Neither was I. My biggest fear was that the blank masks would have an alarm on them, and I picked one up so gingerly that I almost dropped it again immediately when it proved to be free of security magic. Nevertheless, it seemed sensible *not* to bring it back to my own suite, and I spent a little time wandering the manor in search of a conveniently handy nook before it occurred to me that the single most appropriate place for it was indubitably the umbrella stand. From the umbrella stand I could leave the manor at any time, and since servants did not tend to linger in the great hall I was not observed hiding the mask. Nor would I be, I fervently hoped, in retrieving it. If I had my way Lord Pecus would be by far too occupied to notice my absence, but I had no desire for a fracas with any of the servants either. They were quite nice, by and large; and despite a tendency to try and smooth things over with Lord Pecus and I, they were suitably backwards about being forward.

I didn't quite know what to do with myself after the business with the mask. If I had been at home or at the ambassadorial quarters, I could have gone shopping or at least out to tea in order to while away the time. At Pecus Manor there was little to do but wait in quietness for battle to be joined. And I was under no misapprehensions that it would *not* be battle: Lord Pecus, if (or more accurately, when) he found out, was bound to be furious. I was more or less resigned to being confined to one of the cells below stairs after my campaign tonight, and I hoped fervently for poor Papa's sake as much as my own that my meeting with the Earl of Horn was fruitful.

I remained in my suite until I found myself folding and

refolding my evening gloves, and then decided resolutely that enough was enough. Lord Pecus had not yet returned from the Watch House, so I felt myself free to take a turn or two about the garden. The day had not been a pleasant one, more muggy than warm, and now the sky was threateningly overcast. The Glausians were sure to be enjoying it immensely, I thought caustically. Then I had to smile because I had scented the storm on the warm breeze, and for a moment the expectation of the storm mingled with the expectation of an exciting night, bringing a familiar sparking feeling to my chest. I was becoming distressingly Glausian in my sentiments.

The afternoon was a dark one, and I didn't realise how late the hour had become until I saw, with a little shock that shivered from my spine to my toes, that Lord Pecus was striding toward me down the darkening garden path. Bother! There went my opportunity of sweeping grandly into the dining hall. I wasn't even *dressed* for dinner! My annoyance made it easy to quash the smile of welcome that automatically rose to my lips. Instead, I nodded my head coolly in acknowledgement and said: "Good evening, my lord."

What a good thing I had already given Keenan and Vadim their instructions! By now, Keenan should be sneaking into Lord Pecus' office to sprinkle an odourless, heat-activated powder over Lord Pecus' chair of choice. It was Dory Brown, one of the most powerful sleeping drugs I have ever had the misfortune to be dosed with. A relic of one of the far flung countries we visited that had not yet discovered the efficacy of magic, it was happily not well known in Glause.

Lord Pecus, with no idea of his danger, stopped a few feet from where I stood. "Good evening, Isabella."

"Good evening, my lord."

He was silent for a moment, his expression hard to read in the twilight. "Are you coming in to dinner?"

So he was not going to take the hint, was he? I regretfully decided against assaulting him with another 'my lord' quite so soon, and nodded. "I lost track of the hour. My apologies."

I must have gotten into the habit of curling my fingers into the warmth of Lord Pecus' huge arm, because when he offered it to me I had a constant struggle to remember to keep my fingers just touching his forearm, light and impersonal. Once Lord Pecus made an instinctive move to cover my fingers with his own, but recovered the movement in time, and we were able to proceed to dinner without the unpleasant necessity of my dropping his arm.

I ate absently, and little. Twice, I looked up to find Lord Pecus watching me with a frown.

"You don't like glazed ham, Isabella?"

"Hm? Oh, yes, certainly. I find that I'm not so hungry tonight, my lord."

"Isabella—"

"A momentary lapse, I assure you," I told him briskly, trying to ignore the pleading note to his voice. It was no part of my plan to let Lord Pecus think he was forgiven, and it was a little frightening to think how easily it could be done by a mere word from him, spoken in that tone. Lord Pecus had entirely too much influence over me. I considered for an instant what reply would be most dampening, and added: "Do pass the salt."

Suitably dampened, Lord Pecus did so. It was harder to see his face tonight, lending a disagreeable confirmation to the idea that I was well and truly caught up in the love curse. The last month had seen it stretched thin enough to allow me to see his face each time we were together: that it was harder to see tonight was unfortunate but necessary. Love curses are, by and large, an unimaginative and repetitive form of the curse. I had a good idea of what needed to be done to break the spell and no doubts about my ability to break it when the time came, so it didn't seem unnecessarily cruel to allow a setback. I hoped Lord Pecus would see it the same way. He tried, poor lamb. He asked me, determinedly enough, how my day had been; and when a few quiet words informed him, went on to inquire as to Susan's progress. He was not discouraged by my brief replies, but continued to draw answers out of me on a range of different subjects until I found it hard to keep my lips from twitching. No doubt that was his intention. It didn't help that his eyes were on me, glowing with laughter and—was it?—tenderness.

At length, I dabbed my lips with the napkin, laid it aside, and said: "I believe I'll retire, my lord. I'm a little weary."

Besides, I needed the small amount of sleep I could get before setting out to meet the earl. I pushed away from the table, making a small incline of the head in Lord Pecus' direction, and shook the wrinkles out of my skirt. It was perhaps unfortunate that he reached out and grasped my wrist just as the doors opened to admit a footman. Despite the footman, Lord Pecus didn't seem to feel the need to let go.

"Isabella."

The footman stared in a less than wooden manner, a worried crease between his brows and the tea tray unremembered in his hands. I would have been flattered if I had thought the concern was for myself and not Lord Pecus. The servants, although less obvious than Melchior, had permeated the air with a gentle hope during the length of my stay, and it was quite clear that they expected me to break the curse. I fully intended to do so, but there was the matter of the Earl of Horn to be concluded first.

"Let me go, Alexander."

"Oh, have some tea," he said, smiling a little.

I found it necessary to say with some coldness: "Have the goodness to release me, Lord Pecus! I refuse to be manhandled in front of the servants!"

The smile vanished, succeeded by a deep furrow between Lord Pecus' brows; and the footman, coughing in a well-bred manner, was fixed with a narrowed glare that made him visibly whiten. "*What*," said Lord Pecus, between his teeth: "Do you want?"

"The ah, tea tray, my lord."

"Well?"

"Where would you like it, my lord?"

"I think Lord Pecus would like it taken to his study," I said briskly, managing at last to pull my hand away. "He will be taking tea alone tonight."

For a moment it looked as though Lord Pecus would have caught at my wrist again, and I skipped away nimbly, keeping myself out of reach. "Oh no, my lord! I'm still far too cross: we should only quarrel, and I dislike quarrelling. We will talk tomorrow."

"Tomorrow," agreed Lord Pecus, and this time he let me leave unhindered.

❧

"I don't understand," said Keenan darkly. "I fort you didden *want* me to get nabbed?"

"I've no desire to see you er, *nabbed*, Keenan," I replied.

"Well, wot'd I pinch this thing again for?" His tone injured, Keenan presented the Earl of Horn's dynamo.

"It's very simple," I said, receiving the dynamo from him. "Lord Pecus will most certainly know that you've been in his study again: *that* we cannot help."

"I was careful!" protested Keenan, his tone rising in excess of injury.

"No doubt, but Lord Pecus is more careful. Therefore, if we cannot prevent him knowing that you were there, we must by all means prevent him from knowing *why*. If Lord Pecus thinks you are stealing the dynamo, he's less likely to suspect that you've doried him."

Keenan frowned fiercely for an instant before a grin spread across his face. "Oooh, I like *that*!"

"I daresay you do," I said ruefully, reflecting once again on the possible dangers of introducing Keenan to such ploys. "Has Vadim returned yet?"

He jerked a thumb eloquently toward their chamber. "She's pinched someone's clothes."

"Already?" I said admiringly. "How expeditious of her!"

Keenan leaned frowningly against the bedhead and said: "Wot now?"

I had a momentary vision of Lord Pecus, his huge form prone in his brown leather chair as the Dory Brown took effect. "Now," I told him, with a sparkling smile: "We wait!"

Chapter Eighteen

I was able to snatch a few hours of sleep that night, and awoke with the pleasurable sensation of exhilaration that typically comes from an early journey to a much anticipated destination. I have never had any difficulty in waking myself up when required; one of the results of my diplomatic (and sometimes not so diplomatic) adventures, and my early education at Trenthams, which was as comprehensive as it was exciting. I blame Annabel. It must have been all that scrabbling around ruins while people constantly tried to murder us. If it wasn't for Annabel, I would have been a perfectly well adjusted, perfectly well behaved old maid.

In all probability, I would have found it a dreadful bore. I was far from bored at present. Vadim was in a state of high excitement that matched my own, her fingers fluttering restlessly as she set my cap carefully over my hair and tied the smart white apron about my waist, and when I turned to observe myself in the mirror, she was bouncing lightly on her toes.

"Will I do?" I asked, narrowing my eyes critically at my

reflection. I had a lowering feeling that I was by far too thin for the role: Damson was the slimmest of the maids I had seen, and her healthy figure was nothing short of curvaceous. Vadim must have employed a little of her never-endingly useful magic to fit the uniform to my figure: I was sure the pile of material had been much more voluminous earlier.

"If you wear a cloak no one will notice how slender you are," Vadim said comfortingly. "Besides, most of them are in bed by now. Some of the footmen are still cleaning silver, and the kitchen maids are scrubbing pots, but they're all in the kitchen anyway."

"Unfortunate people!" I remarked. "What a time of day to be cleaning silver and scrubbing pots!"

Vadim sniffed. "Cook thought she saw a mouse. Now she won't let anyone go to bed until they've found it and cleaned every last dish in the kitchen. I think the footmen are planning on murdering her with the soup crock."

I wasn't surprised. The kitchen staff were up before most of the other servants, heating waffle pans, scraping crepe irons; and, in short, making life comfortable for everyone else at the expense of their own early morning sleep.

"If I hear the shrieks of the victim, I shall use the distraction to my own advantage," I said, curling my lip slightly. I was feeling too tightly wound to appreciate the humour of it: I wanted to be doing and done. I hadn't felt this much apprehension since Annabel and I were at school.

"Is he—"

"He's asleep. The backup wards took over a few moments ago."

I drew in a long breath through my nose. "Very well. I'll be as swift as I can, but if morning approaches and I haven't returned, I am asleep to all enquiries, up to and including the breakfast tray."

"My lady is not at home to callers," nodded Vadim, spoiling her surprisingly proficient manner with a smirk.

"Exactly." I tucked a single tell-tale red lock back into my cap and gave myself one last look in the mirror. "Make sure Damson isn't admitted, won't you?"

Goodness knew I didn't need a fire laid even during the uncertain autumn, but nothing would convince Damson of that fact, despite my protestations. On particularly warm nights I had taken to locking my door in self-defence, which served me very well now.

Vadim grinned again. "Yes, lady. Are you ready?"

"Ready for what, precisely?"

"I thought you might like something extra," she explained. "I know a Look-Away spell. It won't last more than a few minutes, but it'll help."

"Vadim, have I told you lately what a treasure you are?"

"Yes, lady." This time Vadim's grin was demure.

"Allow me to mention it again. You may proceed."

The spell was short and to the point, and it was not long before I was setting out assuredly down the stairs to the umbrella stand. There was a familiar bulge in the hidden pocket of my cloak, another of Keenan's gifted spells. I found myself somewhat touched by their care.

I might as well have spared myself the anxious thoughts attending my escape from Pecus Manor: not a soul wandered the corridors to test Vadim's Look-Away spell. Fastening my borrowed mask at the entrance of the Manor, I wondered whether I was disappointed or relieved. At all events, my egress from the gates of Pecus Manor was as uneventful as my exit from the Manor itself, proving that even the best security is only as good as its weakest point. If Lord Pecus didn't utterly disown me for this night's work, I would have to mention the matter to him. In a helpful spirit, of course.

Susan was waiting for me outside the gate, dressed in charcoal tones that caused her to melt away into the shadows in which she stood. The first indication of her presence was a stir of movement in the air, and then an arm was flung around my shoulders companionably. A moment later I could pick out the light, one-horse buggy she must have hired to carry us.

"The Adventurers go forth again, eh?"

"Very nice, Su!" I said, looking her over with raised brows. "Where *have* you been obtaining your clothes?"

She shrugged one shoulder elegantly. "Emmett knows a lovely little man in Piccon Street. He introduced me."

"You'll have to do me the same kindness," I remarked, following the line of her coat with a professional eye. Despite the charcoal hue, it looked to be light and cool in the warmth of the night. "Where *is* Emmett, by the bye? I quite expected to see him tonight."

Moonlight showed a wary gleam to Susan's eyes. She vaulted into the driver's seat and took the reins. "The lummox is snoring in the barracks."

"Very wise of you," I said approvingly, climbing into the buggy. Emmett would no doubt have had a difficult choice between care of Susan and apprehension of a wanted, purportedly treasonous earl, if he had been included.

"What about the Beast Lord?"

"Asleep also. However, if my memory of Dory Brown serves, I rather doubt that he is snoring."

"One of these days, Belle, you're going to have to tell me about Dory Brown."

"Certainly not: you're far too young and innocent. Is everything arranged?"

"I'm hurt you have to ask. The earl will be waiting for you

by the fountain, alone; and he's made it clear that he expects you to be likewise."

"Where will you be?"

She shrugged, a slight movement of darkness against the moon. "A few streets away. If you need me, scream."

"I shall do nothing of the sort! I'm quite capable of taking care of myself."

"When you're tongue-lashing, yes," Susan said, turning slightly to grin at me. "Physical assault, perhaps not so much."

I was tempted to reply somewhat heatedly, but the truth of the matter is that I usually *do* rely upon words to wriggle myself out of unpleasant situations, and it seemed disingenuous to deny the fact. Besides, I had a small dagger somewhat excitingly sheathed in my garter, which I could reach by the simple expedient of slipping my hand through a cut I had made in my left skirt pocket. Well, it was *somebody's* left-hand pocket, anyway: I would have to sew it up again before Vadim returned the garment. In any case, if it came to unpleasantness, I didn't doubt that I could look after myself without having to scream for my athletically superior younger sister.

"This is close enough," I said, when we reached the Upper Marketplace. The fountain was a few blocks further in, and I didn't want to risk the earl taking flight.

"Sure?" Susan asked lazily. "The earl was already there when I came to fetch you: I think he was jockeying for the best position."

"And ascertaining that there would be no nasty surprises," I agreed. "Very well, take me another street closer. One would hope that the earl has none of his own surprises planned."

Susan threw me a mischievous look over her shoulder. "You know what I'd do?"

"I shudder to think."

"I'd saunter in casually, just a few minutes late. Make him think I wasn't worried about anything he can do."

"Oh, very good, Su! I see you've been learning a thing or two."

"Ah," she said, not surprised; "That's what you *are* going to do, isn't it?"

"Well, the earl has no reason to kill me—unless one counts slight irritation, of course—and I've never liked skulking."

"What will you ask him about?"

"This and that," I said provocatively.

"Well, I want to ask him what happened to him at the masque," said Susan. "I was told something happened with one of Delysia's footmen, and to think that poor Papa murdered anyone is ridiculous. I talked to some of the people there, and the earl must have been in two places at once if he was with Raoul as well as– you've already thought of that, too, haven't you?"

I shrugged apologetically. "It was a logical jump. Besides, I think Daubney was trying to say something of the kind to me before he was murdered. Vadim confirmed that for me in a roundabout way, and then, as you so sensibly observed, there is the issue of our little Papa."

"Who wasn't where he was said to be, but was branded as if he *was*," Susan finished, nodding. "Only, I don't know of a spell that can do that kind of thing. As a matter of fact, no one I've asked knows a spell that can do that kind of thing. Quite frankly, I would have begun to doubt that it existed if it'd been anyone but Papa. What do the Watch think?"

"Oh, one can never tell with Lord Pecus," I said. "If I were to guess, however, I would say that they're still working the angle that Raoul was dealing in espionage. I'm more than certain he was looking for the leak himself. Two deceased acquaintances of mine had arranged for a meeting with him, quite unaware that he was feeding them useless information."

"Funny, I would've thought the Beast Lord was cleverer than that."

"Lord Pecus is of the impression that everything centres on *me*," I said primly. "According to him, I'm the focal point around which all other facts spiral."

"Perhaps he's not so dull after all. Does he fancy that you're involved in espionage?"

"Goodness knows." I thought about it, and laughed suddenly. "Do you know, I wouldn't be surprised if that really *is* what he thinks. From his point of view, it would make sense."

Susan shot me a shrewd look. "Oh, have you been poking around that great big manor of his?"

"Not at all! In fact, I have studiously avoided doing so."

"Suspicious of you," said Susan solemnly, shaking her head.

"Wasn't it, though? I've been having an immense amount of fun!"

"Still, it doesn't seem to have discouraged him at all," she mused, and I caught the flash of sly humour in her eyes. "Perhaps he thinks he can change your wicked ways."

"Susan, it's my disagreeable duty to inform you that you've become distressingly pert!" I told her firmly. I gathered my skirts together and disengaged my mask, abandoning it on the seat. "Just here will do nicely, thank you!"

"Spoilsport," Susan said, with a grin; but she stopped the buggy at my direction. "Sure you'll be fine, Belle?"

"Perfectly. Mind you keep out of sight, Su: even the main thoroughfares can be dangerous at night."

She winked, making no promises, and drove away at an easy pace, wooden wheels clattering across the smooth urban cobbles. Once she was out of sight I drew in a deep, steadying breath, and shook out my skirts. Across the street light spilled out in untidy patches from a public house that traded through the night, and a few raucous snatches of song floated out into the heavy air, tuneless but enthusiastic. Further down the street there would be another pub—most likely several more—supplemented by a few of the seedier cafes that stayed open all night to accommodate late night drinkers; and all in all they provided enough light by which to navigate the streets safely. Unfortunately, the light would not be enough to deter any of the said late-night drinkers from accosting a lone female in the streets, so I kept to the shadowy side of the street where the light was just enough to get by without stumbling. I made a mental note to suggest to the King that his subjects might benefit from the street lamps that Civet employed to ward off the early onset of winter darkness. No doubt the watchmen would be glad for the assistance. And thinking of watchmen, it would probably be as well to avoid any that were on the beat tonight.

The fountain was in deep shadow when I approached, its decorative wings showing sharply black against the dusky night, and the vague light from a few sporadic windows only served to make it difficult for me to see into the shadows. I was a few minutes late, according to plan, and when the earl stepped from the shadows into half-light, it was not so dark that I couldn't see the line between his brows.

"Lady Farrah."

"Good evening, my lord. I trust you're well?"

He gave a surprisingly genuine chuckle, banishing the line. "Not particularly, my lady. Exile seems to be agreeing with my wife, however, so I can't complain."

"And Lady Louisa?"

The earl's eyes darkened. "I haven't been able to get to her. How is she taking it?"

"Quietly, so far as I've been able to ascertain; and with more dignity than I would have supposed," I said, honestly. I knew Louisa, and so did the earl.

He nodded thoughtfully. "Good, good."

"Thank you for meeting with me, my lord."

"Well, it was only sensible," he said. "But now that you mention it, there *is* a condition to my meeting with you."

"You know I can't promise anything on behalf of Civet— and I certainly can't comment on behalf of Glause."

"You misunderstand me, Lady Farrah: I merely want a word in a few influential ears. I know you have the King's ear; and even I, exiled as I am, have heard that you most certainly have Lord Pecus' attention. I want to return to my estate with my wife and daughter, with all charges dropped."

"Nothing too difficult, then, my lord!"

He was unperturbed. "Reaching, certainly, but not unreasonable, I fancy. I believe my information to be quite valuable. Ah— I would, of course, enter willingly into an oath that there will be no more Charles Black. I will live a quiet life with my wife and daughter, resigning my seat in parliament."

"Your seat in parliament is a hereditary one," I said. "It's not that I don't appreciate the gesture, of course, but I feel bound to point out that the king will almost certainly mention the matter."

"There's nothing to prevent my not using it, however. I wish to be permitted to live peacefully with my family, without fear that Glausian Watchmen will batter the door down at any moment and carry away my wife and child. All I ask is that you mention the matter to the king."

"You can hardly be unaware that I am ensconced at Pecus Manor," I remarked. "I imagine that a word with the king is the very last thing I'm capable of managing at the present."

"Allow me to say that the information I can offer might help you in that regard."

I considered this for a moment. I was quite capable of doing what the earl suggested, and more: moreover, I had been fully prepared for such a demand when I arranged to meet with the earl. It seemed sensible to make him sweat for the answer, however, so I allowed the silence to stretch for a moment longer before I nodded decisively. "Very well: I'll speak to the king on your behalf. I trust your information will bear out my confidence in you."

He took that with a small smile and asked: "Lady Farrah, are you aware of my particular hobby?"

"Not as such. I know you dabble in alternatives to traditional magic, and Louisa mentioned dynamos in one of our conversations. I must admit to a little, *ahem*, investigation of your waterfall room at this point."

He nodded, unsurprised. "I wondered if you understood the significance of the room. The water interferes with the constant magical surveillance the king has on me, but doesn't affect my own gadgets. In fact, some of them require the water as a power source."

I briefly showed him the dynamo that Keenan had recently re-acquired from Lord Pecus' rooms. "One of yours, I suppose?"

"It's one of my more compact, potent power sources, usually for use in a small, handheld communication device. *Not*, however, one that was in use by myself. Some years ago several dynamos were stolen, and a receiver high in the mountains disappeared briefly before appearing again."

"The king?"

"Yes– not that he'll ever admit it. Unfortunately it didn't occur to me that the thief would use them to follow my career. Obviously I'll have to invent a device for finding any of my own gadgets."

"The dynamo was attached to something similar to a detached commlink, I take it?"

"A little. But in this case, both parties have a device, and no magic is used. Sound waves are translated into a kind of energy not unlike magic, and this energy bounces off a receiver somewhere between the two, continuing on to the next person. I mention the matter, Lady Farrah, to make it easier for you to understand what I'm about to tell you next."

"Very well," I nodded, my brain buzzing with ideas. What a boon for a person without magic! Lord Pecus would be fascinated! Well, if Lord Pecus were in the mood to be fascinated with anything I might say, that is.

"Before the *fracas* began with Raoul, I'd been busy inventing a device which would be useful to me in my er, less legal ventures."

"Less patriotic ventures," I corrected.

The Earl of Horn said firmly: "There we must agree to disagree, Lady Farrah. I have always had what I consider to be the best interest of my country and her people at heart. This time I must gracefully bow to the will of the people." He did so, ironically.

"This device I mentioned was what you might call, for the sake of clarity, a scrying mirror."

"Non-magical, I presume?" I said, with some interest.

The earl bowed again slightly, this time less ironically. "Naturally. You may have noticed that I was wearing a pair of pince-nez by a ribbon around my neck on the night of the masque?"

I consulted my memory and was able to inform the earl with perfect truth that I did, indeed, remember. He beamed at me as though I was a star pupil, and explained: "The trick is in the two lenses, my dear. Light flows through them constantly, recording a kind of moving picture for me to play back later if the need arises."

"Eminently useful for your average political spy," I murmured, and was rewarded with a twinkle in the earl's shrewd old eyes. "Imagine the ramifications of presenting evidence of the kind of underhanded, ever-so-slightly illegal dealings between parliament members! All the little cliques and conspiracies exposed with devastating clarity! It doesn't bear thinking of! Frankly, I'm surprised that you've not used the device in any of our conversations."

"It would be less than useful to use my eyeglass recorder with you, Lady Farrah," said the earl dryly. "I have found, much to my dismay, that you invariably tell the truth; and there's no leverage to be got from someone who so persistently and skilfully tells the truth!"

It was my turn to incline my head ironically. I did so, and inquired: "I presume that you recorded something of use?"

"Yes and no. There is a section of very great interest, preceded by a few minutes of confusion in double. As a matter of fact, I took the double frame to be a fault in my calculations for the machine's calibration until I realised that the two frames were of entirely different rooms."

"Is that possible?"

"Strictly speaking, no. And yet, there it was. Do you know what interested me the most, Lady Farrah?"

"I can't imagine!"

"In almost every one of the frames that was doubled, you were the focus of one set of pictures. In fact, it's what led me to agree to this meeting with you."

I remembered poor little Papa's impression that his vision had doubled on the night of the masque, and demanded: "Do you mean to tell me that you have a *visual* recording of the murderer?"

"I have a visual recording of the *murder*," corrected the earl, a little smugly.

"The pince-nez were facing outward," I nodded. "You're intimating that the murderer somehow took over your body momentarily, while leaving you fully conscious. That's the second impossible thing you've told me: would you care to try for a third?"

"Have you travelled into the further reaches of Lacuna, Lady Farrah? Not just the outlying villages, but to the tribes in the rainforests?"

"I've met the tribal leaders once or twice," I told him, wondering where this particular rabbit trail was leading. "I've not travelled into the rainforests, however."

"They have a tradition there," said that well-travelled man, and I fancied that he was just a touch more smug. "They call it the soulstealer: something with which to threaten naughty children. While I was travelling through this area, I was fortunate enough to meet with a very old man who supposedly remembered the last time a soulstealer passed through his tribe. He didn't want to talk about it: seemed to think that it might bring the soulstealer back to ravage the village again. I managed to convince him otherwise, but only after multiple shots of *maska*, by which time the venerable old man was nearly too drunk to be taken seriously. He told me that the soulstealer would appear in multiple forms, usually in the guise of one or the other of their neighbours, and consequently turning them against one another."

"The Lacunan tribespeople have herbal remedies they use to see through that kind of magic," I pointed out. I didn't like to see him so self-satisfied.

"Something I mentioned to the tribesman also," nodded

the earl. "He told me that the remedies don't work against a soulstealer."

"Of course they don't," I sighed. "What more is there to know of this soulstealer? I find myself rather interested."

"I fancied you might. From what the other tribesmen said, the soulstealer visits every fifty years or so, murders his way through a village, and vanishes again. The murders are all similarly bloody."

"You're speaking of a killer with a need," I said, frowning. "A need for the *act* of murder, or a need that *causes* him to murder, do you fancy?"

"I think it might be a little of both. Most interesting still is the fact that the soulstealer appears not to be Lacunan."

My upper lip curled. "How would they know, if he changes his appearance so often?"

"It was not something I was told," said the earl. "It was merely a conjecture of mine, arising from the fact that the tribesman refer to the murderer variously as the soulstealer and the Ghost. Lacunans are not known for their pale skin tone."

"I beg your pardon, my lord, but you seem to be alluding to a single murderer. When the attacks are spanning what seems to be multiple decades, I find myself wondering if that is entirely credible? Even if we allow that our murderer *did* visit a far flung Lacunan tribe some fifty or more years ago, he must be so old as to make it doubtful that he could walk further than the distance between bed and wheelchair by now!"

"Lady Farrah, the further into this tangle I find myself, the less *any* of this seems credible. I do know that magic involving blood and violence is never for any good purpose, however."

"I take that you refer to youth and power spells."

He nodded gravely. "I don't think that the murders have a purpose beyond forming part of a spell, but the murderer is undoubtedly mad."

"*Quite* mad," I assured him, repressing a shiver. The earl was wrong about one thing, however: I was quite sure the murders had more than one purpose. One would hate to seem *conceited,* of course, but one couldn't escape the conclusion, garnered from little pieces of information gained here and there, that the murders — or at least the murder of Raoul — had been to attract my attention. It wasn't a comforting thought, and I found myself grateful for even the slapdash protection of Keenan's dirty little spell ball.

"I suppose that you're willing to give up the recording to the investigation?"

"A gesture of my goodwill," said the earl expansively. He slid a small, pen-like object from his waistcoat pocket and passed it carefully to me. "Point it at the wall and press the button for the picture. When you're finished, press the button again. The picture is quite convincing, I believe. Lord Pecus is a knowledgeable practitioner of non-magical alternatives: he'll know what it is he's seeing."

"I'm glad to find you so confident," I said, a little amused. The earl was being hunted on charges of treason, which held a maximum penalty of death, and he was still playing the fine gentleman. I couldn't help but like him.

"With information so valuable, I should have expected to find you dead! My informants so far have had a distressing tendency to become dead before they become voluble enough to be very much help."

"I've taken precautions," the earl said shortly.

"And Louisa?"

"That was the bargain I made with your enterprising little sister when she first broached the matter of a meeting between us. What a determined young lady! And how very alike you both are! She pointed out that she had no need to make bargains with me when she could simply have me arrested– purely for my information, I imagine, since she did nothing of the sort. She has a little bauble I made especially for Louisa."

"May I assume that this bauble is of nonmagical construct?"

"Certainly," said the earl loftily. "That, Lady Farrah, is the way of the future! I shall not trouble you by explaining how the thing works, but you may be certain that it *does* work. I can personally attest to the fact."

"How very gratifying for you!" I remarked, unable to prevent the slight edge of mockery to my voice. The earl, however, took it in good part, and merely grinned a roguish grin at me.

"Exactly so, my lady! However, as I don't particularly like the idea of spending any longer on the streets than is strictly necessary, I will be so ungentlemanly as to leave you to your own means of returning to Pecus Manor, and depart from whence I came."

"Where can I find you with an answer from the king?"

"An advertisement," said the earl. Suspicious little man! He didn't trust me not to have him summarily arrested. "An advertisement placed in the personal column of the Galhooley Rag should do nicely, I think. Address it to Cedric, with the information that his uncle has sold the mare."

"Any particular mare?" I enquired, with a touch of amusement.

"The chestnut, Lady Farrah," the earl said, with a malicious gleam to his eyes. "The chestnut."

The streets had become rowdier by the time I left the fountain in search of Susan, and I found my hand inching insensibly toward the slit in my pocket that allowed access to my little dagger. It would, of course, be exciting to have occasion to use the pretty little toy, but I couldn't help feeling that such an altercation would leave me in a state of disarray not at all consistent with my dignity. Adding to my general disinclination for a scrap was the fact that the men now staggering out of the public houses all around seemed to travel in packs, and it was likely that I would have more than one assailant to deal with in the event of a struggle. In consequence, I kept rather more to the shadows than I had previously, feeling my way along the shopfronts to aid my balance and realizing crossly as I did so that many of the young men of my acquaintance whom I would normally have enlisted to walk me home were now being disgracefully drunk in cafés and gutters across the road. A few horselords of an unknown regiment, vaguely familiar to me, were being cheerfully sick behind the early morning delivery of fish belonging to one of the cafés, accompanied by two Civetan guardsmen who were laughing at them in loud good humour, but were barely able to stand themselves. Further along the street I passed a couple of other young bucks who were not so drunk, supporting a third who *was*, and who hung in their arms with his sandy head dropped lackadaisically on his chest. It was with some surprise and a little trepidation that I recognised the drunk to be Lord Topher. Had he heard about his young wife, then? If not, I certainly didn't want to be the one to tell him, especially when he was in *that* condition. In the purest self-interest, therefore, I hastened my step in an attempt to gain the corner before the little group could see me. In this, I wasn't entirely successful, for as I darted for the corner, I distinctly heard him burble: "Lady Izz-bella! Many—happy—congrat'lations!"

So Susan's rumours had been spreading, after all. He seemed to find the thought amusing, because he burst into a fit of giggling, and I cast my eyes heavenward as I hurried around the corner.

Susan was right where I expected her to be. Rather, the buggy was, the horse stamping impatiently and tugging at suspiciously slack reins. A cold finger ran down my spine, for there was a lumpy sort of bulge in the driver's seat that was glowing blue. I caught my breath on a tiny sob and darted forward, startling the horse, which reared at me but for once failed entirely to frighten me. Susan was slumped sideways in her seat, buzzing with blue fire and emitting a low, grating hum that set my teeth on edge. Her head was in one piece and where it ought to be, but her chestnut curls had been shaken loose of their tidy confinement and were tumbling around her face, making her appear younger and more vulnerable than usual. I let out the breath I had been holding in a shaking rush, because her chest still rose and fell: she was only unconscious. I didn't dare pick her up with the blue flames licking about her, but by the application of artful shoving I managed to prop her more or less upright until I was able to take the reins myself. The horse seemed to understand that I meant business, for it neither refused to move or attempted to drag me off in an alternate direction of its own choosing, and a very few moments later I was turning the buggy unskilfully but swiftly down the road that ran alongside the horselord barracks, thinking furiously. It didn't seem likely that any of the drunks I had passed tonight could have done this to Susan: even a practised and determined magic user would have found it difficult to take her by surprise. No, the murderer had made an attempt on Susan tonight, and for some reason had been unable to prevail. I shrewdly suspected that his failure had much to do with the unpleasant humming at present growing less around Susan's lax body, and remembered the earl's remark that Susan had something of his for

Louisa. I hoped, savagely, that the device had given the murderer a very nasty shock.

I leapt from the buggy at the entrance of the barracks and rang the bell vigorously three times in quick succession, unwilling to be patient. A sleepy horselord who was unfamiliar to me opened the peephole and showed me a pair of bleary eyes through the rectangle.

"Play your tricks elsewhere, chicky," he said, eyes crinkling with a yawn.

I gave him an awful Look and said coldly: "You will fetch Emmett and Miryum, and kindly address me as *my lady*!"

His eyes widened in sudden recognition and dismay. I could imagine that his mouth opened once or twice in the silence, but the door hid his lower face from my view; and at last he said, in a strained tone: "Yes, m'lady. Sorry, m'lady."

He didn't attempt to stammer out an explanation, which was sensible of him, and if it hadn't been for Susan lying unconscious behind me I could almost have laughed at his consternation. Within a few moments the door was hastily unbolted and flung back to reveal Emmett, who strode out clad only in his blue horselord breeches, shaking his head like a dog. Oh. So when Susan mentioned that he was snoring, she was referring to the fact that she had worked a spell on him, not that she had slipped out. The spell must have failed the moment Susan was rendered unconscious.

"Where is she?" he demanded.

"The buggy. *No*, Emmett, the fire!"

"It doesn't hurt me anymore," he said shortly, picking up Susan as if she was a child instead of a healthily built young woman. "She altered the spell for me. Did you tell her to spell me to sleep, Belle?"

"Of course not!"

"What happened?"

"I don't know. She was like this when I found her. I was hoping you might be able to tell me more."

"Unconscious. She'll come round in a few minutes."

Emmett shouldered past the horselord who kept the door and I followed close behind, almost colliding with Miryum, who looked briefly and professionally at Susan's pale face. She didn't look groggy in the least.

"I'm glad to see that Susan didn't put you all under whole-sale," I remarked.

Miryum smiled grimly. "Emmett's room is beside Susan's. I suppose she thought he would be the most likely to hear her. She'll be fine, Belle. It looks like a simple case of backlash to me, and not too severe at that."

"I'm relieved to hear it," I said, breathing a little easier. I opened the door to Susan's room for Emmett and smoothed the pillow under her head as he laid her on the bed.

"You're looking less fine than usual," Miryum said, in dry amusement. She was lounging in the doorway. "Should we know what you were up to?"

"Possibly not," I said. "You wouldn't like it."

"I suppose that's why she felt the need to spell me to sleep," growled Emmett. There was an angry light in his eyes that suggested Susan would have some explaining to do when they were alone.

My lips curved in a half smile, but I merely said: "I suppose so," and turned my attention back to Susan, who had developed a line between her brows that suggested she wasn't far from consciousness. Nor was she. She woke with a gasp and a start, and tried to sit up, but Emmett pushed her back down with one big hand. A moment later the blue flames flickered and died.

Susan looked up at him cautiously, and said: "Hallo, lummox. I see you're awake."

Emmett sat back and folded his arms across his massive chest.

Susan's eyes narrowed. "Oh, you're giving me the silent treatment?"

"What happened, Su?" I interrupted. They could fight this out by themselves later.

"Your murderer tried to do away with me," Susan said cheerfully. "Who knew, Belle? The earl really does know his stuff! I had my fire up already because I knew it couldn't possibly be Emmett, so he couldn't physically touch me. But *whew!* that stuff he threw at me was strong! The earl's thingummy buzzed and threw it back at the swine, but I copped a nasty backlash as well. I don't remember much after that."

Emmett frowned. "He looked like me?"

"Yes. Don't worry, lummox, I knew right away that it wasn't you: he was smiling at me like an idiot. Got my fire up just in time."

Emmett opened his mouth, presumably to protest the assertion that he never smiled, but just then Susan's face took on the preoccupied look that signals an incoming personal commlink among the magically inclined, and she lost interest in him.

"Oooh," she said thoughtfully, after a short pause. "Belle, I think you'd better get home. The Beast Lord is awake and a bit ticked off, by all accounts. Vadim seems to think he's breaking furniture."

I found that all eyes had turned involuntarily upon me and became defensive. "I assure you all that it's no fault of mine if Lord Pecus is damaging his furnishings! I'm sure Vadim is overstating the case: Lord Pecus *is* older than three, after all!" None of them appeared to be convinced, so I heaved a long-suffering sigh, and said: "Oh well, someone had better drive me home, then."

Susan couldn't forebear to remark that I seemed to have made it safely to the barracks with her, but Miryum grinned and said lazily that she would be happy to drive me, for which I was very thankful. I felt that driving a buggy was a feat not to be repeated more than once a night, or at least not by myself.

I found the manor in uproar. Vadim was waiting for me by the front door with the whispered intelligence that Lord Pecus was on the second floor, staggering grimly toward my suite. The Dory Brown, enough to fell an ox, hadn't worked quite quickly enough to knock out Lord Pecus before he realised what was happening. He'd had time to work a small, desperate piece of magic, which although it did not save him from falling asleep, mitigated the effects to such an extent that he had been able to drag himself out into the hall some forty-five minutes later: from whence, if I were not mistaken, he was roaring at the servants. Vadim gave her report with a worried face, and disappeared gratefully at my order. I wondered how frightened she had been, and felt a sharp pang of conscience. I didn't stay to remove my cloak, but ran lightly up the stairs to find Lord Pecus, maskless and shirtless, surrounded by astonished servants who were alternately trying to assist him to stand and convince him that Lady Farrah was safe in her suite.

"Safe, but not in my suite," I said briskly. "Alexander, I am perfectly whole: there is no need to shout down the house! You're frightening the servants."

Well, perhaps some of them were frightened. The maids were quite frankly ogling Lord Pecus; who, bare-chested and barefoot, was as magnificent a picture as one could hope for. His green eyes, struggling to stay open, fell on me, and an unfettered expression of relief fell on his beast-face. I had expected that, and expected to feel badly about it. I did. What I did *not* expect was for Lord Pecus to surge across the hall and gather me up in a crushing bear-hug. I gave a squeak that didn't manage to sound at all offended, much to my chagrin, and found myself clasped to a bare, hairy chest with my feet dangling indecently short of the ground.

"Put me down at once, Alexander!" I demanded, in a muffled voice. He was still staggering sufficiently for me to fear he would pitch us both lengthways on the hall, which would be as undignified as it was indecorous. I had no intention of presenting such a picture, even if most of the servants had melted away quietly at my arrival. The head footman stopped briefly to enquire if either Lord Pecus or I required anything, and upon Alexander's shaking his head and loosening his arms enough for me to indicate my negative, he left us alone.

"Your servants are remarkably tactful," I remarked, straightening my bodice and skirts with a dignity I didn't quite feel. "Alexander, no! If you attempt to seize me again, I shall be forced to kick you in the shins!"

Lord Pecus gave an unsteady laugh and collapsed sideways into a hall-chair that miraculously managed to hold his massive form on deceptively strong, spindly legs. "Even, now," he said, his eyes drooping.

"Oh no, you don't!" I said firmly. "Up, and to bed with you! I refuse to have you sleeping outside my suite. I'm certain you snore."

He laughed again, more giddily this time, but allowed himself to be badgered to his feet and accepted my help as far as his chambers, where I left him to stagger to bed as best he could. I supposed, biting back a smile, that at least he need not trouble to undress himself.

Chapter Nineteen

Trophy came to see me the next day. I found myself sleepily relieved: if Vadim were to be believed, Lord Pecus was still sleeping, and I found myself a trifle nervous as to his state of mind when he awoke. Trophy was a pleasant distraction, and had the added advantage of being a good-natured buffer between Lord Pecus and I—always assuming, of course, that Lord Pecus did not peremptorily send him away whenever he appeared. I had been reading the *Book of Interesting Excerpts* quietly to myself in the garden, accessing the scrolling guest list from the night of the Ambassadorial Masque in an attempt to map out a consistent graph of individuals at the scene of each murder. It was a task made inherently difficult by the fact that the murderer needed only to touch his victims to murder them. Some of the murders—Raoul's, for example—had clearly been performed on the spot: others had been murdered with a delayed touch of black magic threading back to the murderer. It was a near-to-impossible task, despite the magical and all-inclusive nature of scrolling guest lists, and I wasn't sorry to be interrupted by Trophy's arrival: particularly since he had brought chocolates with him.

"No exciting matters of the constabulary, Trophy? I should have imagined you to be pursuing wrongdoers with great zeal in Lord Pecus' absence!"

He grinned. "No, they're pretty quiet at the moment; I rather think the murderer has them all on the hop. Are you keeping busy, Isabella?"

"Always, Trophy, always! I've enjoyed a scintillating morning of reading in the sun."

"You don't look scintillated," remarked Trophy frankly. "You look half asleep."

"One of the disadvantages of trying to trace the whereabouts of a murderer by the use of a magical book and scrolling guest lists, I'm afraid."

Trophy threw me a look of heartfelt sympathy. "Alexander had me trying to do the same thing, but there were so many difficulties that I started to think that it would be more useful to know where he *wasn't*! I've never had so much trouble establishing a clear chain of events. You know, I don't know why Alexander doesn't just sign you up to the Watch, Isabella: after all, we haven't come up with an idea that you haven't had, too."

"I think you may just have done so, dear boy," I said thoughtfully, eyeing him in wonder. "Trophy, you're a brilliant specimen of Watchman! Of course we should be concentrating on where he wasn't! Book, reference the guest list again to give me a comprehensive list of guests present physically at the Ambassadorial Masque five minutes before Raoul's murder. Cross-reference with a comprehensive list of those physically present ten minutes *after* the murder, and remove all names that appear in both lists."

The Book put up an unusually polite notice of: ***Extrapo-***

lating, please wait... probably for the benefit of Lieutenant Holt, who was gaping alternately at myself and it.

"Can it *do* that?"

"I certainly hope so," I said, curling my fingers around the corners of the book. If only I had thought of this before Daubney, and the washing-water woman! I wondered how many people had died in the meantime, and felt a little ill.

"But why? How will it help to know who wasn't there?"

"I've recently gained a little information about our murderer that suggests he was able to steal another person's body for a time," I told him. "However, instead of simply inhabiting the other body, it seems that he creates another identical but connected to, the host body. What happens to the created body—"

"Happens to the real body," nodded Trophy. "Convenient for your father, Belle."

I raised my brows at him, but his tone was rueful rather than snide. "I know. There will have to be more evidence before it will clear Papa."

"It's finished!" Lieutenant Holt leaned forward eagerly, his head almost colliding with mine. "Oh, very good, Isabella! Only four names!"

Without my noticing, black ink had scrawled out:

Lady Carlisle
Lord Topher
Sargent Ffolkes
Earl of Horn

Below that, in smaller writing, the *Book of Interesting Excerpts* had added: ***The Earl was on both lists, but there were two of him before the murder, so I thought you might like to know anyway.***

"Indeed I did!" I said warmly. That confirmed the information that the Earl's body had been used by the murderer, as did the earl's moving pictures. Only the list, however, proved conclusively that Papa was *not* the one who had used it. I felt a sudden lightness. "Well done, Book! Well, Trophy, what now?"

"Narrow the parameters," suggested a young, boyish voice.

"Good heavens! Lord Topher!"

I wondered blankly what the head footman thought he had been about. Lord Pecus had been very clear on the fact that I was to receive a single visitor, once a day; and although the stricture had annoyed me at the time, I was very willing for it to be enforced when it came to Lord Topher. Hadn't *anyone* had the decency to tell the poor boy about his young wife? His servants at least must have done so, I thought impatiently, and then blinked. Of course they had done so: they could do nothing else. And Lord Topher had most assuredly *been* home, if his tidy cravat and unwrinkled coat were any testament. He certainly didn't appear to be sorrowing, however: in fact, if I were not very much mistaken, there was a light of mischief dancing in his eyes that became more unsettling the more I became aware of it. I began to remember a night when I had seen him like this: the night of the masque, darting back through the door with great wet patches on his waistcoat from the rain, a bright, excited look to his face. Only, it had stopped raining much earlier...

"Lieutenant, I think it's about time for you to go," I said lightly, curling my fingers around the *Book of Interesting Excerpts* and drawing it fractionally back towards myself. Good heavens, how could I have been so blind? Blood on his waistcoat, and I had thought it was rain!

"Oh no! He can stay!" said Lord Topher brightly. "We're going to have such fun! You should narrow the parameters, Lady Farrah; I'm sure you'll find it interesting."

Lieutenant Holt, who was far too well bred to ignore a

dismissal from a lady, looked faintly puzzled but bowed from the shoulders and rose to his feet as if to leave, much to my relief. Lord Topher, smiling brilliantly, put a gentle hand on his shoulder. "I'd like you to stay," he said. Trophy sat down, his face suddenly white, and Lord Topher's brilliant eyes flickered toward me again. "Narrow the parameters, Lady Farrah. *You* know what I mean."

"Compile a list of guests who went home between those two times," I told the Book, with one eye on Lieutenant Holt, who was as pale as a decently tanned Glausian could possibly be.

His eyes were fixed on his own shoulder, his neck stiff, and I thought I knew what he could see, even without magic. There would be a thread of black magic there, connecting the Lieutenant to Lord Topher.

I slipped my hand around his and squeezed gently. "Cross-reference with the list of exceptions and remove all names appearing on both," I said to the Book. I was torn between hope that Alexander would come down to the garden in search of me, and dread that he would do so. After all, he hadn't been so very successful against the killing touch the first time: if it hadn't been for Keenan's little safety spell, it was doubtful he would have come through. I liked Trophy very much, but I would much rather he die than Lord Pecus.

The Book of Interesting Excerpts blossomed with the words: **Sorry about this,** and three names melted away, leaving only Lord Topher's.

"I was *sure* you'd guessed!" said Lord Topher. "You're so clever: that's why I liked you so much!"

"I guessed a little while ago," I nodded. My fingers were very cold where I grasped *The Book of Interesting Excerpts*, stiffly bent around the heavy front cover, and the hand that curled around Trophy's was as icy as his was hot.

"What brings you to visit me today, Lord Topher? It's not that I don't appreciate the visit, you understand, but I am very busy."

He giggled, and then as quickly scowled. "You can't marry that man, Isabella. It's such a waste! Do you really mean it, or were you only trying to lure me out?"

I opened my mouth to reply, but he only shrugged and continued talking, as though to himself. "Oh well, it doesn't matter: I won't let it happen. I can stop you, you know. I can do whatever I want."

"I know," I said calmly, crossing one leg over the other to support the Book without making it obvious that I was wriggling. "You saved Vadim's life that time."

He looked pleased. "I did, didn't I? It wasn't easy, you know: I *really* wanted to do her. She would have popped like a little grapefruit, all warm and salty and *everywhere*. Red suits you."

"Is that so?"

A memory flashed through my mind: the warm, wet shower of blood and brain on my face as poor young Daubney exploded. Lord Topher must have been nearer than I imagined. "I've never thought so, but I suppose I'm a little biased. Blue goes so much better with red hair."

"You're teasing me, aren't you? I like it when you tease me. I knew as soon as I saw you that you were the one I wanted to play the game. That's why I picked that big guardsman to begin with, I knew it would get your attention."

"It certainly did," I agreed lightly, wondering a little hazily if I were going to disgrace myself by losing my breakfast on the walkway. Poor Raoul! His death deserved to mean more than a whim on the part of a madman. "What about your wife, Lord Topher?"

A frown began in the centre of his forehead. "You should

call me Wilfred, you know, if we're to be married. I told you when I called your commlink that we'd be so happy: I think I've been very patient, Isabella."

"Very right and proper, Wilfred," I said, bestowing a sparkling smile on him.

My stomach was doing nasty little flip-flops in an attempt to convince my breakfast to, as it were, abandon ship; but I didn't dare allow such a travesty to occur when Lieutenant Trophimus' life as well as my own depended on presenting the necessary façade. "Now, I think I should like to know about Emily."

"Oh, that was only for the money," said Lord Topher breezily; "You *told* me to do it, Isabella; don't you remember?"

I thought faintly, *Good heavens, I caused that poor child's death!* but I knew it was nonsense. Only a madman would construe the suggestion of a good match as a command to marry a child for her money.

"Only she was getting so *boring,* and then someone said you were marrying Lord Pecus, so I thought I'd better get rid of her and find out what you were up to. What *were* you up to, Isabella?"

"Oh, just the usual tricks. I'm more interested in knowing what you've been up to."

"If you guess some of it right, I'll tell you the rest," he said invitingly.

"Very well, I accept your challenge!" I said at once, and he chortled, eyes sparkling.

"Oh, I *knew* you'd be more fun than the others! Start from the start. No, start from the end! It's more fun if you start from the end."

"Very well. I assume that we will *not* be beginning with today, and proceed to yesterday's debacle."

He nodded, challenging me with a grin. He looked young

and joyous and not at all dangerous, with the light of mischief in his eyes. He was holding the madness in check, but for how much longer could he do so?

"You found Susan last night as she was waiting for me. Disguised as Emmett, you tried to kill her, but I think you hadn't bargained for the earl's interference."

"Was that him? How did he do that? He's a minor magic user, nothing more." He gave me a disarming grin. "It knocked me sideways, I can tell you!"

I nodded. "I thought you were drunk, at first. It wasn't magic, though: the earl specialises in dynamos and gadgets. Well, before that it was Lady Topher: you were one of the servants for a brief time, I believe. That must have been very convenient for you."

He gave a stifled giggle. "She was so surprised! She looked very pretty when I finished, though; all red and gold like you."

His eyes dwelt meditatively on me and I suppressed a shiver, because I knew he was thinking of me in the same way, my brains and blood scattered in a pulpy mess around my shoulders as I lay prone. I added quickly, in hopes of distracting his thoughts: "Putting something from every suspect in the washerwoman's room was very clever. I don't think you ever caught up with the drifter, though, did you? It was a good joke."

A slight frown pinched his brows together. "I didn't expect him to leave that quickly. We might have to find him, Isabella; I think someone warned him."

"Well, he can wait for the honeymoon," I said, with a cheerfulness that brought a sick smile to Lieutenant Trophimus' lips. "Right now we're talking. Why did you frame the Earl of Horn, by the way? I've always been a little curious about that."

Lord Topher shrugged. "He had fingers in so many pies;

lots of secrets to come tumbling out if he was investigated in just the right way. I made sure he was investigated in the right way. I knew *you* wouldn't believe it for a moment, but that only made the game more fun."

"And my little Papa?" I had to work very hard to keep the anger from my voice. "I understand that Delysia's little adventure had something to do with you, but why did you use Papa?"

"Because I had to move quickly," said Lord Topher, scowling. "Did you know that your Watchman asked for your hand that night? I soon put a stop to *that*."

The scowl melted, giving way to a reminiscent, mischievous curl of the lips.

"He tried to stop me but I was too strong for him: silly fool thought that he could catch me with a skin mark!"

He laughed, and I echoed the sound. "That *was* foolish, wasn't it?"

"Yes," agreed Lord Topher, but his mobile face was already darkening with an expression of misuse. "I didn't expect him to imprison you here, though."

There was a flutter of movement over Lord Topher's head, through the door opening onto my balcony. Vadim, if that shade of blue was any indication. I hoped, fiercely, that she would not come down to find me. Another, quicker shadow passed into my line of sight, suggesting that Keenan had popped up for a look and been hastily pulled away by an unseen hand. Now, how had they known that I was in peril? It was to be hoped that they knew better than to try and mount a rescue attempt themselves.

"I must admit that it never occurred to me, either," I remarked, flicking my eyes back to Lord Topher's face with a candid smile. "However, he *did* warn me, and it has been quite useful to be so near to the investigation. Tell me, *was* that your scheme, to attack Delysia?"

He pouted. "It wasn't meant to be her. I left the rose 'specially for you, Isabella: why was *she* wearing it?"

I had a moment of clear recall, Keenan choosing between the two roses. So Delysia's unfortunate incident could be laid at my door also? I would never hear the end of it.

"Those idiots from the Sinkhole couldn't tell the difference between one woman and another," muttered Lord Topher vengefully, without waiting for an answer. His tongue ran unconsciously across his top lip, briefly giving him the look of a satisfied cat, and I had the feeling that there were a few bodies that the Watchmen of Glause had yet to discover.

"But what I *principally* wish to know," I pursued, hoping that it wasn't Lord Pecus' huge form I had caught a glimpse of behind one of the hedges; "Is how you found me the day that Raoul's revolutionary contacts tried to kill me."

"Oh, that was easy! You found the dark threads, or you wouldn't have been able to trace me, but I laid two more traces on you the night of the masque so that I'd be able to find you whenever I wanted to."

"How convenient!" I managed to say. "Your arrival really was most propitious for me: I could have found myself in a rather unpleasant situation otherwise."

To my left, the Lieutenant again showed signs of a rather wan smile. I would have to have a word to Alexander about that boy: he showed signs of remarkable promise under stress.

"That was a good day," agreed Lord Topher, eyes sparkling. "I'm glad you closed your eyes, it would have ruined the fun if you saw me too soon."

"Yes, that's what I thought."

It had certainly been Lord Pecus behind the hedge, because as the light breeze changed direction, I could smell the soap with which Damson laundered his white shirts. I blinked once to steady my face, and tried not to look in the direction of the scent. It was to be hoped that Alexander had a plan, because I was reasonably certain that Lord Topher was a magic user of unsurpassed strength. I wished, suddenly and irrationally, that Alexander would go away, sickened all over again at the thought that I could lose him. A cold little coil in my stomach suggested that it would be a loss I would not quickly recover from.

"You don't look well, Isabella. I think you've been cooped up here too long."

"Oh, no!" I managed one, brilliant smile. "I was merely thinking about something. You grew up in Lacuna, I believe, and your father died shortly before you came to Glause. I wonder, did you and your father often travel among the rainforest tribes?"

Lord Topher giggled. "Oh, you really are clever! But you're not quite right, you know: about Father, that is."

"You haven't had a father for a very long time, have you?" said Lord Pecus, strolling into the courtyard. I closed my eyes for a brief moment, my heart sinking; and when I opened them again, Lord Topher's cheeks had stained furiously red. "I knew there had to be a reason for the deaths beyond your sick enjoyment in them, but blood magic didn't occur to me until it was brought to my attention that the house of Topher routinely sends its scions to Lacuna to die, and its sons there to grow up."

Lord Topher gave a scream of rage. "Shut up! It's meant for her, not you! Shut up! *Shut up!*"

Porcelain teeth gleamed in a grin, but Lord Pecus' eyes were cold through his mask. "Make me, old man. You've had one transfusion too many."

"A youth spell, then," I said quietly, more to myself than to

Lord Topher. The Earl had been right. "But you don't usually hunt in civilization, do you?"

Lord Topher's eyes were still narrowed at Lord Pecus, but he said to me: "That was for you, Isabella, I knew you'd enjoy the challenge. I won't need transfusions again for at least fifty years; this time was just for the fun of it all."

"And very scintillating I found it," I agreed, smiling warmly at him. It had occurred to me that it was possible to get Trophy and Alexander at least out of this business with a whole skin. I stood, stiffly sliding the *Book of Interesting Excerpts* onto the bench beside Trophy. "I think it's about time we were on our way, Wilfred, don't you?"

"Isabella! Do you really mean it?" Forgetting Lord Pecus, Lord Topher took two quick steps toward me, smiling infectiously. "I knew you were the right one!"

"No!" It was difficult to tell if the word had come from Lieutenant Holt or Lord Pecus: I rather fancied that they had both spoken.

The Lieutenant stood, unsteadily, and positioned himself in front of me. "Isabella stays with us, Topher."

"Trophy, sit down!" I hissed at him, but he only smiled at me.

"There are three layers of protection on her," he said to Lord Topher, who seemed to be on the point of giving way to a temper tantrum. "You won't get through those in a hurry."

"She's mine!" countered Lord Topher, his cheeks flushing once more. "I'll show you! Those spells are only good as long as you're alive."

"As are yours," said Lord Pecus, taking another step forward. At that range, he towered over Lord Topher, whose gangly frame was decidedly less impressive in comparison. Lord Topher looked momentarily taken aback, then giggled.

"All right then! Think of it as a wedding present, Isabella:

you can have them both. I'll be back later." He darted at Lord Pecus, and I think Alexander was taken by surprise, because he made no attempt to stop Lord Topher tapping him smartly on the shoulder. "Tag!" he said, with a sparkling smile. "You're it!"

There was a slight huff of air and I heard Alexander gasp, a deep, groaning breath; then Lord Topher was gone, and Lieutenant Trophimus slid to the ground in a stiff heap.

"Trophy! Trophy, fight it!" I seized his forearms, and a touch of colour came back to his face while the red leached from his eyes. Very well. So Lord Topher was still not prepared to have me die? I would use that. A quick glance over my shoulder showed Alexander down on one knee, beleaguered but by no means beaten and entirely without any trace of red to his eyes. Lieutenant Holt, on the other hand, was shuddering, his eyes flicking red on and off; and my fingers were quickly beginning to ache. I didn't dare loosen my grip around his forearms in spite of the ache: Trophimus had shown a distressing tendency toward reckless bravery, and I had no intention of letting him indulge it if I could prevent him from doing so. So long as Alexander was strong enough to keep the black magic at bay there was no reason for either of them to die.

I smiled down at the lieutenant with something more of determination than comfort, and said: "You're going to be fine, Trophy. Keep fighting." Over my shoulder, I tossed: "Alexander? Are you managing?"

There was no reply, and with a cold heart, I said sharply: "Alexander! *Are you managing?* You know I can't save you both, and if you can't manage I will have to leave Trophy to die. Do you understand?"

"Go to him," gasped Trophimus, his eyes very wide and red now. The shudders had grown from a shoulder-wracking pulse to a series of violent twitches up and down the length of his body; a sign, I knew grimly, that meant things were coming to their worst.

He tried to shake me off, but Lord Pecus, admirably in time, growled wearily: "Don't shout at me, woman; I'm not deaf! Stay with Trophy."

I gave a watery chuckle, and said: "Alexander, your address lacks finesse!"

I passed a cold, shaking hand across my brow, and gripped Trophy's forearm again. I was at a loss for what to do, and it wasn't a pleasant feeling; I could only cling to Trophimus and hope that the contact would be enough to save him.

Contact, contact... Yes, *there* was an idea! A tingle started in my scalp and ran rapidly to my toes, making me shiver. "Oh! *Oh!* I am a clot! Trophy, sit up."

He groaned and tried to stir, but I had to wrestle him into a sitting position by main force, propping him against the stone bench. There was a momentary flicker of brown to his eyes, suggesting that Lord Topher had narrowed his interest on us, and I heard Lord Pecus utter a disjointed warning. I ignored it.

"I'm afraid you're not going to like this, Trophy." I slid my hands up his arms to his face, careful to keep contact, and kissed him gently on the lips. His head jerked back but I had a firm hold on it, and after another moment he sat up straight, sliding his arms around me. Then it was I who was being kissed. It couldn't have been Trophimus any longer, because he pulled me to my feet with renewed strength, and kissed me again. This time his eyes were fully brown, right down to the hazel pip in Lord Topher's left eye.

I closed my eyes with a pulse ticking in my ears, waiting until I was sure that Lord Topher had taken over completely.

Then I tore myself out of his reach as Lord Topher looked at me with Trophimus' face, shock and betrayal blazing from his eyes in the split second before they flooded red. I caught my breath for a horrible moment where it seemed that I had made a mistake that would cost Trophy, and not Lord Topher, his life. Then Trophy folded to the pavement, white as chalk, and I dropped to my knees beside him, breathing hard. As I did so he opened gloriously blue eyes and smiled hazily up at me.

"Belle!" His voice was slurred, but his eyes were bright, and I smiled down at him through a sheen of tears.

"Trophy. I'm glad to see you recovered." There was another groan from Lord Pecus, and I had to take a moment to carefully school the joy from my face before I turned to face him. He was trying to rise from his knees. "Yes, Alexander, I'm very well aware that you're recovered as well. May I help you up?"

He ignored my proffered hand. "Lieutenant Trophimus, did I just see you *kissing. My. Fiancée?*"

I was impressed. Said through his teeth, at a growl, just moments after recovering from a decidedly nasty piece of black magic. Lord Pecus was nothing if not resilient.

"Trophy didn't kiss me, I kissed *him*," I informed him. I was feeling a little odd, my ears buzzing, and I thought it best to nip such feelings in the bud with a determined attitude. "Besides, it was technically Lord Topher at the time, Alexander."

Lieutenant Trophimus scrambled to his feet, guilt etched into his features. "I didn't enjoy it, Alexander, I swear!"

"Very flattering, I'm sure!" I said a little breathlessly, in spite of the determination of my attitude. I found it necessary to thread my fingers into the hedge for support, and this annoyed me a trifle. "Alexander, you will have kisses enough for yourself in time. At this moment, however, I wish to know for certain that Lord Topher really is dead."

Lord Pecus' head turned sharply, and I caught a glimpse of curved porcelain lips. "Is that so? I'll hold you to that when I return from locating Topher's body, Isabella."

"I daresay," I murmured, letting go of the hedge as a lost cause. Green and blue swirled together as the horizon merged with the foliage, and the buzzing in my ears spread until my whole body was humming. I made one last effort and addressed Lord Pecus' general vicinity. "Alexander, despite my best intentions I fear that I'm about to faint. Please don't allow me to ruin my dress on the flagstones."

❧

Somewhere above my head, Vadim's voice said anxiously: "Should she still be out, do you think? It's been a long time."

"'Ow should I know?" demanded another voice. Keenan: sounding disgruntled and suspiciously close to tears. I wondered vaguely what he was annoyed about. "Shouldn't have 'appened, anyways, me spell's still all together!"

Ah. Professional pride.

"Stress of the moment, Keenan," I said soothingly, lifting my head from the pillow and blinking a little hazily. Someone had evidently put me back in my room while I was unconscious. "Your spell had nothing to do with it, I assure you."

"*Course* it didden't!" scoffed Keenan, while I experimentally sat up and discovered that the world was no longer spiralling around me. "I knew that! Wot'd I tell you, Vadim?"

"You didn't tell me anything," said Vadim bluntly, darting forward to assure herself that I was not going to fall over again. "You were too busy blubbering about killing her."

"Since no one has, in fact, killed me," I reminded them: "I feel no compunction in interrupting to ascertain if you have yet begun to pack my things."

Vadim looked considerably surprised. "No, lady. I thought... Well, we were just waiting for you to come round."

"Were you so?" I arched my brows at her, prompting a slight flush. I smiled in spite of myself and stood carefully. "Well, I am fully conscious again, and *quite* ready to depart. If we pack very quickly, I think we might even be back in the Ambassadorial Quarters for dinner."

While Vadim flew to remove my gowns from the wardrobe, I turned in front of the mirror, observing myself critically to discover the full extent of the damage to my dress. It was not too severe: evidently one of the gentlemen had caught me before I measured my length on the flagstones, but the right side of my hem was very grubby. I eyed the damage dubiously, and eventually separated one of my more comfortable travelling frocks from the quickly building pile on my rumpled bed, employing Keenan to button the tiny cuff-buttons that sat awkwardly just beneath my elbow.

I was still rebraiding my hair when there was a knock at the door and Damson's head peeked shyly around the door. I found myself surprised and must have showed the surprise, because she blushed as she slid awkwardly into the room.

"I just came to see if you needed...that is, lady are you *leaving?*"

"Certainly I am," I said, smiling at the dismay in her voice. "I'm flattered at your concern, of course, but this was never a permanent solution. As I assume you already know, I was here strictly as a prisoner."

"You weren't a prisoner to us," said Damson, barely audible.

I gave her a faint smile. "Tired of your mask, Damson?"

"Most of us are," she said bluntly, gaining courage. "But it's not so much *us*, lady, it's *him*."

"Lord Pecus will be taken care of, never fear," I told her. "However, it will not be here."

Damson's mouth turned down briefly. "And not you?"

"Well, now; I wouldn't go so far as that. Off with you, Damson, I have all the assistance I need."

"Yes, lady." She nodded her head, but paused long enough to ask: "Will I see you again?"

"Oh, I imagine so!" I said, smiling affably. "And quite soon, I should think."

Lord Pecus returned not an hour later, with the news that Lord Topher's body had been found. He knocked briefly but entered before I had a chance to reply, and informed me of the find while looking around at the general mess with an expressionless mask. He nodded at the pile of baggage beside my bed. "You're very quick off the mark, Isabella."

"I thought it best," I said, shrugging one shoulder. "I will admit myself very much surprised if Papa and Susan are not on the doorstep before dinner, and I would hate to keep them waiting."

"I wish you wouldn't go."

I fixed him with a sharp look. "Alexander, do you or do you not wish to be free from your curse? Really? It has no doubt proved invaluable on the streets, and I think you may be sorry to lose that."

"To tell the truth, it *has* been useful, and if you won't marry me I don't care either way. But I do want to marry you, Isabella, and I'd very much prefer to be wholly human when I do so."

"Very well," I nodded. "Then you will have to trust me. Do you?"

"Yes," he said. "Against all sense, yes."

"Then you may call the footmen to carry my things into the great hall," I said serenely, and preceded him into the stairwell. Vadim and Keenan, each dutifully carrying an overnight bag, jostled each other down the stairs, and I followed.

Lord Pecus' voice followed me down the stairs, with an edge of laughter to it: "I was promised kisses, Isabella! Don't forget!"

Chapter Twenty

A week later I was seated rather glumly at my writing desk, perforating my best writing paper with an aimless pen nib. Lord Pecus, bother him, had *not* called on me as of yet, and I was beginning to wonder if he had misunderstood. Moreover, I had an interview with the King of Glause early that afternoon, and being summoned for an interview with the King of Glause had much the same effect upon one as being summoned to the headmistress' office. One didn't know exactly what it was that one had done, but there was certain to be *something*.

Susan, entering the room in her riding breeches with a half-eaten sandwich in one hand, said: "Good grief, Belle, aren't you ready yet?"

I regarded her frostily. "Of course I am ready!"

"Bored, eh?" she said, with a rude crack of laughter. "I told you that you wouldn't know what to do with yourself. You should have married the Beast Lord."

"That," I said, rising with great dignity and tightening my

reticule around one wrist: "Is a running endeavour. Are you driving me?"

"Like that, is it? Well, I hope it works. Love curses are a pesky business."

"Which is precisely why I wished to avoid becoming involved in one!" I returned tartly. "However, it's no use repining now— Susan, if you think that I wish to be conveyed up and down the streets of Glause by an individual holding a sandwich in one hand and the reins in another, you are very much mistaken! Kindly finish your meal before we begin."

Susan stuffed the rest of the sandwich into her mouth and grinned widely at me with bulging cheeks as if to say: 'Better?' When she could speak again, she said: "You know, you still sound exactly the same as you did when I was in school. You had that same sarcastic edge to your voice that makes people want to curl up in a ball."

"You don't seem to be in any particular danger of curling," I remarked dryly, but smiled in spite of myself. "And I don't seem to remember you being actually *in* school, as such. I remember a great many notes from your teacher, complaining about truancy."

"My mind was too broad to be fettered in the confines of a schoolroom," said Susan loftily, opening the door for me with a flourish. "Well, actually, mostly I was belting about the hills on a pony I broke in, but what's the difference, after all?"

"Oh, nothing at all," I assured her, laughing. "By the bye, why am I being driven by you? What happened to the coachman?"

"He's all right, I just wanted the practise." Susan threw me a sideways look. "When the merger's done the King wants me to stay on with the Ambassadorial staff. Melchior says I can."

I saw the question in her eyes and took pity. "Well, you're going to be busy, aren't you? The king isn't one to let his officers stand still, even if they *are* on loan from Civet: once you're finished with the merger you can be sure that there will be something else. I assume it's to show a unified front to the villages further out?"

"I don't want to spoil the sentiment by using it too much," said Susan thoughtfully; "But I really do love you, Belle. I would have stepped aside if you wanted your job back, you know."

"Oh, I know. But as it happens, I rather think I'm going to be too busy for the job, what with one thing and another. You'll enjoy Glause, I think."

"I know I will," she said cheerfully. "I always did like rain."

It was a testament to the king's fondness (a dubious honour), that I was not kept waiting the requisite two hours for the privilege of seeing him. When I entered the receiving room, he was wandering from painting to painting looking vaguely disturbed; but when he saw me he sat down on a plump green settee and patted the seat beside him. I gave him the requisite curtsey, which he waved away, and settled myself gracefully beside him.

"Good afternoon, your majesty. Lovely day!"

"It is, isn't it?" said the king, narrowing his eyes just a little. "And the weather is fine, the roads are clear, the merger proceeding exactly as planned. Now that we have the humdrum out of the way, suppose you tell me what you and the Earl of Horn found to talk about?"

"Really, you're as bad as Lord Pecus!" I complained. "How ever did you find out about that!"

"I have spies everywhere," he said satirically, but I thought rather ruefully that it wasn't far from the truth. "I heard there was a meeting scheduled, and knowing you as I do, I was certain that it *would* occur."

"It did," I said pleasantly, giving in to the inevitable. I had meant to broach the subject in any case: the Earl's testimony and evidence would still be very useful in legally clearing my father of any involvement in the murders, despite the fact that Lord Topher had been caught in the act. Besides, I had given my word that I would speak on the earl's behalf, after all. "The earl has evidence to offer in the case against my father: evidence that will clear him finally of all charges. In return, he wished me—"

"To speak for him," nodded the king. "I expected nothing less of him. What terms did he offer?"

"An immediate cessation of all action that could be construed as treason to crown and country, as well as the relinquishment of his seat in parliament."

The king smiled sourly. "Which is his by birthright in any case."

"Exactly so. I did warn him that the fact would not escape your notice. He indicated that he would take his chances. If it makes a difference, I believe he'll be as good as his word: he does seem to care very greatly for his wife and daughter, and his concern is all for them. I believe he wants the position more for their sake than his own."

"Well, well." The king leaned back, meditatively tapping his fingers on his rounded stomach with the air of a well fed cat. "After all, he can't cause any more trouble; and he's my most amusing chess partner. I think a royal pardon could be arranged. There is an old saying, Lady Farrah: 'Keep your friends close and your enemies closer'. I like to have mine where I can keep an eye on them. Moreover, it seems wise to root out the rest of Charles Black before they have the sense to know that it's all over. Can you get a message to the Earl?"

I allowed myself a small smile. "Of course."

"Do so. I'd like him back under my eye as soon as possible.

Now then, I hear that I'm to welcome you as a permanent citizen, Lady Farrah?"

"As I said to Susan earlier, it's a work in progress."

"Ah yes," remarked his majesty suavely. "These love curses can be a trial, can't they? I do sympathise most heartily, I assure you."

"Yes, so does everyone," I said. "Most often with a smirk. I have the distinct feeling that they all think it couldn't have happened to a better person."

"However," pursued the king, again regarding one of the portraits with distinct disfavour; "I have to admit to a certain satisfaction in the situation. I may have a job pitched to exactly suit your particular talents, Lady Farrah."

I bit my tongue on a satirical 'Of *course* you do!' and likewise resisted asking him just how long the idea had been under his consideration, the answering of which question might have left me considerably startled. Instead, I merely asked: "Indeed? I would say that I'm flattered, but the truth is that I find myself more apprehensive than flattered."

"Odd. People always seem to like the little jobs I find for them. I was having a chat with Melchior the other day, and he mentioned that we might have a similar problem with informational leaks that seem to be making their way to the Triumvirate."

I restrained myself from nodding knowledgeably and uttering the magic words 'Black Velvet', since the king was one of the few people who would take me up on the comment and I knew very little besides the name. "I know that some rather sensitive information from certain sensitive groups has been finding its way to Lacuna in particular, and that Melchior is worried about the rest of the Triumvirate as well. What exactly is it that you want me to do?"

"Investigate. Make a nuisance of yourself," suggested the

King. "Poke a few bears, as it were. I know you have your ways: particularly effective ones, if I may say so."

"Alexander is not going to like this," I said thoughtfully.

"That's one of the perks of ruling a country, Lady Farrah," said the king, his voice growing a little distant. Oh dear, he had gone head-masterly. "I'm at leisure to command my subjects without unduly concerning myself with their feelings upon the matter."

"Perhaps so," I replied, adding a touch of chill to my own voice to dispel the feeling that I was treading on slightly shaky ground; "But as it happens, I am *not* currently one of your subjects, and may in fact never be so."

To my surprise, he chuckled. It was a fat, rich sound; and one which, to the best of my knowledge, I had not before heard from the king. How worrisome! "Very well, Lady Farrah," he said, but I was under no illusions that the matter had been closed. With all the affability in the world, he added: "We will discuss the matter again if and when you become a naturalized citizen. Until then your sister Susan, a young lady of great enterprise, is making a few discreet inquiries. Do give her my best wishes, won't you?"

He rose as he spoke, and taking the words as a dismissal, I curtseyed myself out. I found myself somewhat amusedly wry. He was threatening to use Susan if I didn't capitulate! Well, the idea *was* after all, an attractive one: espionage at such a high level was bound to be an exciting, if dangerous, pastime. Alexander would not like it, but as the king pointed out, it was not necessary for his subjects to approve of all his actions.

I was still smiling when I rejoined Susan in the foyer.

She raised one brow and said: "He has that effect on me, too. Conscripted you, has he? Something juicy, I hope?"

"The juiciest I could hope for," I nodded, and signalled to

the footman to have the curricle brought around. "Contingent upon my being a citizen, of course."

"Which we're working on," said Susan serenely. "Well, I'm glad to hear that you won't be bored, Belle. The Beast Lord is all very well, but you don't want to have a dull marriage, do you?"

"If I did, I'm afraid I'm destined to disappointment. Oh well, as the old Trenthams adage says, 'Don't put on your boots if you're not expecting to step in the manure'."

"I thought it was 'Always be prepared'," Susan said, grinning.

"Officially, perhaps," I allowed. "Annabel and I found it to be somewhat lacking, however, so we changed it. I asked one of the mucky little brats what the motto was just last year, and she grinned at me with her two front teeth missing, and recited it with great glee."

"It's nice to see that your corrupting influence hasn't waned with the years," she remarked. "Oh, here's the curricle. Where to, Belle?"

I found myself at a loss. "How vexatious! I've no idea! How very dull it is to be an ordinary citizen!"

"You'd better tell the king you'll do it, then," advised Susan, pausing to allow me to arrange myself comfortably before she let the horse have its head. Fortunately, having its head in this case meant a gentle plod, no doubt with the soft, glowing thought of dinner warming its equine mind.

"Perhaps I shall," I said thoughtfully. "Perhaps I shall."

A strange horse was being led to the stables when we trotted around the turning circle before the front entrance. Susan cocked an eyebrow at me and said: "It's not horselord: too big. I think your Beast Lord might have come to see you, Belle."

I felt an odd little tickle of apprehension mixed with

excitement and tried to quell it. After all, I was no longer a schoolgirl. "Yes, I think perhaps he might have done so. Good heavens, is that Emmett, skulking in the archway? You *have* told him that he's not required for guard duty any longer, haven't you?"

"Well, I got sort of used to having him around," explained Susan. "Besides, we're all going to be spending a lot of time together in the near future, so what's a few more days?"

"Possibly a question best put to Emmett," I told her dryly, climbing down with great care. If it *was* Lord Pecus that had come to call, I would prefer not to be smudged during the interview. It might in fact be possible to quickly slip upstairs and change my dress, I thought, weighing the opposing merits of expediency and neatness. Unfortunately the matter was decided for me. The footman informed me, in a louder than necessary tone, that Lord Pecus awaited me in the Blue Room; whereupon, no doubt hearing the announcement, Lord Pecus himself opened the door to the Blue Room and saw me.

"Oh, there you are," he said, for all the world as if I had kept him waiting an excessive amount of time. I couldn't help smiling despite myself: it was surprisingly good to see him again. I would have refused to admit it even to Susan, but this last week I had felt as though I was walking through a world that had a huge, broad-shouldered hole in it.

I nodded to him. "Alexander. How nice of you to call on me at last!"

The porcelain lips of his mask twisted a little, and I found myself wondering if the mask was his remembrance of his own face. It was nothing like his real one. "I suppose it's impossible to discuss this inside the room?"

I sailed past him with my nose in the air. "Certainly we

can discuss it in the room. I was merely surprised. I thought you'd forgotten about me."

I heard the door shut behind me, and found myself picked up—actually picked up!—and hugged to a huge, pleasantly warm body.

"No, you didn't," Alexander said, and put me down again gently. "You can't have. No woman could think a man who proposes to her three times has forgotten her."

He crossed to the fireplace (purely a stalling tactic, since it was not lit) and leant one arm along it, propping one boot against the grate and observing the tip of it. If I didn't know better, I would have thought he was bashful.

But I *did* know better, so I fixed him with a wrathful look, and said grimly: "Alexander, if you do not propose to me soon, I shall break down and cry!"

"Very well," Lord Pecus said, looking up from the boot with a gleam to his eye: "But I'll have it known that you entrapped me. Well?"

I looked up at him innocently, getting my own back. "Well, what?"

This time it was Lord Pecus' voice that was grim. "I want an answer, Isabella."

"But you haven't asked me a question!" I protested, unable to prevent my lips from curling at the corners. Lord Pecus correctly took this as encouragement and abandoned the fireplace altogether to draw me to a sofa big enough to hold the both of us. "Very well," I said, with a fair attempt at sternness. "I will marry you. However, the mask must come off."

Perhaps he was growing used to my odd demands, or perhaps he simply trusted me—a pleasant thought—for he removed it without question. I studied his face carefully until I could see it again: the clear outlines of his human face, growing firmer and more certain while his beast-face grew shadowy.

"Oh, *there* you are!" I said, smiling tenderly at him. "Do please sit still, Alexander."

I slipped my hands around his face, feeling warm human ears with the tips of my fingers instead of fur, and he must have been able to tell the difference, because he looked startled. I drew his face closer in order to kiss him, and he resisted instinctively.

"Isabella—"

I ignored the protest, rising to my knees upon the couch to follow him, and slipped past the beast-face, now only a shadowy cobweb to be torn away. "I've always been partial to dimples," I said, tracing the line in his cheek with my thumb: and kissed him.

Alexander has never been slow to catch on. Some time later, I found myself, in the most elegant way imaginable, no longer kneeling on the couch but sitting on Alexander's lap. Since this seemed indecorous to say the least, I attempted to put some distance between myself and him, and succeeded only in wriggling back onto the couch before Alexander's firm arm prevented me from going any further.

"Oh, no you don't!" he said. "I've spent far too much time wanting to kiss you to let you get away now. Besides, I want to know how you broke the curse."

"It was the easiest thing imaginable! Love curses are all alike, after all: the catch, the kiss, and so on. The catch was obviously that someone had to love you, beast face and all. Once I knew that, it was evident that I couldn't agree to marry you while I was under your roof, since that would technically be considered force. Love curses are always about free will and love winning out over ridiculous odds: quite honestly, it's embarrassing."

Lord Pecus' eyes held a mixture of wonder and tenderness. "This affair has taken too much time from us," he said. "We'll be married tomorrow, Isabella."

"We will do nothing of the sort!" I said, as firmly.

We were still engaged in debating the point when Melchior sauntered in. "What a pity!" he said affably, grinning. "I've missed the juicy part! Oh well, Annabel will be happy: she's been pumping me for information every time we commlink. When's the wedding?"

"Tomorrow," said Lord Pecus.

"Sorry, not possible," Melchior said. "Annabel would kill me, and she's significantly more frightening than you are."

Since Alexander seemed inclined to debate the point with him, it was perhaps as well that we were at that point summoned for dinner by a polite footman who showed no signs of leaving until orders had been complied with. Dinner, in Delysia's opinion, was the bedrock upon which a household fell or stood, and since it seemed doubtful that even my engagement to the mysterious Lord Pecus would qualify as an excuse, we found it wise to comply with a good grace.

AMONG MANY MISCELLANEOUS THINGS THAT ONE FEELS bound to mention is the fact that the *Book of Interesting Excerpts* has disappeared. I've lost count of how many tricks this makes, and since I'm tolerably certain that the circular bookshop will have likewise disappeared, I haven't tried to get it back. No doubt someone will find it again when it's needed.

I find that married life quite suits me. After all, it's nice waking up in the morning to find yourself snuggled in a warm embrace that tends to become somewhat more than warm when the provider of it wakes up to discover himself similarly pleased with his armful.

Alexander is resigned to my role as the king's chief pot-stirrer; but could not by any means be said to be happy with it, which tends to lead to some rather heated arguments. By and large I find that we agree very well indeed. So well, in fact, that our first child will be due in six months: a boy to begin with, or so Alexander tells me.

Perhaps I shall call him Raoul.

If you enjoyed *Masque*, please consider leaving a review on Amazon, Goodreads, or your blog/social media. Sharing the love helps me sell more books, and selling more books helps me write more books!